Tyger

an out-of-this-world tale

Astrid, a young human girl on the alien
planet of Tyger, is thrilled to be invited
to celebrations at the native palace.

But when someone close to her falls for
a local who's completely off-limits, it
sets off a dangerous chain of events that
change her life forever…

Across Time & Space series
The Eternity Stone
Mountain of Glass
Desert of Fire
Desert of Ice
The Hidden Door
Whiter than Snow
City of Light

Fairytale Memoirs series
The Mostly Forgotten Memoirs of Rose Red
Viola Sends her Regrets
Gifted: a Fairytale Memoirs novela

Standalone novels

Breaking the Glass Slipper

Unshakeable

Tyger: an out-of-this-world tale

For information on new and upcoming books,
go to **mmarinanbooks.com**

Tyger

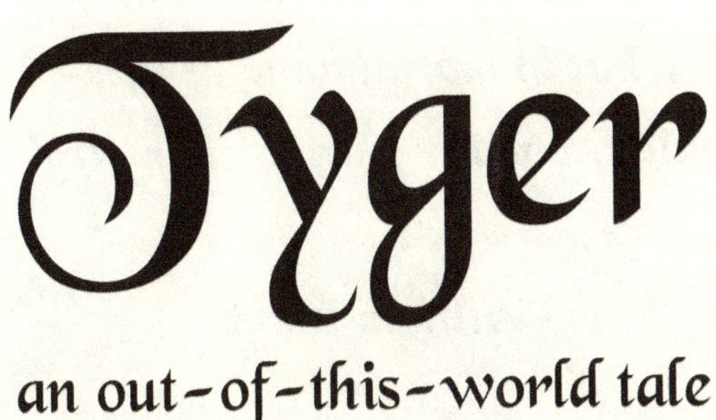

an out-of-this-world tale

M. MARINAN

Silversmith
PUBLISHING

Tyger Tyger, burning bright,
In the forests of the night;
What immortal hand or eye,
Could frame thy fearful symmetry?

- William Blake

First published in New Zealand in 2020 by Silversmith Publishing

A catalogue record for this book is available from the National Library of New Zealand
This version ISBN 978-0-9951196-6-6
Trade paperback ISBN 978-1-99-001400-0

For Paul.
It's not Star Trek, but it'll do.

With thanks to Anne-Marie and Kate.

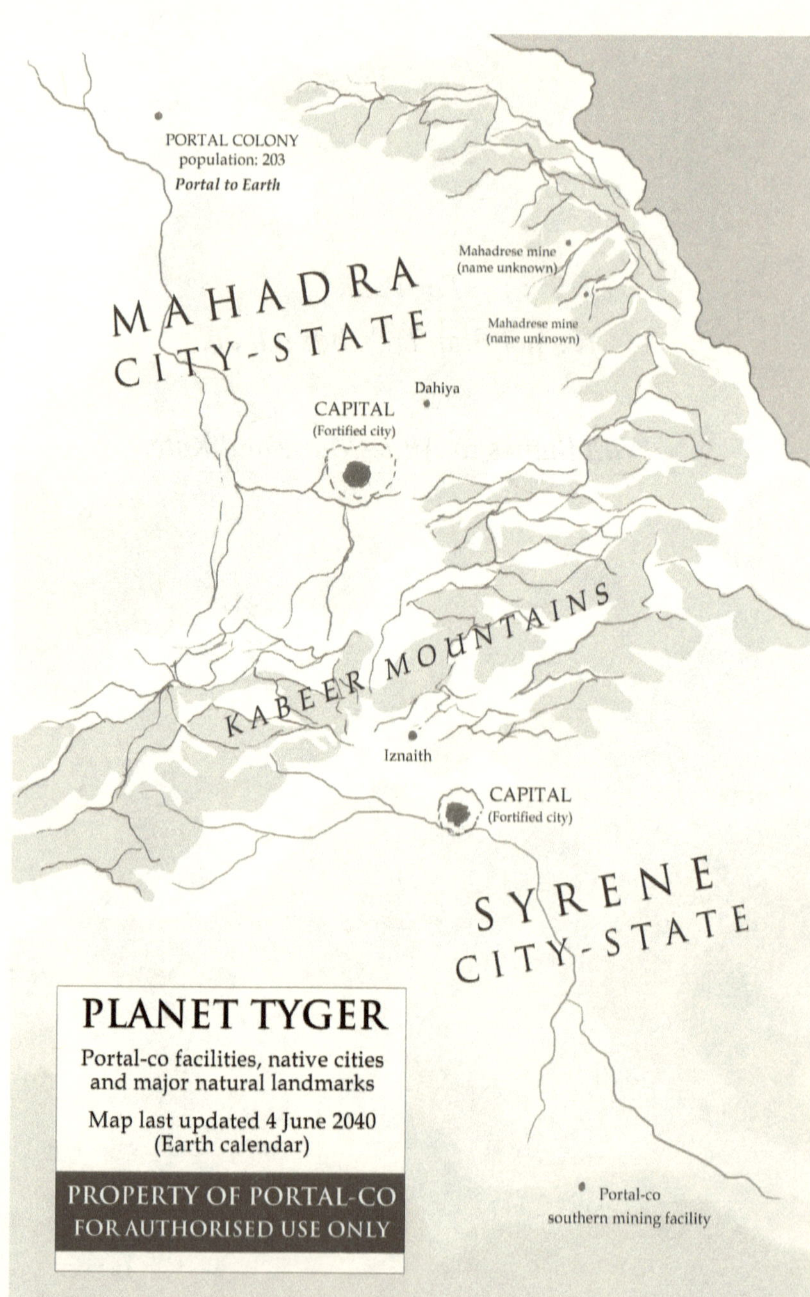

PORTAL COLONY
population: 203
Portal to Earth
MAHADRA
CITY-STATE
Mahadrese mine
(name unknown)
Mahadrese mine
(name unknown)
Dahiya
CAPITAL
(Fortified city)
KABEER MOUNTAINS
Iznaith
CAPITAL
(Fortified city)
SYRENE
CITY-STATE
PLANET TYGER
Portal-co facilities, native cities
and major natural landmarks
Map last updated 4 June 2040
(Earth calendar)
PROPERTY OF PORTAL-CO
FOR AUTHORISED USE ONLY
Portal-co
southern mining facility

Contents

Prologue

Thirteen years ago
Syrene city-state, the planet Tyger
2027 AD (Earth calendar)

The little girl stretched out one hand to her favourite companion, then giggled as the animal wrapped its long, slightly wrinkled trunk around her wrist, its small ears twitching curiously. The trunk moved up her arm to brush over her face, then snuffled up a handful of her reddish-brown hair.

"No, Khoom!" she scolded, trying to pull her hair free, then gave up and scratched him behind those small ears. "You're a naughty raphanta. You know I have to say goodbye. We're going away for a while to see Papa's family in Mahadra. You can't make me late."

But the raphanta didn't respond to her words, only showing some sign of displeasure when she pulled away from him, back towards the sturdy wooden door of his stable. He let out a trumpeting-growl, stomping a solid brown foot on the straw-covered ground, and the sound was echoed by half a dozen other, more nervous raphantas in adjoining stalls.

Outside the stall, the girl's father stood in travelling gear, his arms folded as he waited patiently. His similarly auburn hair was almost fully covered by the hood of his travelling cloak, but his copper-brown eyes were placid.

Next to him, a stableman in a royal grey and blue uniform also stood with folded arms – but his purple eyes looked wide and unnerved. "I don't know how you can be so calm, Malchiel," he muttered to the father. "Not when your child's in a stall with such a beast. Everyone knows brown raphantas are vicious and uncontrollable. I don't even know why the emir insists on keeping one. They give a nasty bite."

"Because they're also extremely fast, and he still hopes he can tame one to race one day," Malchiel replied stoically, but there was a twinkle in his eye. "I've told him that they only ever behave well with girls, for some reason. If he wants a rider who won't be thrown or trampled, he needs to allow females to ride in the raphanta races."

The stableman let out a horrified scoff. "As if he ever would. And what kind of female would want to do such a thing?"

Malchiel shrugged, then called over the stable door to his small daughter. "Come along, little bug. Say goodbye to Khoom, and come out. The wagons are packed."

"I know, Papa," she called back. A few moments later her head and arms appeared above the top of the wooden door. Malchiel reached down to hoist her over, and the brown raphanta went wild.

They left to a chorus of trumpets and rattling stalls – because regardless of how gentle that beast was with one girl, its essentially aggressive nature hadn't changed.

Outside the stable, father and daughter walked over to a wagon laden with goods. An older woman sat at the front, her dark blue hair partially covered by a decorative veil, and next to her was another little girl, almost identical to the first.

The stableman watched them climb up, scratching his chin worriedly with one hand. Then he called out, "Malchiel, I hear the people where you're going aren't so friendly to…your kind. If things don't work out…"

Malchiel didn't blink. "We'll come straight back. I won't risk my family's safety."

The stableman nodded, because what could he say to that? "Best luck, then."

So he watched them trundle out of the palace stables, on their way to a new life. *Best luck,* he murmured again.

They were going to need it.

PART ONE

Tyger

CHAPTER 1
The Holiday

Mahadra city-state, the planet Tyger, 2040 AD

Astrid leaned back in her seat, watching through the airship's small window as the fortified human colony receded into the distance. They'd only been flying for two minutes, but at this speed their small city now resembled a metallic pimple on the dry brown landscape. The ground skimmed by far below them, cracked and barren and mountainous, and she let out a long, happy sigh.

Finally, a holiday. And not just any holiday…

Just then a small blonde girl plunked herself into the empty seat opposite Astrid. Her pretty face was lit with the same excitement that Astrid felt. "I can't believe we're actually going to an alien palace! Don't you just want to burst?!"

Astrid grinned back. "No I don't, Suraya, because then they'll quarantine me for illness and I'll miss out on the Tyger New Year Festival. I haven't lived in the colony for three years just to spend this trip in yet another tiny room. I know I'm lucky to go at all." She paused, then added mischievously, "Maybe I should thank Percy for dumping me in such a public way. If he hadn't, then Anton wouldn't have felt guilty enough to ask me along."

Her recently-ex-boyfriend was also Anton's son – Anton being the human colony's mayor and the leader of this human delegation to the alien locals. Or since this was a different world, she mused, did that make *them* the aliens?

Suraya scowled. "Percy won't get anything except a punch in the nose from me. And I'll never talk to Hana again either!"

Oops. She'd raised the wrong topic, Astrid realised, because Suraya was far too loyal a friend to forget that insult. It had only been three days ago that Percy had decided that the new girl Hana would be a more exciting option than boring old Astrid, and it seemed

Suraya was more offended than Astrid was. But perhaps Astrid was too distracted by the way Anton had promptly invited her along as a last-minute addition, because she almost felt it was worth being dumped. She *loved* anything new and unusual, and this alien festival sounded like it was exactly up her alley.

"Never mind all that," she said quickly. "Let's focus on what's ahead. Aliens, palaces, festivals and exotic food…actual water that doesn't have to be piped in!"

"I just want to see a tree that's not growing in a pot," Suraya said a little glumly. "I tell you, if it wasn't for the great pay here and Brian's job with Portal-co, I'd have gone back through the portal to Earth already. I want to stay with my husband, but I can't imagine living here as long as you and Nathaniel have."

Astrid shrugged, having heard this complaint from her friend many times before. Astrid and her older brother Nathaniel had moved to the colony when their parents had found work with Portal-co several years before. The Earth-based organisation was officially responsible for the only sizeable human settlement on this planet, which in practice meant managing the portal between worlds, trading with the alien locals, and operating both the local mine and the one far south.

The human colony was small and somewhat basic, so as a result the pay for working here was really, really good – plus there was schooling for any children workers brought along. But when their parents had been killed in an accident last year, she'd decided to stay anyway. Nathaniel already worked full-time with the portal and the mines, while she worked part-time in the colony greenhouses around her studies.

"This place is home now," she said in reply to Suraya's comment. "But that doesn't mean I'm not *sooo* excited to go on this trip! We might even meet Prince Raka." She knew next to nothing about the man – only his name and position, and that he was hosting them in the Tyger city of Mahadra – but he was a prince, and that made him interesting, right? If nothing else she'd have bragging rights.

"Emir Raka," Suraya corrected. "That's a closer translation, but Brian says he's a bit of a jerk. He says that if it wasn't for the priceless ambrilene that his people trade then Earth would refuse to have anything to do with him, because his human-rights violations are terrible."

Astrid felt her jaw drop. "Oh yeah?"

Her friend leaned forward and lowered her voice to a near-whisper. "There are only rumours, because the bosses wouldn't let a pleb like Brian find out the real details. But he does know one thing. Emir Raka rules Mahadra, right? Well, Raka thinks that he should also get to rule the next city-state, Syrene. That's 'cos he was supposed to marry the emir of Syrene's daughter, but then she died and her father went crazy – that's Raka's uncle – so now his uncle's nephew is ruling Syrene as regent instead of the real emir."

Astrid felt her eyes cross as she tried to make sense of that. "Wait… Emir Raka was going to marry his own cousin? Is that a human-rights violation or just inbreeding? Besides, they're not human, they're Tygers."

"No, not that, silly! It was the way he-"

"Coming down into Mahadra city-state in ten minutes," Anton cut in via the loudspeaker, his usually calm tones carrying noticeable excitement. "So if you're not wearing your seatbelts, put them on now. And remember, the eleven of us represent Earth to these Tygers. This is the first time we've ever been allowed inside this city, so it's a big deal. We're the aliens to them, yet Emir Raka has invited us to stay for a week. So switch on your translator, and remember that if you mess up, Earth messes up."

"No pressure," Astrid muttered, but her own pulse picked up as she slipped on her translator with its slender curved ear and mouthpiece. She'd lived on this planet for years, yet she'd never mingled with the locals. Except for a small medical team down in Syrene, no one did. They were so insular that she'd never even visited any of their towns or their few major cities, and while she and the others had flown here quickly, that was more to do with the speed of the airship than any true proximity.

Generally, Astrid and the two hundred or so other humans kept to themselves in their fortified city-colony, mostly living off supplies sent through from the nearby portal to Earth, and paying their way by sending back highly valuable minerals. Rubies, platinum…ambrilene. Even though ambrilene could be used for just about anything, Earth scientists couldn't decide if it was animal, vegetable or mineral. It definitely couldn't be mined, that was for sure.

The airship shuddered, and Astrid gripped the armrests tightly, leaning back to avoid the sudden change in pressure. Outside the window she could now see a vast city in the distance: made of the same stone as the surrounding landscape, and lit up pink and gold by the midday sun. She caught glimpses of spiralling towers, patches of greenery and what might have been a river, but too soon they were coming to land and were too low to see anything further.

A few minutes later they had the go-ahead to exit. Astrid crowded into the aisle along with ten others. There were three other women including Suraya, while the rest were male, and all carried that same palpable hum of excitement.

Then they stepped out of the air-conditioned ship and were greeted with a wash of heat from the Tyger summer. It was warmer down here, and the air carried with it the scent of unfamiliar spices and flowers. It reminded her of a Middle Eastern market she'd visited once as a child, and it seemed that the local culture had some similarities too.

She felt a hand on her arm and looked up to see Nathaniel. Older by five years, definitely bigger and bossier, but like her, he resembled their father. Brown hair, brown eyes, and a solid tan even in winter. "Don't forget to stay with me," he reminded her. "The Tyger women don't have the freedom that you're used to, and if you're not careful the locals might think you're…you know. Loose."

"I *know*," Astrid replied a little snappishly. "You've told me that ten times today already."

'Loose', because she was actually out and about instead of locked inside her house, and because she wore trousers. Except today she *wasn't* wearing trousers. She wore – horror of all horrors – an actual dress. Kind of. A long tunic over her nicest tight trousers was a dress, right? It even had slightly puffed sleeves, just like the latest fashions from Earth.

But the biggest joke was being thought of as too permissive, when that was exactly why Percy had left her for Hana.

"Don't get cranky, Az," Nathaniel said mildly. "You know I'm looking out for you."

Except for their aunt Jae who worked as a doctor in Syrene, she was his only remaining family. But she still resisted the urge to stick out her tongue at that nickname, which sounded an awful lot like 'ass'. "Of course you are," she retorted dryly. "And I love it."

But now Astrid could see the city looming up ahead of them, and her brother's overprotectiveness was forgotten. The high walls looked huge; built of the local pale yellow stone, polished by time or skilled masons. The metal gates themselves were just as massive, easily twenty metres high…and closed.

But their group hadn't been forgotten. Music played, something high and melodic, and the gates slowly opened with a groaning sound that told of their immense weight, and of the pulleys that must be working behind the scenes. Astrid's eyes widened and she shuffled with the others to stand in the formation they'd been taught. Most important people at the front, women in the middle. She was at the middle-back next to Nathaniel – she really wasn't important at all – but she could still see what was coming out of the gates.

Wow, wow, wow! An enormous creature was coming into view, one probably twice her height, with wrinkled, pale blue skin, thick legs, and a long trunk that swayed with every heavy step. Its little, floppy ears twitched as if in agitation and its small black eyes darted about, but it still moved steadily towards them, flanked on either side by half a dozen Mahadrese guards in gleaming branzine armour – one of the pinkish-orange metals mined on this world.

"It's a blue raphanta," Nathaniel murmured, leaning down towards Astrid. "It's related to the Earth elephant, but is bigger and seems to be more intelligent."

"Yeah, I've read about them," she agreed excitedly. Raphantas were only one of the fascinating new creatures here on this world that the humans called Tyger, and they weren't the only ones with similarities to Earth animals. Modern humans might have only discovered the portal in the last fifty years, but clearly *someone* had been using it beforehand. Otherwise why would the locals look so very, very human?

As for the raphantas, she hadn't imagined they would be so huge. "Its ears are tiny compared to an elephant's, but look at the size of those tusks! Are they gold-plated?" Indeed the enormous curved tusks did seem to be unnaturally bright and metallic, matching the delicate, spiralling designs curving over its light blue skin.

"Never mind the animal," Suraya whispered from her other side. "Look at the man riding it! Whoar!"

"Oi," her husband snapped from the other side.

"Sorry, Brian."

But Astrid had to agree with Suraya. Forget the raphanta: the man riding on it looked *magnificent*. She supposed anyone would with that level of jewels and gold on their person, but the fact that he was young and handsome didn't hurt. He had golden brown skin and pansy-blue hair tied in a ponytail behind his pointed ears.

It was hard to tell from this distance, but he also looked tall and lean. From what Aunt Jae had said, such colouring was normal for Tyger locals, but to Astrid he was like something from a fairytale. The few photos she'd seen barely did him justice except to show his elegant features…and arrogant expression.

He had to be Emir Raka, she decided. Who else would ride such a fabulously lavish raphanta? And who else would look so stuck-up, she thought a little less kindly. But then maybe if she had absolute power over a quarter of *her* planet, she might be a little arrogant too. Barring Syrene, Mahadra was by far the biggest of Tyger's city-states.

"Not so concerned about human rights violations now, are you?" Astrid murmured to her friend.

Suraya didn't respond, clearly too fixated on the scene ahead. Up at the front of their group, Anton had stepped forward along with his wife, Eirene, and was saying something that was being laboriously translated by their earpieces.

Just then Nathaniel elbowed her in the side. "D'ya see the tyger, Az?"

"Of course I see the emir!" she whispered back. "And stop calling me Az!"

"No, the Tyger local, the *tyger*," he persisted. "The big white cat. It's just to the left of the raphanta, and it's not even on a lead. Can you see it?"

Astrid blinked, leaning sideways to search for the creature between the heads of those in front of her. Then she saw it. A cat sitting nonchalantly not far from the blue-skinned raphanta, with a bored expression on its feline face.

But Nathaniel had been wrong to call it 'big'. It was huge! She'd bet it would be taller than a man standing on its hind legs, and it was marked with faint blue stripes all over that fluffy white coat, just like an Earth tiger.

But unlike Earth tigers, this dangerous animal wasn't locked away, nor deep in the few remaining jungles. "It's not even wearing a collar," she whispered in shock. "It must be well trained." It *better* be well trained. If a cat that size decided to get violent, it could do a lot of damage.

"I think they are," Nathaniel whispered back. "I read that they're sacred to the locals. That's why we call this world Tyger. It's something to do with…some old English poem, I think."

Astrid had a vague memory of such a thing. *Tyger, tyger, burning bright…* The thought made her shiver. What a beautiful, terrifying creature, and it had clearly made enough of an impression on the first human visitors that they'd named the world and the locals after it too.

Just then the big cat looked across at her, and its purple eyes seemed to meet hers. It blinked, then in that way cats did, just held her gaze.

She stared at it for a few moments before looking away. She didn't want it to think she was challenging it, and besides, she'd lost staring competitions to housecats. What chance did she have with this beast? But then her earpiece began translating a new voice.

"…welcome you to Mahadra for the Festival of the New Year. I trust you will find our hospitality to your liking."

"I'm sure we will," Anton began to reply, but the huge blue raphanta was already turning; the emir clearly having decided the conversation was over. Astrid could see the tips of Anton's ears were a little red, but then he shrugged, and in they went.

Syrene

The regent of Syrene stood at the open window of the tower room, his hands clasped behind his back as he looked out over the city. Beyond the stone buildings draped with banners of green and blue cloth, he could see the raphanta track in the distance, currently being prepared for the races in a few weeks' time. It looked busy and beautiful and ugly and chaotic, all of those contrasts all at once.

The Syrenian people were the same: both ugly and beautiful depending on when you caught them. Just look at the way they treated some of the minorities among them. Shameful. He wondered if it was fear or misinformation that made them behave so.

He sighed. "What a mess. Why did you choose me to rule in your place, Stepfather?"

But the man on the bed behind him didn't respond, nor had the regent expected him to. Emir Jireh of Syrene lay flat on his back on the fine sheets, his face slack from sleep and medication, and worn from years of sickness. He was a man of late middle-age, but looked far older.

"The people don't listen to me," the regent continued, still studying the city. "They listen to old Palos your advisor more than they listen to me. And they don't like me either, not how they liked you. Can't you just wake up?"But if Jireh woke up, then he'd be muttering and confused and ranting about invisible dangers. Or perhaps he would just stare blankly at the wall for hours. That was how it had started: a previously fine man and fine ruler had apparently lost his mind over a matter of months.

Just then a tap sounded at the door. "Your Excellency. His Magnificence's evening medicine is ready."

And that was enough one-sided conversation for the day, the regent decided. He smiled at the white-haired nurse then took his leave. It was time to find something to do in this land that neither wanted nor needed him.

Mahadra

Emir Raka's blue raphanta led the way through the massive stone gates, and the humans followed like ducklings after a huge, ugly mother duck. As they filed in, Astrid noticed that the big, white tyger-cat didn't move. It just sat there, watching them walk within mere metres of its own position.

She held back a shiver. It really was as big as she'd thought, and she couldn't shake the comparison to an Earth tiger with its wildness, danger…and teeth. Then to her relief, it got up and loped gracefully back to walk at the feet of the blue raphanta up ahead.

Once they were inside the city, guards came to walk behind them, and Astrid marvelled at the difference in their surroundings. There were wide streets and high, pale stone buildings, but all that she could really see were the people.

Hundreds or even thousands of them lined the sides of the road, packed in like a mosh pit from an Earth rock concert. They cheered as the procession moved through, their curious eyes fixed on the humans, and she watched in fascination as they bowed like a field of wheat blown by a strong wind as the emir's raphanta passed them.

They all seemed to be male, although it was hard to tell with their long hair and loose tunics. So many had dark blue or purple hair, the colour so intense and exotic that she wanted to touch it to see if it was real, or if it would come off on her fingers. Occasionally she'd see a bright silvery-white head amongst the blue. Old age, she wondered, or a recessive gene?

Astrid felt nervous, suddenly aware of her own short brown hair, silky and fine but only just past chin length, and was glad that she'd worn a dress (sort of). Above the crowd she thought she saw a glimpse of veiled faces hidden behind screened windows, but then they moved past and she wasn't sure if she'd imagined it.

She glanced at her brother to see he'd been looking in the same direction, and he caught her gaze with a sheepish smile. "What? Don't tell me you aren't curious."

Curious about what the local women looked like, he meant.

"Yes, but *I* won't get my bits cut off for being too curious," she retorted, half-smiling.

Just as much as Nathaniel expected her to be reserved, she expected the same of him. There were different dangers for both male and females in such an unfamiliar setting, but they'd be careful. None of the humans would be stupid enough to cause offence when they were outnumbered here twenty thousand to one.

Astrid noticed how the dryness of the surrounding desert didn't extend to inside the city walls. There were trees planted everywhere as well as glazed pots of greenery scattered about, while narrow aqueducts ran alongside buildings and spilled out into pools that she could only just see amongst the crowd.

It was a true oasis, and the palace itself was right in the centre, at the end of the long, wide main street. The crowds lined the streets the whole way, and as the blue raphanta reached the palace gates they remained in place, cheering until the whole group had entered the palace and the gates had closed behind them.

Wow, they seemed to really love the emir, Astrid mused. There he was up ahead, sitting straight-backed on that enormous blue animal. He hadn't moved that she'd noticed, nor spoken to anyone else. Maybe he was just focusing on not falling off.

But if she'd thought the city was lush, the palace was much more so. Water seemed to be everywhere, and she'd been so deprived of the sight of it back at the colony that she drank it in with her eyes, wishing that she could jump right into one of the pools that lay alongside the stone paths.

She'd been so distracted by her surroundings that she barely noticed when the emir left, replaced by a small team of what were presumably servants, but who were dressed as richly as she was herself – and she was wearing almost her best outfit. The Tygers obviously weren't minimalists.

Suddenly the group seemed to be splitting off, and Nathaniel gave her a pat on the shoulder before walking away with the other men. "See you at the feast!"

"What's happening?" Had she missed something important?

"You weren't listening, huh?" Suraya said with a slight smirk. "We're going to the women's quarters before the feast."

"Oh." Astrid shrugged and smiled back. "This should be interesting." She, at least, was going to see the famously-hidden Tyger ladies, and chances were they'd be gorgeous. The few photos she'd seen hadn't included *them,* and even Aunt Jae hadn't sent any decent pictures. Nathaniel would be so jealous.

The much smaller group of women was led down halls of the same white stone, marked with elaborate tapestries down every wall and with enormous enamelled vases in just about every spare corner, big enough to climb inside. She hadn't known what to expect, but it was certainly living up to her expectations of what a palace should look like, with a strong Middle Eastern flavour. There was colour everywhere; gold and unfamiliar metallic threads, enormous, bright flowers…

Now they were approaching a set of closed double doors. A Tyger woman waited out front along with two guards, both armoured enough to be unidentifiable, with smooth round-topped branzine helmets. But the woman wore long, beautifully ornate robes with a tidy sash around the waist and chest, and her hair and ears were covered with a turban-like wrap. Astrid estimated the woman was about fifty years old, and apart from her pale purple eyes, she looked remarkably human.

"Welcome to the women's quarters," she greeted them, her words being translated after a brief delay. "My name is Hailene, and I will be responsible for your welfare while you stay at the palace. Your husbands are of course welcome to visit you, or you may visit them when asked, but such requests will need to be made to me. If you would follow after me."

Suraya and Astrid exchanged a dubious glance at the comment about asking for permission, but they kept their mouths shut and followed after. Astrid couldn't help but glance at those guards as she walked through, and narrowed, bright Tyger-purple eyes stared back through the thin gaps in the metal. She lifted her chin and picked up her pace.

They moved through a central set of suites that reminded her of a large hotel foyer, and she barely got the chance to notice that there were women scattered around the room, as well as a few children. Or were there men too? It was hard to tell, since the men wore their hair so long, and except for the guards, they all seemed to wear those long robes.

She found herself studying Hailene's appearance once again. Up close, the Tygers looked so humanlike, but not quite. Perhaps a little taller and leaner than the average human – or her group of humans anyway – and with features that reminded Astrid of North Africa or the Middle East.

They had strong eyebrows, black-lined eyes and that fantastical colouring that they all shared: shades of deep purplish or blue hair that in dim light looked almost black, except for the few that were silver-haired, of course. Perhaps they were albinos – but could she even call them albinos when their skin was as brown as every other Tyger's?

Aunt Jae had debunked a rumour that the Tygers had slit pupils to go with their pointed ears, and Astrid was disappointed to see she'd been right. As far as she could tell, those pupils were as round and boring as her own.

She'd read that the Tyger people were so closely related to humans that they must have originally come from Earth, just like the tyger cats and raphantas. But Earth history had no record of the portal before a century ago, and the Tygers weren't telling.

Plus, it didn't explain the inhuman ears. Astrid's personal theory was that humans had come through the portal before modern records started, and had mixed with Tyger's local population – the true aliens, who'd then died out. She reckoned that the humanlike Tygers must be the inspiration for all of Earth's stories about elves and fairies, too.

Nathaniel had agreed with her for the second part, but popped a hole in her brilliant theory by pointing out that for some ancient humans to mix with true aliens, they'd have to be similar to begin with. Same problem.

Astrid hadn't been able to argue with that, so she'd just punched him in the arm then kept her mouth shut. Ah, older brothers.

Hailene finally came to a halt in another foyer, this one with half a dozen doors coming off it. "This shall be your place of rest at the palace. I trust you shall find it satisfactory."

The slightly awkward translation made it sound like she was describing a cemetery, but Astrid got the point.

They were led to their rooms. Astrid's wasn't as opulent as she would have expected considering the surroundings. It was about the size of her room back home (i.e. small and 'cozy') but with fancier blankets, and a single glass flower in a tall vase. That was a nice touch, she thought. She opened the slatted door next to the bed wondering if there was more to it, but the door only revealed a small convenience.

Oh, well. She was still in a palace, and that was very cool.

Astrid wandered next door to where Suraya was practically squealing in delight.

"Look at this waterfall," Suraya said with an awed sigh. "It's for washing my hands! And this bed! I can't believe I don't have to share it with anyone!" Good point, because although she was married, her husband was located in another part of the palace.

But now that Astrid saw the size of Suraya's room it looked like Astrid had been put in the closet, and she tried to hide her disappointment.

"Let's see yours, then," Suraya declared. She marched to the connecting door, looked in, then did a double take. "What's through the door?"

"The toilet."

"Oh." There was a moment of shared disappointment, then they both shrugged. "We're out of the colony," the older girl said happily. "Who cares about the rooms, right?"

"Maybe it's because I got added to the group at the last minute," Astrid suggested, but she smiled back at her friend. "Shall I thank Percy…?"

Suraya huffed. "Yes, thank him for ditching you before you were silly enough to marry him."

"I wouldn't have married him," Astrid countered. "We were just dating."

"And you were dating him because he was the only one to show interest," Suraya shot back. "It's a small colony, girl, and you were settling."

Had she been settling? She was young, and she always figured she'd go back to Earth to settle. One day.

A servant girl had been quietly placing blankets in the background, and Astrid bit back her response, suddenly aware that the translation devices worked both ways. She could turn it off, but she always thought it was rude to speak in another language when someone else was in the room.

But the girl had heard. "Apologies for your unhappiness, my lady," she said, her voice as quiet as her movements. "We were under the impression you were unmarried."

Suraya and Astrid exchanged a baffled glance. Was she talking about Percy or about the room?

But then the girl clarified very gently, "But of course married women are given the most honour, including the finest rooms in case their husbands should want to visit. Is it not the same amongst your people?"

She was talking about the room size. "Uh…"

"Couples usually share rooms," Suraya said, blushing a little. She'd only been married three months. In fact, one of the reasons she and Brian had come was that they were actually married rather than just de facto like many human couples – that sort of thing would matter to the locals. Astrid figured Suraya was trying to work out how she could have her husband come visit without the whole world knowing about it…but it wasn't like anyone would be surprised.

"Apologies," the servant girl said again. She still hadn't met their eyes, and all Astrid saw was the top of her dark head, with curlier hair than she was used to seeing on the natives. She was small and sturdy for a Tyger, with the kind of sweet round face that would probably make her look fifteen when she was forty. "I can speak to Hailene about moving you if this doesn't suit."

"It's fine," Astrid cut in quickly, embarrassed. The room was at least as good as her room at home, and if she'd had the wrong idea of what it would be like here, it had been quickly corrected. "I was surprised by the difference, that's all. And the location is perfect." She smiled at her friend. "And I'll definitely be borrowing your waterfall."

"What's this about a waterfall?" one of the other women asked as she came into the room, and then they fell into a conversation about their respective rooms (of which Suraya's appeared to be one of the most impressive) and what they were going to wear to dinner that night.

"You'll have to wear makeup," Suraya told Astrid decisively. "We'll be eating with royals, girl. You have to look your best."

Just then there was the tiniest little cough, and the servant girl looked like she wanted to disappear into the floor. "Apologies," she said again. "The unmarried women do not dine with the men, but in the women's quarters after being presented at the feast."

Oh. *Ohh.*

"Surely that wouldn't include you," Suraya said in an aside to Astrid. "Not after coming all the way here."

CHAPTER 2
Differences

"It definitely includes you," Anton said apologetically, briefly reminding Astrid of the servant girl. "Unmarried women don't eat with men. Cultural norms and all that. Sorry, we didn't know until the last minute."

"It's OK," she replied, gritting her teeth. "It's just one meal."

"Actually it'll probably be every meal." He paused. "Sorry."

Ohh. Now Astrid didn't feel OK anymore. Everyone was dressed up for the feast. The men in their tuxedos sent through the portal specially for this occasion, and the women in evening gowns.

She was even wearing a proper dress; one down to her ankles and made of black satin. It was quite plain except for the decorative criss-crossed ribbons across its back, but she'd had to borrow it from a girl at the colony at the last minute. And now she couldn't even show it off properly?

"But why can't I eat with everyone else?" Astrid persisted. "Can't you tell them that it's human custom?"

"We're the visitors here, so we follow their customs. It seems the unmarried women are kept very…protected."

"Restricted, you mean," she said dully. "Fine. As long as I don't miss out on all the fun stuff."

"You'll get to visit for the presentation at least," Anton told her. "By the way, you look nice with your face done up like that. And whatever you've done to your hair."

Not a very eloquent compliment for an hour of Suraya's time spent putting on smoky eyeshadow and French plaits, but Astrid was too disappointed to really appreciate it anyway. She muttered a thank you, wondering exactly what the Tygers thought unmarried girls would get up to if allowed to attend a mixed gender meal. Flirt with all the men? Spit in the food? Take off their clothes and dance on the table?

She briefly wished they'd visited the other city-state, Syrene, instead of Mahadra. At least that way she could have seen Aunt Jae. But Mahadra was the one trading ambrilene, she reminded herself. Syrene wouldn't trade, but allowed in that one small medical team instead.

When they arrived at the feast which was attended by about fifty locals, Astrid realised what they meant by 'presented'. The emir sat at the front of the room under a curtained canopy which must be his 'throne', with several others on either side of him. More locals sat on very low, flat seats down each side of the room, with low tables lined with red cloth runners in front of them.

Astrid stood back with the other humans as Anton and Eirene were led to the canopy and introduced along with two of the other oldest couples. In turn, Emir Raka introduced a few of the most important natives whose names Astrid immediately forgot.

One she did remember, though: a silver-haired young man of about Nathaniel's age, except far snootier-looking. His name translated something like 'Orin the Blessed'. Except for the hair colour and plainer clothing, his elegant features and lean build reminded her a lot of the emir. But when her eyes met his for a mere moment, she couldn't shake the feeling that he wasn't happy they were here.

Then two veiled women stepped forward, and Raka acknowledged them with a graceful wave of one hand. "And finally, my sister, the Most Chaste Lady Tamzyn, and my aunt, the Most Chaste Lady Ruhazia."

The two women nodded in the direction of the clustered humans, and Astrid studied them curiously. If this was the emir's family, she would have thought they would be emiras or even princesses rather than just 'ladies' – but perhaps that was a translation issue.

She'd also expected they'd be well-dressed, and they were. Their long robes were clearly finely-made, and the young one wore a headpiece of beads over her translucent veil. The elder one, who might have been in her sixties, wore a turban rather like Hailene's, but also with a veil so that her features were barely visible.

And there was the problem. Compared to the beautiful colours and ornate jewellery of the other Tyger men and women, these two looked like nuns.

'Most Chaste Ladies'? Maybe they *were* nuns, Astrid pondered. She wanted to debate it with Suraya, or to ask Nathaniel if he thought the women were as pretty as he'd imagined, but it seemed they were being directed to their seats now.

Just then she felt a tap on her shoulder and looked up to see Hailene. "The unmarried women will now return to the women's quarters," she said. Her tone was polite even through the translator, but it clearly wasn't a request.

Astrid glanced back to where Nathaniel stood waiting to be seated. He looked very handsome in his rented tuxedo, and his gaze kept flickering over to her. "Just a moment." She quickly walked over to her brother, trying not to trip in her long, fashionably narrow skirt. "Did you hear?" she asked him. "I can't eat with you guys."

"What?" he replied, but he kept looking over her shoulder.

Astrid glanced back to see the nunlike lady-princesses waiting by the exit with Hailene and two guards, and realised it wasn't *her* he'd been looking at. But then even with that plain clothing, Astrid could tell the younger woman was pretty. Figured. Even alien sort-of-princesses just shouldn't be ugly – it went against every fairytale she'd ever heard.

"Nathaniel, are you even listening to me?"

"Yeah, of course you look very nice."

Astrid huffed out a sigh, feeling more amused than annoyed, then punched him lightly in the arm. "You wally. Ask Suraya what happened, OK? I'll see you later."

"OK. Wait…what?"

But she was now hyper-aware of everyone taking their seats and the segregated singles in the corner, so she just grinned at him, then headed off to join them. Never mind the segregation, she told herself. She was in a palace! An *alien* palace, which was even more impressive. Everyone back at the colony would be green with envy even if she was stuck in the toilet for the whole time.

When Astrid approached the others, they seemed to be whispering urgently under their veils. Hailene looked uncomfortable. The guards looked like tin statues – but was one of them glaring at her under that helmet?

"I'm ready," Astrid said cheerfully. "So you have your own women's feast, is that right?"

"Uh…there will be food served," Hailene replied eventually. Her eyes flicked back to where the others were now seated. "We shall return now, if you will."

"OK," Astrid said a little hesitantly, wondering if she'd done something wrong. But she still followed the woman out of the room and back down the halls. The younger Lady Tamzyn was at her side, and Astrid could swear she was peeking at her through that veil. After a few minutes of awkward silence, she said, "By the way, I'm Astrid Townsend."

There were a few more seconds where it seemed the lady wouldn't answer, but then she inclined her head under that veil. "Yes. *Ass-treed.*"

"Uh…no, *Astrid.* Like, *Azz.*" Astrid tried to emphasize the difference between the sounds, but she just garnered a blank stare. "Ah, never mind. So, you're the emir's sister. Younger, I guess?" Because from what she knew of the locals, they tended to marry very young. Aunt Jae said fourteen or fifteen was normal – and the emir had to be at least in his early twenties.

There was another pause as her words were translated, then the reply came in smooth Tyger. "Are such personal comments typical of your people?"

Astrid felt her cheeks heat, because she couldn't miss the sharpness of that comment. She hadn't meant to be rude, but she answered honestly anyway. "Yes, pretty much. How can you get to know someone if you don't ask questions?"

"Of course." Lady Tamzyn lifted her chin as they approached the double doors to the women's quarters. "I am Emir Raka's *older* sister by two years. As for you, who was the young man that you struck in the feast room?"

For a moment Astrid had no idea who she was talking about. She hadn't hit anybody! Then she realised what Tamzyn meant. "Oh, that's just my brother, Nathaniel. He's five years older than me, and he wasn't listening properly."

Now she distinctly heard the older lady – Rhubarb? – suck in a shocked breath. Tamzyn seemed to choke a little. "And is it…your custom…to strike men when they do not listen properly?"

Oh, so *that* was what she'd done earlier to make everyone look like they'd eaten lemons, Astrid realised. "It was just a friendly punch," she said a little defensively. "Just because he's my brother. I didn't hurt him."

"I see," Tamzyn said finally, but her head turned to face forward. "Your people are not like ours."

Oops. Astrid guessed she'd made a major faux pas, but she couldn't take it back now. She just hoped no one else had noticed. But then she couldn't imagine the supremely dignified Most-Chaste

Lady ever friendly-punching her own supremely dignified brother.

Maybe the Tygers really were different after all.

"Or maybe you just shouldn't go punching people in public," Suraya suggested later that night. They both sat cross-legged on her enormous bed. Suraya's cheeks were flushed pink enough to show that she'd had more than a drink or two at the feast, while Astrid was stiff with resentment over her less than fantastic evening playing checkers…by herself, as the Tyger women had preferred to ignore her rather than engage in conversation via translator.

Yes, *checkers*, because she'd not bothered to fix the broken entertainment app on her laptop, thinking she wouldn't need it here. The old-fashioned checker board game had been added to her luggage as an afterthought.

"It was barely a punch," Astrid countered. "You wouldn't have known about it if I hadn't told you."

"Yeah, yeah, whatever. Do you want to hear something *really* interesting about those ladies?"

"Of course!"

Suraya leaned forward, lowering her voice. "The female royals aren't allowed to get married. That's why they're called 'Most Chaste'. Get it?"

"Why not?" Astrid was baffled. "Don't these sorts of societies use marriage as a way to make connections?"

Her friend leaned forward again until the edge of her nose bumped Astrid's collarbone. "Ow. You're bony."

"That's because you hit a bone. Now are you going to answer my question?"

Suraya sat up again, arching her eyebrows in a knowing fashion. "The female royals aren't allowed to get married, because then their children would be contenders for the throne. That's why. And they can't have kids out of wedlock either. They have to be…um, 'pure and undefiled'."

Lovely. "Contenders…" Astrid frowned. "That's stupid. Surely you'd have the same problem if the ruler had more than one son, right?"

Suraya shrugged. "I 'spose so. Now are you going to leave or what? Brian will be here any moment." And then her cheeks turned even pinker.

Astrid rolled her eyes, but got off the bed. "You have fun *not* being pure and undefiled, then. I'll go make my own fun."

She headed back to her bedroom, but unsurprisingly the small, empty room wasn't any more interesting now than it had been earlier. So rather than spend the evening playing checkers with herself – again – Astrid went to bed.

There was always tomorrow.

It was late enough that the palace had gone quiet, and this world's small cluster of moons hung low enough to cast their pink and purple light over the garden. Nathaniel could smell some fragrant flower – he didn't know its name – but the rich scent just added to the feeling of intoxication.

But the feeling didn't come from alcohol. He'd only had one drink, because getting drunk wouldn't look good for him, or for Earth. And he'd loved the feast with its different foods and the performances by acrobats and dancers and even a fire-swallower.

There'd been just one fascinating face that had stuck in his memory, and that was why he now stood out on the colonnaded balcony of his room where it edged onto the central palace gardens. There was a wall in the distance, just about disappearing in the darkness. He'd guess it was twice his height, and it ran from one side of garden to the other.

Don't go over the wall, Anton had told all the men, as if it even needed to be said. *The women's quarters are on the other side, and the Tygers are rabidly protective of their women.*

As if they'd had to tell him, Nathaniel had thought scornfully. He liked a pretty face – didn't everyone? But he wasn't going to risk his life and his world's trading connections for one, even an alien one. *Especially* an alien one.

Yet the glimpse he'd caught of that lovely face through the shimmering veil had captivated him. As lovely as a Renaissance Madonna, with a hint of sadness that had gripped his imagination.

She's practically a princess, he scolded himself now even as he stared at that wall – a sign of the barrier between them as much as race and position. *Don't waste your time.*

But still he found himself pausing on the edge of the balcony for a few moments longer… then stepping down into the garden.

It was almost midday on Astrid's second day, and the sun sent golden light slanting against the pale walls of the women's quarters. A few rays made their way into her small room, and she angled her small laptop so that the video screen was still visible.

"What was that?" she asked again. "The sound's not good, and I couldn't see what you just said."

Her aunt Jae rolled her eyes from the screen's slightly blurred picture. As Astrid's father's much younger sister, Jae looked like Astrid probably would in fifteen years. She had an angular face dominated by large brown eyes, straight brown hair and a tendency to smile at anything. Jae probably had a few more curves – but then age might add a little weight to Astrid too. Either that, or she'd eventually end up looking as stringy as a soup chicken.

"I *said*," Jae dragged out, "that I'll be able to schedule a few C-sections in, because the local women are starting to trust me. But I'm sure you don't want to know all the gory details."

"I like gory details," Astrid replied. It was mostly true. She knew far more about Tyger life than almost anyone else in the colony, and it was because of these conversations. Jae and the other male doctors in their small medical clinic in the southern city-state, Syrene, experienced far more of the day-to-day life of the local poor than any number of translators.

It made Astrid glad to be where she was – because while it didn't seem like the local women were mistreated, they were certainly cloistered right up until they were married off, usually with a substantial dowry passed along with them. And the whole thing about getting married so young… "You do the caesareans to stop them getting ripped up giving birth, right? Because their hips are too small."

"Precisely," Jae confirmed. "But enough about my day. I'm in a clinic in the poorest part of Syrene, while you're in the Mahadrese palace. A palace, girl! *You* give *me* the gory details."

"I've already told you what there is to tell," Astrid said a little sadly. After getting up this morning with high hopes, she'd been told the outing that day was *also* for married women only. And what could single girls do? Stay in the women's quarters and play checkers. Or in her case, contact her fantastic aunt.

Jae wasn't a replacement mother for Astrid, and she wasn't a friend like Suraya. She was something else, something special, and Astrid was lucky to have her. At a distance, anyway, which was better than not at all. "Any marriage proposals today?" she asked. That was one of the funnier things about Jae's stories – the Syrenians were much more open to mixing with the humans than the Mahadrese usually were, and the proposals were sometimes hilarious.

"Not today," Jae replied with a twinkle in her eye. "They're finally starting to understand that I'm happy as I am. Although there was one last week, where this man had to be eighty-five if he was a day-"

"Ugh!"

Jae laughed. "He wanted me to marry his grandson. The boy was about fifteen, Astrid. And he was watching me with this kind of fascinated horror while his grandfather spoke. I saw him just about collapse in relief when I said no."

It seemed to Astrid that the Tyger people had a lot of trouble understanding the concept of *single*. They thought it meant that she was widowed, or the concubine of one of her male colleagues (God forbid!) or her fiancé had died – multiple times – and then they'd settled on the idea that she must be devoted to her God, like some of their religious women or men. Jae tried to get across the idea that she could *choose* not to marry – and it wasn't a bad thing. Still it seemed like a lot of them thought Jae had something wrong with her. Regardless, they kept a list of the funniest backhanded compliments and proposals.

Like, 'You might be an old alien, but you aren't too ugly. My cousin might accept you as a third wife'. Jae seemed to take the comments as they were intended – well-meaning.

"What had they come in for?" Astrid asked.

"They'd brought a thirteen-year-old cousin who'd cut her foot. I gave her some antibiotics. Except…" Jae frowned. "She was very small, you know, the size you were at about eight or nine. And she's supposed to be getting married next week. It's a disaster waiting to happen, because I know that if she doesn't end up back here in nine months with an emergency caesarean, she'll be another girl with a fistula from a terrible birth, and I told her that. I told her that she should wait two years until her hips are wider, not that the family will listen. Poor things. Hard to believe it's just as bad back in parts of Earth, yeah?"

Astrid cringed. That particular gory detail was hard to listen to. Horror stories about girls getting married too young somehow seemed so much worse when they were happened here and now, on Tyger and even back on Earth. Come on people, it was 2040! Not 1540.

Jae must have seen Astrid's discomfort because she changed the subject. "OK, enough gore. Tell me about your trip. How's Mahadra city?"

Astrid focused on describing what she'd seen so far: how the culture was colourful and unique, and reminded her of Asia and the Middle East in colour and smell, but of ancient Europe in attitudes. Jae had once compared the main Tyger culture as being 1500 years behind modern Earth, and Astrid thought that might be true. "I like it," she finished. "I probably wouldn't live here though. I'd feel like I was stuck in a pretty cage."

"Hmm. The Tygers don't think their women are restricted, do you know that? They think they're protected and cared for, and that we 'Earthers' don't know how to care for a girl." She grinned. "Maybe they're right. You should come down here to visit me, love. We'll dress you in white like me, say that you're my assistant. You'll see a whole new side of things."

"I want to," Astrid agreed. The only reason she hadn't before was her recently finished schooling, plus Percy. He hadn't liked the idea of her visiting Syrene…and now she wanted to do it just so she could rub it in his face. "As soon as I'm allowed. But while I'm here…I'd love to see something. Anything."

After the call ended Astrid put her laptop away and wandered out to the main area of the women's quarters. Here the roof was open with a surrounding colonnade, and the women and children sat about talking quietly or playing, or in the case of one little boy, splashing in the central waterfall and gleefully ignoring his nurse's scolding.

Astrid didn't blame him. There was something about so much restrained femininity that made her want to put on a pair of shorts and run screaming through the rooms, just for the sake of it.

She looked around for someone to talk to, checkers having lost its thrill after the first game. She'd have to move fast – sit right next to them so they couldn't sneakily move away. She just wanted to talk to *someone*.

She spotted the servant girl from the day before, sitting on a cushion in one corner, working on what looked like a tapestry.

Astrid deliberately moved over and sat next to her. "A'sha."

The translation device repeated the word in English – *hello* – and the girl looked briefly startled. "You speak our language?"

"Just hello, I'm afraid," Astrid replied cheerfully. "But maybe you can teach me. I'm Astrid Townsend."

"Yes, my lady."

"Um…I'm not a lady, although thank you for that. Just Astrid's fine. What's your name?"

The servant was looking slightly panicked. "*Esira* Chakandra, my lady."

Talk about a one-track record. "Nice to meet you, ah, *Esira*?"

"*Esira* is her title," another voice interrupted. It was Lady Tamzyn, and she gave the servant a gentle but firm nod of the head. *Esira* or Chakandra or whoever she was fled gratefully with the briefest glance at Astrid. "But it is not her place to speak to honoured visitors. If you have any questions, I might answer them."

Not her place, eh? Astrid's opinion of the emir's sister dropped – and it hadn't been really high to begin with. She might be even more beautiful without that veil and Most Chaste outfit (whatever that meant) but she was also a total snob. "Thank you, but I don't really have any questions. I'm just tired of my own company, and no one else seems to be available to talk."

Tamzyn paused. "You do not wish to play your game with the squares and the stones?"

She meant checkers, clearly. "It's supposed to be a two-player game."

Another pause. "You may come sit with myself and my ladies, then. If desired."

Astrid would have leaped at the invite if it hadn't been so grudging. Even though she was dead bored, she'd rather play checkers against herself than sit with someone who clearly didn't want her there. "That's very kind…" She searched for an excuse. "But I had intended to visit my brother once he was back from the festival." She glanced down at her phone – good timing for a message, Nathaniel – "Oh look. He says they're on their way back now. I think I'll go wait for him in his rooms."

Those sleek dark blue eyebrows arched. "Would you not be required to await his request?"

"Nope," Astrid replied happily, mentally making plans. Nathaniel said he hadn't brought his laptop, but she'd take a look anyway. Last she knew, his entertainment app was working just fine. "I'll go see him now…but thanks for the invite. Maybe another time." *When you don't act like I have leprosy.*

Tamzyn watched the Earther stride away, those immodest trousers covering nothing. Or they would have covered nothing, had the girl not been as shapeless as a half-grown colt. In a few years she might look like a woman, but now, from behind, she may as well have been a lad.

Perhaps *that* was why the Earthers married so late, because they had no beauty until later on.

And the girl had declined Tamzyn's offer of friendship, which she hadn't made lightly. How could the girl be bored here in the palace of the Mahadrese emir?

Tamzyn sniffed, turning away. Of *course* the girl would be bored if she was accustomed to running about wherever she wanted and talking to whomever she wanted. The life of a noblewoman must seem constrained in contrast.

At that thought, she felt a strange, unwanted feeling and not for the first time. It was jealousy, she admitted to herself, and it hurt. She was the only woman of her status in Mahadra – barring her aunt – and she had safety, wealth and beauty. The finest in everything, the best companions (female only, naturally). She lacked nothing…and boredom was so much a part of life that she barely noticed it anymore. In twenty or thirty years she'd still be in these same quarters, just like Aunt Ruhazia. Respected and resplendent, and as frozen and useless as a gilded butterfly.

Tamzyn stared again at the place the Earther had left, then lifted her chin and walked away.

She was a royal sister of Emir Raka, and she'd be jealous of nothing and no one.

Astrid walked to the outer doors of the women's quarters, trying to act like she belonged. Confidence was everything, her father used to say. If you didn't have it, then you should fake it, because other people couldn't tell the difference.

For a moment she actually thought the guards would just let her walk past, but then one spoke. "My lady, where do you go?"

"To visit my brother, of course," she replied lightly. "We have an agreement."

There was a pause where she thought that this was her chance to find out how the Tygers *really* treated women…but then the guard asked, "Do you require escort?"

Considering she had no idea where the others were staying, then yes. "That would be appreciated."

The rest of the humans turned out to be staying very close; just around the corner and down the hall from the women's quarters. The halls were largely empty. They only passed one person on the way; a white-haired male Tyger a year or two Astrid's senior who didn't looked happy to see her at all.

She recognised him from the feast because he'd stared at her in that same way then as well, like he'd spotted a rotten apple on the tree and wanted to remove it before it tainted the others. What had his name been…Erin? No, something less familiar.

Astrid gave him a smile that was more like a baring of teeth, then when his glare became a scowl, added a happy little wave. But then he moved out of sight, and she was left with her usual feeling of both irritation and triumph. When people acted like asses she preferred to get nicer, and nicer, and nicer…because then they *really* got mad, and it left her feeling more in control.

Then they reached what had to be the men's rooms, and she set herself to forgetting grumpy Erin, and finding Nathaniel's room. It shouldn't be too hard; these rooms fanned out from a central hall just like hers and Suraya's. At the end of that hall was the entrance to the main garden, as well as what seemed to be the other side of the massive stone wall that blocked off the women's gardens.

Astrid wandered from room to room until she recognised Nathaniel's distinctive black and silver suitcase, a gift for his fifteenth birthday nine years before. She recalled it well because at the time she'd been small enough to fit inside, having the idea that jumping out to surprise Nathaniel might be funny. But somehow she'd managed to lock it…

Luckily he'd found her within a few minutes, because suitcases weren't supposed to thump from side to side and make screaming noises. She wasn't scarred by the experience – much – but it was fair to say she wouldn't be climbing into any more tiny dark spaces. Especially lockable ones.

The rooms were all empty, and Astrid's search for her brother's laptop came up empty. Maybe he'd left it at home after all. She settled herself in his armchair to wait instead; his room being large enough for a hefty chair, although not as fancy as some of the others. She wondered how they'd allocated the rooms. They were all quite similar, but it did seem like the married couples had bigger rooms – even if husbands and wives had been separated.

One upside of Nathaniel's room was that it had a small window with a view of the garden. The scent of the blooming flowers wafted in, and from this slightly raised spot she could see over the white wall and just make out the women on the other side, sitting outside under the colonnade and doing whatever it was they did. Astrid spotted a familiar, elegant figure in plain brown – Lady Tamzyn in miniature, chatting with several other blue-haired women. She wondered if the Tygers had meant to give her brother such an interesting view. She wondered if *Nathaniel* had noticed the view.

After about half an hour of waiting, Astrid was lying upside-down on the chair with her feet propped against the wall when her phone dinged.

We've been invited to visit one of the noble's homes. Will be about two hours – don't wait up.

Don't wait up! Was he crazy? It was barely mid-afternoon and she was fainting with boredom. Having to wait another two hours would be *torture!*

Astrid threw her arms over her head in frustration, but managed to lose her balance instead, falling out of the chair and landing in a pile on the ground.

"This is the worst," she told the mosaiced ceiling. "If I was a boy, this wouldn't be an issue. I'd be out there, having fun." Not that she wanted to be a boy in general. She quite liked being a girl, actually, but here in this moment it wasn't doing her any favours.

Just then from her upside-down position she saw a pair of Nathaniel's boots, half hidden under the bed. They looked a lot like her own comfortable shoes, only somewhat larger. She stared at them for a long moment, and then a terrible, sneaky, wonderful idea came into her mind.

Ten minutes later the palace guards watched as one of the visiting Earthers strolled out of the gates of the palace, his clothing loose and comfortable around his lanky form.

The boy wore a plain hat with its brim low over his face, and the whole effect was so plain that he could have passed for a servant, especially with his oddly-coloured hair covered. Didn't the Earthers know that New Year festivals were a time for the *best* clothing to be worn?

One of the guards wondered absently why the boy hadn't gone earlier with the rest of his people, then decided it wasn't his job to wonder, and so promptly forgot. And then the Earth boy was lost in the crowds.

CHAPTER 3
Whales & Pit-fights

Crime paid.

Or at least, sneakiness paid, Astrid thought. Because what else could she conclude when a simple change of clothes (and rather more restrictive underwear) meant that she could be out here, seeing things, buying things and eating things…not necessarily all the same items.

She even had a chance to use the spending money that she'd been given for the trip, since no one had realised that most of the invites wouldn't include unattached women.

She bought a blue stone bracelet at what might have been too high a price, judging by the glee on the stallholder's face, and ate a kebab with alternating spiced fruit and meat, hot enough to make her nose run. In the centre of the thronging main street was a performance, so she stood and watched while two stocky, moustached men fought in a choreographed way on the back of a patient grey raphanta with swirls of gold and blue painted on its smooth sides. It was smaller than the emir's blue raphanta, and perhaps not as pretty. That wasn't saying much.

But the performance was over far too soon, and Astrid groaned with the rest of the audience when the performers took a bow.

"Enjoy that, did you?"

The words took a few moments to translate in her earpiece, and by the time they'd translated – and she'd connected the words with three boys standing nearby – they looked puzzled by her lack of response. The three of them had dark, dark blue hair in various styles and were dressed almost identically in festival finery.

"The performance," the shorter boy in the middle elaborated. "You looked as if you liked it."

"I did, very much," she replied, and saw the surprise on their faces as the translator repeated her words in its unisex tones, in their own language. She coughed, realising her own voice sounded too high in comparison, then lowered her tone. "I've never seen fighting like that before."

"Oh, that wasn't fighting," one of the other boys boasted. "It was dancing with swords. Do you want to see some *real* fighting? We're on our way now."

Astrid hesitated. She'd been away for only half an hour or so, and thought she could fit in another twenty minutes before having to head back to the palace. But there was just something about the boy's tone… "Is it legal?"

"Of course it's legal," the first boy huffed. "The emir even provided the prize himself, didn't he? But only men can watch it because it's so brutal. They have to have it away from the street so that children and women don't see it by accident. Hand to hand fighting, until only one fighter remains. But perhaps your people wouldn't consider you old enough to watch."

Soothed by knowing the emir approved it, and stung by the boy's implication that she was a child, Astrid lifted her chin. "Of course I'm old enough. But I've only got fifteen minutes or so before I have to return to the palace."

"Looks more like he's from the stables," one muttered to the others.

"Each bout only takes a few minutes," the first boy said, ignoring that last comment. "Especially if it's the champion fighting."

"Wael the champion!" one of the others cheered. "Two years running. The man's a genius."

Whale?

"So are you coming or not?" the first boy challenged.

Astrid thought it over, and really, there was only one answer. "Of course I am. Let's see this fighting genius of yours."

As they walked, she quickly learned that the shorter, talkative one's name was Zethus, and his brothers were Zabi and Zev. Apparently their parents had thought alliteration was a clever idea – but Astrid figured it might make postage confusing, since their initials would all be the same.

She gave her own name as Ted. It was her father's name, and she figured he would forgive her borrowing it, especially for something like this. He'd always enjoyed those classic films where everyone was fighting and doing backflips all over the place. He'd tried to learn some martial arts himself and even had her and Nathaniel enrolled in Krav Maga lessons.

Astrid had attended for a while before losing interest – she didn't have the discipline to be really good, even though she was quick. But she didn't need to know how to fight here, she just needed to watch.

She followed the boys under a canvas roof, packed full of screaming men, and almost got an elbow to the face more than once as they squeezed their way to the front of the crowd. No one seemed to look at her twice as she finally got close enough to see what was going on – then almost fell forward as her foot hovered over empty air.

Wow. It was a *pit* fight – one without a fence, since she'd come within inches of falling in. The pit was about five feet deep and ten feet across with white sand on the ground. Inside, the two male figures circled each other in plain white shirts and dark trousers. One of them was stocky and bald with a moustache like a walrus and a distinctly grim expression. She didn't much see the other's face, because within moments the moustached one had moved in and – *punch punch* – knocked the other to the ground.

Astrid screwed up her nose at both the violence and the speed. Was that it?

But no, the fallen man was still trying to move and the moustached one had grabbed him around his shirt collar and was repeatedly punching him in the face. The second grappled at Mr Moustache's legs, and was kicked solidly for his efforts. And yes, Tyger blood was as red as human blood.

Yuck.

"What are the rules?" Astrid asked the nearest Zee in fascinated horror. She had to ask a couple of times before he could hear her over the noise, and he laughed.

"Only rule is no biting, no killing." He paused thoughtfully. "And you can't target the groin."

"Oh."

That left a lot of other, painful options, which Mr Moustache was using to the best of his ability. And then finally the other man was flat on the ground, and he raised one hand and made a gesture like a star opening and closing.

"He's surrendered," the boy said.

"He can't," another countered – Zabi, perhaps? – "Because he hasn't passed out yet."

Ugh. *Ughhh.* Some poor woman would be getting her husband

back minus his looks tonight.

By now the other man had passed out, or was doing a good enough impression of it for Mr Moustache to be named the winner.

"And Wael wins again," Zethus cheered. "If he holds in there 'til sunset he wins the prize. Either that, or beats twenty challengers. Better move back before the next bout."

"What?" Astrid asked. But suddenly the crowd was pushing against her from all sides, and she found herself forced closer to the edge of the pit. "What?" she tried to call again, but she'd lost them. Ah, well. Perhaps one more bout, she decided, then she'd better head off before she was caught out.

"Next challenger!" someone was shouting. "Who'll face Wael the Champion?"

Someone who didn't value their pretty face, Astrid through wryly. But just then she slipped, her foot almost falling over the edge of the unfenced pit. Her heart pounding, she caught herself and elbowed whoever was behind her, trying to make a space to move back.

For a moment she succeeded, but the crowd was swaying like in an Earth mosh pit and suddenly she felt a hard blow at her back and stumbled forward. She didn't even teeter on the edge – one moment she stood there in the crowd, and the next she was on the floor of the pit, standing opposite Mr Moustache AKA Wael the Champion, who looked much larger, bloodier and scarier than he had from up above.

The crowd roared, and Astrid squeaked. She quickly turned up her translator to max volume, then raised her hands as if in surrender. "I don't want to fight you! I just fell in!" Or was pushed in, but that was something to consider later.

"You don't watch unless prepared to fight!" someone shouted from outside the pit, and Wael glowered at her.

"Five seconds, *Earther*. If someone takes your place, you go. If not, you fight. Five…four…three…"

He swung at *two*, and she panicked. She ducked, and the punch knocked off her hat and grazed her cheekbone. There was a roar from the crowd as it became clear to everyone that she was foreign (if not female – thank God her hair was short by their standards) and suddenly she felt the intense sense that they wanted her to lose, and lose badly. Or 'him', rather. But then everyone would cheer on their own side, wouldn't they?

Wael stepped forward and struck again. He was fast and strong, but she was panicking and had the agility learned from nineteen years as an annoying younger sister. She dodged again and this time he punched air. It just made him angrier (or maybe he always looked like that?) and she ducked and dodged and ran around behind him, tripping him as she did so. That wasn't on purpose, but the crowd went wild.

"Fight like a man!" Wael shouted furiously. "Not like a little girl!"

Well, she was closer to a little girl than she was to a man – but there was no way in all realms she was going to say it. Something told her that it would be better to be pummelled black and blue than to admit she'd sneaked into a men's event, dressed as a male.

Astrid wasn't a fighter. She didn't even like arguing with people, because wasn't life so much nicer when everyone got along? That attitude didn't fit here, though, and she did all she could to recall that Krav Maga training from years ago. *Thanks, Dad, for trying to get me trained...but it was a shame that you didn't try harder to make me pay attention!* Because now all she could think of was that kicking him in the groin would be super effective, and also super not-allowed.

Then suddenly they weren't alone in the pit. There was now a big, angry, familiar figure pushing between her and Wael the moustached champion.

"I'll fight you," Nathaniel said clearly.

Wael looked startled, but jutted out his chin. "You've lost your chance to swap. I finish this one, *then* I fight you, Earther."

"My *brother* is only a child by our laws," Nathaniel countered. "He has no right to be here. He did not have permission."

Suddenly Astrid felt the weight of a hundred judging eyes, and welcomed it if it meant she could leave. "Nate," she tried to say, but he turned on her.

"Leave it, *brother*," he snapped. "Wait for me on the street, and try not to get in any more trouble."

And that was that. Dozens of hands hauled her out of the fighting pit and through the scowling crowd, and within thirty seconds she found herself unceremoniously dumped on the street. "No children!" someone scolded, and then turned back to the fight now taking place. She gained a couple of curious glances from passers-by, but otherwise it was much the same as when she'd walked in with the three Zees. Nobody out here knew what had happened. She'd almost been pummelled by a Tyger-slash-walrus!

Astrid paced back and forth with her hands in fists, jittering with agitation as the crowd roared from inside the fighter's tent, too loud for her translator to separate the sounds and let her know what was going on. She wanted nothing more than to go back to the palace and put something cool on her throbbing cheekbone, but equally she wanted to see Nathaniel in one piece, to know he hadn't been knocked unconscious like the fighter before her. He always had paid better attention to his own training than she had. That had to mean something, right?

The crowd roared again and she tensed, imagining a dozen different outcomes, each worse than the last. And how would she explain Nathaniel's injuries to Anton? *I'm sorry, but my brother was trampled by a rampaging fighter-walrus...but don't worry, they say he should regain feeling in his legs within twelve to fifteen months...*

Astrid was so tense that when she heard a snicker and saw who it was, she went mad. "You!" she shouted. "You pretended to be friendly and you pushed me in there, and now my brother's having to fight Wael the champion!"

The shorter one of the three Zees backed off a little when he saw the expression on her face. "I didn't push you in. He did." He pointed at the sulky taller one unsuccessfully trying to hide behind a fruit stand.

"You shouldn't have come if you weren't willing to fight," the taller boy said petulantly. "It's the rules."

Astrid couldn't remember any of their names, and she didn't care. "I didn't know that was the rules, and you knew it!"

"You said you weren't a child!" he countered.

"I'm not!" Astrid paused. "I'm nineteen, so I bet I'm older than you. But Earth law says twenty-one is adult. It's an old rule, even though no one really takes it seriously." Except for certain substances, marriage without parental consent, voting...

"Stars," the shorter Zee muttered. "You're only fourteen, Zabi."

She ignored that. "If my brother's seriously injured because of you..."

"Then you'll what?" the short one mocked. "Run circles around us and never throw a punch?" He rolled his eyes. "Calm down, Earther. Last I saw your brother was still standing. He's got a kick like a mule."

Well, thank God for that. Now feeling sick of the whole situation and especially of these three, Astrid turned her back on them and watched the crowd anxiously. Still no sign of Nathaniel. What happened to those who were knocked out?

"You're going to have a black eye."

"Are you *still* here?" she burst out, glaring at the middle Zee.

"Don't you want to go in there and prove you're a man?"

"I *am* a man," he retorted. "I'm getting married next week."

"Really?!"

"He's been betrothed since he was six," the boy's brother added helpfully.

Astrid was briefly fascinated, then remembered she was annoyed with them. "How nice for you. But you didn't answer my question."

The boys looked sheepish. "Didn't want to accidently get pushed into the pit."

Oh, for heaven's sake. She gave them a withering glare. "That seems to happen a lot."

"There's always such a crush at the end of the competition," he continued obliviously. "Because that's when you can win the prize. You get less money, though."

"The last one standing at the stroke of four gets the trophy," Zabi added in eagerly. "And thirty gold coins for every contender they've beaten! If you start in the morning and last all day like Wael, you end up rich as a noble!"

"And if you fight all day then lose at the last minute?"

Zethus threw his hands up dramatically. "You get nothing."

"So everyone wants to fight at the end of the day," Zabi explained. "Except that the fighters get even more vicious, because they've got so much more to lose. If Wael wins this one, then he'll have… eight wins?"

"I heard it was eleven," his brother said.

They kept talking, and Astrid turned away again, watching the tent. Then she heard the countdown, because the whole crowd began to shout out the numbers, and her translator struggled to keep pace. "Ten…nine…eight…seven…six…five…four…"

No one was even watching her now, and she joined the boys in pushing into the crowd, trying to see who'd won. But there was nothing except a sea of backs and necks, and the occasional hard elbow in her gut. Feeling near tears, she backed away and tried to see from another position.

And then finally, finally Nathaniel came out. He had a bloodied nose and lip and his hair was spiked haphazardly from his head, but he was still standing. To Astrid's surprise he also had a gold chain of some kind looped over his chest and neck, and when he saw her, he stopped and stared at her for a long moment.

"Let's go," he said finally.

He didn't wait for her to agree, just started walking, and she had to run to catch up with him.

"What happened? Why didn't you come out sooner?"

"They don't *let* you come out 'til you're done," he snapped, turning to look at her with those eyes so like her own. Right now they seemed to be in a stranger's face; a big, angry, bloodied stranger. "But I thought you would've known that."

What could she say to that? "Did you win?" she asked instead.

"Don't sound so surprised." For a moment Nathaniel almost grinned, looking more like her usual cheerful big brother, then seemed to recall that he was still angry with her. "Those guys obviously hadn't come across our fighting style before. After the third one, no one would challenge me. And then the time was up."

Astrid sagged in relief. "What about Wael the champion? It's hard to imagine him surrendering."

"He didn't surrender so much as pass out. Packed a good punch, though, before I managed to get in that last kick." He pulled a mashed brown thing from his side pocket and shook it out, then stuck it on her head. It was his soft sunhat that she'd 'borrowed' which had been knocked off in the pit.

There was a silence, and she took the hat off again. It was clearly ruined. "I didn't mean to end up in there," she said earnestly. "I just wanted to see the festival, and these boys asked if I wanted to see a real fight, and-"

"Those boys?" Nathaniel pointed at the three Zees, as she now thought of them, who were watching from a safe distance.

They flinched as they realised he'd seen them, and one yelled, "What about your prize?"

"I don't care about a bloody-" Nathaniel began, but then saw there was a Tyger standing behind him, an old man with a grey-blue beard.

"Your prize, sir. Where would you like it to be delivered to?"

Her brother didn't answer at first, and she realised in dismay he was planning to turn the prize down. "The palace," she told the man. "We'll be there five more days."

The Tyger waited for Nathaniel's agreement, and she nudged him in the side. "You don't want to offend them by acting like the prize is worthless," she whispered, putting her hand over the mouthpiece of her translator. Besides, think of all that gold!

Nathaniel nodded at the Tyger, who seemed happy just to be

given some direction. He left, and the two siblings headed back towards the palace.

"So," Nathaniel said finally. He'd removed his translator completely, Astrid noted. "You didn't want me to offend the locals by not taking their gold. But you weren't worried about offending them by *dressing as a boy and going to a men's event?*"

She removed her own translator. "I was so bored," she replied, and hearing her own words made her cringe. She sounded like a selfish child. But she tried to explain, "Everyone else got to go out, even Suraya, and she's only a few years older than me! And they kept me in there, and no one talked to me, and all I did was play checkers for the last two days because the entertainment app on my laptop is broken, and I thought no one would care if it was only an hour…"

"You mean you thought no one would know," he corrected grimly. "What did Mum always say, Astrid? About trying to lie, to sneak around?"

"Everything that's done in the dark will come into the light," she echoed dully. Celia Townsend had said that frequently, meaning that no sneaky deed was ever permanently hidden, but now she was truly feeling the truth of it. "But you promised me you'd take me to see everything, and you haven't taken me anywhere!"

"Is it my fault that the culture here is even more strict than where Aunt Jae lives? And was that an excuse for you to lie? To risk so much just for…for what, Astrid? An hour of entertainment?"

"I didn't tell any direct lies-"

"You lied with your appearance, and by omission! What if someone had found out, Az? They're not like us. They might've hurt you!" He frowned, touching her swollen cheekbone. "And you'll have a decent black eye as it is, even if we treat it early. Man, I'm glad I kicked that guy in the head. What a brute."

Astrid stared at him in shock. "You kicked the champion in the *head*? Was he lying down at the time?" That didn't sound like her brother.

He grinned briefly. "Nah, it was a scorpion kick. Perfect aim, and he didn't see it coming. Don't ask me to do it again, though. I just about split myself in half." Then he scowled at her again, his dark eyebrows pulling low over his brown eyes. "And as for you going out, we've been invited to a feast in another noble's home. All of us, and they made it clear the invite was for you, too. It was supposed to be in two days, but I can't see that happening now. What are we supposed to tell them, that you fell down a flight of stairs?"

"Walked into a lamp post," she suggested. "Hit in the face with a flying apple, tripped over my pet dog…it's not *that* bad, surely?"

Nathaniel grunted. "It will be."

"Ohhh…" Astrid looked up at her brother beseechingly. "We'll use the medi-kit and a bunch of makeup. I've been *so* bored, Nate; I told you I've been playing checkers all day, every day."

"That doesn't sound so bad-"

"Against myself!"

He sighed. "Let's see what we can do for that bruise."

In the women's quarters, Lady Tamzyn sat with her friends around a low table full of the usual dinner fare. As before, they only had their own company – the alien girl had chosen to sit alone. Again.

"I hear the brown-haired Earther is *ill* tonight," Naima said delicately. She was one of Tamzyn's long-time companions, and one of the higher-ranked ladies in this court. "That's why she eats in her room."

"Mm." They all knew what 'ill' meant, especially after they'd seen the girl come skulking in a few hours earlier. Her short, fine hair had fallen in front of her face, but Tamzyn hadn't missed the shadow forming around her eye and cheek. She was familiar with that kind of thing. Most men she knew were lenient with their wives and female relatives, but there were a few who got nasty when they drank too much methuo juice. Or, like one or two she knew, who just had nasty tempers and would lash out at any given moment. Those people might look good to outsiders, but any who knew them also knew to tread carefully at all times.

"I suppose she shouldn't have gone to visit her brother without permission," Naima continued. She had an expression of satisfaction on her face that Tamzyn found difficult to see, especially when she felt it echoed in her own heart. The Earther girl's brother was handsome in an alien way, in spite of the odd brown colouring and rounded ears. But then Tamzyn knew that looks rarely had any connection to character.

Perhaps she felt satisfied disappointment, she wondered, because the Earthers weren't any different, not really. And even if they wore trousers like men, the women's lives weren't all that different. She wasn't missing out on anything.

Really.

The next day was as sunny as the last, with only a slight breeze to break up its warmth. Astrid sat outside under the sheltered colonnade of the women's quarters, her hair falling over her bruised cheek as she studied the still-blank laptop screen. Aunt Jae hadn't replied to her message, but then she was probably busy nursing sick children and doing emergency caesareans and so forth.

Astrid let out a heavy sigh from boredom and frustration, mostly at her own actions yesterday. Nathaniel had been right when he said she'd have a black eye. The whale-inflicted bruise from her cheekbone had extended up into her eye socket, leaving a multicoloured purple mark even with the help of the medi-kit. All the makeup that Suraya could provide couldn't quite cover up the shadow, although it made her look less ghastly.

At least her face wasn't swollen. She was desperately hoping that it would fade by tomorrow night so she could attend the dinner, but in the meantime she was all alone…again.

Astrid prodded desolately at the closest black checker where it sat on its white square. Right now she'd even welcome a stilted conversation with the unfriendly Lady Tamzyn, but the other women avoided her much as they always had. Even the little curly-haired servant never came near her, and she could only play checkers so many times. If only she'd taken the time to get her entertainment app fixed, because right now her laptop was good for communication only. She couldn't access any of her books or films or games or *anything*. What a waste.

Sigh.

Astrid was so busy feeling sorry for herself that she didn't hear the quiet footsteps approach until a shadow fell over her table. She looked up to see a Tyger male standing there next to her. He was young and handsome, with an elaborate white and purple robe and dark indigo hair falling loosely around his shoulders. He was watching her curiously with eyes a few shades lighter than his hair.

"What is this that you do?" he asked.

The translator kicked in a bare moment later, around the same time that Astrid recognised him. Emir Raka, and he was talking to *her*! She just about swallowed her tongue. "Ah…"

Luckily he didn't take offense. Instead he let out an unexpected laugh and sat down on the vacant seat across from her. "But of course it is a game," he said with a slight smile. "I have watched you play it, both the black and the white pieces. But you have lost interest?"

Argh, the emir was talking to her! Astrid finally found her voice. "Maybe I've played it too many times," she managed to choke out, her eyes fixed on the table in front of her. She was hyperaware of her bruised face and plain clothing, and ducked her head further so her hair would cover that cheek. Besides, Raka was *definitely* better-looking than Percy. More bravely she added, "It's actually a two-player game."

The emir nodded sagely. "I knew this already. We have similar games here in my kingdom. I am very good at them."

Modest too, she thought wryly.

"Teach me this game," he said imperiously. "What do you Earthers call it?"

Feeling pleased but quite discombobulated, Astrid found herself giving the rules for checkers without even asking how long Raka had been watching her, or why he was even in the women's quarters at all, talking to a young, unmarried girl. Not that she cared, but it seemed a big deal to the locals. But then she figured the rules probably didn't apply to royalty.

"So if your piece makes it to the other side without being captured, it becomes a king," she finished, turning her piece over to demonstrate. "See how the other side is a different colour. Then you can move it in any direction."

"A…king?"

"The boss. The ruler," Astrid explained. "Kind of like an emir, I suppose."

"And is it so easy for a commoner to become a *king* in your world?"

Her head shot up in surprise, but he was still studying the board with narrowed eyes, seeming engrossed in thought. Had he been joking?

"No, it's not easy at all," she replied cautiously. "But this is just a game." In case he hadn't noticed.

"Hmm. And what does the winner gain from the loser?"

Good question. When Astrid played her brother, the winner

would strut around saying 'I win, you lose, ha ha ha' or something similar. They didn't *get* anything out of it except mocking privileges.

She studied the emir warily, but he didn't seem to have any inappropriate motives. "I suppose you could play for a prize, but we just play for the fun of the game."

Raka blinked, then nodded decisively. "Very well. We shall play for the glory of winning. I will go first." And then he moved his first piece – the black one – into the middle of the board.

Argh. Astrid debated whether to correct him or whether to ignore his painfully wrong move, but someone spoke from beside them. "You must move only one square at a time, nephew."

It was the older lady, Rhubarb. She stood quietly back in the shelter of the colonnade along with a couple of other women, and Astrid hadn't even heard her approach. Second time in one day – either the Tygers were really stealthy, or she needed to pay more attention.

The emir studied his aunt with narrowed eyes, then inclined his head. "I bow to your greater knowledge, Aunt Ruhazia." He picked up the black piece and then moved it a couple of places back to a correct location.

Ah. Not rhubarb, then, Astrid realised. And the emir had won some brownie points with Astrid by listening to his aunt here in a culture where women were so cloistered.

Trying to ignore their growing audience and the fact that clearly someone had been watching her earlier, Astrid focused on playing the game. She played to win, of course (because otherwise why play?) and Raka didn't make any more missteps, but it was clear he was taking the game very seriously. When he captured her first piece, he smiled and nodded. When she captured two of his in one move... well, he wasn't smiling. The game ended with her still having six pieces on the board.

"Not bad since you've never played before," she said lightly. "Maybe you can teach me one of your games."

"No. We play again."

There was a slight murmur from their audience – the three ladies had grown to half a dozen, and a couple more approached as Raka spoke. A guard or two was watching from a distance.

"Um. OK." Had he never heard of saying 'please'? She reset the board.

"You go first this time," the emir said flatly.

So Astrid went first, and this time she didn't play as carefully, but she still took her chances when she saw them. She won, but just by a margin of two. She looked up at the emir expectantly. He still had that same intense, taut expression, and it was fixed on the board rather than on her.

"Again. And this time, play to win."

Astrid jolted in surprise. She hadn't realised that he'd noticed, and she wasn't sure if she liked his attitude. But hey, at least she wasn't playing by herself anymore, and maybe after he grew tired, someone else would play.

The emir waited while she set out the pieces once more, then moved to take the first turn without a word. It looked to be a thoughtful move, and he watched her hands very carefully as she placed her own piece. "You have played this many times, yes?"

"Since I was a child."

He grinned, his teeth looking very white against his golden-brown skin. "Then not for very long. You appear barely out of childhood, yet they assure me you are a woman."

Ouch. Some of the watching Tygers didn't smother snickers, and Astrid felt her cheeks warm. "That depends on who you ask," she said lightly. "By most human – *Earther* laws I'm not an adult until I turn twenty-one." There was an expectant pause, and she added, "In two years."

"And yet you were betrothed." Raka took his turn.

She froze. Betrothed to who, Percy? *I think not!* "I don't know who told you that," she replied carefully. "There was never any formal arrangement in place. As I said, I'm not considered a legal adult for two years. Even if I'd agreed…the marriage wouldn't have been valid."

The emir waited for her to move, then placed his own piece with obvious satisfaction as he jumped over one, two, then three of her pieces. "And so they bring you here, for an adventure."

Or for a punch in the face and incarceration, more like. "I'm very lucky," Astrid replied, and in that moment she thought that perhaps she was. After all, she was the only human who got to play checkers with a royal.

She studied the board – damn, he really had just made a good move – then smiled. She took one of her pieces that had languished at the side of the board, then jumped once, twice – right to the other side.

King.

"Hmm." Raka leaned in, his eyes narrowed.

But while the emir put his full attention into the game, Astrid saw something white move out of the corner of her eye. She turned to see a tyger – a real one, a big, striped cat – sauntering across the blue-green lawn towards them. Once she'd spotted it she couldn't look away. It wasn't wearing a collar, and while it wasn't as big as an Earth tiger, it wasn't a housecat either.

The emir's irritated cough caught her attention again. He'd made his move – making one of *his* pieces a king – and she'd not even noticed he was waiting. Meanwhile the tyger-cat sat itself down not ten feet away and watched with unblinking purple eyes. No one else seemed bothered so she tried to turn back to the game, but her move was haphazard. She turned back to the tyger-cat again. It yawned, displaying a pink tongue and large, needle-sharp white teeth.

When Astrid finally turned back to the game, the emir was watching her with an amused smile. "The *beini* frightens you? He will not bite."

He, she, who cared! It was a giant, possibly man-eating cat. It didn't *need* a gender.

She smiled awkwardly under her curtain of hair, making her own move carelessly. "We have similar creatures back on Earth, but they can't be tamed. We'd never have them running free." Not with all their teeth intact, anyway.

"But this is not your Earth," Raka said. He moved his king back over the board, taking one, then two of her carelessly placed pieces. "And here a *beini* will not dare to bite. Ah, and I do believe I have won."

So he had. Astrid looked at the board in surprise, then back at the white tyger. It stood again and sauntered off towards the wall separating the women's quarters from the rest of the accommodation, then crouched and leapt over in one smooth, impressively powerful movement. She turned back to the emir, who was clearly expecting some kind of congratulations. "Well done," she told him politely.

He stood, looking pleased with himself. "Yes, but it was only expected that I should win once accustomed to the game. You will attend dinner with your people tonight."

It was clearly a statement, not a question. Luckily Astrid had already discussed tonight's open dinner invite with Suraya and Nathaniel. Her bruise was going down, and with enough makeup and her hair covering her face, she'd be able to get by. "Yes, Your Magnificence. I'm very glad to be attending." And she was…except for the awkward bruise.

The emir nodded then turned to leave. A couple of the guards turned to go with him. They'd been standing behind her the whole time and she hadn't even noticed. A few of the women who'd been watching moved as if to leave as well, and the remaining silence made her realise that the whole time, everyone had been just as quiet. Except for the emir's aunt at the beginning, only she and the emir had spoken the whole time.

Feeling a little uncertain (had she really just played checkers with a royal? Cool!) Astrid began to gather the pieces to put them back in their little carry bag. A shadow fell over her in a repeat of an hour earlier, but this time she looked up to see Lady Tamzyn. The girl stood with her hands folded in front of her in the ornate pleats of her dark grey robe, and wore a sober expression on her oval face.

Oh, what had Astrid done *now?*

"If you wish," Tamzyn said delicately, "you may join my ladies and I for our midday meal."

Astrid just stared at her for a moment, forgetting to even hide her bruise. Was that an invite?

Tamzyn's cheeks darkened in a faint blush. "Or perhaps you have something better to do."

Astrid suddenly realised she'd been terribly rude, and that the girl was actually being friendly – for her, anyway. "No, of course I don't. That would be…very nice."

Tamzyn nodded in much the same way as her brother had, then turned to walk away. It seemed that Astrid was expected to follow, so mentally shrugging, she put the checkers back in their carry bag and folded the old board in its resting position. Lunch with another royal, she mused – even if it was dry crackers, she could add *this* to her bragging list too.

CHAPTER 4

A Meal with the Monarchy

Tamzyn saw the surprise on her friends' faces when the Earther girl followed her into their dining room. They'd all had the idea that the Earthers were sulky and standoffish – but perhaps even sulky, standoffish girls occasionally wanted company.

Still, the ladies were always well bred, so they quickly stood, hiding their surprise behind politely serious expressions. They'd be talking about it later, though.

Tamzyn sat gracefully on the dining carpet, folding her legs under her, and Leyna, Naima and Zahra followed suit. She saw the Earther pause for a moment, then sit down in an empty space. She briefly looked uncomfortable, then settled herself into an awkward pose with her legs crossed beneath her.

The Earther said something, and a moment later her odd translation device repeated it in Tyger. "Thank you for inviting me to share a meal with you. I've never eaten with royalty before."

The women all exchanged surprised, mildly amused looks. Clearly the girl hadn't, or she would have known that the highest ranked person must speak first. Had she not noticed that from the game outside, where she'd been honoured by Raka?

"But of course you have not," Tamzyn replied graciously, giving the unspoken signal that the others could also join the conversation. She didn't need to tell the servants to make extra food – it was already done. "I hear that Earthers have no emir."

The girl looked pained, then shrugged in a very undignified way. Her movements were all expressive, open; she didn't hide what she was thinking. "My people aren't ruled over by emirs – or kings or princes, if that's what you're asking. But some of the other nations back on Earth have hereditary monarchies. Most of them have no power, you understand, but the people enjoy the tradition."

Across the dining mat Naima almost spilled the goblet of spiced tea that a servant had just handed her. "Royalty with no power?" she burst out. "What is the purpose of that?"

Suddenly the girl grinned, showing straight, white teeth and the potential for some beauty if only it was tended. "It's mostly to wave to the crowds at festivals, and to attend the best parties so the hosts can boast about it afterwards."

There was a pause where they all took that in, and Tamzyn had the odd thought that Raka really better not hear this conversation. Royals without power, indeed. (Well, she had no power, but that was expected. But the *emir…*) "And you," she asked the Earther delicately as she selected a dried fruit pastry from the tray offered to her. "Will you boast about this particular meal?"

As if suddenly realising she'd misstepped, the Earther flushed bright red. It was the oddest thing where her skin changed colour from the neck up to the hairline, and Tamzyn watched in fascination.

"Yes, I suppose I will," the Earther replied with a shrug. "Even if this goes badly, I can say that I ate with a royal princess."

"And is it going badly?" Zahra asked politely from the other side of the dining mat. Her expression was as soberly polite as always, but there was a gleam of mischief in her eye. She'd been attending Tamzyn ever since her marriage to one of the higher nobles three years earlier, and while she was always respectful, she also had a sharp tongue.

The pinkness faded from the Earther's face, and she lifted her chin. "I have no idea," she answered frankly. "I don't understand your customs, even though I'd like to, so I don't know what's good or bad. But you haven't fed me to the tygers yet, so that has to be a good start."

There was another startled pause, and then Tamzyn felt her lips curve into a real smile. Naima let out a little giggle which she quickly stifled, and suddenly the atmosphere in the room relaxed. Perhaps the Earther wasn't so unfriendly, Tamzyn concluded. Just ignorant.

"We will teach you our customs," she said kindly. "But I can promise you that we don't feed *anyone* to the *beini,* ever." By the heavens, that would be quite, quite unethical, and even disgusting. The Earthers might have some wonderful machines and weapons, but they certainly didn't know everything about this planet they were visiting.

Some time later, politely barbed conversation had morphed into something more genuine. The other women had faded off into the background, having an intense discussion about wall hangings by the sound of things, but Lady Tamzyn had stayed to talk. Astrid found the food was different but interesting, and the customs were also different but interesting. Spiced fruit kebabs and pink herbed grains were all very well, but one thing was for sure, she and the other humans had no idea about some very important things.

"So you smile to be *polite*," Tamzyn exclaimed in surprise, her delicate dark brows arching high above her eyes. "How very odd. We only smile to show happiness."

Well, *that* explained a lot. Astrid tried to think of how she could explain human culture to someone whose was clearly very different, then realised that actually there was no human culture. There were still two hundred or so countries in the world, each with its distinctly different customs and politics, and some were at open war for various reasons. She could only describe her own culture, as the Tygers seemed to think of all 'Earthers' as the same.

"It's just another tradition," Astrid said with a rueful shrug. "But then you certainly have some that make no sense to us." Oops, that was probably rude, she realised. She tried to backtrack. "I mean that are unfamiliar."

Tamzyn looked amused. They didn't smile widely, these people; instead they would show emotion in more subtle ways than Astrid was used to, but it was there. Within the palace Emir Raka was the only local that she'd ever seen laugh properly. "Unfamiliar or makes no sense, it is much the same. What is it that confuses you?"

Astrid tried to pick something that wouldn't be insulting. "The place of women is different," she said finally. "I knew that women here are more…protected, but I wasn't expecting to be so sheltered. At home, and on Earth, we pretty much go where we want. Well, within reason, and when we have permission. We can't do just *anything*."

Lady Tamzyn suddenly seemed fascinated by the hem of her robe. "So you did not have permission to visit your brother yesterday?"

What an odd question. "For the most part, he doesn't need me to ask permission," she said. "Especially here when we're visiting another city, and he knows I haven't been able to get out much."

"But he was not happy," Tamzyn persisted, glancing up and briefly focusing on Astrid's cheek. The bruised cheek. "Even the most doting brother would be unhappy at having his privacy intruded upon by a younger sister."

Astrid frowned. Nathaniel never minded when she visited. Or at least if he did, he hid it well. "I wasn't-" she began, but then an idea struck her. She lifted a hand to her bruised cheek. It still ached, though she knew the mark was barely visible. But it wasn't *invisible*. "My brother didn't hit me, if that's what you're thinking."

Tamzyn's gaze skittered away from hers. "I would never venture to comment on such a thing. It is not for me to discuss how other females are disciplined."

Disciplined!? Now feeling quite worked up, and feeling the need to defend Nathaniel, Astrid continued urgently, "But he didn't! He'd never do that. It's against our law to strike another person, and besides, he's not the kind. He's very gentle." When he wasn't scorpion-kicking walruses in the head.

"Very well." There was a pause. "Yet you are bruised."

Astrid sighed heavily. "That's another story, and none of my people had anything to do with it."

The Tyger's gaze sharpened. "Who, then? One of my people?"

Oops, that was even worse than the previous comment, Astrid realised. "I'm no longer comfortable with this conversation," she said quickly, trying to think of something, anything else to discuss. "Here's an obvious change of subject. I hear your cousin rules the neighbouring city-state. Does he ever come to visit?"

As a distraction it worked, because Tamzyn actually laughed aloud, startling that familiar curly-haired servant who'd quietly come to pick up the used dishes. "The current regent of Syrene is very young, and he is not my cousin, Earther. He is merely the child of the Syrenian ruler's deceased wife. But he is not…friends with my own brother, and I expect he will not visit in this lifetime." Her expression sobered. "Perhaps if you find yourself speaking again with the emir, do not mention that subject."

"Oh. Alright." Astrid frowned, thinking of the mountain barrier that split Mahadra in the north from Syrene in the south. She hoped it proved a true barrier, because when rulers had disagreements, that was grounds for war. Just look at Earth's history. "But there's peace between your city-states, yes?"

"Women are not aware of such things," Tamzyn replied delicately. Astrid raised her eyebrows in disbelief, and she added, "but the men talk, and we listen. I believe all is well."

"Oh," Astrid said again, but in relief this time. "Good."

Because what use were fine tapestries and feasts if an army was at the door?

Orin waited quietly at the entrance to the royal chambers. He didn't make any sound to notify the emir of his presence; it wouldn't be appreciated. Instead he stood outside the fine, waving curtain that separated the chambers from the resting hall, listening to the faint sounds of movement within.

He could hear gentle conversation from the women's quarters drifting across in the afternoon air. From this window he could also see right across into the women's garden and even the colonnade where they often sat to enjoy the fresh air. That was no doubt why the previous emirs had chosen such a location for their own rooms.

Finally, quiet footsteps approached the curtained entrance, and he stepped aside. A girl walked out, her curly head bowed in respect for his station. But then as one of the *esira* slave class, even he was above her, no matter how many times she might visit the emir's chambers. His half-brother did have odd tastes.

A moment later heavier footsteps sounded, and Raka pushed aside the waving strands with an impatient hand. He was wearing one of his casual robes and had clearly just bathed. "Oh. It's just you."

He turned to walk back into the room, and Orin followed him. "What was that about earlier?"

"What was what about?"

"The Earther girl. You were showing her favour."

Raka turned to face him, his usual impatient arrogance displayed on his elegant features. He'd taken after his royal mother. Orin, on the other hand, looked more like his decidedly unroyal mother – although he'd been lucky enough to have their father's silver-white hair from birth. That special colouring had saved him where many other royal bastards hadn't been saved. "I was mastering a new game, as well as showing kindness to the least of our new friends, in the presence of many. There was nothing inappropriate."

Friends. Also known as the mysterious foreigners who paid with weapons and unfamiliar goods, which were always appreciated in a realm where war was imminent. Orin heard the bite to his brother's voice and lowered his own head submissively, hiding his expression. "What if the Earthers accuse you of seducing her? They won't pay you so happily then."

Raka grinned, that open, friendly grin that won him so many friends from those who didn't know him. "They would be fools to accuse me of any such thing, but in truth they value the ambrilene so highly that I could string the girl from the ceiling by her toes, and their leaders would whistle and look the other way."

Ambrilene. *Ugh.* Orin wouldn't touch the filthy stuff with even the sole of his boot. It smelled so strange, and Raka still wouldn't reveal where he got it from. Not even to his own brother. But Raka also seemed happy with the payments that the Earthers brought, and in turn the Earthers seemed to love it. "What do they use it for?"

"Anything. Everything. Who cares? They pay, and that's all that matters."

Raka sauntered over to the large open window that overlooked the city, setting his hands behind his back in a familiar pose. His long dark hair fell over his shoulders, blending in with the dark embroidery on his robe. Orin wondered again what would have happened if he had been born to the royal wife, and Raka to the chambermaid. Well…Raka wouldn't be standing in this room, that was for certain. Perhaps he wouldn't be standing anywhere. Mahadrese royalty didn't like their heirs to have any competition, not even from bastard half-siblings. If it hadn't been for his lucky white hair…

"They'll be here for another two days," Raka continued, his tone now cheerful. "Plenty of time to discuss trading more *significant* items." He looked up past the edge of the distant city walls to the blue-brown mountains that lay beyond them. Past those mountains was the area once known as the other half of this city-state, now called by a different name and ruled by a different person, who incidentally Raka couldn't stand.

More significant items. Orin knew Raka meant bigger weapons, better ones that would enable him to take back the land that would have been his had the young Syrenian princess not passed away of a fever two years earlier.

Orin didn't wait. He excused himself, not wanting to hear yet another lengthy monologue on why the people across the mountains truly wanted to be ruled by Raka and were disappointed by their weak new regent, and why they'd be doing the right and honourable thing by reclaiming the land.

Orin didn't know much about right and honourable, and he lacked interest for hearing Raka's self-righteous musings. He changed the subject as he moved to leave. "I'm certain that inviting the Earthers into the city for the New Year Festival will go a long way towards making ties, but I can't see how it will get us access to their greatest weapons, Raka."

"Because you have no concept of how far charm and simple good manners can take you!" Raka snapped back. He sighed. "But what can I expect from a simple bastard, no matter how closely we've been raised? Never mind. You just do as you're told, and it will all work out. It cannot fail to."

Orin AKA the simple bastard didn't respond to the jibe, his closed expression remaining unchanged. But then he'd heard that many times too. So he just shrugged. "As you say." After all, there was plenty *he* had going on that he'd never let his brother know about. For all of his alternating flaws and virtues, Raka, emir of Mahadra, would be most unforgiving if he was ever to discover Orin's private plans.

Nathaniel didn't know how long he'd been standing at his balcony. If he stood just like *this*, then he could see just past the garden into just the narrowest sliver of the women's quarters. And not just any women's quarters, but what looked like the sitting room of the most beautiful girl he'd ever seen in his life.

She was even lovelier without all that makeup that the Tygers seemed to like wearing. Her wavy, purple-black hair fell down her slender back past her waist, and every movement was delicate, graceful. He didn't mean to stare. It was more that he couldn't seem to stop himself looking...

Just then the girl turned, and even across this distance he knew she'd seen him. Her dark, pansy-purple eyes met his just for a moment, and then-

Bang bang bang. "Nathaniel!"

He jumped, and the girl fled from sight. He stomped over to the door, not even trying to hide his irritation. "What is it, Astrid?"

Her made-up eyes widened at his tone, and her hand fell from the door where she still held it in knocking position. "It's time to go. You know we're having dinner at some noble's house outside the palace.

Anton told me to come and get you." She tried to peer around him into the room as if she'd catch him doing something exciting, but of course there was nothing to see. Not anymore.

"Well, you've got me," he said brusquely, then softened his tone. It wasn't her fault that he was infatuated with an alien angel. "What's all that stuff on your face?"

Astrid wrinkled her nose, brushing a hand over her plaited hair self-consciously. "It's makeup, of course, and not just to cover my bruise, although it does do that too. And you're supposed to tell me I look nice."

"You look nice," he parroted, moving towards the door. Damn, he hadn't realised how late it was. He'd been too caught up staring. "And it does cover your bruise."

His little sister scrambled to follow, looking happy for the first time since he'd found her with that beast in the fighting pit. But then this was her first outing – her first *sanctioned* outing, anyway. "Sound like you mean it!"

"You look smashing," Nathaniel repeated in a false British accent. "Now aren't you going to compliment *my* gown?"

She laughed, just like he'd known she would. "You're simply gorgeous, my dear," she repeated in a dreadful accent that hovered between Spanglish and Scottish. "All the Tyger women would fall head over heels for you – if they were allowed to see you."

Nathaniel sighed at the truth of that, and if it was a little too heartfelt, Astrid didn't seem to notice. Then they caught up with the group, and he put on his social face. After all, there was no point focussing on impossibilities. They were going out for dinner at one of the noble's homes, and it was a great honour. It was a great honour even being allowed in this place, and he wasn't going to mess it up for their colony and Earth.

But as they all moved down the wide tiled hallway towards the palace gates, one of those giant white cats stopped to watch them walk by. Nathaniel found himself quietly stepping between it and Astrid, who was obliviously chattering with Suraya. The big cats might be considered lucky by the locals – their name for them, *beini*, even translated as 'blessed' – but there was something about their intent predator's gaze that made him *very* uncomfortable.

Several hours later they were retracing their steps back into the palace, tired but definitely fuller. The food had been opulent, the entertainment good: dinner and a show for the 'Earthers'. Astrid had loved it, and she was still chattering about how she'd liked *this* food, and *that* dance. He felt a lot more settled letting her walk back to the women's quarters.

But when Nathaniel headed back to his own room, he found himself detouring into the shared garden. Here fragrant, overhanging plants mingled with beautifully carved statues, each picking up the white light emitted from glowing stones placed here and there – a sort of natural energy enjoyed by the locals, but too weak for Earth to bother trading for. It was enough to act like moonlight here on this different planet, which had a scattering of small moons but nothing as large or as lovely as Earth's moon.

Nathaniel sat quietly on the stone bench closest to the wall, much as he had the last two nights, and waited. And then just like the last two nights, he heard quiet footsteps across the colonnade and onto the grass, and the small sounds of someone settling on a similar seat on the other side of the wall. The other side adjoined the women's quarters and was a mirror image of his own position.

It was the same person as last time, he thought. It had to be, because no one walked quite like that, and no one wore that exact same scent. Yet he found himself peeking over his shoulder and through one of the hand-sized holes carved in the stone wall.

She was looking at him already, and he jumped in surprise. She let out a small sound that could have been distress or humour – it was hard to tell with these people – and moved as though she would leave.

"*Shen zha*," he called out, his voice low but still echoing across the quiet garden. 'Wait.'

The girl froze, turning to peek at him through the gap once more. She wore a veil around her head and under her chin, and he could just see the outline of her hair and shoulder through it. "You speak our language?" she asked, clearly surprised.

Nathaniel swallowed, then answered as carefully as he could in the Tyger tongue. "Just a few words, oh lovely one. But perhaps you might teach me more."

Her purple eyes creased in a smile that barely touched her lips. "What did you just call me?"

"*Soo nak-au?*" he tried again, quickly switching on his translator. "Is this not a compliment?"

Now she definitely giggled. That didn't need translating. "You called me a dish-washer. Perhaps you meant *shau-nikau.*"

This time it translated as 'beautiful one', and Nathaniel felt caught between amusement and embarrassment. He decided to go with the first option. "You are most definitely *shau-nikau*. I would not know if you are also *soo nak-au*. Are you?"

"I've never washed dishes in my life!" she exclaimed. But she didn't sound offended, still watching him with those bright Tyger-purple eyes. "Do you know who you're speaking to?"

He should have looked away then, but this was the first time they'd spoken. Every other time she'd sat in silence and then left, and he'd not even tried to speak. "I know," he said quietly. "I hope I haven't overstepped."

The girl let out a dismissive huff. "Your sister dined in the royal chamber today. It appears that overstepping is something Earthers do easily."

Nathaniel cringed internally, wondering what Astrid had done that was so memorable.

But the Tyger girl continued, "And yet I find I cannot dismiss you entirely. You do know that we should not even be speaking, Earther?"

He still couldn't look away. "Then perhaps we should stop."

"Yes. We should." There was a long silence where he waited for her to stand up and leave – after all, how long could they talk here unnoticed? What kind of consequences would it have? But then she spoke again, and her tone was almost abrupt. "Will you tell me a story, Earther? One about your home?"

"What, the colony?"

"No, your *home*. Earth."

Ahh. He leaned back against the stone wall, listening to the sound of the Tyger girl's breathing on the other side. "Only if you'll call me Nathaniel."

She paused, and he waited. Then finally she whispered, "Very well. Nathaniel."

Astrid was practically bouncing as she made her way back to her small chamber. What a great night! Finally she was seeing what she'd come here for; the colour and the smell and the *difference* of this place, and it made her feel a bit sad about going back to their dry little colony of two hundred.

She'd have to make arrangements to see Aunt Jae after all. Anton had said that she might be able to, even though Percy had thought she'd never be allowed to go anywhere except back through the portal to Earth. He'd said it would be too dangerous.

In your face, Percy. Now the challenge would be to let him know how much fun she was having without actually having to talk to him, and without letting him think she cared about him anymore. Which she didn't.

OK, maybe a little bit, but she mostly had hurt feelings over the way he'd ditched her so quickly and easily for a newer, more permissive girlfriend fresh from the portal, and complete with attractive foreign accent. What a jerk.

Inside her room Astrid saw that her laptop was on with the messenger program open, just as she'd left it. A blinking white light showed a message had been received. She cheered as she saw it was from Jae, then sat down on her soft bed and opened the video message with a grin.

But as the video played, her grin faltered then disappeared entirely.

"Nathaniel. Nate!" Astrid banged at her brother's door, her hand shaking a little as she did so.

This time he answered his door quickly, and he must have seen the look on her face because he didn't tease her or tell her off for coming back. "What is it, Astrid?"

Astrid mutely held out her laptop with the replaying video, and they went inside his room then sat down to watch it.

In the centre of the screen was Aunt Jae. She looked tired and a bit pale, but that could have been from the traditional sheer Tyger veil she was wearing over her head and shoulders. Her doctor's clothing had also been replaced with a loose grey robe that went up to her collar.

"Sorry about the late reply," her recorded self said. *"We've had a bit of trouble down here. A lot of trouble, really, and I'll be going to a court hearing. It's all about a thirteen-year-old girl who was meant to get married within a few weeks. I recommended she didn't marry so soon because she was too small and would be risking her health…*

Well, she listened, and she told her parents, and they panicked and agreed she should she wait until she was fifteen. But then the groom took

*offence, and he and his family blamed it on us. The girl's gone missing –
I think her family took her. I hope her family took her – but we're being
accused of bride stealing."*

Jae let out a wry smile, and as Nathaniel looked at Astrid, she
saw her own confusion and unhappiness mirrored in his expression.
"What's this, Az?"

"Just wait," she murmured.

Back on the screen Jae was still talking. *"But since they think I
can't steal a bride, they're laying the blame on the male doctors. You know
they're both married, but the locals are just looking for someone to blame. We
haven't done anything except speak the truth and try to save a young girl
from misery, but we'll still need to appear before a local judge."*

She looked down at her lap, and Astrid could still see how she
was trying not to cry. *"I don't know what will happen. Maybe nothing.
Maybe we'll have to leave. Maybe…well. I'll just have to let you know. And
don't worry, most likely it will all turn out to be nothing."*

The video slowed to a halt, showing it had finished, and Astrid
turned her worried gaze on her brother. "I've never seen her like that
before, Nate. Do you really think it will turn out to be nothing?"

He was staring at the screen with a numb expression that she
knew meant he was still taking it in. "I don't know, Az. Maybe. Life
really is different here. Some of the people are really different. Maybe
she'll end up having to come back to the colony."

"I hope not. She and the others have put so much effort into that
medical centre, it'll break her heart." And there really weren't enough
sick and needy up in the colony to justify a full-time doctor. Jae would
probably end up returning to some of Earth's poorer areas, and then
they'd barely see her at all.

Nathaniel patted her on the shoulder. "We'll talk to Anton
about it."

Ten minutes later, Anton had watched the same video message. He
shook his head, his brows low. "There's nothing we can do. The
doctors all knew what they were getting into, and that if something
went wrong they'd have to sort it out themselves." He gave Astrid
what he no doubt thought was a comforting smile. "But the Tygers
hate to hurt females. I fully expect your aunt will be fine."

That didn't actually answer her question. "But what about the
other humans mining further south, in the cold lands?" she persisted.
"Can't they go up, send someone legal to help them out?"

"Already done. As I said, they'll do what they can do, and we'll find out the results." He shook his head. "I told Jae she should settle up here near Mahadra where the wealth is, but no, she wanted to go to where the 'need' was. This is what comes of stubbornness." What a *douche*, Astrid thought angrily. She was about to tell him so when Nathaniel suddenly rose to his feet, grabbed her by the arm and picked up the laptop.

"Thanks, Anton," he said quickly. "We'll keep each other updated, right?"

"Of course." The mayor nodded at them genially, unaware of how close he'd been to getting an Astrid-sized handprint on his face. "You're looking better, Astrid. But don't walk into any more tree branches!"

She didn't even respond, instead giving him a tight smile. But once they'd left she turned to her brother. "Does he even care?"

Nathaniel sighed and kept walking her back to her room. "You know Anton's a mixed bag. But he's here because he's negotiating for more ambrilene, and he was kind enough to let you come too. But I really think Aunt Jae will be alright. As he said, the Tygers are rabid about protecting their females."

Their females. Not 'Earther' females. But Astrid couldn't argue, because really there was nothing she could do. There was only a day and a half left of this trip anyway.

She went to bed.

Politics, politics, bloody politics. The trip was coming to an end and they'd said their goodbyes and got back on the ship, but all everyone could talk about was the interaction between Mahadra and Syrene.

In Astrid's opinion, Syrene was far less friendly than Mahadra, since they flatly refused to trade with Earth. Well, they let Jae and the others set up a medical centre, which was more than what Mahadra allowed, but they'd shut the door to actual goods being exchanged.

"And Syrene's current ruler is only a regent," Suraya was saying in a very intelligent sort of tone. "Because his father Jireh is mad, so he can't rule properly. And they say that if the Jireh's daughter hadn't died then Raka would have married her and ruled Syrene too. It would have become one giant city-state, the biggest on the planet by far. He could have ruled *everything*."

"Emir Jireh is the regent's stepfather, not his father," Suraya's husband Brian disputed. "Though you're right about the other part.

But did you know that Mahadra and Syrene used to be ruled by the same man anyway? Only a generation ago, or so I was told at dinner last night, until the emir died and split his land between his sons, which gives us the current city-states, plus a couple of others further to the south-east."

They continued on in that vein, but Astrid wasn't paying attention. She was reading and re-reading the short message she'd received an hour earlier from Jae. It was good news, right? Maybe…?

The hearing went well, the regent is quite reasonable. Heading south anyway for the next quarter until things settle down. XOX.

It was even written rather than videoed, which showed that she'd *really* been in a hurry. But Astrid was happy that Aunt Jae hadn't given up entirely and come back up north. She really loved her aunt, but she didn't want her giving up on her dream.

Nathaniel came back from the bathroom and sat in the comfortable ring of seats along with Astrid, Suraya and Brian. He'd disappeared almost forty-five minutes before.

"There you are!" Astrid exclaimed. "Did the food finally disagree with you?"

He gave her a very grown-up look. "I went to sit up front for a while, that's all. Any new messages?"

"Just the same one," she replied desolately, turning to watch the scenery fly by beneath them. Brown…greenish-blue…brown…more brown. Rocks…

"It wasn't *bad* news," he said reasonably. "Aunt Jae will be fine, and she'll let us know when something new happens. You know her, and you know the reception in the south of the continent is terrible. It's too far from our cell tower."

Terrible reception, freezing winters and roasting summers. Believe it or not, the colony was actually located in some of the *better* unclaimed terrain. "Yeah, I suppose so." But then something different tickled Astrid's nose. "Hey, are you wearing cologne?"

"Of course not," he replied, but he wasn't meeting her eyes.

She leaned forward, shoving her face into his neck. "You are, or maybe you just ran into someone who's wearing it. It's a nice smell, but kind of girly…"

"Get off, you weirdo." Nathaniel shoved her none too gently away and into her own seat.

Astrid didn't take offense, instead finally took part in the conversation with the other two. "Yes, I'd totally come back here," she said, "but I'd wear a pair of trousers the whole time, or a fake wedding ring. You guys had so much more fun!"

She hadn't told anyone about what really happened to her eye. She wanted to tell Suraya, but then Suraya would tell Brian, who would tell another one of the guys, and it would get back to Anton. Then Astrid would never be allowed to leave the colony again. She might even be sent back to Earth. So instead she'd told people that she'd walked into a tree branch in the gardens, and if there had been any doubts, nobody pushed for more detail.

The group got into a hearty conversation about the highlights of the trip and their favourite souvenirs, and Astrid managed to forget about her face and about Aunt Jae for just a moment.

But she wasn't *that* into the conversation. Out the corner of her eye she saw Nathaniel fidget and finally stand, stretching his arms in an exaggerated movement then wandering away. Her eyes narrowed, and she waited a few moments before excusing herself too.

Either her brother had a terrible case of the runs, or he was up to something.

CHAPTER 5

Stowaway

Syrene

Not guilty.

The verdict handed down by the regent had been fair and appreciated, but it had sparked a riot. Jae Townsend put her head down and barrelled through the raging crowd, following after Dr Kunas' white-shirted back. They were surrounded on every side by guards provided by the regent to help them get out safely, but the crowds were loud and angry and pushing on every side.

In fact, some of the locals around them looked so *furious* and capable of any violence that Jae was actually frightened. And to think it all came from giving out real, valuable health advice. She'd been so happy here, she thought desolately. The people had seemed so friendly and so grateful…right up until they weren't anymore.

Then finally the metal sides of the shuttle came into view, and the door began to open, right into the writhing crowd. Some of them were pushed aside by the manually controlled electric forcefield – the pilot wouldn't let anyone inside who shouldn't be in there.

Jae saw Dr Sye Kunas, the oldest of the three doctors, struggle his way up the low stairs and onto the platform of safety, and a moment later he disappeared inside the shuttle's door with a clear expression of relief. Soon enough she'd made it too, and she turned to look back down at the crowd and to Dr Bill Chirnwood where he followed just behind her. He was about fifteen years older than her, with a thick salt and pepper moustache and a forehead that seemed to grow taller every year. But she'd never seen him look like this.

Afraid.

Bill reached the edge of the steps and he was reaching for her hand when the blow came. Something – it looked like a rock – bounced off his temple and sent him sprawling sideways, stunned.

A trickle of red ran down into his ear. The guards leapt to attention, shouting at the crowd and trying to force them back. It wasn't clear who'd thrown the rock, but it was clear that more were coming. Bill stumbled to his feet and Jae tried to step back outside the forcefield to pick him up, but it wasn't letting her through.

"Open the forcefield, damn it!" she shouted to the pilot, and a moment later the shimmering blue vanished and she grabbed her friend from where he stumbled, yanking him through into the platform with an intense feeling of relief. One of the guards had fallen through with them, and there was a brief moment of surprise before he nodded at her with those typical Tyger-purple eyes, then stepped back out into the crowd.

The doctors raced inside the shuttle, and the door closed behind them with an audible clang. The stones were flying thick and fast now, bouncing off the metal hull and barely leaving a mark before falling back into the crowd.

"They're mad if they think those rocks will make it through the walls," Sye muttered. His fair hair was damp with sweat, and he dabbed at it as he watched nervously through the one-way windows. "This stuff's stronger than titanium."

A bare moment later a lump of *something* hit the same window and stuck, leaving a spiderweb-shaped pattern with the projectile as its heart. They all jolted, and Jae exchanged a shocked glance with Sye.

"Go, go!" someone shouted, but the shuttle's engine had already shot up to full, with the powerful thrusters sending the nearest rioters flying backwards. The shuttle shuddered, then abruptly lurched upwards and away. Jae looked out the window to see Syrene shrinking to a miniature version of itself: the large, regal law buildings in their typical brown stone topped with gleaming paint, the clusters of greenery so carefully planted by the locals and nourished by the many aqueducts that carried water from the mountains; the crowds themselves, both male and female, some still looking furious, some confused, one or two crying…

She sucked in a breath then turned away from the scene, unable to watch any longer, and set herself to mending Bill's bloodied head.

"It's just a flesh wound," he joked, and when she stared at him blankly he persisted, "Get it? Just a flesh wound?"

"But it *is* just a flesh wound," Sye said from across the shuttle. "How is that a joke?"

"It might be a concussion too," Jae said grimly, dabbing at it gently. She'd got the Monty Python reference, but she didn't think it was really the time for old humour. "Do we have the handheld X-ray?"

The others looked glum. "We left it at the medical centre," Sye replied. "Like everything."

With that reminder Jae's mood sank even lower. When they'd left the centre for the hearing, she'd been hopeful. The regent was young, but rumour had it he was also fair, and she'd been confident of a good result. Well, confident-ish, anyway. He'd given them their 'not guilty', but there'd been that mob who'd been stirred up by the former groom's family and perhaps by some some anti-foreigner sentiment, and it had become clear that they couldn't return, not yet. Perhaps not ever.

Jae sighed. "This is going to need some attention, Bill, and it's eight or nine hours back to the colony. I don't like that timeframe."

"Oh, we're not going to the colony yet," Sye corrected her. "There's not enough fuel for starters, right Liz?"

The pilot gave them a thumbs up from the front seat, almost hidden behind the protective plexi-glass. She'd flown here specially from the southern mining station to retrieve them.

"That means we can't go," Sye explained to the others. "We have to go south to the mining station, and then someone from the portal colony can come down to get us. We'll have to contact them first, though."

Liz the pilot made another hand gesture, and Sye frowned. "OK, maybe someone already has contacted them? But whatever. We're going there, then we'll go to the colony, and if we're lucky we'll even go back to Earth."

Jae looked at him in surprise. "I thought you liked it here. We're not in exile, you know." For most of them, being here was an incredible adventure. Jae would always think of Earth as home, but this place had become increasingly familiar and comfortable – except for the obvious issue, of course.

"Bloody well feels like it," Sye muttered. But he shrugged and turned his attention back to the pilot, and Jae couldn't do anything except wait for their arrival in the cold, lonely, desolate location where a few humans manned massive machines, churning up the unclaimed ground in search of something useful.

Southern mining station, here we come.

Astrid crept down the short corridor after her brother, her steps silent on the non-slip floor. She followed him past the bathroom and then around the corner to a small, round metal door. It was the smaller entrance to the cargo hold, which they weren't supposed to visit while the airship was in flight.

He paused outside the door, and she quickly ducked out of sight as he turned to glance over his shoulder. *Phew.* She knew he hadn't seen her, but he was definitely up to something. She waited around the corner until she heard the door open then close again, then quietly moved towards it. It hadn't shut properly, and a thin ribbon of light was visible through the narrow gap.

Well, well, well. What was he up to?

Astrid pressed an ear up against the thin gap, trying to make out what was happening inside, but she could only hear vague murmuring. He was talking to someone. But why would he hide it from her? Unless there was something he was afraid to tell her about…

An idea sprang to mind, and Astrid pushed through the small door full of righteous fury. "Nathaniel Theodore Townsend," she announced, "who are you talking to?"

The murmuring abruptly silenced, and a moment later Nathaniel stepped into sight from behind stacked containers of goods, his face pale. "Astrid? Did you follow me?"

"Duh," she replied sarcastically, then quickly added, "Are you talking to Jae? Did you hear what happened to her? Is it bad news? Because if it is, I'd really rather know about it now than have you keep it a secret-"

"Astrid!" he snapped. "Keep it down, will you?"

She lowered her voice. "Well, is it?"

"I haven't heard anything new about Jae, alright?" He stomped past her, closing the door so their conversation was in private, then moved to stand between her and the containers. "And not everything is about you!"

Astrid slumped. "Then what are you doing down here?" she asked weakly. "It looks weird."

That was his brotherly cue to say, '*you* look weird', but instead he replied, "Did you tell Suraya about how you got your black eye?"

"Of course not," she replied indignantly. "It would've got back to Anton, and I'd rather not be sent back to Earth in disgrace. What's that got to do with anything?"

He paused. "You keep my secret, I'll keep yours."

"OK," she agreed eagerly, certain he'd never tell on her regardless. "What's your secret?"

Nathaniel gave her an arch, grown-up look. "I didn't say I was going to tell you, just that you shouldn't ask any more questions about it. Capiche?"

There was no 'capiche' about it, but something else had caught Astrid's attention. A very faint sound from one of the storage containers, as though something had banged against its metal side. She froze – but in curiosity, not fear. "What was that?"

Nathaniel leaned casually onto the container, blocking her path. "What was what?"

"That sound!" She tried to move around him, but he just moved with her, still blocking her way. "There's something down here, isn't there? Is it an animal? Oh my gosh, you stole an animal! You know we can't trade for live goods yet, not without testing for disease. What is it? Not a tyger?"

Her brother let out an awkward chuckle at the last part. "Ha ha. You always leap to conclusions."

Oh yes, she was leaping, and she leapt onto this one. "It *is* a tyger! How did you get it on here without anyone knowing? Did you shoot it with a tranquilliser? Did Brian help you? 'Cos I don't think you could have carried one of those on your own, and there's *no way* one of those cats would just wander in here on a leash."

"I didn't…" Nathaniel stood up straight. "Actually, Emir Raka did gift us a tyger cat for six months or something. It's tranquillised in a cage around here…"

"Really?!" But even though that was fascinating if it was true, Astrid hadn't been distracted from her real source of curiousity. She feinted left, then dodged around and under his arm. He caught her by the scruff of the neck, but she'd already seen it.

A dainty slippered foot, bent sideways as though its owner sat curled up on the floor.

Nathaniel saw the moment when Astrid realised. She froze, and the air of naughtiness she'd had left. She turned on him solemnly, her brown eyes wide. "Who did you smuggle in here, Nate? Please tell me it's not a girl."

He wished he could tell her that, but unfortunately it would be a lie. So he just stared back at her, trying to convey the urgency of the situation with his expression. "You mustn't tell anyone, Astrid. It's life or death."

"Whose, yours?" she retorted, pulling herself free of his grip. "You know Anton will kill you if he knows you helped someone leave, let alone a local. It's a servant girl, right? You're doing your white knight thing, since you can't stand to see anyone in bondage."

She stepped around the corner to see the inside of the storage crate currently being used as a home, and Nathaniel followed.

"I'm sorry," he told its occupant, and he knew that the small, quiet translator he'd loaned them would be interpreting every word. "My sister is nosy, but perhaps she can help us."

But his nosy sister was still staring, and staring. "Damn," she said finally. "I wish it *had* been a servant."

The Tyger girl drew herself to her feet, pulling her cloak/veil around her shoulders and face. He now knew the gesture was to cover her nervousness. "I have no wish to cause trouble," she said haltingly. "But can you not see that I had no future there, no life? I only wish to be free." Then she turned those big, beautiful eyes on Nathaniel, and he felt his heart clench with answering emotion. "Free, and with my husband."

Astrid's eyes bugged out like a Chihuahua's, and she exploded, "*Husband!?* I sure don't remember being invited to any ceremony, Nathaniel! You are so *dead!*"

"But he said your leaders will not kill him," his wife said anxiously. "Nathaniel, you said you would be unharmed!"

"They won't hurt me," he assured her. "She means they'll be angry – if they find out." Then to Astrid he explained, "The Mahadrese consider marriage sacred from the time the agreement is put in place. Tammy has agreed to marry me before witnesses, and so we're married under Tyger law, even though we're not *actually* married yet."

But they would be soon, he hoped. It had to happen, because there was no turning back now.

Astrid just stared at her brother. Her big, crazy, idiotic brother who stood there next to the tall, elegant 'Tammy', their hands held tightly together, and looking at her with equally beseeching expressions.

Tammy, also known as the Most Chaste Lady Tamzyn of Mahadra, the one and only sister of the all-powerful Emir Raka. And her brother, who wasn't usually so stupid that he'd want to marry a girl after knowing her a week – and who'd probably removed the lady from her 'most chaste' state.

Nice one, Nathaniel.

"You're mad," she declared. "You're absolutely mad." And if he replied with something like 'madly in love', she was going to punch him.

But her brother saved himself from a surprise black eye by answering, "I know it's stupid, and it's a big risk, but it's done now and we're not turning back. We can't. We just need to get through the portal and we can claim refugee status."

Claim refugee status! "It's not like your life is in danger," Astrid snapped. "You can't just pretend to be a refugee."

"Oh, but my life is in danger now," Tamzyn countered earnestly. "I can never return home, or Raka would have me killed. And your brother also, of course."

"Seriously?" Astrid looked to Nathaniel for confirmation, and he nodded solemnly.

Tamzyn continued, "It's because I disobeyed his express orders and the tradition handed down from our father. The sisters of the emir must not marry nor bear children, for it would create rivals to the throne, particularly if the children were legitimate. They say it is for our own purity, but that's not the truth."

Astrid just stared at her open-mouthed, trying to reconcile the charming, arrogant, checker-playing Raka with the ruthless tyrant described. "Have you killed?" she echoed again. "Are you quite sure?"

"Aunt Ruhazia's older sister Elysha was walled up in a tower twenty years ago for taking a guard as a lover. He was quite painfully executed, of course. I was just a child at the time, but I was shown clearly what would happen if I misstepped. Yet I have chosen to do so."

Urgh. Walled up – that didn't sound so bad, just lonely and dark. "Wait…walled up, as in without food and water?"

Tamzyn studied her with what looked like pained condescension. "Yes, Astrid. One can hardly starve to death if one is being fed."

Urrrgggh. Astrid didn't know what she would have said to that – something inappropriately flippant to cover her horror, perhaps – but just then the door to the cargo hold creaked and opened. The three exchanged horrified looks, then Tamzyn ducked out of sight, disappearing into what looked like a very large suitcase and pulling a cloth down to cover herself.

Nathaniel grabbed Astrid's arm and yanked her away towards the entrance, then said loudly, "There's no way I'm going to take the fall for this, Astrid. You need to confess!"

Astrid froze, and whoever had walked into the cargo hold went still and quiet. A moment later, a slightly amused-sounding male voice said, "Oh dear, have I walked in on a domestic?"

At the sound of that infuriatingly familiar voice, she felt the hairs stand up on the back of her neck like a dog threatened by a rival. She couldn't see the intruder – Nathaniel still gripped her arm, holding her facing him – but he said in a lighter tone, "Percy. What are you doing in here?"

"I came up for the return trip, of course," Percy replied casually. "I was sitting with the pilot, getting the best view. I was sent down here to check the cargo before landing. And what does Astrid need to confess about?"

She exchanged an urgent look with her brother, and she could see Nathaniel pleading eloquently with his eyes. *Don't give us up. Please.*

Well, bogger. "None of your business what I did or didn't do, Percy," Astrid replied flatly, turning to face him where he stood in the doorway to the hold. "We're trying to have a private conversation, which is why we're down here."

Percy was an older man at age twenty-one, a bit taller than Astrid and with a similar lanky build. He was dark-haired with narrow, handsome features which at the moment looked a bit uncertain. "That's fine, but you'll need to leave before we land. You know that's policy."

It took a concerted effort for Astrid's eyes not to slide to Lady Tamzyn's storage box but she managed it, instead striding towards the door and stepping widely around Percy as though he was toxic. "I suppose you're going to finish securing the boxes," she called back to Nathaniel, trying to retain her 'irritated' expression. It wasn't difficult under the circumstances.

"Yes, I'll check them all, and we'll finish this conversation in the Greenhouse," he called back, referring to the sizeable glasshouse in which the colony grew their food, and where Astrid often worked.

"Fine." Astrid stepped out the door, and luckily Percy followed her. He might be an ass at times, but he didn't have the guts to be alone with Nathaniel, not after how he'd treated her right before the trip. She'd find it funny if she didn't have more important things to worry about.

She headed quickly along the corridor, her thoughts whirling. Nathaniel had abducted a precious Tyger royal! Well, helped her escape, anyway. And he thought he was *married* to her? And they were going to have to get through the *portal*?

There might be a way of doing that if Tamzyn was happy to stay in the box, and if the portal guard was particularly terrible at their job, but otherwise Nathaniel was going to be in serious trouble. As it was, Astrid was supposed to be pretending that *she'd* done something bad, which she kind of had…

"Astrid," Percy said, sounding wounded. He'd been striding to keep up with her, and she'd almost forgotten he was there. "I know you're angry at me, but it's childish to ignore me like this."

"I actually didn't realise you were speaking," she snapped back, "because I had other things to think about."

"What things?" His expression turned sly. "Something your brother was bawling you out for, no doubt. What did you do, kick a Tyger in the jewels?"

"Sure, that's exactly what I did," she replied sarcastically. "Now did you have something to say, or are you just going to keep asking stupid questions?"

Percy paused as if regrouping. "I just want you to know that I still care for you, and I'd appreciate it if we could be friends, for the sake of our history and for the people around us."

Now Astrid stopped in her tracks and stared at him incredulously, but he looked completely sincere. "Two weeks ago," she said. "Two weeks ago you showed up to the under-twenty-fives gala with Hana May on your arm, telling everyone she was your girlfriend, but without the decency of first telling me that I *wasn't*. And now you want me to be nice to you because you're feeling…what? Guilty?

Uncomfortable?"

Now he looked both. "I never meant to hurt you, but Hana...it must have been fate, because she swept me away, and I realised that you and I were never meant to be."

No, he'd been swept away with desire for another girl who was far more glamorous and free with her affections than Astrid had ever thought to be – or so she'd heard. Astrid hadn't bothered to find out if the gossip about Hana was true. It was easier to think that it must be, rather than that there was something really wrong with *her*.

Astrid had known Percy for years. He'd already been living at the colony when she'd first arrived with her family, but they'd never had more than a casual friendship. Then about four months ago he'd started to pay her more than just friendly attention, and she'd been flattered. No one had ever shown her such interest, and she had to admit she'd been infatuated.

Now Astrid was just hurt and embarrassed at how he'd left her waiting in her room on gala night, dressed in a new, Earth-made gown and not knowing that he'd simply taken the most expedient method of losing an unwanted girlfriend.

After half an hour of waiting she'd concluded that they'd mixed up their meeting place, and she'd gone to the party herself. She remembered the awkward confusion on their friends' faces, and Suraya coming up to her and saying, *'I'm so sorry Astrid, why didn't you tell me?'*

'Tell you what?' Astrid had asked. Then she'd seen Percy with Hana hanging off his arm, looking glitzy in a tight, shimmery, rather low-cut dress (Hana, not Percy), and the truth had begun to dawn on her. She'd ended up confronting him and having a nasty, public argument, then had gone back to her room and cried like her heart would break.

That had been only two weeks ago, and she was certain Anton had included her in the delegation to Mahadra out of pity. Funny, because now she'd seen Tamzyn in the hold her petty issues with Percy seemed like nothing.

But to Percy she said, "I don't believe in fate. I believe in character and good choices, and you don't have what it takes to stick with a relationship. I won't be your friend, Percy, but I'll be good enough not to kick you in the shin when I see you. How's that for an agreement?"

His jaw dropped, and she took the opportunity to hurry away. This time he didn't follow her.

Nathaniel watched as the one and only human colony loomed closer through the viewer screen, looking small and symmetrical and very tidy from the air. It had been built from natural and imported materials, intended to both match the surrounding pale dirt and compliment it. Within its round, smooth wall were rows and rows of neat little streets, with small apartments that were enough to house the two hundred inhabitants. The numbers had increased over time as the colony was able to feed them.

He wondered what Tammy would think of his home there. But then he realised she'd never see it, because if things went to plan, she'd go straight from the hold to the portal room. It made his gut twist to know that he too might never see this place again after tonight.

It was worth it, though. Tammy was worth it.

Nathaniel thought back to the first time he'd seen her face to face with her veil lifted. Before that, they'd met up night after night to talk quietly through the holes in the garden wall, but he'd never seen more than glimpses of her. He'd fallen in love with her quiet dignity, her laugh, her subtle and sly sense of humour…the sheer differences between their people had made their strong connection seem strange, yet so very much more real.

Then two nights ago, they'd been up talking for hours. No one had noticed them – no one had said a thing. Tammy had asked if he wanted to meet in person.

Well, yeah!

Of course Nathaniel had wanted to, but he'd been worried about how it might look. How it might impact on her…on both of them. And she'd told him that even though she would be alone for the rest of her life, she'd never forget him. She wanted to make sure he'd never forget her either.

It had just about broken his heart to think of someone so lovely and vibrant being kept here like an involuntary nun. Of course he'd said yes.

So she'd whispered instructions of how to go to a particular place in a particular hall and to wait there quietly. He had…and there she'd been, clothed head to toe and with her face covered. Then she'd lifted her veil…

Nathaniel shook his head at the memory. He'd only thought he'd been growing attached before that. The moment he'd seen her, really seen her, he'd fallen so deeply in love that it almost felt like a fairytale. He never thought that kind of thing would happen to him.

He hadn't been able to help himself. He'd blurted out, *"I wish I could marry you."*

And she'd said, *"I wish I could marry you too. But you'd have to take me away from here, because my brother would never allow it. The consequences would be severe."*

Then they'd just looked at each other. For him, now that she'd voiced the idea it seemed so possible. A long shot, a daring choice, but possible.

"I can't give you this kind of life," he'd whispered. *"I'm not rich. We'd have a small house and plain clothes…no servants."*

She'd put her hand on his and said, *"It would be worth the sacrifice. Wealth and position are worth little when one is alone."*

Well. Everything that had happened since then seemed like a blur, like something in someone else's life. Nathaniel had been running on adrenaline ever since Tammy had gone to get two trusted witnesses – a friend and a servant – and then they'd repeated that agreement in front of the two. And that was a Tyger marriage, easy as that.

Then he'd had to plan how to get her out of the palace and through the portal to Earth. It had been so hard, yet somehow they were halfway there…

"You alright Nate?" Brian asked cheerfully. "You've been quiet."

Nathaniel resisted the urge to jump at the sudden interruption. Instead, he forced a smile and scrambled for a reply. "It's just strange to be coming home. It feels like we've been away longer than a week." And his whole world had turned on its head.

Astrid met his eyes from across the table. Hers were dark and reproachful in her lean face, but he stared evenly back at her. What he'd done, he'd done for love, and to give Tamzyn a life she'd otherwise never have. All Mahadrese women were restricted, but the royal women unbelievably so. And some of the things she'd told him about the palace… What they'd been shown wasn't the full story by a long shot. He wasn't sorry to have helped her leave, but it was just a shame she had to start her new life in a box marked 'fragile'.

The airship landed with a slight shudder, and a moment later a blue light flashed overhead, signalling it was safe to get out of their seats. He stood and stretched deliberately, doing his best to look casual. "You need a hand with your luggage?" he asked Astrid.

"Sure, why not," she replied flippantly, and he followed her to the small room where they kept all their suitcases, waiting for the queue to thin out. Other colonists had begun to flood in, greeting those who'd been away and helping with the luggage.

"Your eye looks better," he said. "I almost can't see the bruise."

"Oh, did Astrid get hurt?"

Nathaniel turned to see the speaker – a short, pretty girl about Astrid's age with curly, intensely red hair. She wore an expression of sympathy, but he wasn't buying it.

"Hello Hana," he said flatly. He had to be polite since the colony was too small to carry feuds, but he didn't have to like her. She'd come to the colony just a month earlier – two weeks before quite deliberately and quickly seducing Percy's affections away from Astrid. The boy wasn't such a catch in Nathaniel's opinion, but they should have gone about it differently. "Can I help you?"

"Just being friendly," she replied with that slight, undefinable accent, tossing her hair over her shoulder and eyeing him up from head to toe. "I'm a friendly person."

Astrid had already taken her suitcase and left the room, and Nathaniel followed suit, grabbing his own and propping it on his shoulder. He looked at Hana, who was still watching him with a pout she probably considered sexy, then gave her a brusque nod before following after his sister.

He finally caught up with Astrid well into the entry terminal, grabbing her arm with his free hand and pulling her aside into a quiet alcove. "You know I need your help," he said in a low voice. "We've got to move through the portal tonight. The longer we stay, the riskier it becomes."

Astrid stared at him, then shook her head. "I hate subterfuge, and the more I think about it, the less I like it. We should tell Anton, maybe he'll help us."

Nathaniel was appalled. "Maybe he'll send us straight back to the Tygers-"

They paused as a few others passed just by the alcove, giving friendly smiles as they did so.

Nathaniel swore. "It's too public here. I'll meet you in the orchard greenhouse at eight tonight."

"Anton will still be doing the presentation from the trip."

"That's exactly why it's the best time to meet." He looked at his sister intently. "Please, don't let me down on this one."

She sighed, looking away. "Fine."

It would have to do.

They stepped back out of the alcove to find Hana standing a mere five feet away. She gave Nathaniel that same once-over then shrugged insolently, and he just about sighed in relief as he realised she hadn't heard anything. Then he and Astrid went their separate ways.

He had plans to make.

CHAPTER 6
The Portal

Astrid had fully intended to meet her brother that evening, even though she knew they'd be in trouble if their absence was noted. But here she was a mere hour later, seeing him again in an unexpected location. They'd both been called to Anton's office, and their leader did not look pleased.

"You know that I'm fond of you both," he began, linking his hands behind his back in that way that meant he'd prepared a speech of sorts. He started pacing back and forth in front of them. "I've seen you both grow into fine young people, and I was good friends with your mum and dad. Broke my heart when they passed away, the both of them at once."

Nathaniel and Astrid exchanged panicked glances. Had he found out so quickly about their stowaway?

"And I was happy for both of you to be part of the delegation. I always thought you were sensible kids – especially you, Nathaniel, although I confess I never thought you the sort to jump into a pit fight." Anton smiled briefly. "You showed those Tygers that we're good for more than just our weapons, and I hear you won a pretty penny for it too."

That was true, Astrid acknowledged. She'd forgotten about the gold. At least Nathaniel could use that to get started back on Earth – if it came to that.

"Thank you," Nathaniel replied politely.

"Yes. Yes," Anton continued. He stopped pacing and turned to look at them both very seriously. "Which is why it troubles me to hear what I heard today. I need honesty from the two of you. If you've done anything back in Mahadra which impacts the safety and security of this colony, I need to know about it."

Astrid felt her stomach drop into her feet. "Was it Percy?" she asked hoarsely. "Did he say something?"

"Or Hana?" Nathaniel asked next to her. "Did *she* say something?"

Anton raised his eyebrows. "It doesn't matter who said anything, if there was there something to say."

Astrid knew that meant it had been either Hana or Percy. There was a long, terrible silence where she desperately wanted Nathaniel to speak up, but didn't dare do so herself. She wanted to throw their situation at Anton's mercy, but quite frankly she didn't trust him to side with them. He could be quite unsympathetic at times – just like with what happened to Aunt Jae.

When they didn't immediately respond with confessions of guilt or protestations of innocence, Anton prompted, "Astrid, I understand something happened back in Mahadra that you were hoping we wouldn't find out about, and that Nathaniel is angry with you for. Now if it's personal I'll leave it at that, but if it affects the whole colony, I'd appreciate it if you'd speak up."

It had definitely been Percy, then. What an ass, Astrid thought furiously. A double ass! And that was a nice little speech from Anton, but she knew from experience not to take him at his word. If she said it was personal, Anton would look displeased, and then she and Nathaniel both would be watched even more carefully until 'the secret' was revealed. And that would make Nathaniel's position even more impossible…

Nathaniel looked terribly pained, and opened his mouth to say… she didn't know what, but she butted in quickly. "It was me. I did something stupid, but no one except Nathaniel knew, and I thought it would be better for everyone if it didn't get around. I mean, we could tell you, but then you'd be angry…and we wouldn't want it to go any further," she finished lamely, feeling her stomach twist anxiously. Funny how earlier she'd been convinced she'd never have to say a word, and yet here she was, confessing.

"Oh?" Anton's eyebrows began to twitch as though he was trying not to react, but was failing. "And what is it that you didn't want to get around?"

Astrid looked down at her feet, suddenly feeling tears prick her eyes. This particular secret was nothing, but with Jae's troubles, and with Nathaniel and Lady Tamzyn…having to deal with public disapproval made it even worse. "I didn't hit my face on a tree branch," she squeaked. "I got the bruise because I sneaked out of the palace dressed as a boy and was punched in the face by a Tyger in a pit fight."

There was a moment where Anton just stared at her, his light blue eyes wide. Then his face went very red. "I beg your pardon? A pit fight? I thought *Nathaniel* was in the pit fight."

"He came to rescue me," she explained, her voice coming out as small as she felt in that moment. "I was tricked, pushed in, and I couldn't get out. But Nathaniel came and fought the man instead, then took me back to the palace. It was a stupid thing for me to do, but we didn't tell anyone because we thought the Tygers would be really upset."

Anton still looked incredibly startled. Whatever he'd been thinking, it clearly wasn't that. "Well," he said finally. "Thank you for your honesty, Astrid. I'm sorry to hear that you took such a foolish course of action. There will of course be consequences for you, but you're correct that the Tygers would be upset, and so I won't be passing this information on or risking them hearing about it."

"Am I going to be sent away?" she whispered.

"That's unlikely," Anton replied briskly. "But you certainly won't be going on any trips anytime soon. Now, I've got things to do and people to see, so the two of you should go back to your duties until I tell you otherwise. Nathaniel, you're on portal duty tonight, aren't you?"

Nathaniel nodded, and Astrid shot him a startled glance which he didn't return. He was going to be watching the portal, located a mere two minutes from the colony, to make sure he passed on any urgent messages or greeted any unexpected visitors…or smuggled through any unexpected goods. She wondered how he'd managed to arrange that so quickly.

"Then you get yourself to that. Shame you'll miss the welcome home dinner, but that can't be helped. And Astrid – you do whatever you're supposed to be doing."

Which was nothing, because even though it was only three pm, her regular duties didn't resume until tomorrow. For Astrid that would mean a mix of high-level correspondence classes along with a few others her age, and chores that were shared evenly between the colonists.

But finally they were allowed to leave, and they walked away down the hall in silence, Astrid's face hot with frustration and embarrassment. Nathaniel lightly squeezed her hand. "Thank you."

"Yeah, you owe me," she muttered. "We still meeting at the greenhouse at eight?"

"Better make it the portal," he replied, his voice very low. "I won't be able to leave."

Astrid sighed heavily, suddenly feeling exhausted. She scrubbed a hand across her forehead, swiping her fine hair out of her eyes. "I suppose I could help unpack the hold," she offered.

"I've already got our valuables out earlier," he countered, and she knew he meant Tamzyn. "But there are a lot of volunteers, what with the tyger that Raka donated. Everyone wants to see it before it gets shipped through the portal to Earth. You could sleep until later. You look like you need the rest."

She glanced at him in surprise, only now remembering the big white cat being among the gifts they'd been given upon leaving. It had sat quietly with a jewelled collar and solemn purple eyes in a wheeled metal cage Raka had proudly provided. "To Earth?" she echoed in surprise. "I thought we were supposed to keep it here. Wasn't that one of the conditions?"

Nathaniel shrugged. "Don't ask me, ask Anton."

Astrid didn't want to talk to Anton for a year if she could avoid it, but suspected it would be much sooner with her 'punishment' being dished out. She'd say that Nathaniel owed her big time, but in truth if she'd never made that stupid decision to sneak out, there'd have been nothing for her to confess to.

So she went for a nap instead, thinking that the Mahadrese had made a poor choice sending one of their precious sacred cats away with the humans. She bet ten to one that either it would be experimented on for cloning, they'd try to breed the thing with one of the few remaining Earth tigers…or it would end up a pretty rug on some rich person's floor.

Two hours later Astrid excused herself from dinner, claiming she felt exhausted from the trip.

"Must be from all the activities that you did," Suraya said dryly, and the other girls watched in envy, not knowing Suraya was joking.

At ten to eight Astrid slipped out of her room in a comfortable hooded sweatshirt that mostly hid her face, and at eight o'clock she arrived at the entrance to the portal room. It was a big, secure metal door with a ten-digit pin and a thumbprint key that for the most part wasn't used, because there was always someone on guard. Right now the door was closed, but she'd barely stood there for a minute when it opened from the inside.

"Come in," Nathaniel said. He was wearing his best clothes, and was jittering slightly with either nerves or excitement. She felt the same way herself…or maybe that was just dread.

She entered and he closed the door behind her. Now she was inside a large room, which had boxes stacked down one side, waiting to be transported through to Earth. They were of all shapes and sizes, as well as multiple tiny bright blue chests that she knew held the precious red-gold ambrilene.

The portal itself was a mechanical oddity taking advantage of a pre-existing natural 'wormhole' that had been officially discovered twenty years ago, but unofficially, was probably discovered thousands of years earlier. It was an incongruously plain wall marked with a big circle, and there was a matching circle on the floor.

The portal's power came from the location, not the machine itself – on the Earth side it opened into a carefully guarded building inside a quiet green area. But here on the Tyger side, a small, brightly-coloured, open-topped transport vehicle sat on the circle. The vehicle was empty of goods but its two seats were ready for occupants.

Then Astrid saw that they weren't alone. One other person waited quietly at the side of the room, covered head to toe in what looked like paint-splattered overalls, complete with face mask and hood. Not one inch of skin showed. Judging by the tall, curvy figure it had to be Lady Tamzyn, and she wasn't preparing to paint, but rather to travel.

One of the oddities of the portal was that it splashed vivid colour all over anything that moved through, colour that took weeks to fade from your skin, and sometimes never washed out of clothes. It was clownish-looking rather than toxic, but everything transported had to be very well covered, even people.

As Astrid stared, the other girl nodded politely, lifting her mask to show her anxious yet excited face with a translator still attached.

"Hi," Astrid said blankly. Then to her brother, "So you changed your mind about taking her in a box, hmm?"

Nathaniel began putting on an identical suit. "It made more sense this way, but I'm going to need your ID bracelet," he said matter-of-factly. "For Tamzyn, so they'll think it's you and I going through."

"She doesn't look a thing like me," Astrid protested.

"The people on the other side don't know that," he pointed out reasonably, sealing his suit with its front closure and pulling up the colour-splashed hood. "If she has the ID bracelet they won't even think to check for weight, height, or DNA."

Astrid looked down at the silver bangle she wore around her left wrist, as did everyone else here. She'd worn it for so long that she would feel very strange having it removed. Not only for identity, it also worked as a tracker in case she got lost.

"We don't have much time," Nathaniel urged her impatiently. "I'll need you to make sure we get through properly, then wait here until Sean comes to take the next shift at midnight. Tell him I went through to see family – but don't say who I went with."

"But the records will say two people went through," she pointed out, feeling increasingly cold. Was he really leaving so quickly? Except for Aunt Jae, he was her last close family member. "And I'll still be here."

Nathaniel sighed, scrubbing a hand over his face tiredly. "Sean's not detail oriented. He'll just do what he's told, and spend his time on his hand-held player. Will you do it, Astrid?"

"Of course," she said in a small voice, feeling tears prick at her eyes. She fumbled to release the little-used catch, then handed the bracelet over. "When will I see you again?"

Her brother sighed again, then suddenly leaned in and gave her a tight hug before kissing her on the forehead. He hadn't done that since their parents had died. "It won't be long. I'll get in touch within a fortnight, just as soon as things are settled on Earth. Then either we'll arrange for you to come back as well, or…I don't know. We'll see."

We'll see. Talk about painfully vague words. Feeling like her world was falling down around her, Astrid watched as Nathaniel carefully buckled Tamzyn into one of the seats, smiling tenderly at her in a way that she'd never seen him do with anyone else. Then he put Astrid's bracelet on Tamzyn's wrist and slipped her mask back into place. He slipped his own mask into place too and sat down next to Tamzyn, then gave Astrid a nod.

Astrid walked around the circle, checking that nothing hung over the edges, then walked to the other side of the room and tapped once on the 'open' button. This portal had been designed to be used by anyone, since it was meant to be a regular channel to transport goods. They'd had everyone's DNA uploaded just in case of emergency – in case they needed to escape back to Earth. Astrid had refresher courses on how to use this thing every year, but until now she'd never touched it in earnest.

The button blinked red once, twice, then turned green as a

humming noise filled the air like a swarm of bees was nearby. Coloured lights began to shimmer over the vehicle and its occupants. That meant the portal was ready. One more thumb tap and they'd be through. She gave Nathaniel one last querying look – would he change his mind? – but he just gave her a thumbs up. Next to him the Tyger girl leaned over as though whispering into his ear – two masked figures miming a conversation – then he turned and shouted something at Astrid.

"What?" Astrid called, her hand resting over the button. "I can't hear."

He made some kind of gesture with his hands, like a 'crocodile', and pointed at something behind her. She turned around, trying to see what he meant, but there was nothing but boxes. "What-"

Just then her hand accidently brushed the button once more, there was a flash of light, and the vehicle and its occupants abruptly vanished. They'd already be on Earth. "Shoot," she muttered. "I hope that wasn't important."

Even though Astrid was unnerved by the sudden changes and quite frankly, feeling miserable, she kept her word, plunking herself down on one of the worn chairs usually used by the portal guard and waited. And waited, and waited.

After about fifteen minutes she grew bored, so got up and began to inspect the many boxes stacked to go through, making a game of trying to guess the contents. She'd made it quite far into the stacks of boxes before she noticed one particular one. It was big and made of ornately-shaped metal, and it sat right at the back, separate from the others.

It was also empty. Astrid's breath stopped and she suffered a moment of intense, painful fear before realising that the humans must have moved the tyger into another, better enclosure. It was probably already on Earth if she judged by the size of the boxes remaining, and what Nathaniel had said about people being keen to help move the creature.

Huh. Nothing exciting to think about, then, except for the impending disaster that would rush down on them just as soon as the full story came out. So she glumly sat back on the chair and waited for Nathaniel's replacement to show up.

Sean meandered in a few hours later at five to midnight, looking mildly surprised to see her.

"Nathaniel wasn't feeling well," she told him. "He asked me to watch the portal." The second part was true, anyway, and the first part was debatable.

But just like Nathaniel had predicted, Sean just shrugged and took a seat next to her. "That's fine. Did you get to see the tyger?"

"Not the one in the cage," she replied.

"Huh."

And that was all he had to say, so she went to bed.

"Astrid, are you paying attention?"

No she wasn't, actually. Astrid jolted to attention, fixing her eyes on Gillian, the young adults' teacher. Well, the one who made sure they showed up and did their correspondence education, anyway. "Sorry," she mumbled. "What did I miss?"

"It's time for your twenty-minute break," Gillian replied impatiently. "Everyone else has already gone."

Indeed, the room that served as a classroom for the two dozen students of Astrid's age was now completely empty except for the two of them. Astrid had been so deeply worried about Nathaniel, about being discovered, and about Anton's impending punishment for her trick back in Mahadra that she hadn't noticed. "Oh. Sorry."

"They've mostly gone to see the portal," Gillian said a little more kindly. "Even though I clearly said that we were to keep a distance."

The portal. "What about the portal?"

"Good grief, you really were out of it, weren't you? As I said before, someone came and trashed the portal keys at about two or three this morning when the guard had fallen asleep. Hard to think anyone could sleep through that, yet they did."

"Trashed it?" Astrid exclaimed. "How?"

"Pushed the buttons in the wrong sequence, tossed around the boxes..." Her voice dropped. "They tried to set fire to the chests of ambrilene, but you know how hard that is to damage."

Ambrilene, the thing that Earthers valued most. And could it be a coincidence that this happened right after Nathaniel and Tamzyn went through the portal? Astrid's stomach sank, but she managed to summon the appropriate response. "Wow. I wonder who would do that?"

"Someone who's been drinking, I expect. They'll review the recordings just as soon as they've managed to repair them."

So they'd managed to damage the camera as well. Hmm. Feeling shaken, Astrid couldn't even smile. She'd known there was a chance that the recordings would be checked and that Nathaniel and Tamzyn's escape would be seen, but she'd thought it was unlikely. She'd thought it would take longer before it came out that they'd 'borrowed' an alien princess. But the timing of this attack wasn't good. No, not at all.

Gillian was watching her carefully. "You know, I actually said all of this only ten minutes ago, but clearly you haven't taken in a thing. You're worried about your aunt, I expect, but you needn't be. She arrived safe and sound at the southern mining station yesterday."

"Who told you that?!"

"Walt, who came to bring a message from Anton. He wants to see you at eleven, probably about the same thing." Gillian looked up at the large digital clock on a nearby wall. Ten-forty. "There you go. You've still got time for your break."

Astrid smiled tightly, thanking the older woman and getting up to leave even as she felt a mix of numbness and dread. Would she confess about Nathaniel and Tamzyn? It very well could be a clue to why the portal had been damaged, but she also couldn't imagine that an angry Tyger (the person, not the animal) could have got into that closed-off area so quickly without setting off all kinds of alarms. No, it had to have been a human.

But Gillian had reminded her that she was also worried about her aunt, so she took her handheld viewer and found a quiet spot outside the building to check her messages. Yes! There was a new one from Aunt Jae! But Astrid's joy faded into frustration as she realised the reception was so poor she couldn't even open the thing. If Jae was sending from the southern mines, then they'd be using just a single cell tower to cover all that distance. It clearly wasn't working.

Astrid's gaze fixed on the tall silver pole that stuck up from the hillside just outside the city walls, and she briskly tucked her viewer back in her pocket and headed for the nearest exit. There was a small side gate, and she pressed her thumb against it for the two seconds needed to open it before heading up the hill. The area was lightly forested with small trees and plants brought from Earth. The colonists had planted them to create a more homelike atmosphere, and it had worked.

She made it to the base of the cell tower. Up close its base was as wide as the portal itself, and it went up, up, up into a tiny pointed tip over ten metres above her head. The tower's build looked deceptively fragile as it didn't tend to sway in the wind – it was a mix of titanium steel and ambrilene, and it was sturdy.

Her message was downloading! *Yes.* If she was going to face Anton and have her punishment, then she would do it with the knowledge that at least Aunt Jae really was alright.

Finally an image showed on the small screen. It was Jae, wearing a brown cap and jacket that Astrid had never seen before, and smiling at the camera with animation. "Hi, darling. I hope you weren't worried about me."

Even though it was a recording, Astrid still answered. "Worried? Why would I be worried?"

The recording of Jae went to speak again, and just then there was a rustling in the nearby bushes. Astrid froze, looking around with wide eyes. She technically wasn't supposed to go outside city walls without permission – but she seemed to be good at doing what she wasn't supposed to do. "I'm just checking my messages," she said loudly. "I'll be back inside in ten minutes."

Just then a small, squealing animal ran from the underbrush, skidded across her booted foot, then disappeared in the greenery on the other side. Astrid just about leapt out of her skin, then realised it was only a heathpig and rolled her eyes at her own foolishness. The little native creatures were barely a foot long, half as high, and looked like hairy mini pigs right down to the snouts. They had no tusks and weren't at all dangerous.

Aware of her limited time, she bent back down to her viewing screen, but then an odd thing happened. Her vision flashed white and then grey, and blackness rushed in suddenly from the edges.

What the-

The southern mining station, Tyger

"Well, I think it's a great outcome considering," Jae said staunchly as she watched Bill Chirnwood get carried onto the ship sent down from the colony. "You know I don't want to settle back into colony life, and the fact that there are locals here who need my help means I have a reason to stay, at least for the short term."

"Refugees, not locals," Sye corrected. "No one chooses to live down here. It's far too cold."

Jae suspected it would be quite warm in summer, but he was right. No one chose to live down here, and the shanty town they'd discovered not five kilometres from the facility was populated with Tygers who'd been forced out of their homes. She figured it must be an ethnic thing. She'd never before seen Tygers who had naturally red hair – even a ginger-brown shade, like this lot had – although she hadn't had a chance to ask them for details yet. She hadn't managed to do more than a basic food and blankets drop while waiting for more supplies to come from the colony. They'd arrived today with the ship that came to get the others.

"Even so," she responded cheerfully.

Sye rolled his eyes good-naturedly, giving her a brisk hug, then moved up the ramp onto the ship. "You stay and enjoy your impoverished, disease-ridden refugees, then come back to civilisation when you finally get bored."

"Thank you. I plan to."

Jae waved as the doors closed and the ship rose, a brief puff of wind sending the dust flying into her face. Ugh.

Darren, one of the miners who was also a techie, grinned at her. "You have to step back when it takes off, since there's no proper landing strip here. We're still working on it, because most of our supplies are sent in and out by drone."

It seemed an awkward way to run a mining site, but then Jae knew that this place wasn't even three years old yet. Still, she would have thought a proper landing site would be a basic, important thing to build. But she was only a doctor, so what did she know?

Jae headed towards the small standalone building they'd designated as her new clinic – not that she'd been able to use it yet – checking her messages as she did so. There was still no reply from Astrid or Nathaniel, which was surprising as she knew they'd been worried about her, and it had been a whole week since she'd sent her last message.

Jae decided to give them the benefit of the doubt. As it was, she switched her army cap for a more local-friendly head scarf, which was actually warmer, and slipped a long tunic over her trousers. They had more blankets and food to give out, and she was going to do it, whether they wanted her to or not.

Somewhere in Mahadra city

Astrid sat huddled on a stone floor, her head swimming and her limbs feeling as heavy as lead. She could barely see three feet ahead of her, and darkness seemed to be in every direction. She'd woken up here mere minutes before, scared and alone and confused. It felt like she'd been sleeping for ages, waking for brief periods and having the most bizarre dreams…

"Hello?" she whispered, and her voice came out in a croak. Ouch, sore throat. Sore everything, and the whole place smelled kind of musty. Where on earth was she?

Just then there was the sound of a door opening followed by light footsteps. A moment later a small figure came into sight. It was the servant girl from their visit to Mahadra, the one with curly hair and a long name, who Astrid hadn't been allowed to speak to. Her head was down and she held some kind of tray.

Astrid stared at her in amazement. "What are you doing here?" she tried to ask.

The girl didn't meet her eyes, but tapped at her own cheek.

Astrid moved her hand in an answering gesture and realised the translator was once again in place. She hadn't worn it since she'd got on the ship from Mahadra yesterday – they didn't need it, and she definitely hadn't put it on herself.

But had it really been only yesterday? It felt like much more time had passed – an eternity.

The mouthpiece of the translator was glowing dull red, signalling it was off. Astrid fumbled to turn it on again, then once the tell-tale green symbol lit up, she tried to speak again. But her voice was more than hoarse; it was almost non-existent.

"You will be thirsty," the girl said, kneeling in front of Astrid and lifting a small jug off the tray. It also held bread, Astrid noted, and a piece of fruit cut and displayed like the petals of a flower. "Save your voice."

Her words translated almost seamlessly as the translator did its job. Astrid took a drink. It was something like milk, and it felt merciful on her poor, poor throat. But as she drank, her mind and her eyesight grew clearer, and a very nasty realisation crept in.

She was in a stone room that – well, looked kind of like a dungeon, except not too dirty. Light came from a window high above, and what might have been a rug hung down over the brown stone walls. There were no other furnishings, not even a chair.

"Thank you," she murmured when she finally felt like she could speak again. "Please tell me, what happened?"

The girl stared at the tray, carefully unloading the contents onto the floor next to Astrid. "There is a chamber in the corner of the room if you have need."

A chamber? Astrid followed her pointed finger to the low seat with a hole in its centre barely two feet away. A long drop, probably, and an explanation for the vaguely unpleasant smell of the room. She was no stranger to such things since at the beginning parts of the colony were very primitive, but that was years ago. Now, every last convenience was imported directly from Earth: shiny, clean and most of all, flushable.

But never mind that – she knew the humans didn't build out of local stone. Only the natives did that. And considering the fact that there was a native girl *right in front of her…*

"Was I kidnapped?" Astrid asked hoarsely. But how had they got to her so quickly?

But the servant only stood to her feet, moving quickly to the exit with the tray in her hands. There was a curtain covering it, Astrid now saw. She tried to stand to follow the girl, reaching out as if to hold her back, when *clunk.* Something grabbed her ankle and tugged her back as hard as she'd pulled, and she could only watch the servant leave.

She'd been chained into place.

The servant left the Earther alone in her cell, still calling out those unanswerable questions in her hoarse, odd language. Her master was waiting outside the entrance to these lower rooms, with an expression of impatient expectance on those features she'd once thought majestic. He wouldn't sully himself or any of the Mahadrese women by sending them into the dungeons.

"Well?" He didn't add *'esira'* but he didn't need to. His opinion was etched into every expression and every movement that he made in her presence.

She finally looked up to meet his gaze, fixing her eyes on the space between his dark eyebrows. Strangely enough he insisted on this contact when they were alone, but she never could bring herself to truly meet his eyes. She wouldn't be able to hide her true thoughts if she did so. "She knows nothing."

The emir leaned back on his heels, satisfaction now radiating from every pore. "And so it should be. Let her wait, and let her wonder."

He turned to leave and she followed as she knew she was supposed to. After these last three years she could read him like a book. But as she went, she couldn't help pitying the Earther, who didn't understand the situation she'd been pulled into.

Crap. Crap. Crap. Astrid tugged at the chain frantically, but all it did was make her ankles hurt where the hard metal was shackled. OK, to be fair the shackles did seem to be covered in cloth of some kind, but still – shackles, like some kind of prisoner!

After a few moments of panic, she closed her eyes and lay her head back against the stone wall, trying to even out her breathing. So chances were that she'd been kidnapped by the Tygers because *her brother had run off with the emir's sister.*

Damn, Nathaniel. Why?

That idea lined up with the damaged portal, but how would the Tygers have known so quickly? It was several hours by airship, and while the Tygers rode raphantas in the same way some humans rode horses or camels, it would still take days for them to travel, to follow her even if they'd immediately noticed Lady Tamzyn's absence. Now either they'd been on the ship the whole time – seriously unlikely – or they'd had some human help.

Astrid didn't like either of those ideas. And she didn't like being kidnapped! What were they going to do with her?

That last thought sent a cold shudder down her spine, one that lingered. She knew she was no beauty, especially not by Tyger standards, but she knew what angry, vengeful human men could do when they thought their women had been insulted. Surely Tyger men wouldn't be any different.

Except, the Mahadrese wanted to stay on good terms with the 'Earthers' who paid big money for their ambrilene…

That knowledge sustained her through the next few hours as

Astrid tried pointlessly to remove the shackles, then finally gave up and just waited. She made use of the chamber pot and ate the plain food that had been left for her. It was one of those times where she didn't realise how hungry she was until she started eating, and then she felt ravenous, wolfing down the bread and fruit and then looking for more.

There wasn't any, of course, but she did notice something else – her clothes were clean. Of course she put on clean clothes every day, but she had the feeling that at least a couple of days had passed, and there was no smell of sweat. Instead there was a faint, unfamiliar smell to the fabric that implied her clothes had been cleaned in some unfamiliar substance, most likely by the locals.

Damn it, that was even worse. It meant someone had probably seen her *naked,* since her underwear was just as clean.

Ugh.

But finally she heard footsteps once more, and the curtain was pushed aside to reveal the servant girl again. "You will come with me now please," she said, bending down with what turned out to be a key.

"So you can't tell me what's going on?" Astrid asked quietly.

The girl didn't respond, just shook her head briefly.

"Well, do you have a name? I can't remember what you told me last time."

For the first time the servant looked up and met her eyes. The girl's were unusually coloured: red-brown in the centre and purple at the edges, the first Tyger Astrid had seen with irises like that. "My name is Chakandra, but you may call me Chay, if you must call me anything."

Shay. "Not *esira*?" Astrid joked feebly.

Chay looked away, focusing her attention on unlocking the shackles. "*Esira* means captive or slave. It is not a true name."

Yet the others had been calling her that. Astrid suddenly felt cold. "I didn't think the Mahadrese kept slaves."

The shackles slipped off, and Chay helped Astrid to her feet. "There are always exceptions. Follow me please, and do not ask any further questions. If in doubt, be silent."

The words sounded harsh, but Chay's tone was gentle, and Astrid realised why the girl was so quiet all the time – she wasn't allowed to speak. So Astrid rubbed at her ankles where they were exposed by her cropped pants, then stood to follow. Through the curtain was a door, then outside the door was a stone hall full of other doors just like the first – it was clearly a dungeon as she'd surmised. Two guards in full armour waited outside, only their eyes visible. They silently moved to flank her and Chay first through more stone halls, then up narrow stone steps until they reached a tiled floor and new, more elaborate halls.

These grew more beautiful and ornate the further they walked, and there were people everywhere. Some wore simple clothing like Chay, some wore lovely, expensive-looking clothing, and every last one of them watched as the procession moved by. Some of the women even lifted their veils to cover the lower parts of their faces as they passed.

Astrid stared right back, and it removed the last of the doubt in her mind. They were definitely in the Mahadrese palace – they'd just passed the familiar entry to the women's quarters.

As if there had ever really been any doubt.

Finally they moved through yet another familiar set of double doors, until they were inside the hall where she and the others had been briefly presented at the beginning of their trip. The walls and floors were richly decorated, with columns of fine white stone spiralling up each high wall, and a throne sat squarely at the top of shining wooden steps. The hall was full of people, crowded on either side, but the direct path to the throne was quite empty.

Chay led her halfway into the room, her head down so far that it seemed she shouldn't be able to see where she was going. Then she bowed even further towards the throne before backing away to disappear into the crowd at the sides. Then it was just Astrid with the guards on either side, seemingly alone in a crowd, and with the throne's occupant looking right at her.

It was Emir Raka, of course. Who else? And for a moment his expression looked so severe, so serious that she thought he was about to shout 'off with her head!'. Just behind him to his left stood that familiar white-haired young man who watched her with a narrow, hate-filled stare.

But then the emir broke into a sudden, unexpected smile. He rose to his feet and held out his hands as he walked down the stairs. "Ted Townsend," he cried genially. "Welcome back."

CHAPTER 7

Hostage

Red Townsend, Raka had called her.

It took a moment for that to make sense in Astrid's head, and she just blinked at him dumbly across the short distance to where he stood. Was her translator not working properly?

He saw her confusion, chuckling as he stopped about five feet away and put his hands at ease behind his back. "Ah, you thought I did not know about this. Foolish, proud Earther, thinking she can hide such a thing from the ruler of Mahadra. Foolish girl, thinking she could try to fight a Tyger man and come away unharmed. Our women would not even think to do such a thing!"

Astrid just stood there dumbly, because what could she say to that?

But she didn't get a chance to speak anyway, because the emir carried on, leaning forward. "Your leader Anton told me four days ago in our video conference. He was most concerned that we had been offended by your unseemly behaviour, and advised that you had fled back through the portal to Earth in shame three days before that. However, I assured him that our business relationship remains intact."

Damn it, Anton! What had he been thinking?! "They think I left a whole week ago?" Astrid whispered. "Was *that* why you took me, because I offended you?" So at least she now knew how much time had passed, and why she was so hungry. Four days since she'd left the colony. What had they been doing with her all that time, dragging her unconscious body around on the back of a raphanta?

She'd known the Tygers would be upset if they found out she'd dressed as a boy to attend their festival, but she hadn't thought they'd *kidnap* her because of it. And Anton thought she'd gone through the portal! If he didn't know where she truly was, then how would he even try to get her back?

Raka brushed a hand through the air dismissively. "Offended me, bah. You Earthers cause offense like you breathe. You cannot help yourself. No, the reason you were taken is that we require a hostage pending the return of my own beloved royal sister."

Ahh *schnit*. Astrid felt her hopes sink right through to the floor. Could this be any worse?

As he'd spoken Raka must have made some signal, because the room emptied, all except for the guards, the hateful white-haired guy, and a couple of servant women. "What a shy thing you are," he mused. "It is hard to believe you ever had the courage to disguise yourself as a man, although I can see why the disguise worked. You are what we call half-grown." He looked her up and down. "Although perhaps just outwards rather than upwards, hmm?"

Rude. But Astrid wasn't shy, she was just scared stiff. "If you didn't tell Anton that I'm here," she said very carefully, "then how can he exchange your sister for me?"

"Aha!" the emir shouted suddenly, making her (and at least one of the guards) jump in surprise. "So you admit that you stole her! My precious older sister, kidnapped by foreigners pretending to be friends! For *shame*."

Now she was just confused as well as frightened. The hairs on her arms were standing on end, but her voice remained even. "I didn't steal anybody. *We* didn't take anyone against their will. That would be against our laws. Wherever Lady Tamzyn is, she's there willingly." Or so Astrid hoped.

"Your laws! The same laws that mix male and female and dress them as though they were the same? The same laws that *vote* a leader into position as if that can ever compare with the hereditary, heaven-granted right of a monarch? *My sister* left this palace without my permission, and has been defiled simply by spending time amongst your people. I say she has been kidnapped, and therefore she has been kidnapped!"

The emir nodded his head decisively, as though simply by speaking he created the truth, and turned back towards his throne. "We held back the knowledge of your capture until you were safely brought here, and we could send a memento to encourage your people's assistance. That is assuming they want you back."

There were so many things she could say now, like *what an ass*, or *this is totally illegal,* but instead she settled for, "Memento?"

"Perhaps…a hand?"

Astrid gasped in horror. The surrounding Tygers didn't react, except for the white-haired one, who none-too-subtly rolled his eyes. Raka didn't seem to notice, instead letting out another roar of laughter. His moods were as changing as a newborn's nappies.

"Just my little joke," he assured her. "We will take a lock of hair instead – assuming you can spare any."

He indicated to the female servants, and one of the older women stepped forward with a pair of scissors. Another grabbed her from behind to hold her still – unnecessary, because Astrid would *far* rather give up some hair than a hand. Hair at least tended to grow back.

A few seconds later the women stepped away, one holding a hank of brown hair in one fist. Astrid felt cautiously to the space behind one ear – instead of a lock of hair, they'd taken a good-sized chunk.

Raka waved his hand again. "Take her back to her cell." And as before, the guards and the women leapt back to attention. Chay had vanished, and one of the women grabbed her wrist as though to pull her along. (Also rude, but what did you expect from someone who butchered hair like that? Astrid didn't have long hair, but it was healthy and most of all, it was *hers.*)

"Wait!" Astrid called out desperately, setting her feet in place and turning back to look at the emir.

He raised a dark eyebrow arrogantly. "You wish to beg for your freedom? You shall not have it."

Duh, she knew that. Astrid straightened, feeling a little irritation blending in with her fear. "I just wanted to know how you brought me here, that's all."

Raka made a dismissive sound. "Your Earthers are so happy to share your devices, but you never expect that they'll be used against you."

Devices. They'd traded all kinds of things – goods like saucepans and fabric, but also minor weapons like stun guns. If you used those consistently, someone would stay unconscious until they died of thirst… *Damn it, Anton!*

But then there was no more time for questions, as she was pulled out of the room.

Near the southern mining station

The small shuttle hovered uncertainly above the cave and tent dwellings as the humans waited for a response from the cave's inhabitants, for good or for bad. As for Jae, she couldn't see anything moving amongst the brown rocks and few straggly trees.

She turned to the pilot, raising her voice to be heard over the hum of the engine. "Marco, are they gone?"

Marco was the colony's pilot/security guard, a middle-aged man with a moustache and an apparent inability to smile. He shrugged. "Who can tell. You want to go down anyway?"

"Yes, please."

The shuttle gently lowered to a halt on an empty patch of earth, and Marco held up a hand. "Give me a minute to check the area's clear, then you can come out."

If the area was clear, then there was no one who needed help, Jae thought irritably, but didn't argue as he stepped out of the vehicle, weapon at the ready and his eyes narrowed like a cowboy out of an old film. A few moments later he gestured for her to come out. "Nobody here."

She climbed out into the chilly, open air, squinting a little at the bright sunlight. "We should–"

Suddenly a burst of noise filled the air, and Marco spun around, weapon at the ready. But Jae had already seen what had caused the sound. "Don't!" she cried. "It's just a bird!"

A moment later he lowered his weapon. "That's one hell of a bird," he muttered. "It's as big as a condor."

It was the biggest bird Jae had ever seen, not counting the flightless ones. Its wingspan must have measured fifteen feet across, and its body looked as large as ten-year-old's. It was copper brown to match the landscape, and it watched her steadily with golden yellow eyes from its perch on a nearby tree stump.

"It's an acrypid, a bird of prey," she said more evenly than she felt. She'd seen this kind of bird up north, but only on people's walls as a kind of display. They'd been a lot smaller too. "Look at that hooked beak. You wouldn't want that thing around your kids. Perhaps that's why they've gone."

"They might still be 'round here somewhere," Marco offered, gesturing at the tents where they'd been set up over the openings of a series of caves. "Give a yell on your device."

He meant her translator, and she did so, setting it into place and making sure to amplify her voice just enough that anyone nearby could hear, not enough to be frightening. These people might not have come across humans and human technology before, and they might not react well.

"My name is Doctor Jae Townsend," she said for the benefit of anyone who might be listening. "I'm a healer, and I'm here because I want to help. I will leave some food and blankets for your use, and if any of you wish to talk about health issues, especially the females and children, please come to see me. There is a new building on its own near the other Earthers, and if you come there you will not be harmed." She paused. "I'll be staying for at least one month."

Nothing but silence greeted her. The bird watched her for a moment longer, then turned to fly off across the brown land, each wingbeat as loud as a helicopter starting up. She and Marco watched it go, then she sighed. "You think I'm talking to the wind, don't you?"

He shrugged, pressing the combination of keys to release the load of food and blankets. It was more of the same things they'd dropped off last time – which she noted were no longer in view. That was a good sign, because it meant someone was using them.

"Don't see what else you could have done. Just a month, is it?"

She sighed. "There's not much point staying longer if no one needs my help. We'll see."

Marco raised a grey eyebrow. "That we will."

But when they checked the site the following day, the supplies had vanished.

Astrid had spent what felt like days sitting in that cell, tapping her fingers on her knees to entertain herself. She'd thought that playing checkers alone had been bad? Checkers now seemed like a luxury, because every time someone came to bring her food and water (plain, she noted, although plentiful) they didn't speak. They never responded to her requests.

However, she counted only two periods of darkness. It couldn't have been more than two days, but she was this close to turning the chamber pot upside down and playing drums with it for fun. It wasn't like she'd smell any worse – she hadn't been given any means to clean herself this whole time.

But on the third day, after someone had already brought her daily meal, she had another visitor. It was Chay, and she bore gifts. Well, kind of. Along with a couple of other female servants, she'd brought a bag of clothing, a comb, a big bowl of water and a wash cloth.

"You will need to be clean for your visit with the emir," Chay said, her eyes lowered as always. Did she even know how to make eye contact? "We also have new, clean clothes. Your own clothes will be laundered, and you may have them back."

"Hallelujah," Astrid muttered, looking down at her grey, grubby tunic and trousers. They had been cream once, but no longer. She pulled out the clothing and held it up to display. It was rather like what she wore already, except the tunic had a big bib-like section with intense purple and black designs, almost like what she'd seen on the walls in the palace. She looked up at Chay curiously.

"So that you are not mistaken for a servant or a guest," Chay said with a hint of apology in her voice. "Will you require help with your hair?"

"What's left of it," Astrid muttered. "No. No, I'll be fine." But she found it interesting that the emir wanted to see her again. Maybe she'd be able to get some useful information out of him – or maybe she'd come back missing a hand. "Chay-" she began, but the girl had already ducked out of the room.

Ten minutes later Chay returned just as Astrid was smoothing down the front of the borrowed tunic. No matter what she did, it still looked like she was wearing a big baby's bib, as though she was afraid to spill food on her clothes. She looked up at Chay with a rueful smile. "Will I do?"

Chay nodded, moving forward with the key again. She didn't speak.

"You know," Astrid said conversationally as her shackles were released once more, "I don't talk to you just to hear the sound of my own voice. I don't want to hear state secrets or anything, but it would be nice if you'd speak back."

The servant's cheek dimpled in what might have been a hint of a smile. Then she said so quietly that Astrid almost didn't hear it, "I have been forbidden to speak unless spoken to, and unless in pursuit of doing my duties." She made a meaningful gesture towards the doorway hidden behind the curtain, then tapped her ear.

"Oh." Astrid dropped her own tone accordingly. "Someone is

listening?"

Chay didn't speak, but her mouth shaped the word. *Always.*

Well, poop. That made this place a whole lot less pleasant than Astrid had imagined, not that she thought it so wonderful in the first place. "Why are you here?" she asked in barely a whisper. "Were you born here in this palace?" Here in slavery?

The servant just shook her head minutely, then said in a normal tone, "You are ready to go. Follow me, please."

And that would be all she'd get out of Chay, Astrid mused. She didn't want to get the girl in trouble, but she was more curious than ever. How had Chay ended up in such a position? What *was* her position? There must be some trust there if she was sent in to unlock Astrid's chains like this.

Chay reminded her of someone, Astrid decided. She couldn't work out if it was her manner or her looks – not that she'd had a good look at her face, since it was almost always pointed at the floor. And whose rule was it that servants (or *slaves*, because it didn't seem like there were any others quite like Chay) couldn't have a simple friendly conversation if they were asked? She bet it was Raka's rule, that arrogant asshat.

Speaking of arrogant asshats, this particular one was sitting at a table in what looked like a parlour. He was alone, hunched over with his attention fixed on a familiar black and white board.

Oh, *no.* He wanted to play checkers *again?*

Emir Raka looked up as she entered the room, one dark eyebrow arched arrogantly. "Sit."

Astrid sat, noting as she did so that the board didn't hold the familiar flat pieces. No, instead it held pieces of various sizes and shapes. Chess – but not quite. She could see a little blue-painted raphanta where the knight usually would be, no doubt yet another gift from Earth. "Have you heard back from the colony?" she asked politely.

"They will not have even received the lock of hair yet," he replied dismissively. "And you will address me as Your Magnificence at all times."

Good thing he couldn't read minds, because what she was thinking was far less polite. She swallowed her irritation. "Your Magnificence. Perhaps if you told them by video conference, as they've clearly given you that equipment-"

"Enough." He waved a hand dismissively. "We shall play chiss now. You are familiar with the game?"

"Chess."

"Chiss. As I have said."

This, Astrid told herself as she went through the rules for yet another classic human board game, was going to make a great story one day – assuming she ever got out of here to tell it. "…and then when you capture the king, you win," she finished. "It's a game of strategy."

"All games are strategy," Raka said. "And life is simply a game to be won."

She looked at him in surprise for a moment – yes, he was serious – then shrugged a shoulder. "If that's the case, then I suppose you're winning at life."

"This is true," he replied modestly, moving his first pawn to mirror her own move. "I have not captured the king yet, but I will."

She had the strongest feeling he wasn't talking about this particular board game.

Two hours later they finished their third game. Raka won (by some very careful manoeuvring by Astrid so that it wouldn't look like she'd let him on purpose) but he still scowled at the board like a child told to go to bed early for no reason. "You say I have won," he accused, "yet you have more pieces left than I do. I have only six. You have nine."

"The number of pieces doesn't matter," she replied, not for the first time. "You could have one piece left, and you'll win as long as you capture the other player's king." It was a bit more complicated than that, but she'd never claimed to be a genius at chess. Or 'chiss'.

"And yet I do not feel as though I won by enough of a margin," Raka said. "Set the board again."

It was better than playing drums on her chamber pot, she thought, but barely. "I need to go to the bathroom," she blurted out suddenly.

Raka and the guards standing quietly at the corner of the room all looked at her in surprise. "Is this an Earther custom?" he asked suspiciously. "To wash halfway through the day? I did not notice that the others did such a thing."

Astrid realised he thought she wanted to bathe, which meant the translator wasn't working entirely as it should. Feeling her cheeks heat, she tried again. "I need five minutes of privacy before the next game. Your Magnificence."

There was a long pause where it looked as though he would argue, then understanding dawned. "Oh. Why didn't you say so, then?" He clicked his fingers and the guards snapped to attention.

A moment later one of them was leading her out of the room and down the hall, then deposited her outside what was clearly a washroom – and in this case not for washing.

The guard pointed at the little room with its little door that she could see right under. "One minute."

Astrid studied the toilet cubicle dubiously. It looked better than her own chamber pot – just – but there was definitely no sense of privacy. There was even a little window at the back with a patterned screen, but she could see the garden right through it. It definitely wasn't like the windows back in the women's quarters. "I'll need more than a minute," she told him with dignity. "I'm a woman. We can't just whip it out like you can. And I'll need you to turn your back, because otherwise I'll be too nervous to go."

The guard looked displeased, or so she guessed from the way his eyes narrowed under his helmet. "I was not intending to stay. You may have two minutes only." And with that he turned and left the room.

The irony was that she didn't really need to go. She was just coming up with an excuse for a break. Funny to think that playing board games with royalty could be so strenuous – but she'd been given a wonderful opportunity.

She wasn't even wearing shackles.

The little screen covering the window was pushed off without difficulty, and a few seconds later Astrid went tumbling out the other side like a baby elephant being born. (Yes, she'd seen that once and it was memorable). She landed on soft, dry grass with a scattering of pink flowers right by her face. She was in the emir's private garden, full of trees and flowering plants, with a fair bit of space to walk in. Over one side she could see what had to be the women's quarters, and on the far side was a wall that she knew led to the city proper. She was alone.

Heavens, this was too good to be true. Standing to her feet, Astrid tugged a few times at her distinctive 'bib'. It came off in her hand, and she flipped it to the reverse side which was plain black, before wrapping it around her head. She might have been able to pull off 'boy' again with her short hair, but here, the plain brown colour was far too distinctive, and there weren't supposed to be any human visitors in the city at the moment.

She started off at a brisk walk for the far wall, her breath coming fast and shallow from fear and excitement, and she reached it without any difficulty. It even had handy notches for her to climb – too easy!

But she was halfway up the wall, so close to freedom, when *smack*. Something slammed into her from the side, sending her flying off the wall and back onto the grass. She hit her head with a jolt, feeling like the breath had been entirely knocked out of her, and with shock making her head spin. Something heavy was pressing on her back, pushing her into the grass, and there was a rumbling sound right in her ear.

It felt bad. Very, very bad, and if she'd really needed the bathroom, she would have just gone right then, forget her dignity.

Slowly Astrid lifted her head, turning to look over her shoulder, and there it was. A tyger face leaning right into hers, its teeth bared in a snarl. It snapped at her, and she was too scared to scream. She whimpered, frozen where she lay, until finally interminable minutes later a pair of boots filled her vision. The weight eased off her back, and the guards hauled her to her feet before dragging her back towards the palace.

The tyger followed alongside, its white tail twitching with every movement and its purple eyes fixed on her as if she'd make a good supper. It followed all the way into the palace, down the hall and into the emir's chamber where he stood by the open window, his hands casually arranged behind his back.

"Ah, there you are," he said calmly, returning to his seat. "Come. I do not like being made to wait."

The guards pushed Astrid back towards the empty chair, firmly shoving her into it, then returning to their places by the doors. The tyger sat back on its haunches not ten feet away, now looking bored and placid...but somehow still terrifying.

As for her, she was still stunned into silence. The blood had drained from her face, and her hands were shaking. Emir Raka didn't seem to notice. He pointed at the board. "I have removed the pawns to make the game faster. Here, make your move."

Did he not know what just happened? Astrid looked dumbly down at the 'chiss' board, which true to form had been remade to suit Raka's wishes. It seemed he'd made the first move for her too. How thoughtful, and how like him to make his own rules.

"Fine," he said lightly. "I'll make your move." He took her queen and moved it directly up to the top of the board opposite his, then took his own piece and knocked hers over. "I take your queen. Ha. See, it pays to pay attention."

Astrid looked at him, at his arrogant, oblivious face, then at the guards who stood stolidly by the doors, then at the tyger which still sat in the same place. As if it had seen her looking, it yawned, displaying needle-sharp fangs. They were all acting as though nothing had happened, but everything had. She'd forgotten. She'd thought it was just the people that she had to worry about, but she was clearly wrong – and those were the best trained big cats she'd ever seen.

She took a deep breath, picked up a random piece, and made her move.

It was the worst game of chess Astrid had ever played. To be fair she hadn't played much, since she'd always preferred the deceptive simplicity of checkers. But after fifteen minutes Raka made a sound of frustration and abruptly shoved the board off the table. The pieces scattered, and one of the blue carved raphantas fell onto her lap. She quietly picked it up and set it back on the now empty table, but Raka pushed it off too. It skidded away to hit the nearby wall and fell with a clunk on the floor.

"You're not even trying!" he shouted. "How am I supposed to savour winning if my opponent puts in no effort?"

If she put in effort, then he might actually lose, and he wouldn't savour that at all. But Astrid just looked at him, and finally he let out a mighty sigh, waving his hand dismissively. "Take her away."

Clunk. That was the sound her shackles made when they landed on the floor of her cell, once more locked around her ankles. *Riip.* That was the sound her make-shift veil made when it was pulled off when they grabbed at her translator, and then finally the curtain fell closed, leaving Astrid alone in her cell and without any means of communicating with the people around her. Well, the people out in the hall, anyway. There wasn't anyone around her right now.

Finally Astrid found the strength to speak. "Schnit," she said to herself. "This just gets worse and worse."

Back in the emir's chambers Orin watched patiently as the guards melted away, leaving the two brothers alone. The emir was muttering to himself and picking up the now slightly dented pieces once by one, returning them to their places on the board.

A moment went by, then two, and when Raka was finally satisfied with the board's layout he turned to his brother. "She really was terrified," he said matter-of-factly. "Did you have to frighten her so much?"

Orin didn't answer for a moment. "Revenge, as discussed."

"But entertaining," Raka continued. He tapped a finger on the now set-up board. "I think I may have to teach her some Mahadrese games."

"You must take care not to create expectations of the Earthers," Orin found himself saying. "Or is that your intention? A trade of females to cement relations? After all, they already have your royal sister."

Surprisingly the emir didn't take offence. "Intentions, as in that I would wed that alien child? I think not, although perhaps in time she might make an acceptable wife for some man."

"But if the Earthers think-" Orin began, then tried again. "But perhaps you no longer wish for their approval. You certainly do not need it. You already have strength far outweighing the other city-states, and perhaps you have seen that to mingle with the aliens-"

"Better that they trade with us than with Syrenius," Raka snapped. "Leave the thinking to me, simpleton, and keep to your duties. If you had been faster in your original instruction, then the loss of my sister would have been a short one. As it is we will have her back, and we will have revenge, and we will have what was stolen from me by that weak, useless boy-regent. Unless you have a better idea?"

The questing was clearly sarcastic since Orin always had ideas, but they were rarely voiced to this particular person. Raka was too arrogant – oh, so arrogant – and mercurial and in some ways so childlike. Easily manipulated in some ways, but stubborn and cunning in others. "No," he replied. "No, I have no better ideas."

The shackles were unmoveable, and Astrid's lock-picking skills weren't up to the task with only her now twisted earring as a pick.

She'd lost the shock-induced numbness she'd had since first arriving, or perhaps that had feeling had been leftover from whatever they'd used to keep her unconscious for the journey here. Now she felt angry: angry and desperate, and depressed.

So when Chay finally returned the next morning, Astrid just spoke her feelings, never mind the lack of translator. "I don't know what they want with me," she said desolately. "Playing games, seriously? I don't think Nathaniel will ever give Tamzyn up freely, not if he truly thinks she's in danger, but I don't know whether to believe that or not. I don't know what to believe. I do know that Earth is going to be furious if there's any break in the supply of ambrilene, and they'll blame Nathaniel and I for it. It will be our fault, I suppose.

"And even if I could get out of these shackles and somehow climb up to that window, I'd probably just be chased down by one of those freaky cats." She was lucky her throat was still intact, and she definitely didn't want to repeat that experience.

She sat back against the wall in despair, studying the servant as she did so. Chay was small and soft-looking, with pretty, rounded features, delicate hands, and curly purple-black hair where it showed from underneath her simple servant's veil. It was her face that reminded her of someone, Astrid decided, not her manner. But who?

Chay met her eyes briefly, giving her a nod of what might have been sympathy, then set back to unloading the tray of that day's food and water.

That was when Astrid noticed something new. It might have just been the light – but no, it couldn't be. As Chay bent down in front of her, the roots of her hair appeared to be red.

"Hey," Astrid said in surprise. "Do you dye your hair?"

Chay finished unloading the tray and gave Astrid a polite nod, murmuring something in the Tyger tongue before standing to leave.

"Bye," she called as the girl left.

Chay paused by the doorway, then said haltingly, "Bye."

"Well," Astrid murmured to herself with a glimmer of humour. "That's one way to get past the language barrier." To actually learn the other language. How novel.

But that wasn't the last time she saw Chay that day. Judging by the dimming light it was probably evening when the girl came back, this time accompanied by two other women and with what looked like a suitcase of cosmetics. She didn't argue as they stripped her and cleaned her and put her into rather a nicer outfit – this one loose-fitting and purple, but with the same ugly bib.

"This is a good sign, right?" Astrid said aloud. "I wouldn't be getting changed if I was going to sit here for another week."

Unless they were taking her to her execution...

Then a new, much nicer idea occurred. "Hey, am I getting traded back?"

The Earther chattered away as Chay and the other women dressed her. She had to know that they couldn't understand a word she was saying, but Chay could sympathise with the desire to be heard, even if not understood. She didn't even have that much.

"Where is her translator?" she asked the other women.

"The emir ordered it removed," Neema replied, frowning as she studied the alien girl's chin-length brown hair. "By the stars, who would allow a female to cut her hair so short? She looks like a boy."

"I saw the males," Jianne said with a superior tone. "They're practically bald, so it must be relative."

"The hairpiece, please," Chay requested, and her tone came out more brusquely than she intended.

Jianne handed over the elaborate jewelled comb which Chay knew had come from the royal collection – she'd been sent to get it. Such an odd position she held her, with everyone knowing she was merely *esira,* yet also knowing she held the emir's trust...and rather more.

She wondered why the emir was doing this anyway. It had to be something to do with the contact he'd just had with the Earthers on the new device they'd gifted him, like a big moving picture so that they could communicate. And he'd been in that room, talking to them on the device and then having poison whispered in his ear by that blessed, bastard brother of his...

But when the Earther let out a cry of pain as the comb was placed, Chay muttered apologies that she knew weren't understood, and wondered why she was acting like this. Almost...jealous. She had *hated* her master. Absolutely hated him for what he'd allowed to be done to her people, and for keeping her here like he had, for treating her as he had. Yet had she now forgotten that she was a captive, and had she begun to think of herself as a treasured pet instead?

Foolish, Chay told herself. Utterly, utterly foolish, as was this jealousy she was feeling.

But then she'd never been in such a position before, had she? She'd never had this new secret, and as she thought that, a new pang of fear and hope went through her. She had to tell him. She knew she had to, because she certainly wouldn't like to be surprised with such a thing. And maybe, just maybe, she'd graduate from *esira*.

Astrid wore no shackles today as they moved through the palace. No, she'd graduated to handcuffs linked with a fine chain between her wrists, which somehow felt a bit easier. The sun was low and sent golden beams through the corridor screens as the guards walked her through the palace, with Chay leading the way. It must be near the end of the day.

But this time they didn't lead her to the emir's parlour, which she thought of as the 'chiss' room. They took her somewhere else entirely, up winding steps that grew narrower and narrower until she knew she was in a tower. They went up and up until they finally reached an open door and stepped through into a round room.

It was rather nicer than her cell, that was for sure, with an actual bed, a large window at about chest height showing a view of the city, and what might have been a bathroom hidden behind some screens. Emir Raka stood at the window, looking out with his hands clasped behind his back. It seemed to be a common stance for him.

The guards melted away, leaving her standing there alone with her hands chained and in new, purple clothing, and feeling just as off-balance as she had before. There was no game board in sight, but there was a bed. She did not like that there was a bed.

Raka raised a supercilious eyebrow and said something in Tyger. She just stared at him, and he repeated himself, looking irritated.

"I don't have my translator," she explained a little apologetically. "It was taken away yesterday."

He scowled at her, then shouted something. There was the sound of scurrying footsteps from behind, and after a minute of silence something was shoved into her hand. The translator. She set it into place around her ear, then tried to look appropriately interested and grateful. "Sorry, Your Magnificence. What was that you said?"

He let out a sound of frustration. "You always have to ruin things, don't you?"

She did? "Sorry?"

"Come over here. Look out the window, and tell me what you see."

Feeling awkward, Astrid cautiously followed his instructions. He moved aside, and she looked out to see that she was way higher than she'd first thought, and it was nerve-wracking; there appeared to be a pool of swirling black water directly underneath the tower; and Raka was standing too close. "Um…dirty water?"

"That's the waste water from the palace laundry," he snapped irritably. "Look further. What do you see?"

She looked. "The city and the city wall. Uh…desert? A bit of greenery? Mountains…"

"The mountains," he repeated in exasperation. "The Kabeer range marks the line between my land and the land that should be mine too, but which was stolen from me and is now ruled over by a halfwit in lieu of his insane stepfather, my uncle. The goods your people trade with me are what will enable me to take back what's mine."

So *that* was why he was so desperate to trade with Earth, Astrid realised – and why he was after the weapons. Of course. She hastily scanned her memory and came up with, "Syrene?"

"Yes, Syrene," he agreed sarcastically. "What else would I be talking about?"

She bit her tongue, determined not to respond in kind even though (in the words of her late mother) he really could do with a flick around the ear. "Forgive my ignorance, Your Magnificence," she said tightly. "Most of Tyger culture is a mystery to me."

"Then you're going to have a wonderful time watching the city over the next few years," he said.

Astrid paused. "You're returning me in a *few years*?" she squeaked. At least he hadn't said he'd kill her. She'd rather be somewhere high up than trapped in that little cell for the same length of time. She was starting to get bruises on her backside from the stone floor.

"No," he replied. "We're not going to return you at all. You're going to stay here in this tower until you die of old age, or some other cause."

Her heart stopped for a long moment, then started again – beating at double-time. "Pardon?" she croaked, turning to look him full in the face. He just stared back at her, a careless, arrogant sneer on his handsome features.

"You see," he began conversationally, taking a couple of steps back towards the door, "I spoke to your people this afternoon, and your leader assured me that not only are they unaware of where my royal sister might be, but that they've no way of returning her should they be able to confirm she was taken. He says that they do not condone the actions of a single, misguided young man – that is, your brother – and they insisted again that you yourself had fled through the portal to Earth ten days ago and haven't been seen since. But they don't want it to affect our trading relationship."

"Fled through the portal...?" Astrid echoed dumbly. But she'd been *seen* the following day at school! Even if they had managed to recover the records of who'd travelled, they would have known that it couldn't have been her.

"Indeed," Raka bit out. "They seemed to have little interest in my avowals that we did in fact hold you, and when I offered to send something more solid than hair they just looked confused and reminded me of our trading agreement. I should have expected it, of course. I knew how much your people would trade for the precious ambrilene they love so much. So – we have traded, inadvertently it seems. A most chaste royal...for you."

Her heart sank through the floor. Did this mean her people weren't trying to get her back, or were they just playing until they could sneak her away?

"And so I told them," he continued, beginning to pace back and forth across the room with his damned hands behind his back, "that we would further cement our agreement. A wife for a wife. They seemed happy with that."

"A wife?" Astrid squeaked. "But you said-"

"I know what I said!" Raka shouted suddenly. He strode over to where she stood at the window, then grabbed her face in one hand. She hadn't thought he was particularly tall, but now he seemed too big, too strong, and she'd never been so scared in her life.

"Did you really think I would take such an odd creature as my wife?" he raged. "That I would gift the Earthers with being part of the royal Mahadrese line? Never! So you shall have the punishment that my sister would have borne if she had been returned – and which she will bear, when we finally find her. You will remain in this room for the rest of your life, and think carefully on how your people valued you so little!"

Raka released her abruptly and she staggered back to hit the windowpane. "And when they ask how you are," he continued in a low voice. "I shall give them the regrettable news that you have taken ill and passed away. Poor, poor girl, unable to stand an ordinary Mahadrese illness. And they'll be satisfied, and I will continue to give them ambrilene until I've gained the weapons needed to take back Syrene. But you won't know about that. You won't see anyone. You won't speak with anyone. You will be completely alone…forever."

If Astrid could have replayed that moment she would have done something daring. She would have punched him in his stupid face in spite of her handcuffs, or said the right, cutting thing, or…she didn't know what.

But in this moment what she actually did was just watch him silently as he left the room, her eyes wide and hands still chained.

He paused in the doorway, speaking to one of the guards. "I want that window boarded up at once," he told him. "We wouldn't want any *accidents*."

The door slammed shut and locked into place, and then she was alone. It was the first day of the rest of her new, solitary lifestyle, if they had their way. And while there was no way that Astrid would give up that easily, she'd never felt so miserable before. "Land," she said desolately to herself. "Land and bloody pride."

"Driving forces," a new voice said, and she just about leapt out of her skin. A young man stepped out from behind the screens that divided off one side of the room, his expression cold and dismissive, and his white hair falling straight to his shoulders. He wore a jewelled pendant and a plain white robe, and he looked at her like she was an insect about to be crushed underfoot.

"You!" she choked out. "You're the one who's always glaring at me. You had something to do with this, didn't you? Why are you even here?"

He just looked at her. "My name is Orin the Blessed," he said flatly, "which you'd know if you'd been paying attention at the presentation. My royal brother did think about keeping you as a concubine, but I talked him out of that. I explained that different doesn't mean exotic, and that touching you in any way would be beneath him."

His *brother*? Astrid studied the man again, remembering at once how she'd thought he'd resembled Raka…but had been told Raka had no legitimate brothers. No competition for the throne – so this one must be illegitimate. "You talked him into this?" she whispered. "Into locking me in a tower until I die? What kind of malicious monster are you?"

She shouldn't ask questions like that, she thought later. Because Orin didn't move. He didn't, but still he changed. His regular features rippled and twisted until they were like an old All-Hallows mask; until his teeth were big and sharp and his face was a muzzle with white hair sprouting over every surface.

"*Not a monster,*" the creature hissed. "*Blessed.*"

Astrid screamed and stumbled back against the window, and the beast stepped forward. Then there was nowhere else to go, and it set one white-clawed hand firmly against her purple-bibbed chest and pushed.

She tumbled over the window ledge, free-falling, and screamed all the way down, until she couldn't scream anymore.

CHAPTER 8
The Fall

Orin let his features morph back into human form, moving over to the window and looking out. The swirling black pool of water below showed only the occasional ripple as a sign that something had fallen in, although no one could have missed that scream.

He waited a few minutes, watching to see if by some miracle she'd bob back to the surface, but there was nothing. This particular pit of dye-filled darkness led straight down the carefully built sewer system that came up outside the city, then flowed into the river that led into the foothills of the Kabeer mountains.

The guards posted outside the door finally noted that something was wrong, and one of them opened the small hatch that would enable food and water to be passed in. Better than they'd done for Aunt Elysha, whose finally resting place was in the tower opposite this one. She'd taken a mere four days to expire from lack of water, but then it had been in an unseasonably warm winter.

The funny thing was, this girl had been lucky, because they'd actually planned to feed her. But Tamzyn, if she was ever found, wouldn't be so lucky. The royal females must remain chaste – pure and undefiled. It wasn't just a title, and the punishment for doing otherwise was always capital.

"Sir?" the guard ventured. He looked an inch away from asking, "Aren't you supposed to be out *here*?"

Orin turned away from the window, setting his features into a most solemn expression. "Regrettably the girl chose to throw herself to her death rather than face her sentence. I shall notify my brother."

The guard looked both appalled and relieved – but then it would be far better for someone else to pass the message on to Raka. "Yes, sir," he stuttered. "Shall I send someone to find the body? It might surface upstream, outside the city."

"Leave it for the fish," he answered coolly. "The aliens deserve no better."

"Yes, sir."

And so he headed down to his brother's chamber, still solemn in expression, but inside feeling a most comfortable satisfaction. Easily manipulated, indeed.

The sun was setting, casting pink light over the palace's pale walls, but the white glow-stones kept the emir's chambers as light as day as Chay quietly went about her tasks. As for the emir, he'd been uncharacteristically silent for at least thirty seconds after his brother gave the news.

"I do believe I'm actually disappointed," Raka said finally from where he sat in the deep bathing pool, then let out a short, unhappy laugh. "Throwing herself out like that a mere minute after I left, and when the door hadn't even been bricked up or anything! It wasn't as though we'd threatened to starve or beat her. I would've thought she'd have more courage."

"She was a foolish girl," the Blessed One said, standing blank-faced at the edge of the bathing room. "But you had already told her of your plans. Perhaps she lost hope."

"Huh. Well, I might have changed my mind. It was novel playing mind games with a female."

"A dead female now. I heard her skull crack as it hit the tower on the way down."

The emir played games all his life, Chay thought as she worked silently at the side of the room, preparing his clothing for bed. She felt cold and shaky, and that last comment had made her want to retch. The Earther was dead, and so suddenly?

Chay knew of other women who'd killed themselves rather than surrender their virtue, and until a minute ago she'd thought that the Earther wouldn't have been one of those women. Even though the Earther had fallen silent in front of the emir (but who didn't?) she seemed to have courage when they were alone. And to dare to dress as a male…

The white-haired brother waited silently, then when Raka didn't say anything further, suggested, "There are others who could be taught to play games." He gave Chay a meaningful glance.

Raka let out a short laugh. "Play games with a mere slave, Orin? I'd as soon marry one. No, I do believe that ship has sailed." He paused, pouting. "I shall teach one of the courtiers to play chiss instead. The Earther barely put in any effort after you startled her the other day."

Chay flinched, but neither male noticed. How could he be so heartless? To joke around when a girl had just died – and to casually crush her own hopes while he was at it. And to think Chay had been jealous of the Earther, had imagined she would take that place Chay herself wanted; that of a woman who belonged. Concubine or wife, it wouldn't have mattered.

But now the Earther was dead, and wouldn't become either. The Blessed One had convinced Raka not to defile himself with the girl, but Chay knew that Raka could have changed his mind at any moment. It was too late for that now.

Then finally the *beini* left, and it was just the emir and her, as it was every night. He chattered away as she helped dry him and laid out his clothes; a service that only the rich required. Everyone else just dressed themselves.

"The nation of Raka. Or perhaps I shall just rename the city-states to Mahadra North and Mahadra South, with this of course remaining my capital." He paused. "Do you have an opinion?"

On these rare moments when he actually asked, he always expected a reply – agreement. "Any of those would be suitable, Your Magnificence." But her voice shook.For once he actually noticed, stopping halfway through slipping into his robe. "Are you upset?" he asked in disbelief. "Over the Earther?"

Chay looked at her feet, then forced herself to lift her head even as she felt his hand on her chin. She fixed her eyes on the point between his eyebrows. "Perhaps a little, Your Magnificence. She was very young." And gone so quickly. So, so quickly. So perhaps it was grief that made Chay venture, "The general belief was that you intended to take her as a concubine as recompense for Lady Tamzyn's… kidnapping."

"I changed my mind," the emir said simply, studying her face in that way he sometimes did when they were alone, the way that made her think that perhaps he did care. He didn't look at anyone else that way, did he? "And I do not need a concubine. I have you."

Chay, who didn't get the honour of being labelled 'concubine', since that would elevate her to the protected position of half-wife. She knew, she *knew* she would never be a real wife, not to him, probably not to anyone now, but perhaps the other…? She couldn't keep her eyes on his face. She looked down at her feet, small and barely clad in simple slippers. "Yes, Your Magnificence."

But the emir didn't let go of her face, squeezing her cheeks a little. "You've grown plumper these past few months."

"Have I?" Now would be the perfect time to tell him. She just needed the right words.

"Hmm. It is not unattractive, but still…you're not with child, are you?" His tone was sharp, and Chay sucked in a breath. "Because I'd hate to have to replace you so soon."

Was it soon? For three years she'd been his plaything in this palace, from the age of sixteen when most girls would be married. But his tone told her everything she needed to know before she even had to ask. He would *not* be happy to know. "I take the herbs every day as instructed, Your Magnificence."

"Good." Emir Raka seemed satisfied with that, letting her go and studying her with his usual possessive gaze. She'd thought that gaze meant she was valuable, meant she was safe – but perhaps she'd just been fooling herself. The emir was not a man who liked to lose *anything*.

But later, when he was sleeping, she stared up at the dark ceiling and wondered what in all the heavens she was going to do.

The river that fed Mahadra city was one of the longest in the continent. After starting somewhere to the far north, it flowed past the city, losing much of its bulk to irrigation, then twisted its way well into the foothills of the Kabeer Mountains. By this point it was narrow, deep and occasionally treacherous if one didn't know the safe passages.

It was also good for fishing, which was why Jazir and Vuyani were currently sitting on the rocks at this quiet part of the shore, waiting for their catch to cook. They'd taken just enough for lunch plus tomorrow's breakfast, as fish didn't keep well in the warmth, and there'd always be more to catch.

"Huh," Jazir commented to his sister. "Look at that."

It wasn't a fish that had caught his attention, but something rather larger and in a solid shade of purplish-blue, rather like a shakberry. The thing – person – dragged themselves out of the smooth water onto the rocks, blue hand by blue hand, before collapsing rather dramatically.

Vuyani gave him a disbelieving stare. "Well, come on then! He could be dead!"

"He's not dead, he was just moving," Jazir argued, but grumblingly followed his sister's prompts. They wandered over to the now still form, then prodded at one limb. The figure groaned and spewed up a mouthful of dark water, briefly dyeing the pale rocks lavender. "Huh. Well, that explains the colour. He must have fallen in a vat of dye."

Vuyani looked at him in disgust. "How would he have ended up here, then?"

"Someone pulled him out of the dye, and threw him in the river to clean up, obviously!"

"There's nothing obvious about it!"

But while the siblings were arguing, the blue youth rolled over and opened his eyes. Both siblings jumped in surprise.

"Ugh," Vuyani said. "Now that's just creepy. *Brown* eyes."

"Dunno," Jazir countered. "They could be pretty in the right head. Weird, but pretty." His sister gave him yet another disbelieving stare, and he argued, "I said in the right head!"

But Vuyani had turned back to their 'driftwood'. "It must be a Dragonfly. He must have thrown himself in the river to escape from the soldiers." She crouched on her hindquarters and prodded the boy in the arm. "Hello there. You alright?"

Jazir didn't argue over whether the kid was a Dragonfly, since it actually made perfect sense – Mahadra had grown extremely dangerous for Dragonflies these last few years. "So he was trying to dye his hair blue to match everyone else, but fell into the vat."

His sister didn't comment on that, and neither did the Dragonfly kid. He just blinked big brown eyes which looked even weirder in his dark blue face, and struggled to push himself into a sitting position. He muttered something incomprehensible.

"What did he say?"

"How am I supposed to know? I don't speak Dragonfly."

Vuyani elbowed him in the side. "Dragonfly isn't a different language. They speak Tyger, just like anyone else. They just look different." She poked the boy again, speaking slowly and loudly as if he was an idiot. "Helloo theere. Caan yoou uunderstaaand mee?"

Perhaps the boy was actually an idiot, because he just stared at them blankly, looking confused. Then he slapped at the side of his head, feeling around his jawline as if searching for a sore tooth.

Jazir grabbed his blue hand, pulling it away. "Don't do that, kid," he told him kindly. "You'll knock out the few wits you've got left."

The boy just looked depressed, and Vuyani sighed. "Well, blue simpleton or not, we're not leaving him here. We can bring him along with us, drop him off somewhere in Syrene. I'm sure he'll be good for *something.*"

Well, she wasn't dead. She didn't even have any broken bones. Except for the fact that the palace's foul wastewater seemed to have dyed her skin indigo, Astrid was quite unharmed – and being helped along a rocky river path by a couple of Tygers who seemed to think she was an idiot. Probably the fact that she'd lost her translator added to the confusion.

They were about her own age, no older than late teens, but were dressed more casually than anyone she'd seen in the streets of Mahadra on her last visit. They both wore loose, cheerfully-coloured clothing, and the girl had a white cloth loosely wrapped around her hair. Astrid could still see the dark blue ends and roots, unlike the carefully covered nobles and servants she'd previously met.

"Jah-zeeer," the boy said slowly, tapping on his chest, then pointing to the girl. "Voy-ah-nee." He pointed at Astrid. "'Sha?"

Her knowledge of the language might be very limited, but that seemed clear enough. She opened her mouth to introduce herself, but stopped. 'Astrid' was on the run, and 'Ted' and 'Nathaniel' were just as off-limits. And it wasn't as if they'd know if the name was male or female, right?

She sneaked a brief look down at her front. The outfit was now an unbroken shade of blue-black, causing the ugly bib to blend in for once, but it had done her a favour. It hid her limited curves so that perhaps she *could* pass as a boy. A blue, simple, brown-eyed boy.

The Tyger boy looked exasperated, and said something to the girl, who shrugged. They chattered on for a bit with Astrid straining to identify more than a word or two, and then as one they turned back to her.

"Tam," the girl said. She pointed at Astrid's chest. "Tam."

Astrid pointed at herself. "Tam?"

The girl – Voyani, or whatever her name was – nodded and looked satisfied. "Tam."

And that was that. Through gestures and speaking slowly (which really didn't help, by the way) they managed to give the impression that they wanted her to travel along with them. They had a small cart hitched to a hairy ox-like creature called a karak, and were following a narrow, winding path that led through this deep valley.

The two of them sat up front, chattering away to each other as they travelled along, then occasionally glancing back to give Astrid big, fake-looking smiles. She fake-smiled back, and they seemed happy enough with that.

But her thoughts were racing. She remembered what felt like hours of being tossed about in a washing machine, feeling an inch away from drowning and then from giving up out of sheer exhaustion. Before that she remembered falling out of the window, falling and falling and *knowing* she was going to die, and then hitting the water so hard that she must have passed out.

But before that…

Had the white-haired Tyger *really* changed into a monster, or had she just imagined it?

No, not a monster, a *tyger*. A literal big white cat, with equally big white teeth. It made her shudder to even think of it.

Jazir turned to grin at her from his seat up front, then gestured to the road ahead of them. "*Syyy-reeene. Sa'snaa ree-ooo.*" He held up a hand with all five fingers outstretched. "*Sa'sna reo.*"

Well, Astrid did know her Tyger-language numbers at least. Five days to Syrene, was it? Which meant they must be leaving Mahadra, which meant they were travelling through the Kabeer mountains…

Oh, thank *God* for that. Jae had said several times that the Syrenian regent was a reasonable person, which compared to Raka must make him simply normal, but perhaps he could arrange to get her back to the colony.

But if Raka had been telling the truth then her people were happy enough to leave her here, if not to die then at least to be the plaything/chess partner of a probably unstable emir.

Astrid let out a heavy sigh, slumping onto her hand, and caught the attention of one of the travellers. He said something which she didn't understand, then made a hand gesture that was even more incomprehensible. She stared at him blankly and he shrugged, turning back to face the path ahead of them. Communicating was too hard, the gesture seemed to say, and she had to agree.

But at least this was better than being walled up in a tower.

Some time later

"Two days to Syrene now," Jazir said in slow Tyger, holding up the same number of fingers. "Two."

Astrid just looked at him, tempted to roll her eyes as this was the fourth time today he'd told her. But instead she smiled politely and nodded, repeating his words as well as she could in the same language, and trying to keep her voice low. "Two days."

Goodness, it was amazing what she could pick up when the translator was missing in action. Chances were that the words were already in her head, what with hearing them a hundred times through the translator, and were only now being used.

She'd also worked out that Jazir and Vuyani were some kind of salespeople. They seemed to have household objects and possibly spices in little bags in their cart, as well as a variety of handwoven blankets. She *thought* that they travelled between Mahadra and Syrene, sleeping in their cart and finding food as they went, but she might have misunderstood that.

As for her, she was still purple, unfortunately. Her skin had faded to a depressing light grey, a bit darker around the nails, but her hair had soaked in the colour and was almost black. That wasn't entirely a bad thing, since her 'exotic' brown hair was no longer showing.

She'd given up on trying to ask about the 'beini' thing, having put it to the back of her mind. Trying to mime, 'do men sometimes turn into animals?' had ended up with her looking rather sillier than she already did. She'd keep that question to herself until her Tyger was more fluent – at which point she might be able to explain that her name wasn't Tam, either. But for now it would do.

Astrid focused on learning basic words, careful to keep the same simple expression. She wondered if she'd ever mixed up 'foreign' with 'stupid', because these two sure did. Even so, they were kind, and by the time they came out of the mountains and into a green plain she was almost normal-coloured, except for her hair, and felt confident that she could make herself understood if need be.

She'd heard that Mahadra was the biggest city-state on the planet, but if that was true, then this must be the most beautiful. As they came down from the mountain road she could see a wide plain, sheltered by mountains on one side and dusted green with plants and scattered grass. A wide river ran through the plain, splitting off into several smaller canals, and with buildings clearly clustered around its edge. She could see what looked like irrigated crops, and beyond those, the high white walls of some kind of city. Except for its setting, it looked like it could have been Mahadra's twin.

"So this is what Raka would kill for," Astrid murmured to herself. "It's surprisingly pretty." And lush. Really, really lush, in that bluish-green colour typical of the local vegetation.

The road widened and became busier as they passed a few isolated homes, then came into a built-up area full of people and business. The two travellers came to a halt and immediately set themselves to arguing high-speed with a local merchant (or perhaps that was just their way of doing business: they always sounded like they were arguing to Astrid). She began to wander around curiously. She had such a limited knowledge of Tyger culture, and of course back in Mahadra she'd only briefly seen the city during its festival.

But here, swarthy men in white robes and caps argued over trays of vegetables and crates with fat, flapping birds inside; children ran through the dusty road, laughing and playing; and more interestingly, there were women. They wore long, draping robes like the ones back in Mahadra, and either veils wrapped tightly around the backs of their heads like a hippie from Earth decades past, or half-covering their mostly dark blue or purple hair.

There were quite a few with silvery-white hair like horrible Orin, and Astrid found herself transfixed by one girl who was perhaps her own age, but with reverse colouring: light hair and dark skin. The girl looked up and saw her watching, but instead of being offended just raised an eyebrow.

Astrid glanced away, not wanting to insult anyone. But she couldn't help wondering again about what the locals called 'blessed', and what she thought she'd seen back in the tower. It was so noisy here, which was probably a good thing, but she just didn't know what to do next. Make it to the capital, perhaps, then try to find transport south…

Just then something tickled the back of her neck, and she scratched at it irritably. The tickle stopped, but then started again. She slapped at the back of her neck, and something slapped back, grabbing onto her hand.

Astrid let out a shriek of surprise, turning to see a hairy brown face right in front of hers, and a long brown limb wrapped neatly around her hand. She tugged her hand away, and the limb followed her, prodding at her hand and then her face. *What the...?* There was laughter around her from the locals, so clearly she wasn't in danger, and she realised a moment later what it was. A raphanta, one barely taller than her and in an unusual brown shade, as brown as her own hair usually was. It seemed to have taken a fancy to her, plucking at her collar and her dyed dark hair with its curious long trunk.

Astrid finally got over her fright, letting out a laugh. "You're a baby, aren't you?" She stretched out a hand, letting the trunk wrap around her wrist like they were shaking hands. "Well, hello there."

The raphanta opened its mouth and let out a sound that might have been happy, but sounded like a deflating balloon. It also revealed several rows full of needle-like teeth, very unlike those of Earth elephants. Also unlike an elephant, it had tiny, floppy ears, long, slender legs, a slightly humped back, and what looked like a saddle dragging along behind it.

An escapee.

Astrid patted the ugly, hairy head. "Don't worry," she told it in English. "I understand completely."

The marketplace of Iznaith was as chaotic as ever, but Jazir loved it. He loved the noise and the smells and the sights after two solid weeks of travelling alone with his sister (and Tam), and he particularly loved the raphanta races that Iznaith was known for. The racetrack here was second to none, and every time the biannual races came up he'd make a point of being here.

While Vuyani finalised their agreement with the local spice trader, Jazir found his gaze wandering. Here and there he could see raphantas being led towards the track, or fed and painted in advance so people could recognise who they were betting on.

There were mostly the solid greys, which weren't that fast but could be trusted not to throw you off a cliff; then a few of the royal blues for those who could afford them and who'd put up with their sensitivity, and- oh, stars, there was a brown viper! It was a deceptively small breed of raphanta, but anyone who knew raphantas knew that nothing could beat it for speed – assuming it didn't maul or kick you first. Brown vipers had tempers worse than Vuyani on a bad day. And who was that stupid kid who was *petting* the damn thing?

A moment later Jazir's eyes bugged as he recognised their simple Tam, rather less blue but also showing his cluelessness, as he stroked the brown viper's trunk and then its shoulder. Amazingly it didn't kick him in the chest, crushing his ribs, or even bite his hand. It actually seemed to like the attention.

Jazir patted his sister on the arm. "Vuyani. Vuyani."

"Stop it, Jaz! I'm busy."

"No, seriously, look at this!"

Finally she looked up, and they both watched as the viper *fondled* Tam's head with its trunk, and the silly boy laughed.

"Should we save him?"

"I don't know." Jazir just stared. "It seems to like him."

"Brown vipers don't like anyone. You just hope that they'll let you ride them, and pray they don't throw you."

Case in point: a trio of weary-looking men ran over, holding a bridle and ropes, with one visibly limping. Tam looked surprised to see them, then horrified as they grabbed at the raphanta. It threw back its trunk, trumpeting angrily and showing those sharp viper teeth, and then let loose with a solid kick, sending one of the men flying dramatically backwards.

The other two tried to hold its head but it furiously shook them off, slapping one in the face with that long trunk and then stomping heavily on the other's foot. As the man howled, the raphanta trumpeted again, sounding almost like a laugh, then took off at great speed.

"Shame," a boy murmured from beside Jazir. About Jazir's own age – late teens – the boy wore simple grey clothing and had a generous beard that seemed too thick for someone so young. "That was the rider, too."

Jazir looked at him curiously. "Which one? The one with the broken teeth, foot or ribs?"

"The one who was kicked first. The owner put everything into running Kopa in the next race, but without a fit rider he'll lose the entry fee." The boy looked sympathetic at that prospect. "Kopa's just too young, not tamed yet."

"How do you know all of this?"

The boy shrugged airily. "I know the management. I'm Benn."

Jazir introduced himself and his sister, then they watched as Kopa – a name he knew meant 'vicious' – did a circle of the whole village, then trotted up behind Tam again and prodded at his neck with its trunk. Tam jumped, then turned with an expression of surprised delight, muttering to the beast in his unintelligible language.

Benn watched the scene curiously, his dark eyes narrowed. "You know that guy?"

"Um…does it pay to know him?" Jazir hedged. "Or is he in trouble?" There was a long silence, then he sighed. "We brought him here, but the kid's as simple as a two-piece puzzle. He barely speaks Tyger!"

"Then what *does* he speak?"

Jazir shrugged. "Dunno. He mutters nonsense to himself, mostly, and he doesn't even know well enough to avoid a brown viper."

Benn looked thoughtful. "Simple enough to ride one?"

"Surely you're not suggesting we offer him as a rider," Vuyani cut in. "Look at him."

They were already looking, and Tam was laughing as the curious brown trunk prodded his dyed blue hair and then tapped him on the nose.

"Hmm," Jazir mused. Then to Benn he began, "Hey-"

But the boy was gone.

Astrid wasn't sure how it happened. One moment the brown raphanta was being chased off by those bullying men – or it chased them off, rather – and the next it was back, playing with her hair and poking in her ears like a curious child. She got over her nervousness since it clearly wasn't going to hurt her, but then noticed that she'd gained an audience.

Jazir and Vuyani stood at a slight distance along with one of the men, the one who was now nursing a bloodied nose. They were having a fervent conversation – not to mention that half a dozen other locals were watching her with either smiles or curiosity. She dropped her hand where she'd been playing 'handshake' with the raphanta, then lowered her eyes as well. She didn't want to get anyone's attention, not until she was home and safe.

She wondered how much she would have to pay someone to take her to Aunt Jae down south. It would be a long walk…or ride, if she could get hold of one of these creatures *and* actually point it in the right direction. But it would be extremely easy to get lost, then die of exposure.

Feeling irritated again at even being in this position, Astrid resolved that she was going to learn the scorpion kick, and if possible use it on Raka the next time she saw him. It wasn't Krav Maga, but damn it would be satisfying.

But now her two traveller friends were approaching along with the man with a bloodied nose, smiling and nodding and speaking to her in that slow way that they always did, and accompanying the speech with hand gestures. She wasn't sure what they wanted, except that they kept pointing to her, then to the raphanta, then making weird shapes that she didn't understand.

"Copper," Jazir kept saying, pointing to the raphanta, then to her. "Tam. Copper."

Tam being the nickname she'd picked up when they'd first met, whatever that meant. Astrid looked at the raphanta which was still trying to plait her short blue hair with its trunk. "Copper?" Was that its name?

Lots of frantic nodding proceeded all around. "Copper," Jazir agreed, then rattled off a series of words she couldn't understand.

Astrid stared blankly, and they looked frustrated, finally gesturing for her to follow. So she did, and Copper the raphanta followed behind her, its trunk tugging at her hair like it was being pulled by a rope.

They took her to a place not far from the market, except *this* place was teeming with raphantas, just teeming with them. There had to be at least thirty of the things, grey and blue and with swirls of paint over their sides that even Astrid recognised as Tyger numerals. There were flags everywhere, what looked like a wide track marked out, and people *everywhere*. The noise level was intense.

Jazir pointed very slowly at a nearby blue raphanta, its sides painted like a stained glass window, and the rider looking very small indeed on the top. "*Zasi.* Tam, Copper, *Zasi.*" Then he pointed at the track, which stretched all the way past the village and into the foothills before reappearing quite some distance away. "Tam *zasi Kopa.*"

Finally understanding dawned. "You want me to *ride* it?" Astrid looked at the brown raphanta, and it looked back. "Zasi Copper?" She made an exaggerated gesture – 'why'? Wasn't it a baby? And she was lean, but she wasn't exactly a lightweight.

The other three looked frustrated again, then started babbling again, gesturing at the racetrack and making hand signals that were probably very meaningful, but meant nothing to *her*. Finally Vuyani grabbed her by the hand, dragging her over to a colourful tent nearby. On either side of the entrance were guards, and at the back wall of the tent a series of sparkly things were displayed. Some gold, some silver, some wooden; some looking very valuable and some perhaps not so much.

Vuyani pointed emphatically at the sparkly things, then at Astrid, then at the raphanta still following cheerfully behind. "Tam *zasi Kopa a vitez, avah jayiza.*"

"Jay-eeza?" Astrid pointed at the sparkles questioningly.

Vuyani made an expression that looked something like 'maybe' and waggled her hand side to side.

"You know," Astrid said to her flatly, "I really wish I knew what you were saying, because it sounds important."

The Tyger girl let out a heavy sigh, and she and Jazir set to having an energetic argument with the bloody-nosed man throwing in the occasional comment. Astrid found herself a quiet spot on the ground nearby, leaning against a wall, and watched. Her friends seemed to be arguing quite desperately for something to do with *her*, and losing. Finally the bloody-nosed man threw his hands in the air and stomped up to where Copper was happily stealing straw from another raphanta's manger through the slats of a nearby fence, grabbed at its sagging bridle and got a slap in the face as a reward.

Silly man, didn't learn.

Just then Astrid felt the brush of something against her arm. She turned, but there was no one there. But there *was* something on the hard-packed dirt next to her though; something familiar. She picked up the small grey item with a sense of disbelief, turning it over in her hand, and a series of tiny lights blinked green as she held it. Green meant *ready*.

It couldn't be…but it was. A translator, just the earpiece, but apparently still functioning if the lights were correct.

CHAPTER 9

A Day at the Races

There was a translator sitting in the dirt, just as if it had been left for her.

Suddenly wary, Astrid looked around suspiciously for whoever had dropped it. There was no way it could be a coincidence. It wasn't there, and then it was; ergo it had been left for her, and someone knew she was from Earth. No doubt they just wanted her to use it, to prove that she was human, because no one else would know what to do with it. And then they'd grab her, and take her back to Raka…

But the surrounding busyness showed nothing out of the ordinary, no one watching her with evil intent, and she began to feel a bit silly. No one was even looking at her at all, and she began to wonder if the earpiece had been there the whole time and she just didn't notice. Even so, she was cautious and slow as she slipped the thing onto her ear to hide it underneath her chin-length bob.

There were a few seconds of confusion when the translator tried to pick up every sound from around her, blasting her ear with nonsensical chaos, but then it clicked into gear and began to translate cleanly from the nearest conversations. As always there was a moment where she had to learn to listen to the whisper of the translator rather than the surrounding noise, but then she was in and listening in fascination.

"Half a year's wages," Jazir was saying emphatically to Vuyani. "First place gets half a year's wages, and Xever said he'd give us half if Tam successfully rides Vicious! You just need to *explain* it to Tam, and I'm sure he'll agree! We can offer him half of our half, yes? That's a good deal." His voice lowered, growing more excited. "And we can use the prize money to fix the house, to give it a new roof and to re-dig the well. It'll be incredible!"

That was a bit sad, Astrid thought, and it showed the siblings' financial situation if they were getting excited over re-digging a well.

"I don't think he's got the wits to understand," Vuyani replied flatly. "I showed him the prizes and he just looked blank. He doesn't have the wits to be wary of a brown viper, that's for sure. And who's to say Tam could even ride the thing at all?"

Tam. For the first time the word translated as 'blue' and Astrid had to hide a smile. As nicknames went, it could have been worse. But what were they talking about, riding 'Vicious'? She looked across to where the brown raphanta was now drinking from another raphanta's trough – the same one whose straw it had stolen – and realised that she'd also renamed the creature.

"I prefer Copper as a name," she murmured to herself, then had a brief moment of surprise where the translator repeated her words aloud in the local tongue, right in her ear. It was the same language that they spoke in Mahadra, but with a slight accent.

Brilliant! Even if she couldn't manage to repeat the words aloud, at least she could now understand what was going on around her.

Just then Jazir and Vuyani looked over at her, and she gave a wave, trying to look just a little more intelligent than she had before. Thoughts were racing through her mind, of whether riding a raphanta would be like riding a horse, 'cos if so she hadn't done that since she was a child back on Earth, and whether she'd get enough prize money to pay someone to take her down south, down to the Earth-run mines and Aunt Jae…and whether Copper would even let her ride it, or whether she'd get herself another black eye just when the first one had faded.

But she had to at least try, didn't she? Her other option of trying to do the same thing moneyless didn't sound pleasant, although she could always try to beg for the help of the regent, assuming he wanted to give it…

No, Astrid decided. No more depending on Tyger royalty, since in her experience so far they tended to be insane. So she stood up, confidently walked over to Jazir and Vuyani, and said in her limited Tyger, "Yes. Tam ride Copper." And maybe she did sound like an idiot, but it was the best she could do.

Jazir's jaw dropped, and Vuyani looked dubious. "Really?" she asked. "What changed your mind?"

Now Astrid definitely didn't have the vocabulary to explain, so she just waved a hand in the direction of the prizes. "Those."

"So he *did* understand," Jazir muttered to Vuyani. "He's just slow to process."

In a manner of speaking, yes.

Turning to Astrid, Jazir said, "So you can ride, can you?"

They all looked across at the brown raphanta, who was now struggling to shake off the bloody-nosed man and a friend who'd managed to get a rope around its neck. The men had a brief moment of triumph, before once again Copper did a mighty kick with those long back legs, booting one of the men in the unmentionables, and causing the other to back away in alarm.

Hmm. If Copper should ever decide it *didn't* like Astrid…well, at least being kicked in the unmentionables wouldn't hurt quite as much.

But when they approached Copper's owner Xever and made their offer, he was desperate enough to accept. He looked at Astrid (or 'Tam') with a dubious expression, then shrugged. "I can't take getting kicked again, and I don't have anyone else offering to ride the little beast. You want to, lad, go for it." Then as one, he, Vuyani and Jazir all took a distinctive step back from the raphanta who'd almost cleared out the previously full manger.

Astrid approached warily from the side, preparing to duck in case of sudden trunk/foot attack. "Hey Copper," she crooned. "You don't want to kick me, do you?"

Apparently not. The raphanta paused eating its meal, then turned to give Astrid's face a happy stroke, leaving behind a handful of hay as it did so. So far, so good.

"Straighten the saddle," Xever hissed frantically from his safe distance. "Straighten it then tighten it, and you should be able to get on his back. The first race starts in fifteen minutes!"

OK. Straighten the saddle…Astrid brushed off her faceful of hay then crept closer, stroking a hand over the raphanta's leathery brown shoulder and sliding back to where the saddle had slipped under his belly. There was a pause where Copper seemed to decide if he'd allow that, and Astrid waited to be slapped in the face – but then Copper went back to eating, and Astrid slid the saddle gently around his barrel-like belly until it sat on his back.

"How did you catch the thing in the first place?" Vuyani was asking Xever. "I thought these always run too fast to be caught, and you can't hunt them without penalties."

"Some lying scum sold him to me drugged, making him seem far more placid than he actually is. And we thought that since brown vipers are so fast we had a good shot at the prize – until we realised he had the temper of a viper too. Good thing he likes your lad. But we haven't even got close enough to paint his sides. Let's hope we go fast enough that it doesn't matter."

Good thing, too. Maybe Copper liked the smell of human, or maybe the smell of dye. Who knew. By this point Astrid had worked out how to tighten the saddle. It didn't have stirrups, rather the saddle hung low and had stiff ledges down at its lowest point that would serve for the same purpose. But how on earth did you steer the thing?

"Good one, lad," Xever called across to Astrid. "Now climb on up, grab the bridle and we'll see about pointing you towards the starting line."

She shot him an alarmed look. She hadn't ridden a raphanta *ever*, and she was supposed to start with a race? She sent up a silent prayer that she wouldn't fall and be trampled – God still existed on other planets, right? – and then grabbed the saddle, hoisting herself into the air and up onto the raphanta's back. Copper froze, then shook a little, lifting his head, then trotted away from the manger. Astrid finally managed to sit upright, but there was just one problem.

"You're facing the wrong way!" Jazir shouted. He looked alarmed but was hiding a smile, and Vuyani was covering her mouth. Xever had covered his eyes, shaking his head.

"Thank you, I know," Astrid muttered in English, trying to ignore the laughs of everyone around her as she had a very backwards view of riding a raphanta who had now decided to actually go somewhere. He didn't want to race *now*, did he?

But Copper only walked a few metres before stopping again, and when Astrid finally managed to turn herself to face forward she saw that he'd just moved on to the next unused stall and was chewing away at what looked like a bucket full of scraps. "Seriously?"

"Good, good," Xever encouraged her. Unlike the others, he wasn't laughing. "Now take the rope, and wrap it around both your hands. You'll need it to hold on."

"But how do I steer?" she asked plaintively in English. Of course he didn't understand, but her translator helpfully repeated her words in Tyger, so she did the same.

"Wow, that's the longest sentence I ever heard him say," Jazir murmured to Vuyani.

"You don't steer," Xever replied. "You just hold on and let the raphanta take you. They're usually very well trained."

They all looked dubiously at the brown viper, and Xever repeated, "Usually."

"All they need is a competitive spirit," Vuyani explained. "Then they chase the others."

Except Copper's competitive spirit was nowhere to be seen, because other raphantas passed and headed towards the racetrack, and all Copper did was eat. Eat, and drink, and occasionally poop – but at least Astrid wasn't facing backwards anymore to see that. She was thankful Copper had no interest in throwing her off, but they couldn't win her transport money if they didn't *go* anywhere. Astrid tried nudging him in the sides and using the rope that passed as a bridle to lift his head. She even tried various 'race' words as supplied by Xever, all of which were happily ignored.

"That's it, then," Xever said, sounding utterly defeated as the horn sounded for the first race. From here they could see the first set of racers head off down the wide raceway, starting off slowly but then gaining speed with those long legs. "There goes my entry money, because that was my only chance. Wasted away on a brown viper."

"There's always next year," Vuyani said, but she was clearly disappointed too. Jazir had already sneaked towards the racetrack and was enthusiastically watching the other riders, each raphanta looking distinctive from a distance with their multicoloured painted sides.

Astrid slumped in dismay, leaning her forehead onto where her arms rested on Copper's back. "It's all a game to you, isn't it?" she muttered in English. "Now how am I going to get to the mines?"

Just then there was the sound of intense trumpeting from further up the track as a blue shoved aside a slightly smaller grey, causing it to fall sideways and trapping its rider. The excitement of the crowd intensified, and then abruptly Copper's head lifted, almost smacking Astrid in the forehead. "Ow."

But he wasn't just curious. Suddenly he stepped away from the food, pointed his head towards the chaos of the raceway, and charged.

The spectators of the seventy-ninth annual Iznaith raphanta races watched in amazement as a small brown raphanta charged *through*

the fence marking the entryway to the race course, then swerved dangerously close to the screeching crowd before turning and heading at full speed up the track towards the greys and blues in the distance. Its sides weren't marked and its rider was dressed plainly, and from the brief glimpse a few people had before it was lost into the distance, the rider appeared to have his eyes shut.

"Hooray!" Jazir shouted, waving a fist in jubilation. "Do it for our new well!"

"Go Tam!" Vuyani shrieked.

As for Xever, he was just relieved the beast had actually got onto the track, and was hoping he wouldn't be completely humiliated. "Hey, he does know how the race works, right? He knows he has to collect the flags?"

Jazir and Vuyani glanced at each other, then said in unison, "Um…"

Finally Astrid understood why someone would go to the trouble of buying a little, ugly, foul-tempered raphanta rather than one of the big beauties, and it wasn't because it was cut-price. It was because when they ran, they *flew*. She had her eyes shut in pure terror, and her teeth clenched so she couldn't even scream as Copper sprinted down the rutted dirt track, his long legs pistoning with every move.

Finally she managed to open her eyes and saw that they were at least heading in the right direction, and in fact the large rear of a trotting grey raphanta was right in front of them. Copper swerved at the last moment, ducking around the grey and passing it, and Astrid had a moment of seeing the outraged expression on the grey's rider before they'd left it behind. If they were making people angry, they must be doing alright. *She* wasn't doing anything. She sure couldn't steer – all she was doing was hanging on. Perhaps Copper wasn't so horribly trained after all.

Minutes went by where Astrid's backside grew increasingly numb, and Copper passed two, then three more greys as the track turned and curved into the barren foothills. Then a big blue rear loomed up ahead – it was one, no *two* blue raphantas, their broad sides painted in matching swirls of red and white, one just ahead of the other on the increasingly steep path. Their riders were perched on their broad backs like baby koalas on their mothers, and both had an array of red and blue flags tucked under their seats.

Copper slowed down, picking his way more carefully, and perhaps his smaller size was a benefit here where the path was steep and narrow and so very, very rocky. Up ahead the blue raphantas were moving slowly now too, and she saw the closer one's rider glance over his shoulder.

He must have seen her since his mouth moved as though he was speaking to the first rider, then the first raphanta slowed just a little to allow the second to catch up. Now the two blues were almost side by side, and Astrid could clearly see the gap between them narrowing. Soon they'd be blocking the path, as the rocky walls on either side began to close in. She wouldn't be able to overtake them until the other side of the chasm where the path grew wider.

Copper must have seen the same thing, but had a different reaction. He picked up his speed, almost stumbling on the loose rocks as he charged for that narrowing gap. Astrid gave a squeak of dismay, pulling her feet out of the way just in time as Copper squeezed his way in between the two far-larger blue raphantas before popping out on the other side like a bizarre parody of childbirth.

The blues' riders shouted something unintelligible at Astrid, and shaken, she just responded with a crude Anglo-Saxon hand gesture. Copper turned and roared challengingly at the closest blue, slapping it with his trunk, and then all hell broke loose.

The blue raphanta threw up its own trunk with a panicked bellow, then reared up on its hind legs, almost unseating its rider. The second blue reared away too with a high-pitched squeak, causing a flurry of swearing from its rider as it slammed against the rock wall to its right.

Copper was dancing about, waving his trunk and roaring at the two much-larger raphantas, and he seemed to be enjoying himself. But Astrid wasn't enjoying herself at all – she was desperately trying not to fall off or get knocked out by any flailing blue trunks, and she could see the greys they'd just passed catching up further downhill.

"Damn it, Copper!" she shouted, tugging at the rope. "Forget them, just go!"

Finally Copper did decide he'd won that encounter, as he turned and pointed himself in the other direction, starting to run again. He scrambled over the uneven rocky path that curved through the foothills before finally the path turned and Astrid could see the valley in front of them again – or *below* them, rather. The path dropped steeply into the valley floor, which would be the perfect time to tread carefully. Further down she could see the track marked out by varied blue and red flags on poles, each with a person or two standing by, and what must have been the finish line in the distance with that massive crowd.

"I think we're coming first," she said in surprise. Now all they needed to do was make it to the end without killing themselves or Copper attacking random spectators.

Her raphanta let out an excited trumpet, throwing up his trunk and then – yes, ran for it, right over the end of that horribly steep path, and all Astrid could do was hang on.

All they needed was the energetic theme song to that old TV show Bonanza. They charged down the too-steep path, right down the hill until they hit flat ground. There was half a moment where time seemed to slow as Copper caught his balance, then on they went, past one, two, three flags until finally they reached the finish line. They charged through to the roar of the crowd, and Copper barely slowed. He swerved *through* the crowd – Astrid didn't *think* he trampled anyone – and then skidded to a halt beside the river before sticking his head down for a drink.

But the stop was too sudden for Astrid. She lost her grip on the rope and went flying over Copper's head to land with a splash in the water.

Graceful as always, she thought. But hey, they'd won! That was a miracle in itself.

She dragged her sodden form out of the river, trying to wring her clothing out as she did so, but she could feel the grin stretching her face. Whew, the adrenaline of it all! And to have won!

But when Xever and Vuyani ran over to her, they weren't smiling. They were pointing back at the finish line to where the blue raphantas were trotting through, one after the other, their riders clutching handfuls of red and blue flags, and Astrid got a sinking feeling.

"You had to grab the flags!" Xever shouted. "The flags! Don't you bloody know how to race?"

"The flags?" Astrid echoed in their language, feeling her elation very quickly turn to disappointment, then anger. They'd never said anything about flags!

"You had to grab the flags as you went by," Vuyani said in a low voice. "Red means two points, blue means one point. You were first through the end gate, that's ten points, but it won't be enough to get to the next round."

Astrid felt like she wanted to cry, especially when Jazir walked over with a distinct slump to his posture. "We came third," he said glumly. "Those two royal blues came first and second by a mile. They were slower, but they got the flags."

He didn't scold Astrid for not getting them, but she felt like she was going to burst. Why hadn't they told her such an important piece of information? "You did not say," she gritted out in a low tone. "You did not say…the flags."

Xever began moaning pathetically, Vuyani and Jazir looked incredibly disappointed, and Astrid felt like she'd let everyone down. Only Copper was still slurping away happily, unheeding of the commotion.

"Kopa's sides weren't marked anyway," Jazir commented flatly. "That's three points down too. We'd still beat the greys, but who cares about *them*?"

"But his sides are marked," someone unfamiliar said from the edge of their group, pointing. "Look, white and red."

Indeed, Copper's sides were smeared with swathes of blurred paint from when he'd squeezed between the two blue raphantas, and when Astrid had almost lost her legs.

"Where did that come from?" Vuyani asked curiously.

Astrid shrugged dully, trying to find the words. Her Tyger vocab was growing by leaps and bounds thanks for the translator, but she still struggled. "Two blue raphantas. Mountain path." She held up her hands side by side, moving them together in a clapping motion.

"They tried to squash you?" Jazir exclaimed.

She shook her head. "Tried to…stop."

Xever's head shot up, his dark eyes holding a maniacal gleam. "They tried to block you on the path, is that what you're saying."

She shrugged a shoulder. "Yes."

It seemed that was a bigger deal than she'd thought, as a minute later she was being dragged by the sleeve to what looked like the management.

"Those two blues tried to block Kopa from passing!" Xever announced, waving his arms dramatically. "I demand that they be disqualified!"

As it happened the riders were actually nearby, celebrating that they were moving on to the next round. But once the allegation was made, they objected ferociously. "You're a liar!" one of them accused Xever. "You're just sour that your viper and its idiot rider were too stupid to grab the flags as they went by, so you're trying to stir up trouble!"

Xever's face went purple, but the management – a slim young man with a neatly-trimmed beard – held up a hand. "Do you have any evidence of this?"

"Only that my viper has *their* paint smeared on both sides of his body, and my rider says they tried to block him going by on the mountain path. Isn't that enough?"

The management gave Astrid a querying glance. "Is this true?"

Realising by now that it was quite important, she nodded. "Yes," Astrid replied carefully in Tyger. "They tried to block the path, but Copper...ran. Squash." How to say 'caused a fight?' She made another gesture with her hands, trying to show the face-off between the raphantas, then finished, "Then Copper ran."

"Look at him," one of the riders sneered. "He can barely speak. How can you trust a word he says?"

Astrid flushed pink with anger and embarrassment, growing tired of being treated like a fool, even if she'd accidently acted like one.

But Jazir stepped up, acting as her white knight. "This kid almost drowned a week ago," he said hotly. "He's clearly been injured, but he still outraced *you*. You're the one who's sour, and you're a bad sport!"

Ah, that was sweet – and would be sweeter if she didn't know he was thinking of his new well. But the management finally stepped in, stopping what might have become a fist fight by saying, "Let's take a look at the royal blues, shall we? They won't have been washed yet."

So they all trotted off to where the two raphantas were being cared for after the race. As it happened they *hadn't* been washed yet (was that a thing they were supposed to do?) and the smeared paint on their sides matched that on Copper's, no surprise to Astrid.

"Disqualified," the management said flatly. "You're in the next round then, Xever. Make sure your rider knows the rules."

"I will," Xever replied rapidly. Then as the man walked away, Xever fell to his knees with his hands dramatically raised to the heavens, and mouthed something like the Tyger word for 'thank you'.

You're welcome, Astrid thought, since he clearly ought to be thanking her too.

Now all she had to do was win the next round.

The southern mining station

Jae studied her handheld screen in disappointment. She'd finally had a reply from Astrid, but surprisingly it was text rather than video, and very brief.

Sorry, I've been busy. I'm glad you're well. Will make contact once I have time.

The message was brusque compared to Astrid's usual bubbly chatter, and Jae had to admit she felt a pang of hurt. After the upheaval she'd been through, she would've thought her nearest kin would actually care that she was alright. But maybe Astrid was reaching that age where she pulled away from family, and Nathaniel's contact with Jae had always been irregular. Sighing, Jae began to compose a new text message of her own.

"*Jae!*" Marc's familiar voice shouted through her walkie-talkie.

"What?" she shouted back. You always had to shout with these things or you couldn't be heard. Funny how technology on Earth had graduated to complex devices the size of pinheads, but here on the colony they were fifty years behind.

"*Someone's here for you!*"

Jae stood and went to her window, lifting the curtain and squinting out into the dimming afternoon sun. Days were short down south at this time of year. She could just make out a hulking dark shape waiting at a distance from her front door. She couldn't see them well, but her heart leaped as she realised it must be a native. Someone needed her help! Maybe she wouldn't have to leave so quickly after all!

She quickly wrapped her head scarf into place, just tied around the top of her head and her ponytail rather than covering all her hair as many natives would, then clipped her translator into place and practically ran out of the door.

The man turned to face her. In the dim light he almost looked like he wore a big pair of wings, but as her eyes adjusted it was rather disappointingly just a cloak. "You are the healer?" he clipped out.

"Yes, yes I am. I'm Jae Townsend. Are you ill?"

He was silent a moment, his stern Tyger features unreadable. "Not I," he replied finally. "A child."

"OK. Is the child here?"

There was another long moment of silence – wow, the man really seemed reluctant – then finally he turned and gestured, and another figure appeared from behind the shelter of the trees. It was a woman dressed in brown, almost blending in with the landscape, and she carried a small figure in her arms, slumped over her shoulder. The small figure was far too limp, even for a sleeping child.

"He doesn't talk, doesn't eat," the man said grimly.

"How long has he been like this?"

"Three days. We thought he would heal, but he grows worse."

Jae switched into medic mode, suppressing her curiosity about these people and their situation. The man's head was covered, as was common for the locals as the air grew colder, but she wondered if it was true that their colouring was different to other Tygers; who they were and why they were here. "Bring him inside and I'll tend to him."

The woman hugged the child to her chest, her eyes wide, and the man shook his head. "No. Out here."

Seriously? What did they think she was going to do in there? But Jae hid her irritation, nodding politely. "May I touch him?"

The man shrugged, which looked like a yes, and the woman didn't push her away, so Jae gently moved in and felt around the child's small neck. His skin was cold and dry, with hard patches around the hairline that almost felt like scales.

She frowned. Except for the texture, she would have said it was a common disease that affected Tyger children who didn't have adequate nutrients, and which was similar to a human disease that had largely died out except in the poorest areas. But his skin…

She went back inside the clinic and came out with a hand-held injector to take a blood sample, but when she moved back to the boy, the man blocked her. "No. No devices."

Jae couldn't hide her frustration. "I can't treat him if I can't use these devices. I need to test his blood to confirm his illness, because then I will know the right treatment to give."

The man paused reluctantly. "Test my blood. It is the same."

"But you're not ill!"

Finally the woman spoke up, her voice small and tired. "Why are you unsure if it is a particular illness?"

Jae explained the symptoms, finishing with, "But the skin on his hairline is hard and scaly. I haven't seen this before, and I don't want to give him the wrong medicine as it could harm rather than help him."

"His skin is not scaly."

"I just touched it," Jae began, but the woman lifted back the child's fallen hair.

"Look again. Not scaly."

And what did you know, the child's skin now looked smooth and healthy, right up to the hairline.

"No scales," the man repeated sternly. "So he has this illness. Will you give him medicine?"

"If he does have it," Jae began slowly, "then I know how to help him. But as I said, I cannot give out medicine if I can't be sure he has the right illness. I need to test him first."

"And then what?"

"And then I'll take the test inside the clinic, and after about ten minutes I should have a diagnosis. Then I can give the medicine."

The couple exchanged a telling gaze, then the man nodded. "You test, but I will come with you."

Whatever. At this point Jae was just hoping they wouldn't walk away without that medication – children had died from this.

She quickly took the sample, pressing the tester against the boy's exposed neck and waiting for one, then two drops of blood to emerge, then taking the third drop for testing. "I'll be back shortly," she told them.

The man followed Jae silently through the door into the clinic. It was just about dark outside now, she saw once back inside the bright indoor light, and she couldn't even see the mother and child huddled outside. After snapping the blood sample into the tester device, she handed the silent man a blanket and a water bottle. "For the child. It's cold outside."

He just blinked. In the light she could see his eyes were a golden brown, almost orange – something she'd never before seen on a Tyger. He was bulkier than the average Tyger too, but perhaps that was just all the layers he wore. Even his hair was hidden under a brown cloth wrapping. "You wish me to leave the room."

"I wish you to trust me," she replied in a low tone, "and to see that I'm trying to help, not to harm. What are you so afraid of, anyway?

What harm have we caused you?"

"What harm?!" For a moment the man just looked stunned. "How can you ask that?"

Jae just stood there holding the rejected gifts. "I ask because I have no idea what you're talking about. The Syrenians were happy to have our help, given because we *want* to help, but you're acting like we're monsters, and I really don't know what we've done except be foreign, and I can't change that."

The man stared at her with those unusually coloured eyes, then abruptly turned and left, the door clicking shut behind him. Jae's shoulders slumped and she let out a disappointed sigh. Her temper didn't usually get the better of her, but then she wasn't often treated with such suspicion – or not quite. She'd had to fight for respect in the beginning with the Syrenians, but she'd mostly done it with good grace.

Suddenly the door swung open again, revealing the man, his wife and the child. They silently moved into the room, and the man moved forward to take the blanket and water bottle. He wrapped the blanket around his wife's shoulders, and handed her the bottle. "Is it still testing?" he asked.

Pushing past her surprise, Jae snapped shut her hanging jaw and quickly checked the progress of the sample. "Uh…yes. It is. But in the meantime, would you like something to eat?" Hospitality was a big part of the Tyger culture, but they were so suspicious that she made a point of eating a sample of the packaged food before handing it over. Although, introducing oneself was also a big part of the culture, and they sure hadn't done that part.

The couple studied the dried fruit sticks with suspicion, sniffing at them before taking a bite. The man asked, "Why would a woman have a home out here all on her own, offering aid to those who are not her people? Are you in exile?"

In a manner of speaking. "Not in exile," Jae replied carefully. "My people would welcome me back, especially as I'm a trained *doctor*." The word translated as 'healer' in Tyger. "And there are many Earthers who don't have medical help nearby. But here on Tyger, there are *no* Earther doctors besides us, and so no Earther medicine. And Earther medicine…" How to say it without being rude? "…can help in ways that Tyger medicine can't."

"But you are down here," the woman said quietly, her eyes wide. They were golden brown too, Jae noted. "There is no one here. No one except us."

"I was in Syrene for four years," Jae explained a bit sadly. "Then some people didn't like something I said, and I had to leave along with the other doctors there. The others returned to our people, but I saw…well, I saw your people's camp. I don't know why you're here or if you even want Earther help – it seems like you don't – but I thought I had to give you the chance."

"And what if we don't want your help?" The man's gaze was challenging, then his mouth curved in a smile as if he'd realised the contradiction he'd just made. After all, they were here too.

Jae shrugged. "Then I'll go home. You must make your own choices."

"We did not choose to be here," the woman said with a bit of heat for the first time. "We were forced here from the south of Mahadra. Even Syrene was not safe for us."

Finally she was getting somewhere! "Why?" Jae asked quietly. "Why was it not safe?"

The man scoffed. "Because we are *branzinos*, Earther. That is all."

Branzinos. The unfamiliar word was interpreted as 'dragonfly' in Jae's ever-present translator. She frowned. "What's that?"

The couple stared at her incredulously, and if the child had been awake, no doubt he would have as well. "You don't know?"

Clearly not!

And then they told her.

CHAPTER 10
Foolish

The royal palace, Mahadra

Orin leaned back against the wall of Raka's outer room, waiting. The scent of flowering lilies wafted through the screen window, and inside the inner room he could hear the sounds of low conversation between Raka and one other.

A few minutes later the 'other' came out, footsteps as quiet as always, eyes fixed on the ground. She saw Orin there and barely restrained her urge to jump, but he saw her reaction just the same. He always saw things like that, just like how he'd seen the red roots of her curly dark hair the other week before she'd dyed it. He knew what it meant, too.

"Blessed one," she greeted him formally. "His Magnificence is ready for visitors."

Her tone was even, but he knew she hated him. He could literally smell it. And what did he care what a single female slave thought, and a Dragonfly at that? She was probably the last one in the kingdom if he'd judged correctly. But still he ended up saying in a near whisper, "Does Raka know you're with child?"

The *esira*, small and rounder than before, froze. Her head barely reached the top of his shoulder, but he could sense the fear emanating off her. Fear, and perhaps a little something else. "I don't know what you're talking about."

"So that's a no, then."

There was a long silence where he saw her jaw working nervously. "Are you going to tell him?"

Orin shrugged casually. Indecision always made them so much more fearful. "Shouldn't he be able to tell for himself? After all, he… knows you far better than I."

The girl's voice came out very low and tight. "He has no children, and he is of age. He should be happy."

"For a child with a slave? One of uncertain blood?" He stood, moving past her towards the inner room's curtain. "If I were you, I would ask what happened to Xandrea."

He walked through the curtain, and he heard her murmur under her breath; *"Who's Xandrea?"*

Raka turned to face Orin as he moved into the inner room. Raka wore a robe and the relaxed expression that indicated he'd just taken his daily bath. "Is there a problem?"

"No," Orin replied casually. "Not at all."

But he could still hear the *esira* hovering outside the curtain.

"Jianne," Chay asked in an intentionally casual tone, "who is Xandrea?"

The older woman barely looked up from folding sheets, but she tensed. "Where did you hear that name?" Chay didn't respond, and Jianne carried on, "Someone trying to warn you off, I suppose, not that there's much point. Xandrea was a servant here at the palace. She often attended the emir directly."

'Attended'. Just like Chay. "Oh?" Chay asked lightly. "*Was* a servant? Was she promoted?"

Jianne laughed harshly. "Sure, if you call dying a promotion. She died three years ago of a putrid stomach. It was sudden, but you can't help sickness, can you? But perhaps that was just before you arrived."

A putrid stomach, so she'd eaten something bad. Chay wrinkled her nose. "That doesn't sound so unusual."

"Yes, well." Jianne's voice dropped, and she fixed Chay with a penetrating gaze. "But they say it wasn't a putrid stomach. They say it was poisoning, but it could never be proven, and who'd investigate a mere servant's death? But the worst part was this." Chay waited with bated breath, and Jianne leaned in. "The poor girl was pregnant, and the babe died with her."

Chay's heart skipped a beat, and she had to wait a few moments before she could speak again. "Surely it must have been an accident," she said weakly. "Surely no one would want to kill a harmless servant, especially one who was with child."

"The *emir's* child," Jianne retorted knowingly. "And would

have been his only heir, even if the mother had never been named concubine or wife."

If the baby had been a boy, of course. Girls were meaningless, unless they were pretty. Then they could be sold off as concubines or wives.

Chay fell silent then, but she was thinking deeply. Raka hadn't liked the idea of her being with child, but she struggled to believe that he'd have his own servant poisoned. He wouldn't need to, since he could order their death for the flimsiest of reasons. She'd seen him do it before with others. Xandrea's sickness was probably just a coincidence…

…Just like the coincidence that Orin the blessed bastard was also Raka's only heir.

"You're quiet tonight," Raka commented. He was lying back in his tub, his dark hair spread out over the smooth floor while Chay carefully brushed and oiled it. "You're not still thinking about the Earther, are you? It's been…oh, *weeks* since she died."

Barely one week, actually. "Not the Earther," Chay replied honestly, hearing her voice shake a little. She swallowed, a handful of dark hair gripped between her fingers, then tried again. "I haven't thought of her at all." And apologies to the Earther's spirit, should it be listening, but it was true.

"Then what?" Raka studied her, the upside-down pose making his otherwise handsome face look a bit foolish. But his eyes were steady on hers. "I know you. You're brooding about something."

When he acted like this, acted like he *cared*, she'd almost forget her position. She'd almost forget that his last servant-mistress had died under suspicious circumstances, while pregnant with his child. She'd almost forget how he'd responded when he thought *she* might be in the same situation.

But she couldn't lie, so she diverted. "Someone mentioned a girl named Xandrea," she said finally, and she couldn't meet his eyes. "They said she…served you before I arrived here at the palace."

Raka's eyes narrowed. "Who mentioned such a thing? Never mind, it doesn't matter. Are you jealous, girl?"

Was that it? Hardly! But Chay leapt onto that explanation, feeling her cheeks heat at even the idea. "I would not presume to be jealous," she said haltingly. "A most noble ruler will always have many… servants. I consider myself…*lucky*…to be here."

She'd choked out that last word, but in a way it was true. She was lucky to be here instead of 'disappeared' like the rest of her family. Lucky that she wasn't quite like the rest of the Dragonflies, and as a result had been allowed to live in slavery instead of being given what she assumed was a quick, nasty end.

Or was that luck? Chay wondered. Some might say she would've been better to die rather than be dishonoured. But there was a stubbornness inside her that made her fight to live, to push her way through ugly circumstances, if it meant living another day. Why, she didn't know. Perhaps it was the hope that things might become better…

Raka laughed suddenly, taking on that youthful, joyful handsomeness that would so often distract her. "Be jealous all you like, little Chay, but it changes nothing. Xandrea served me, yes. But she was a foolish girl, and now she's gone." His expression suddenly went grim. "You are not foolish, are you Chay?"

She gulped. "I try not to be, Your Magnificence. But…in what way was Xandrea foolish?" At his dark expression she quickly added, "I ask only so that I might avoid the same situation."

He studied her again, then smiled. "Xandrea did not take her daily herbs, and so she was foolish. But you are not so foolish."

The herbs that were supposed to stop conception, but which didn't always work. Chay forced a shaky smile. "I'm not foolish," she agreed, then set her head down and focussed on massaging his scalp.

She'd hoped it was otherwise; that someone else had wanted to remove royal offspring. But it seemed that Raka had followed the path of his own father, who had declared that there should be no competition to his own son taking the throne and ruling his whole inheritance. The former emir had forbidden his sisters to wed, and had had one killed when she'd taken a lover.

Rumour had it that he'd forced his concubines to take poison rather than birth another male. Orin the Blessed – curse his wicked soul – had survived only because his mother had hidden, and by the time she'd been discovered, he'd been born, white hair and all. The mother had died for her crime, but he'd been allowed to survive. After all, it was unlucky to kill a sacred, shapeshifting *beini*.

But now Chay knew something for certain. She'd been 'foolish'…
…and if she didn't leave soon, she'd be dead too.

Iznaith, Syrene

Astrid collapsed gracelessly off Copper's back, her whole body feeling bruised from this third and final race, and handed the three flags she'd managed to grab into Xever's waiting hand. She accepted the drink shoved at her from Vuyani, then sat back on a large rock.

Did they win? She thought probably not, because even though Copper was by far the fastest on that final race, he was also aggressive, unsteerable and single-minded. She'd managed to grab the flags – more by luck than any actual skill – and then Copper had charged for the finish line. There was no doubt that they would have won then, except he'd taken offense to one of the big blue raphantas quietly tethered off at the side of the track. It turned out it was one of those that had almost blocked him the previous day.

Astrid hadn't known the blue's history at the time. All she'd known was that her noble steed had swerved off track to get into a raphanta fist-fight (mostly trunks, actually, and a bit of foot-stomping) with this random, *much* larger animal. It had taken all her strength not to fall off, and then when Copper finally realised the other racers were passing him, some had already gone over the finish line. They'd come in seventh in the end, but perhaps captured enough flags to place anyway…?

They all waited with bated breath as the points were tallied, and then heard, "Kopa of Xever, fourth place."

Astrid slumped in disappointment – they hadn't won a prize – but Xever and the others didn't look too upset.

"Ah, well," Vuyani said pragmatically. "The gold for fourth place is still nothing to scoff at. Our portion won't buy us a new well, but it might help get the materials."

Astrid looked up in surprise, then watched as the awards were handed out. Most of them were medals in shades of gold or silver or branzine-copper. Theirs was gold, a medal that was placed around her neck amid half-hearted cheers from the crowd.

"That went far better than it could have," Xever admitted afterwards. "I thought I wasn't going to get a single silver back for that beast, but now we've at least paid for our travel here. The next set of races is next week in the capital. The prizes aren't quite as good, but they're nothing to scoff at either."

They were a group of five now. The one Copper had trampled had rejoined them some time ago. Astrid now knew he was Xever's brother. The third man had been the jockey, and had been a local hired for the race only. He'd already left, presumably deciding that the promise of riches wasn't worth getting regularly beaten up by an animal.

Vuyani and Jazir turned to look at Astrid expectantly at the statement about more races, and she raised her hands in the air out of pure weariness, then pointed at Copper. "Needs training." More importantly, how was more racing actually going to help her get home?

"Of course he needs training," Xever agreed pragmatically. "But so do you, lad, and you'll get it."

Right. 'Lad'. Astrid just shrugged, then turned to find the nearest bathrooms, because lad she was not. There were long-drops in a wooden shack out the back of the stables (where the smells were all equally bad, so no one would really notice a bit more stench) which were just fancy enough to have a bit of reflective metal pinned up inside.

She checked her reflection, noting that her skin had reverted to its usual tan colour, but her hair had retained a lot of that gunk from the wastewater. If she squinted it could pass for Tyger-blue, but not for much longer. She resolved to dye it properly, and in the meantime to find herself a hat.

Astrid came out to find a young man standing casually between the toilets and the stables, almost as though he was waiting for her. He was lean with dark blue hair in a low ponytail – in his late teens perhaps, except that he had a big, thick beard obscuring the bottom half of his face. She nodded at him politely and went to move past, but he stood to attention, holding up a hand to halt her.

"Good race. I hear you came fourth."

There was nothing wrong with his hearing then. Astrid smiled politely, nodding once more. "Yes."

She tried to move past again, but he walked with her. "I'm Benn."

She gave another smile, a dismissive one this time, but he wouldn't be dismissed.

"More of a listener than a talker, are you?"

Obviously.

"But perhaps having the other half of the translator would help with that."

Astrid froze, turning to stare at Benn in shock. He looked just as unassuming as he had before – barring that beard that looked like a fluffy blue cat was assaulting his chin – but there was knowledge in his purple eyes. "I know you've got it," he continued. "I left it outside the stables, and I watched you put it on, so there's no point pretending you don't know what I'm talking about. You're an Earther, aren't you?"

Oh *schnit*. What was the bet he was working for Raka?

Perhaps in that moment Astrid had a few choices: to bluff it out, to ask more questions, to admit the truth. But she did none of those things. Instead she panicked, suddenly pointing at something behind Benn's shoulder with an appalled expression that she didn't have to fake. He fell for it, turning to see only a grey raphanta relieving itself on the side of the stables, and she bolted.

Two minutes later Astrid reached the cluster of Copper's owners and her acquired friends. "I will race," she huffed out, bending over to catch her breath. "Next week in city."

"Great!" Xever cheered.

"We go now."

"Now?" he said in alarm. "We just finished. Let's relax, try out the track here…"

"Now, please! Try out the track in city."

The group of Tygers stared at her, and she tried to convey her urgency while hiding that anything was wrong – not an easy task.

But suddenly Jazir said, "I think we should go now too."

Xever's eyebrows shot up. "Any particular reason we have to go right away?"

Jazir glanced rather obviously at Astrid, and his cheeks flushed. "I just think we should go. Please."

He was a terrible liar, Astrid thought, but he seemed to be acting on her behalf.

Copper's owner sighed. "Very well. If our jockey wants to go now, then we'll go now."

He and his brother moved to gather their things, and Astrid sat down behind the cart, stretching her legs as though she was relaxing, but feeling the exact opposite. She kept looking out for the bearded guy who'd given her the translator, but from here, every Tyger face just looked the same.

A few minutes later Jazir came to sit beside her, followed by Vuyani who took a seat on her other side. "We've been talking," Jazir said in a low voice. "You know we're your friends, right?"

Astrid blinked at them as the sentence translated. "Yes," she replied in her limited Tyger tongue.

"We'll keep being your friends," he continued. "Here, or in the city. Whatever you need."

Astrid blinked again, frowning. She had no idea what he was talking about. Did he mean because she could ride the raphanta, and perhaps bring in gold? "Friend because I ride Copper?" she ventured.

"No," Vuyani cut in, rolling her eyes. "He doesn't get it, Jaz. Tam, we're saying that we know you're hiding, and who you're hiding from. And we'll help you, OK? We won't let you get hurt."

Astrid felt her eyes bug this time. Her disguise seemed to be falling away, but how had these two worked out she was human? They seemed so clueless. "How?" she asked finally.

"Your eyes are brown," Jazir replied. "Only Dragonflies have brown eyes. You've clearly come from Mahadra, and everyone knows about the persecution there. It's not hard to work out."

Dragonflies? Persecution? "Uh…"

Jazir clapped her on the shoulder. "But we'll all be moving on to the city now, OK? We'll tell Xever that you need to rest down here out of sight, and you can jump in the cart when you feel safe to do so. Any time you need us, we'll help."

The siblings stood and looked down at her, clearly expecting an answer. But even though their conclusions were all wrong, their attitudes were all right, and Astrid felt tears well up. Someone was looking out for her…someone was being kind to her just 'cos? It was unexpected, and it was wonderful.

"Thank you," she croaked out, then ducked her head to hide the tears.

She could do with a friend or two right now.

Near the southern mining station

Jae couldn't believe what she was hearing. Or she *shouldn't* believe it, because it was far beyond anything she'd ever heard before. And this hulking man with his rough clothes and his sick child and their strange, amber eyes…they were saying it, and she found that in spite of everything, she did believe them.

"So your people – the Dragonflies – have been forced out of the cities," she repeated back carefully, trying to make sure she had understood correctly. "Because you're different from the other Tygers."

"They're afraid of us," the woman said quietly. "Because we can be strong, if we choose."

That was one way of putting it. "Because you can take other forms," Jae repeated, the words sounding strange on her tongue. "And you say that the Tygers can do the same."

"A few Tygers can take one additional form, that of a large cat," the man shot back, for the first time sounding arrogant. "All Dragonflies may take many forms. In Mahadra these last few years, they tried to drive us out of their towns, to turn us into slaves for their mines. In Syrene, the emir protected us while he was well. But now he can do nothing, and we're treated as though we are dangerous. But we don't want to cause harm. We want to live in peace with our families."

"Doesn't everyone." Jae stood for a few moments, flexing her hands at her sides, then glanced up at where she knew a camera filmed everything that took place within the building. It was Portal-co policy at quiet outposts like this. But their audio wasn't so good… "I need you to show me," she said finally. "Would you show me, please?"

The man and woman exchanged a glance, then he shrugged. "We've told you, so we will also show you." Then he stretched out his bare arms from underneath that cloak, showing that the fabric was loose rather than fitted like a jacket. For a second they were just bare, brown human arms, then suddenly his flesh rippled and they were wings. Two giant, golden-brown wings, just like that bird she'd seen at the refugee camp. He blinked those similarly coloured golden-brown eyes at her. "Will this suffice?"

"Uh…" Jae let out a breath she hadn't realised she was holding. "Yes."

The man lowered his arms as they returned to their humanlike state, but kept watching her with that same intent gaze. Her mind was whirring frantically, trying to make sense of everything they'd said. They *were* shapeshifters – heavens above, they were! – and the Mahadrese were persecuting them, forcing them out of their cities just as they'd said, and forcing the able-bodied into work camps. And worse, even worse, was the truth about ambrilene.

A golden-brown substance, mined from 'somewhere' on this planet, that would change to suit whatever substance it was paired with. Need metal repairs? It would become shining and hard like metal. Need wood repairs? It'd become like wood. But ambrilene always did best with organic substances. It could even be used as emergency medical supplies, because when pressed on a wound, it became exactly like skin…

A sudden wave of guilt overcame Jae. "We didn't know," she said in a low voice. "We didn't know where they were getting it from. We thought they were mining it, just like we mine for metals and precious gems."

"Mining the bodies of our ancestors from our graveyards?" the man murmured. "Indeed."

That just made her want to throw up all over again. She'd handled ambrilene once or twice, but generally it was sent through the portal to use however Earth saw fit. Oh, and Earth paid well for it. Paid Raka, that was, but Syrene refused to trade. "I swear to you, we didn't know." Now her voice was shaking with horror and sincerity. "If we'd known, we wouldn't have bought it. We wouldn't have *used* it. I'll make sure everyone knows, and that this will stop!"

"I believe you," the woman said quietly. "You know that whether or not you Earthers had come, the persecution would have continued? It began before you arrived, but had become worse since Raka came into power. He organised for our villages to be cleared out, for our people to be collected. So many of them lost, taken into the mountains. We only just escaped."

The man scowled at the reminder. "May Raka die a thousand deaths."

Jae felt her eyes widen, but based on what she'd heard, she couldn't disagree. But at least the persecution of this minority wasn't *only* because of the ambrilene trade with the humans.

She glanced through the open door to where their surroundings looked increasingly cool and dark. "Will you stay overnight? It's warm in here. I can give you food." She'd given their child the medicine he needed, but it wasn't enough. She had to do more.

The man shook his head. "We should go now."

"Very well." Jae watched them walk outside, then called, "Do you have names?"

"Malchiel," the man called back. "And my sister is Rechal."

Sister. Huh. Jae wondered briefly where the woman's husband

was – because the locals didn't 'do' single parenthood – then realised after everything they'd said, he'd be dead or enslaved somewhere.

But she watched until their figures vanished from sight, then turned towards the mining station.

She had to talk to someone.

The Royal Palace, Mahadra

Orin stood at ease in the small, quiet meeting room, his hands resting behind his back and his face set in a neutral expression. Raka and General Naim were talking at length, and he knew his input wasn't required.

"I don't see why we cannot speak by using the Earther devices rather than you having to travel all the way here," Raka complained. "You have one now, do you not?"

The general was a slim man in his early sixties, with a thick moustache typical of many of his age, and watchful eyes. He'd served under their father, and still held a position of power. Unlike many others, he'd managed not to irritate Raka. He was also in charge of the successful programme removing the undesirables from their land and repurposing the survivors as free labour…the *Branzinos*. "The Earther devices should not be used for private information," he replied smoothly. "My spy assures me that the Earthers can and do listen in, if they wish."

Raka scowled, turning to glare at the nearby gifted viewing screen as if he wanted to throw it out of the nearest window. "Then it's good for nothing but speaking to the Earthers. But if I remove it, then they will know there is a problem."

That was the thing about Orin's brother; he wasn't stupid. Arrogant, difficult and selfish, yes. But not stupid.

"It changes none of our plans," General Naim assured him. "We should be ready to go in four months, if the Earthers trade the rest of their weapons as expected."

"If?" Raka spun around to stare at his general. "Is there any reason why they wouldn't trade? You assured me that the Earthers are not concerned about the missing girl. Why would they not?"

General Naim blinked, and Orin could tell the general knew he'd misstepped. "They are not concerned," he said slowly, "but they are expecting certain quantities of ambrilene. Our stores are running low. We may need to supplement our offer with gold or branzine, which they also value-"

"Ambrilene, Naim!" Raka interrupted. "You assured me that after the clearances there should be enough for everything we needed! Are you now saying there isn't?"

Clearances? Orin's attention fixed on that one word, and he glanced sideways to study his brother. Raka had never said where the ambrilene came from, even though Orin had guessed. And perhaps he should have guessed there'd be more coming, too, considering how violently the Mahadrese Dragonflies had been forced out of their villages over these last few years. He'd heard that even Raka's pet *esira* had lost her family in such a way.

"The substance isn't the same as what we initially found," General Naim finally replied, his voice low. "It seems that in order to become useable, it must go through a certain process. Or perhaps the Dragonflies from our villages are not the same as these older ones..." Suddenly his eyes slid to Orin, who did his best to look bored. "Is it acceptable to speak of this now, Your Magnificence?"

Raka waved a hand carelessly in Orin's direction. "Forget the bastard. He does what he's told, and he keeps his mouth shut."

The general didn't look convinced, but nodded. "Perhaps it is only time that changes the substance, Your Magnificence. Or perhaps it is a ritual they themselves undertake. But either way, I strongly recommend you make plans as though we will *not* have the ambrilene to trade."

Raka scowled. "And this is your report for today, General?"

General Naim paused for a moment. "Indeed it is, Your Magnificence. While it isn't all good news – it should not affect our ability to achieve our goals."

Raka turned away, waving a hand dismissively, and the general clearly knew he was released. He bowed neatly. "Until next time."

Once he'd gone, Raka slumped into a nearby chair. He was still scowling: his eyebrows low over his eyes and his mouth turned in a flat line. "Nothing is going right, Orin. Why?"

Orin wondered if his brother expected a real answer. "Life has many challenges. The strongest can overcome them."

"And the smartest avoid those challenges in the first place," Raka snapped back. "No ambrilene, he says. So either I'll have to give up my branzine metal stores, or else delay getting those weapons. My royal sister is off being defiled by some pit-fighting alien, and I've got no one to play chiss with! I hold you responsible for those two last problems, Bastard."

Orin blinked, biting back the surge of anger that rose every time he was called that name. "I do not think I could have retrieved Tamzyn without alerting the Earthers to our blessed secret. You instructed me very firmly that they should not find out. They have too many advantages otherwise."

Orin was still resentful that the situation had ever occurred. He'd allowed himself to be given to the Earthers as a 'gift' in *beini* form after the recent festival – but of course that was before they knew Tamzyn had been stolen. He was supposed to study the Earther fortress from the inside, and to check whether Naim's spy was telling the whole truth before escaping.

Was it undignified to be caged like an animal by aliens who knew no better? Yes, but one didn't say no to Raka. But then when Orin had finally realised what was happening, that *Tamzyn* had been in one of those other containers and was being smuggled away, it was too late. He was too slow to escape, too slow to retrieve her.

He'd been furious, and had damaged the portal device in an attempt to get through. In the end he'd simply waited for a chance to take an Earther in turn, hoping to use them as a hostage. But the Earthers hadn't cared, had they?

"And the Earther girl?"

Orin just looked at him. Raka didn't know what had truly happened in that tower, and he wasn't going to tell. "I was too slow to catch her. She was quick." And couldn't Raka just teach someone new to play that stupid game?

"See, *you* were too slow. Too slow for Tamzyn, too slow for the Earther. I can set you another task – but will you be quick enough for this one, *beini*?"

"If it's possible, I will do it."

"Bah. Possible. It's always possible, Orin. The question is whether *you* are capable – or whether Father should have just disposed of you at birth, and saved himself the disappointment of seeing what he'd created."

Orin didn't allow his expression to change, having heard such comments many times before. "What do you want of me?"

Raka leaned back again on his chair, studying him with narrowed eyes. "Go to Syrene and dispose of the so-called regent."

This time Orin couldn't help it. He felt his eyes flicker and widen. "You wish me to assassinate Emir Jireh's stepson?" He knew that Raka hated the regent for taking the place Raka believed should be his, but he hadn't realised it was such an intense, murderous hatred.

Raka spread out his fingers as if to say 'of course'. "If there is no regent, there will be no war between the two city-states."

Orin was silent a long moment. "But even if the regent is gone, our uncle the emir of Syrene still lives." And the Syrenians would never allow Raka to rule over them when their beloved Emir Jireh still lived, no matter how sick he was.

"You think they will choose another regent rather than be ruled over by *me*?" Raka countered, sounding outraged.

Definitely. "Possibly. They do not know what is good for them."

The emir huffed out a sigh, tapping his fingernails on the hard arm of the chair. "I also have my spy in the Syrenian court, and you may be right." He paused. "You will dispose of my uncle also."

That was no small request. To assassinate the neighbouring city-state's regent, plus its ill emir… "If I'm caught…"

"Then my spy will ensure you are not harmed," Raka snapped, rolling his eyes. "But I tire of this conversation. Where is Chakandra?"

Orin couldn't hide his emotions this time, so he ducked his head in a show of obedience. "I believe she's in the hall, waiting for your command."

"Send her in."

Orin turned to leave, and Raka called after him, "One question, brother. Is the *esira* with child?"

Raka asked because Blessed Ones could scent such a thing, and Orin was the only one trusted to give such information. He didn't hesitate to answer. "I smelled nothing but herbs and soap. No, she is not with child."

Chay had heard the whole conversation through the thin wall. They hadn't even lowered their voices as if to stop her hearing, because *esira* were not considered a threat. They were barely people, perhaps more like part of the wallpaper. But she heard the *beini* lie to the emir, and as he left the room, his lavender eyes met hers for just long enough to show that he knew, that she knew.

He'd helped her, perhaps. But why?

CHAPTER 11
Problems

Earth

It was evening by the time Nathaniel finally got back to the small but tidy motel room on the third floor. The tiny bedroom and living area were both empty, but the glass door to the balcony was open. He could just see Tamzyn standing outside on the balcony, her hair covered by a scarf for warmth as well as habit, and a long robe draped around her curvaceous form.

He set down his bag on the hard tabletop with an audible *clunk*, and she jolted in surprise, turning to stare at him. As always, her lovely face caught him by surprise over and over. Someone like that, and she'd chosen *him*?

She hadn't had any other choices, he reminded himself. She'd been locked up in the women's quarters like an imprisoned nun, and he'd been the only one stupid enough to talk to her. "Good evening," he ventured.

"Good evening," Tamzyn said in halting English. She smiled at him, but he wondered if the smile was a little tight. It didn't extend to those beautiful eyes. "Did you have good success today, husband?"

Now this was a happy subject. "Yes, I did. The Ministry for Women's Rights has agreed to take on your case. We had to argue a bit since you weren't born on Earth, but they've agreed that since your DNA is human, you should have the same rights." Funny thing, upon closer inspection, the Tygers were practically human. There were almost no biological differences that they could see, past the ears and the colouring.

Tamzyn blinked, and two little lines appeared between her eyebrows as the translator worked slowly. "So they will not send me back?"

Nathaniel grinned, coming to stand beside her on the balcony.

Their building was in a cheaper part of the city, but near enough to the outskirts that they had view of mountains and trees along with the typical grey of manmade structures. The sun had just set, and the sky was just dark enough to show a couple of pinprick-sized stars. "No, they won't send you back. Officially you're not even here. I'm here with Astrid."

"Astrid. I hope she is well."

"She'll be fine," he said, reassuring himself that it must be so. He felt a little guilt at leaving her to deal with the aftermath, but she understood what was at stake. If Tamzyn went back, she was dead. Simple as that. If she'd never left the palace in the first place, she never would have truly lived.

Poetic, yes? But that guilt came over him again. She was a royal princess, and he'd brought her to what? A tiny motel set amongst concrete? He couldn't look after her. He was twenty-four years old, and he might have committed a crime bringing her here. He didn't even have a *job*.

"You know," Nathaniel said slowly, "I've been thinking about us. You being here."

"Oh?"

"Well…" This was hard to say, but it was for her benefit. "You know we're married by Tyger custom only, and you said your brother could have the marriage annulled if he wished. By Earther – *human* custom, we're not married. We're only engaged, and we haven't even…" Done the things that would mean a real marriage. "You're not stuck with me, I mean," he finished lamely.

Tamzyn looked appalled, and tears welled in her eyes. "You wish for an annulment?"

"What! No! Tammy, I love you. I just don't want to take advantage of your lack of choices. You've never even met any other men before me! How can you say that you've chosen me, when really you've never known anyone else?"

The tears seemed to dry up a little, but she lifted her chin as if suddenly angry. "Nathaniel Townsend, I *have* met men. Many, many men came to visit their wives in the women's quarters, and I watched them all. I watched how they talked to their wives, their mothers, their sisters. I saw how *my* brother spoke to me, and I saw how you spoke to your sister. I also saw how she spoke of *you*. She admired you greatly, and swore that you would never hit her-"

"You want me because I don't hit girls?" he cut in, dismayed.

"Tammy, it's against our laws to hit another person." Outside of organised fights, anyway.

"It didn't stop you kicking that Tyger fighter in the head!" She huffed out a sigh, scrubbing her hand over her face. "Nathaniel, I have chosen you, and I do not regret it. If you have not chosen me, then you must tell me now, before we complete your human customs and you stop sleeping on the couch!"

He felt his cheeks heat, but his gaze was intent on hers. "I chose you the first moment I saw you. But what can I give you, Tammy? Not a palace. I'm afraid that one day soon you'll look back, and you'll regret coming with me."

Her expression softened, and she stepped towards him, taking his hand and holding it to her heart. "Never. Never will I regret this, even if we *do* stay in a strange little house where everything is grey. And maybe one day, in years to come, we can return. But if that never happens, I will still not regret this choice."

She meant it. He knew she meant it, and he let out that deep breath he'd been holding, leaning in to wrap his arms around her. "Then I'll do everything I can to make sure you don't regret it, starting today. What would you like to do, Tammy? Travel somewhere? Learn to drive a car? Learn English?"

Tamzyn leaned back to study his face, and now she looked very solemn. "Teach me to fight?"

Nathaniel's eyebrows shot up and his jaw dropped. "Uh…sure. You mean self-defence? Or you want to learn how to kick someone in the head?"

"Perhaps just the first," she replied demurely. "Then progress to the second."

She was smiling, but she also seemed serious. Nathaniel was an inch away from clearing the small lounge to make a temporary training room when his phone went off. He quickly checked it. "Hey, it's Aunt Jae! She must have got someone in the colony to forward her message," he explained to Tamzyn.

But then the further he read; the less sense Jae's message made. "Oh. It's not from the colony. It's straight from…somewhere to the far south. But what's this about Astrid?"

Tamzyn was watching curiously over his shoulder now, even though he knew she couldn't read the text.

"My aunt says that Astrid isn't responding to her messages," Nathaniel explained. "She asks if she's well." He went to respond with 'of course', but then realised that actually, he didn't know. He hadn't heard from her himself in some time, except for a very brief text message the previous week. "I'll send a message to Az' directly," he decided. "I'll request a video call."

Syrene

"How is he today?"

The nurse finished tucking Emir Jireh's blankets closer into his sides, then looked up at the regent. Merima was an older woman, a widow with lined features, silver-white hair under her headscarf and steady hands, and her expression was solemn. "He grows weaker, Your Excellency. He has not fully woken in three days."

The regent closed his eyes briefly, sucking in a deep breath. That was longer than any other time. His stepfather truly was growing worse. "He's not old yet. This shouldn't be happening."

"Sometimes people grow ill," the nurse said softly. "And our medicine is not enough to heal them."

The regent paced over to the open window, standing with his hands behind his back and studying the vista. It helped him to think. "Even the Earther medicine was not sufficient," he mused.

There was a silence. "Earther medicine, Your Excellency? When did His Magnificence have Earther medicine?"

He glanced at her over his shoulder. "Palos told me the Earthers were consulted two years ago when my stepfather's illness became so severe. They said they could not help."

Merima's eyes dropped, but her lips curved unhappily. "If the venerable advisor Palos advises such, then I'm sure it must be true."

Palos was a similar age to the emir's own father, and had been his long-time friend and advisor. He'd had influence in determining the laws for many years, and was the first point of contact for the regent himself. But this nurse – she too had been caring for the emir for many years, and the regent had known her since he was a child.

"You do not recall this?"

"No, Your Excellency." She frowned, then glanced up to meet his eyes. Anxiety was clear in her own dark ones. "But perhaps I was away at the time. I am not told everything."

"Of course," the regent agreed quietly. He turned back to the window, his thoughts whirling in his head. The Earthers had recently fled, but he still had the means to contact them if needed.

But was he really doubting Palos? The advisor had been in the palace long before he'd arrived with his mother, and most likely would remain long after the regency ended. Palos was as much a part of the surroundings as the pillars holding up the roof of the main building. In fact, Palos himself supplied the medicine that kept the emir alive but quiet.

But still the regent found himself saying, "Merima, I do not want you to give my stepfather his medicine today. Not for three days, you understand?"

"But Palos…"

"Tell him that you've administered it, but in truth you must put it in the chamber pot." The regent sucked in a breath, briefly closing his eyes. "I am not doubting Palos, just perhaps the medicine is… ineffective, or incorrect. I want to see what happens if he is without it. Will you do it, Merima?"

It was a genuine question rather than an order. The regent was well used to 'his people' smiling and nodding when he spoke, then turning to ask Palos what they ought to do. He'd eventually given up on trying to make any actual changes to this land, instead focusing on what he could do – making occasional judgements and watching over the emir.

But out of everyone in Syrene, this nurse was best placed to see how Emir Jireh fared day to day. And so when she finally nodded her agreement, he believed her.

"Thank you."

"And where will you go now, Your Excellency?"

The regent glanced across the city again to where a large track was visible. It was crowded with people even from here, and he could hear faint sounds of cheering or perhaps weeping – depending on how the spectators had placed their bets. "The raphanta races, perhaps. I understand I'm to give out the prizes."

"Yes, Your Excellency. His Magnificence always loved the races."

And so Jireh had, which was why the regent had upkept the traditions as well as possible. He turned to leave the room, but as he did so, he felt a strange vibration in his wide robe pocket. Slipping into a side room and checking it was empty, he pulled out a small silver device and tapped once at the screen. "Yes?"

The face of his Mahadrese spy looked up at him, small and blurry on the tiny, fantastical screen of the Earther device. A secret means of communication, and one that was his lifeblood. But today he definitely looked unhappy. "We've got a problem."

Mahadra

Two days after Emir Raka had asked if Chay was with child, and she'd heard Orin the bastard lie in response, she found herself alone with the latter. She was emptying out the emir's bath, bowl by painstaking bowl, as Raka had long left. Then she'd heard a sound, so she'd looked up to see him there, watching her with those calculating eyes.

She couldn't help it: she jumped in surprise, then hated that she'd jumped. "Blessed one," she greeted him politely, averting her eyes. "His Magnificence has gone to lunch."

"I know." He paused. "I'm here to see you."

Chay felt herself go stiff from head to toe, and it was all she could do not to tremble. What did he want? To threaten her more? To blackmail her for some no doubt appalling reason?

But when she didn't answer, she saw him move closer from the corner of her eye. "What must it be like, being the last Dragonfly in the city-state? Most unpleasant, I imagine. And to hide your true self this whole time…" He tutted. "It surprises me that you're still here."

Her hands clenched into fists at her side, and she ducked her head so that she couldn't accidentally meet his eyes. It sounded like he was threatening her. "As you well know, I am *esira*. I cannot go anywhere until the emir orders it so." Then she added a little more daringly, "and His Magnificence knows what I am. He knows I only have this one form; never mind what colour my hair might grow."

"Hmm." The *beini* watched her with one hand under his chin, that face so similar to his brother's. "A defective Dragonfly. How unfortunate. Or fortunate, perhaps, if you are still here when the others are gone."

How long must she listen to this? Chay raged internally. The reminder of everything she'd lost was most unwelcome, and she turned away from the man, even though it was explicitly against anything she'd been taught through painful lessons in this very palace. She picked up her deep bowl and dipped it into the almost-empty bath. "If you'll excuse me," she murmured. "I must finish my tasks."

There was a brief silence, then the *beini* stirred. "As must I. In fact, this very day I'm setting out for Syrene on a…trading mission. A quiet, quick one, you understand. So you will not be obliged to see me for some time."

She didn't answer. She'd clearly heard Raka say it was an assassination, but she was never expected to comment.

"I'm taking several large chests full of valuable cloth and so forth," he continued. "In fact, the last one is in my chambers, ready to be loaded onto the wagon within the hour. It's not even half-full though. What a shame to bring a nearly empty chest to our dear neighbours across the mountains. I daresay it could fit…oh, another forty to fifty *bac*."

The measurement of weight was almost exactly Chay's own size, and she found her head shooting up to stare at him incredulously. "Are you trying to get me to leave, Blessed One? Because it would be on your own head if you were caught doing such a thing. Even if you are the emir's heir and stand to benefit by my absence, surely you must know that much!"

The *beini*'s purple eyes met hers without blinking, rather like his catlike form. "Yes, I *am* the emir's heir until such a time as he marries and provides one to replace me," he said smoothly. "And I would never suggest such a treasonous idea as to try to remove any servant of his, even one who has been…foolish. Although I have a distaste for how His Magnificence dealt with his last foolish servant, I merely commented on my own imminent travels." He stood from where he'd been idly leaning against a pillar and casually made his way to the door. "But *esira*, of course you have made arrangements to deal with your own…foolishness, yes?"

With those parting words he left, and Chay just stood there for some time, the half-full water bowl still clutched in her pale hands.

Of course she hadn't dealt with her 'foolishness'. How was she to do such a thing? There were medicines that would rid of the body of…*mistakes*…but even in her terrible situation, she couldn't see her baby as a mistake, or even 'foolishness'. No, she'd have to leave, but she hadn't thought of how she could do so. Everyone knew her, and she couldn't just walk out of the palace. But she could hide in a chest, covered in cloth, and be carried out…

But the *beini* would benefit from her absence, Chay reminded herself. If she didn't bring this child to full-term, then he'd remain the only Mahadrese heir – simply because there were no other options, not because a bastard would ever be truly welcomed on the throne. But then he could have had the same result only by waiting to see if Raka took the same action he had with poor Xandrea – assuming he'd been responsible for any poisoning.

A distaste for how His Magnificence dealt with the last foolish servant.

Chay found she was short of breath, and her hand slipped to cover her belly, which was still flat even though the rest of her had become rounder. She didn't want to be dealt with. So even though the risk of leaving was terrible, it seemed the risk of remaining would be far worse.

So she found herself setting down the water bowl, and quietly making her way towards Orin's chambers.

Syrene

Astrid had spent so much time carefully examining the new race course before she had to ride it – trying to memorize where each of the flags were, where the dangerous corners were, where Kopa was most likely to get distracted by food and/or other raphantas.

But when it came down to it, she'd just clung onto Kopa's back and tried not to fall off as he'd charged around the enormous, hilly track at high speed. He was still generally vicious, unsteerable and so, *so* fast.

He'd made occasional detours out of curiosity or to challenge other raphantas who looked at him the wrong way (or so she assumed), which meant *all* raphantas, and a couple of times Astrid had almost found herself in tears, afraid she'd be thrown off or accidentally bludgeoned by thrashing, sinewy trunks.

And then the other racers would catch up and pass Kopa…so naturally he'd forget whichever random bystander he'd been fighting with, and would charge after them. Astrid had managed to grab a few flags along the way out of pure luck rather than any skill, and when they finally made it across the finish line near thirty minutes later, she literally had no idea what the outcome would be.

But this time, rather than heading straight for the nearest water trough, Kopa slowed down and began a sort of prancing circuit around the busy field, waving his wrinkled trunk and letting out the occasional trumpeting noise as if convinced of his own success. Astrid waited for him to slow down, then when that didn't happen, just waited until he was near a fence. Then she grabbed onto it with one shaking, exhausted hand and hauled herself off his back.

No need to stand up, she told herself. *We'll just stay here for a bit, clinging onto the fence.* But she took off her big floppy Tyger hat to let some air onto her sweat-damp, newly dyed blue-purple hair. (Thank you, Vuyani.) Astrid still didn't know what a Dragonfly was, but she knew it meant someone would help her get a disguise, and that was good enough.

The others quickly found her. "Great race!" Jazir enthused. "You got what, five flags? And you didn't let Kopa maul anyone!"

"There was the blue raphanta near the entry," his sister pointed out. "And the two greys about halfway along the track."

"Fine, Kopa didn't maul anyone to the point of being sued," Jazir corrected. "I don't think."

Astrid had kept up with the conversation pretty well even if she hadn't had her translator, but as always, her reply was brief. She didn't yet have the vocabulary for full sentences. "We win?"

"Uh..." Vuyani made a waggling gesture with her hand, the universal sign for 'maybe'. "We'll see."

Just then Xever came to join them. "Good going, Tam," he told Astrid. "But can you catch Kopa next time? He's taken off. My brother's gone to get him, but you know how that always turns out."

Astrid slumped against the fence, but nodded wearily. She *did* know how that would turn out – with someone getting kicked in the gut, and Kopa doing his version of a wicked laugh. "I get," she said, even though she knew that her not-so-noble steed wouldn't listen to her any more than the others. He just didn't maul her, which was pretty useful, she supposed.

She headed over to where Kopa was taunting some horse-like creatures that were locked behind a high fence, and tried to grab for his lead. While she would have sworn he wasn't looking at her, he suddenly ducked just as she was about to grab him, then took off into the crowd amid screams (the trampled) and laughter (those not realising they were about to be trampled).

"Thanks a lot, Vicious," she muttered in English. She slapped her hat back on her head, then began to jog after him.

About half an hour later, after Kopa had finally allowed her to catch him, Astrid made her way back to the stables where Xever and the others were waiting.

"They've tallied up the points," Jazir announced, never one to let someone else do the talking. "It looks like you came second. That's some decent money, Tam! What do you think about that?"

Since Astrid still struggled to translate costs from dollars to the local currencies, she didn't think much of it at all. But they seemed happy, so she smiled. "New well?"

"Definitely a new well," he enthused. "But what will you do with your cut?"

This was a topic they hadn't really discussed yet, because she hadn't had the words to ask, and wasn't sure if it was safe to do so. But now she ventured, "South."

"What?"

"Go south," she tried again, but just then there was a loud trumpeting noise – the sort that came from a horn rather than one of the many raphantas around the track. Naturally it was echoed by *real* trumpeting, and when the din finally died down, she saw that everyone was moving towards one end of the track.

"Time for prizes," Vuyani told her, the others already having disappeared up ahead. "Come on, Tam. You might even get to go up on stage!"

'Tam' *definitely* got to go up on stage, Astrid found out shortly afterwards. Much in the way her own culture gave awards, they'd started with the lower prizes…and they still hadn't been announced. Then fourth, third…second.

"Second place to Kopa of Xever, with sixteen points!" the presenter announced. Then Xever was making his way up the front through the cheering crowd, and someone was shoving a flustered Astrid after him. She followed him up to the low platform where the prizes were being given, and watched as a young man in rather splendid gold and blue robes hung a thick golden chain around Xever's neck, then murmured something unintelligible. Xever smiled and bobbed in a Tyger-style bow, and then the young man was looking at her.

He was holding another, smaller gold chain, and he smiled. It was a nice smile, and he had a nice face with regular features – the sort that maybe wasn't immediately gorgeous, but was nothing to complain about either. He kind of reminded her of someone. His straight, navy-blue hair fell to his shoulders and almost blended in with that ornate robe.

Astrid smiled back awkwardly. Sure, he was a good-looking guy, but she was a girl dressed as a boy who'd probably raced illegally, and currently in hiding from a Tyger despot. She was desperate to get off the stage, to get back to the place where no one could look at her properly, and where she had less opportunity to mess up horribly. But she tried to copy Xever's bow, then reluctantly moved forward and let the young man put the chain around her own neck. It briefly got caught on her ear under her loosely-tied hair, and she lifted a hand to lift it off.

The man's gaze froze on her hand, and she realised in dismay that she might have exposed her *other* different feature – those distinctly rounded ears so very unlike the locals'.

Uh oh.

But he didn't seem to notice. "Tam, was it? Good race." His voice was as ordinary and pleasant as his appearance, and it too seemed familiar even with the benefit of the translator.

Astrid just forced another polite smile. "Yes, sir." Then she went to make her way off the stage, but he reached out one hand as though to stop her.

"Do you know who I am?" he asked mildly.

She blinked at him in confusion.

"I'll take that as a no," he said, smiling a little and revealing a dimple in one cheek. "I'm Alsair Benn Syrenius, currently regent of Syrene while my stepfather Emir Jireh is indisposed. But you can call me Benn."

Astrid sucked in a panicked breath. She didn't have the words to reply, and had she offended him by not knowing? Or wait…was this a good thing? Jae had described him as reasonable…

"We met at the races in Iznaith," he continued quietly. "I was in disguise, of a sort." He touched his clean-shaven face, and she realised that previously he'd been wearing a thick blue beard, typical of many Tyger men. Emphasis on *wearing* – it must have been fake. And he was certainly the one who'd given her the translator, which meant he knew who she was.

The regent. The *regent*?

"Oh," she said weakly. "Good?"

Just then there was a cheer from the crowd, and the regent glanced over her shoulder. "Ah, here's the first-place winner. Would you please wait for me, and not flee this time? I need to talk about a most important matter."

A moment later the translator did its work and Astrid gave a brief, stunned nod, barely moving out of the way as the first-place owner and jockey made their way onto the stage. She shuffled off to the side, her thoughts churning and confused, but also feeling hopeful.

The regent of Syrene was awarding prizes at the races. Or at least he'd *said* he was the regent, and why would he lie about such a thing? He really did have a nice robe, Astrid mused.

But she thought of Raka and the pageantry surrounding him everywhere he went, and Benn the regent of Syrene seemed… ordinary in comparison. But in a good way, more like he wouldn't have you executed or locked up or forced to play board games until you looked like you'd genuinely lost, like Raka would.

Hmm.

But then Astrid felt a hand on her arm, and Jazir was pulling her off the stage entirely, back into the crowd. "Come on, Tam. You've had your turn."

Ah, because he thought she was dim. Of course. But she dug in her heels before he could pull her too far into the crowd, and gestured at the young man still on stage. "Regent."

"Yes, that's the regent," Jazir agreed, not sounding nearly as impressed as he ought to. "Well spotted. Now come on, let's show the others that chain you've got there!"

But Astrid set her hand against his, trying to free herself. "Talk regent," she said, hating that she was so restricted in her speech. "Talk…after."

Finally he seemed to understand something was different, and his blue eyebrows came down low over his eyes. "You want to talk to the regent?"

"Yes!"

"Because of…" Jazir waggled his eyebrows meaningfully. "*You know.*"

He no doubt thought it was something to do with 'Dragonfly', but close enough. "Yes," she replied instead, then folded her arms. She wasn't going anywhere. Not when a solitary trip to the human southern mining station would get her lost or frozen or both, and not when a reasonable regent wanted to talk to her.

So Astrid stood at the side of the stage, watching as the first-place winners proudly held their prizes in the air. But her attention wasn't on their admittedly impressive winnings. No, it was on the quiet young man on the other side…who seemed to be watching her just as she was watching him.

Then finally the ceremony was over, and as she made her way back towards him she heard someone say, "What a great prize! It's just a shame that Emir Jireh couldn't present it like usual."

"Oh hush, you know he's still sick in bed," the reply came. "For now, the boy is better than nothing."

"I suppose." But the first speaker didn't sound convinced.

Just then Astrid met the regent's eyes where he stood just behind the speakers, and he smiled ruefully, clearly having overheard the whole conversation. In that moment she realised they'd been talking about *him* – and it hadn't exactly been respectful.

The others wandered off, and then it was just the two of them, somehow alone in the middle of the crowd.

He was the first to break the silence. "As you see, my people greatly admire me," he said dryly. Astrid didn't know how to answer, and after a few moments he added quietly, "That was a joke, but I suppose it didn't translate very well. You must be Astrid Townsend."

She felt her eyes bug. "How…?"

"Long story," he replied more seriously, "and not one for this place, never mind that no one seems to be listening. Can you come somewhere private?"

Even though she wanted to trust the regent, she instinctively rebelled at the idea of being alone with anyone who knew who she really was. She glanced over her shoulder to where Vuyani was watching her wide-eyed. Behind him Jazir seemed to be arguing with Xever – or perhaps just talking enthusiastically. It was hard to tell sometimes with the way they spoke with such fervour.

"You'll be safe, I swear it on my own life. Or would you like to bring your…minders?"

Minders, because the others thought Astrid was simple. So right then she made a decision. She pointed at Vuyani, then when she had her attention, pointed at the regent and gave a thumbs-up with a cheesy smile. Vuyani smiled back, looking a little uncertain. Then to the regent Astrid said, "Yes. Talk in private."

He paused, then with a slight smile added, "And I can bring the other half of the translator, perhaps?"

Oh, yes!

The southern mining station

Jae felt shaky with her new knowledge, like she was bursting with it, desperate to share it and yet afraid to do so. It wasn't the best attitude to bring to a very important meeting, but it would have to do. So when she came back from the medical centre after being told that new, terrible truth, she went straight to the mine's head, Ellin, and step by step, blurted out the whole thing.

"So you see that we can't possibly keep buying ambrilene," she finished emphatically. "The Mahadrese are enslaving a minority, even killing them, and selling us the bodies. The Syrenians might not be killing them, but they're pushing them out, and not allowing anyone new to settle. We're supporting a genocide!"

Ellin was a short, solid, straightforward woman who commanded respect by giving it, and by being scrupulously honest. Or that was Jae's impression in the few days since they'd met. But now her mouth was hanging open, and her dark eyes were round and a little glazed.

"Ellin? Are you OK?"

Ellin snapped her mouth shut. "Shapeshifters, you say?"

"Yes! It sounds unbelievable – and I *know* we've never come across anything like this – but I saw Malchiel change right in front of me! He was an acrypid: the same huge bird that Marcus and I saw when we visited yesterday. If you need proof, we've got the conversation on video."

They found the recording of her conversation with the Dragonflies. The audio and video weren't perfect, but they were enough to convince Ellin. "Holy *#%@," she muttered, her eyes bugging. "This better not be altered."

"It's real," Jae said fervently. "If you need to see Malchiel shapeshift in person, I can talk him into coming here to show you." She paused. "OK, it'll take a lot of convincing. The Dragonflies are understandably very wary of us, but we're lucky that they blame

Raka's regime rather than us. And once we show you, we can get a better recording, and take it back to whoever's in charge of trading. The sooner the better!"

Ellin went silent for several seconds, then said slowly, "It's not that I don't believe you, Jae. It's just this will all be a bit easier to take in once we see it ourselves – in person – alright?"

"Yes, of course." She'd expected as much.

"And even if your story is true, and we shouldn't be buying the ambrilene, we're also not really responsible for what happened." Ellin seemed to be working through the idea as she spoke. "The Tygers already hated these others…these 'Dragonflies', you say. We didn't start that."

"We just profited from it," Jae retorted. "What does Earth history call those people who sold weapons to the Nazis, Ellin? Or who bought stolen goods? Complicit. We *must* stop it at once! And we must do everything we can to make up for what's happened." Maybe they could put pressure on Raka to release the Dragonflies they were keeping as slave labour in their own mines. Malchiel seemed to think he knew where they were…

The other woman took on that slightly panicked look again, and she raised her hands, palms outwards. "Alright, alright! Just…let me talk to Anton back at the north colony, alright?"

"Alright." And in the meantime, Jae would do what she did best.

Heal…and ask questions.

CHAPTER 12
The Blessed Ones

Earth

Nathaniel blinked at the tiny black and white figure on the screen. While video calls on Earth were such high quality that it was almost like being in the same room, video calls through the portal to the colony weren't nearly as advanced. But nothing changed.

Suraya's tiny face creased with concern. "Did the reception just cut out, Nathaniel?" she asked. "It sounded like you said Astrid's not with you."

"I did!" he exclaimed. Beside him, just out of view of the camera, Tammy sat with a similar worried expression. "Suraya," he continued urgently, "I've jumped through hoops just to get this video call to talk to Astrid. She did *not* come through the portal three weeks ago. She stayed behind-"

"But Anton said she did," Suraya cut in. "He said she ran off suddenly, didn't even say goodbye. Are you *sure* she's not on Earth, and just hasn't made contact?"

Nathaniel paused, second-guessing himself. Was that possible? But then he shook his head. "I just checked a few days ago. I got a message confirming she was in the colony still, but it was brief." He frowned, feeling dread creep up his spine. "This isn't good, Suraya."

"I'm sure there's a good reason," she said, but even she didn't look convinced. "Have you spoken with your aunt?"

"Jae?" Nathaniel latched onto that idea like a lifeline. "I'll ask her. She's down at the southern mines at the moment, but Astrid would definitely try to contact her."

"Hmm. I was just wondering...you know how the portal was trashed the night you left? And then Astrid left the next day." She frowned. "But...Anton said you and Astrid left together. That doesn't make sense."

His eyebrows shot up. "Trashed? What do you mean?"

Suraya explained how just after the human delegation had arrived home from their visit to Mahadra, some unknown person had tampered with the controls to the portal back to Earth, and had left it unusable for several days. "Then there was the tyger," she added thoughtfully.

Nathaniel glanced nervously at Tammy, knowing that the other girl couldn't see her. "Oh? Which one?"

"You know, the *tyger*. The big cat that the emir gifted us. It was in a cage in the hold, drugged of course. Don't you remember?"

Now she'd mentioned it he did, but he'd forgotten amongst everything else that was going on at the time. "Oh yeah. What about it?"

"It went missing," Suraya continued. "The same night the portal was trashed. Anton said it was taken through to Earth, but Brian told me privately that he couldn't find a record of it. He said-"

But then her tiny, black and white figure froze, and after a moment the screen went blank. The call had cut off – pretty normal for contacts through the portal.

"That's not good," Nathaniel mused aloud, but his thoughts were on his sister. "A tyger running loose in the colony?"

But next to him Tamzyn had gone white. She leaned forward, her translator at her ear as always. "Did someone say a *beini* was taken by your people, Nathaniel?"

"Uh…yeah. Emir Raka gifted it to us for six months."

It was an offhand statement, but she was shaking her head in response, her big dark eyes too wide. "No, no, no," she muttered in Tyger. "No, not a *beini*. And they say that the…portal was destroyed, yes? Oh no, no, no. He must have seen me go through…"

"Who must have seen you, Tammy?" Nathaniel asked in confusion. "Emir Raka?!"

"The *beini*! The…*tyger*, you called him." She leaned forward, grabbing him by his shoulders, and showing more urgency than she'd shown even when she'd feared her life was at risk. "Nathaniel, you must forgive me because there are things I have not told you. Things I thought better not to tell you – but now I see that was a mistake. Your people know the *beini* are sacred to us, yes?"

"Yes…"

"But you do not know the most important thing," she continued emphatically, "that the *beini* are *us*."

"Er…?"

"The silver-haired among us are skin-changers, Nathaniel," Tamzyn said urgently. "They are not animals. They can take the form of a great cat, but their minds are the same as always. If my brother the emir gifted your people a Blessed One, then Raka surely intended the *beini* to act as a spy. He must have seen me get taken through your portal, and then tried to come after me, but caused destruction instead." Her already wide eyes widened further. "Or he is already here! Oh, Nathaniel! What if he has hurt your sister?"

Nathaniel's eyes were twitching from the effort of trying to keep up with what she was saying, and her nails dug painfully into his shoulders. "Um…Tammy," he said finally. "Are you saying that your people believe that some of you can…turn into these cats? Um… spiritually, you mean?"

"I do not know this 'spiritual'," she snapped irritably. "And there is no believe or not believe, Nathaniel. My illegitimate half-brother Orin is a blessed one, a skin-changer, and I know this from what I've seen with my own eyes. He came to greet your people at the gate to Mahadra city when you first arrived. He was in *beini*- cat form. My royal brother Raka was on a blue raphanta, do you recall?"

"Yes, I do." But he was thinking of all the times he'd seen one of those enormous white cats watching them in the palace. Just watching…those eyes looking so intelligent, and if it was on its hind legs, then it would be as tall as…a man…

Nathaniel swallowed. Could the humans really have missed something so significant about these alien people? And if so, then what did it mean for them, and for Astrid who'd been left behind?

"I'm going to talk to Jae," he said finally. "We'll get to the bottom of this."

Syrene

Benn slipped off his ornate robe and handed it to the race's manager, who moved to put it away. Now wearing a disguise of his own – 'ordinary Benn' – he led the Earther-in-disguise away from the bustle of the racecourse, and around to a quiet place behind the stables.

Here a cluster of trees grew in an unruly but pleasant tangle, and the patch of shade that they cast was currently occupied by a white *beini* in cat form, stretched out on its side.

He blinked. *Her* side, he meant, for the *beini* was female. "Good afternoon," he greeted her politely. "Might we have this space for a few minutes?"

The *beini* sat up and blinked back at him, then seemed to shrug before walking away. He watched her, ensuring she'd gone from hearing distance, then sat down himself. He gestured to the Earther. "Take a seat."

The Earther warily watched the *beini* go, then turned back to Benn. "You…talk *beini*?"

Benn couldn't help grimacing. The words had been pronounced well enough, but he'd seen by the expression on her face that even she knew her speech was horrendous. So he slipped his hand into his pocket and pulled out the little silver shape he'd been carrying for weeks, ever since he'd seen her back in Iznaith. "Would you like this?"

She took it, then only briefly glanced around before removing her hat and pulling off the translator that had been hidden, hooked over one strange round ear. She messed around with the two pieces for a bit, trying to fit them together, then finally set the whole thing back into place over her ear.

"Are you finished?" Benn asked politely.

"Yes," the Earther said in his tongue. "Thank you."

This close up he could see the fine bones of her face; those big brown eyes that even the shade of her hat hadn't been able to hide. She looked rather like her aunt, he decided, but much younger. Rather…gangly, like a half-grown colt. But pretty. And odd…but definitely pretty.

Several moments passed, and Astrid's eyebrows lowered. Then she leaned forward and said something in her language. A few moments later, the strange voice of the translator said in Tyger tongue, "It's better that Vuyani and Jazir don't hear this conversation, because I think they'll be safer in ignorance of my true situation. But why did you want to speak to me, sir?"

Benn couldn't help smiling at the slight disconnect between her mouth moving and the translator's words. He wanted to answer, *because I find your people fascinating,* but instead he said, "I need your help…and it seems you need mine too."

Astrid studied the regent carefully. It would be hard to believe it really was him if the others hadn't confirmed it. He had a nice face, she decided, and one that appeared honest. By providing her with the translator, she felt like her whole world had opened up. But what he'd said wasn't so easy to understand.

"I see why I need your help," she answered finally. "If you know my name, then you must know I'm not exactly safe right now. But how could you possibly need my help?" She paused. "Wait, how do you even know who I am? Do you have contact with my people? Can you contact them now? Because I'm in *serious* trouble."

He'd been studying her face carefully while she spoke and the device translated, but now he seemed a little dumbfounded. "Ah… you have a lot of questions."

"Sorry," she muttered, ducking her head. "I just haven't spoken properly to anyone in weeks. Vuyani and Jazir think I'm an idiot, and I didn't have the vocab to explain myself anyway."

But when she looked up, the regent was smiling at her. "Don't worry. I understand how it feels for people not to listen to me, for they love my stepfather the emir, and would rather listen to him instead. But I myself listen very well. I have a friend in Raka's court, one who tells me all that goes on, especially that which concerns the peace between our nations. They especially mentioned the Earther girl who'd been stolen away as revenge for Lady Tamzyn's kidnapping."

"She wasn't kidnapped!" Astrid blurted out. "She wanted to leave! She might be a royal, sir, but she wasn't allowed to do anything! And we don't kidnap people! *Your* people do that."

The regent's dark eyebrows shot up, and she cringed back, realising she'd overstepped…again. But he just replied, "I did ask you to call me Benn. And I would hope that my people – the Syrenians – don't kidnap anyone. But if you say that Lady Tamzyn was not stolen, then I believe she was not stolen. What of you, Astrid? How did you come to be in Iznaith, then here in our city?"

Astrid studied him warily, trying to work out if he really was as calm as he appeared to be. But when nothing further happened – not even an eye twitch – she let out a slow breath. If Jae had said this guy was reasonable, then he was probably her best bet at getting home safely, right?

So she took the plunge and told him about everything, right from the start where she was allowed to join the delegation because Percy had dumped her. How she'd made mistakes in Mahadra, how she'd not realised there was anything wrong until she'd seen Tamzyn in the ship's hold. How she'd been grabbed from outside the colony, had been imprisoned in Mahadra and forced to play board games, and how she'd been pushed out of a window.

"On that point," Astrid said suddenly, "I could swear that this guy turned into a…um, *beini*. Or just a little bit, anyway. I don't *think* I imagined it, but I also noticed that you spoke to that *beini* just like they were a person…" Her voice trailed off anxiously, as she was caught between spelling out what she was asking – *are beini actually people?* – and wanting him to reassure her that they weren't.

The regent – Benn – was silent for a few moments. Then he said, "This man, he pushed you out of a window?"

"Yes!" Astrid still felt annoyed thinking about it, although annoyance was far too mild an emotion for attempted murder. "So perhaps I imagined the…change. The situation was rather stressful."

"Hmm."

She waited for him to elaborate, but he just watched her, and she was embarrassed enough that she didn't pursue the topic. "I fell into some kind of filthy water," she continued, "and was washed along. I almost drowned, but then when I realised I might be able to escape, I just kept swimming underwater where I could. I went along with the current for…oh, hours, I think – then when I felt like I was far enough out of the city, I got out of the water. The riverbank was all rocky, and I was coloured kinda blue from whatever I'd fallen into, and then I met Jazir and Vuyani. They think I'm simple-minded because I can't speak your language without the translator, but they've looked after me. I was very lucky."

"The traders," Benn mused. "The boy is very fond of racing. They were lucky to have met you too, maybe, as you raced for them. Second prize is nothing to scoff at."

Astrid shrugged a shoulder, unsure of how to think about what had happened. Sure, she'd done them a favour, but it was little in comparison to saving her from Raka. Well, maybe not saving her, but they'd willingly helped her along when they'd had nothing to gain.

"Then we were both lucky," she said finally. "As for the racing, that was an accident. I travelled with them up to Iznaith, and that's where this little raphanta took a liking to me. Xever – that's the owner

– was desperate for someone to ride it so he didn't lose all his money, and I thought that I could use any winnings to pay for my passage down south."

He met her eyes. "You want to go to the Earther mine, do you not? To your aunt."

"Yes! Yes, I do. Er…how did you know that? Have you been in contact with her? Can you call her now?"

Benn smiled a little, just a curve at one side of his mouth, and she realised she'd been babbling again. "If you mean call her on one of those Earther devices, I'm afraid I cannot do it right now. But I could do it back at the palace, if you would come with me. And…"

"What?"

He looked as though he was about to say something, but then shook his head. "You look very much like your aunt," he said finally. "A fine woman. That was how I recognised you, that and Kopa."

Astrid sat back, confused. She understood the first part, but… "How did Kopa help you know I was an Earther? I mean, a human?"

"You know that Kopa is a brown raphanta, yes? A particular breed known for its small size, bad temper and speed."

"I thought he was a baby," Astrid said honestly. "A naughty baby raphanta."

Now Benn broke into a smile – a full, white-toothed grin. "A naughty baby, hmm? Not death on four legs?"

"Er…" If she'd known of Kopa's reputation, she wouldn't have dared to touch him. "I think my poor vocabulary is responsible for that," she said with a scowl. "So what does this vicious, death-on-four-legs brown raphanta have to do with you recognising me?"

"Well. My stepfather, Emir Jireh, was very fond of raphanta racing." Benn paused. "I mean, *is* very fond of racing. He encouraged racers to be housed and even bred at the royal stables, and he would spend a lot of time with the raphantas. One of his stablemen would breed brown raphantas, and Jireh saw how mild the creatures would be with the man's little daughters. He was convinced that all brown raphantas simply preferred females, and would be much more manageable if only females were to race them.

"So when I saw you in Iznaith riding this nasty- pardon, *naughty* brown raphanta even though you clearly had no idea what you were doing, I thought to myself, 'wouldn't that be funny if she was a girl?' Then I saw you closer, and realised that you looked rather like this Earther woman Jae Townsend, right down to those lovely brown eyes."

"Er…thanks." Astrid couldn't help blushing.

Benn didn't seem to notice, continuing, "Of course I knew that you yourself were missing from the Mahadrese palace due to my… friend there. It seemed like too much to imagine, but I put down the translator just in case. Then you picked it up and proved I'd been right all along."

Astrid blinked at him. "Oh. That's…logical." And lucky. Oh so very lucky.

He shrugged. "I am known to be logical." Then as if that statement would be too boastful, he added a slight smile. "I do have the means to contact your people, and even Jae Townsend where she is staying in the south. They can retrieve you when you are ready."

Hallelujah! She felt like squealing with excitement or crying with relief, but instead just nodded. "Thank you." The words didn't come close to reflecting how she was feeling. "But what can I do for you?"

Benn was silent a moment, his smiling lips tightening into a straight line. "Help me to avert a war."

Astrid felt her jaw drop. She'd been expecting Benn to say 'help me get a trade deal' or even, 'is your aunt single?' but not 'help me avert a war'. "Uh…how can I possibly do that?" she exclaimed. "Not that I don't want to help. I just don't want to over-promise."

The regent studied her for several moments, then sighed. "What I am about to tell you is very important, Astrid. I need your help, but I also need your secrecy."

"Well I need *your* help, and I need to not be grabbed back by Raka," she replied bluntly. "You seem like a good guy. What do you need?"

There was another pause. "My stepfather Emir Jireh is unwell," Benn said finally. "His illness is the reason I hold my current position. And while that position might seem of little importance, it still gives me the ability to stop his nephew Raka from become regent himself. Raka believes Syrene belongs to him just as much as Mahadra, because his father was the older of two brothers, but his grandfather chose to split his empire rather than have Raka's father rule it all. He was to marry my stepsister Iryz – Jireh's daughter and Raka's cousin – but she died of a fever some years ago."

He shrugged, his smile now gone. "He sees Syrene as his birthright, and has been amassing a store of weapons in order to invade. Unless Jireh comes back to health, I believe this invasion will take place before year's end."

Astrid's jaw snapped shut, and she couldn't hold back a squeak of dismay. "That's not good," she said feebly. "But Raka was engaged to Iryz, you say? Did Jireh not know what sort of person he is?" Not to mention they were first cousins…

"The betrothal contract was signed when Iryz was an infant and Raka a child," Benn replied. He sighed heavily. "She would have been fifteen this year."

"I'm sorry."

He shrugged again. "As am I, but we can do nothing about the past. It's my stepfather the emir who concerns me now. I will contact your people, but I would like your aunt to bring her medicine here. In secret, you understand, as my people do not always accept outside help."

Astrid couldn't hold back a disgusted snort, thinking again of how the doctors had been run out of town. "But you won't even trade with us," she pointed out. "Why wouldn't you, if you knew there was a problem with Raka getting Earther weapons? Didn't you know you'd be desperately out-gunned?" There was a pause as the translator struggled with that last word, and she amended, "I mean, you wouldn't have the weapons to fight back."

"We wanted to trade," Benn explained. "We would have traded branzine and gold and precious gems mined from our mountains. But your people want ambrilene above all else, and only Raka would provide that. My friend tells me he refused to trade with the Earthers if they were also trading with us." He raised both hands, palms upwards. "We had no choice unless we wanted to dig up graves and deal in the dead like he does."

It made sense to Astrid that Raka would insist on being the one-and-only, but that last sentence made her mouth dry. "Excuse me… deal in the dead?"

Benn met her eyes in a long stare, then looked around him as if checking no one was watching. "You Earthers are strange but interesting," he said. "But perhaps it isn't well known that the ambrilene you prize so much comes from the graves of our *branzinos*, the bronze ones. They're often called Dragonflies, and they're a dying breed in Mahadra…and even here, I regret to say. By law they are safe, but in practice they've been shunned these past few years while my stepfather slept."

She couldn't believe what she was hearing. "What?!"

"Dragonflies," he said again, more slowly as if she hadn't understood the first time. "They have odd brown colouring and unusual abilities, and over time their bodies break down into a substance that the Mahadrese have been calling ambrilene. We here in Syrene explained that touching the dead would defile both ourselves and those buying such things, but your people didn't care."

"What do you mean, they didn't care?" Astrid burst out. "Are you saying they *knew*? Our leaders *knew* about this?"

Benn just blinked at her. "But of course. Emir Jireh himself spoke with your leader years ago, then I did the same when I became regent and realised the problem. There is no doubt that they know…but now we Syrenians will trade anything for care for the emir. Anything except ambrilene."

Astrid sat back on the dry grass, a horrible sinking feeling building in her gut. Could it really be possible that the humans been greedily buying up corpses? When she thought about human history, and what had happened to most Egyptian mummies once the gold had been stripped off, she was sure she knew the answer. "I think we need to make some calls."

"As you wish. But I see we have company."

He pointed across the grassy field, and Astrid looked up to see Jazir and Vuyani meandering in their direction. She recognised their expressions as curious but concerned, and made a decision. "Come," she called to them in her limited Tyger. She had the translator now, but she felt wary of even these two finding out her real origins.

"What is it, Tam?" Vuyani asked warily. She gave the regent their version of a curtsey, which involved touching her hand to her head in a little bow, and Jazir echoed the movement. "Your Excellency."

Astrid glanced at Benn, then back at her lovely, clueless Syrenian friends. "Good news," she told them heartily. "I go palace. You want come with?"

Their jaws dropped. "Uh…"

"Of *course* we want to come," Jazir exclaimed not too long afterwards. "A palace! We've never been in a palace!"

"We're too poor, and we look it," Vuyani commented baldly, not sounding at all sorry about it. "It's lucky that the regent wants to buy Kopa from Xever now that Tam won't be racing again."

Jazir glanced back to where Tam was still speaking with the regent, somewhat separated from everyone else so the conversation couldn't be heard. But their sweet, silly Dragonfly was gesturing energetically and talking with more enthusiasm than Jazir had ever seen him show, and the regent seemed to be listening. "What do you think he's talking about, Vuy? What could he possibly have to say to the regent?"

His sister studied the two of them with narrowed eyes, then glanced back to where Xever and his brother were celebrating. They'd been pleased enough to offload their vicious little beast for a good price, good enough to buy a different raphanta to race in its place. Perhaps a sturdy grey who could be trained to take any rider, and who could actually be steered towards the flags and away from other racers.

As for himself and Vuyani, Jazir supposed they should actually do some trading, which was the whole point of them being in this area. But then he thought of the gold they'd won – or that Tam and Kopa had won on their behalf – and dismissed the idea.

Palace first, *then* trading.

Mahadra

The large caravan of riders and well-laden wagons moved slowly along the rutted road, heading away from the city. There was safety in numbers, so these groups of merchants would travel together several times a year over the mountain road between the two major city-states.

It had been easy enough for Orin to arrange an extra rider, an extra chest of cloth to 'trade'...a chest which had been noticeably heavier when lifted onto the wagon. He wondered how long it would be before his brother would notice the missing *esira*. Some time tonight, he figured, but Raka wasn't likely to make the connection with Orin's 'special mission' to Syrene.

Or so Orin hoped. The emir was so arrogant he wouldn't consider that someone so close to him would rebel, even in the smallest ways. *I am the emir, and I get what I want.* He trusted Orin as much as he trusted anyone, except…Orin still didn't know who Raka's spy was in the Syrenian court. Could be anyone, really, and they'd be watching out for him when he arrived for his special task. He didn't like that kind of surveillance, preferring that he was entirely anonymous on this occasion.

He unhappily pondered that idea as they approached the mountains, but as they reached the first of the foothills, he pulled his wagon aside, allowing the rest of the caravan to pass. He glanced across to the heavy chest, then said to no one in particular, "I just need a few minutes of privacy."

No one answered, of course, but did the silence from the chest seem just a little heavier? If there was no response by the time he'd returned, then he'd open it, he decided.

A few minutes later Orin came back out of the bushes to find the chest closed, just as he'd left it. He sniffed at the air, because something wasn't quite the same. But then when he opened it, it was empty, lined only with rumpled cloth and the lingering scent of the girl…and fear.

"Esira?" he called quietly, aware of the other wagons up ahead. "Chakandra?"

There was a faint rustle from the other side of the road, and he glanced up to see a reddish-brown form suddenly dart from the bushes, then head deeper into the rocky area that made up these mountains. It was a hartdeir, a sturdy horned beast that was common in the mountains. But they were usually grey…

For a few moments Orin couldn't think at all, he was that surprised. He debated whether to pursue her – perhaps to suggest she take predator form rather than prey – but realised that this was his purpose, wasn't it? Free the captive. If she'd chosen this form of freedom, then that was up to her.

But he couldn't help thinking of what she'd told him earlier. *I have no other form. Raka knows this.*

Raka 'knew' his little *esira*, did he? Apparently not so well. So in spite of everything, in spite of where he was going and what he'd been sent to do, Orin threw back his head and laughed.

The southern mining station

Jae moved as quickly as she could, replacing her precious medical instruments in their cases then stacking them into their carriers. She'd have to take everything, because there'd be no way to order anything in if she was short.

Emir Jireh is dying, Astrid had said. *If he dies, chances are Raka will sweep in and take over Syrene, and no one will stop him. Can you come straight away?*

Of course she could! Now she knew about how the Mahadrese had driven out or enslaved all the Dragonflies, she certainly wouldn't want them ruling this planet's second-largest city-state either. But an equally important question was, what on earth was Astrid doing in the Syrenian palace!?

Jae felt her eye twitch again at the memory of that brief conversation just an hour earlier. The reception had been pretty good considering their locations, and she'd recognised her niece at once, even if she *had* done something funny to her hair.

I'll explain everything in person, Astrid had told her in hushed tones. *Please don't tell anyone I'm here. There's something fishy going on.*

"Fishy indeed," Jae muttered aloud as she picked up a handheld body-scanner. She debated whether to add it to her rather large collection, then shrugged and added it anyway. It wasn't like anyone else would be using it back here, not now the other doctors had left for the colony.

"What was that, Jae?"

She jolted a little, then smiled wryly at Marc, who was standing in the doorway to the small medical centre. "Oh, hi. I guess you finished with the first load already."

"That I did," he agreed, studying the new pile in front of her. "Taking the kitchen sink too, are we? Looks like you're planning to be away for a while. I guess you've given up on your refugees."

Jae felt her eye twitch again. "I haven't given up on them," she countered. "I just have something really important to do."

"Ah, yes. The emir is sick." Marc raised an eyebrow. "You know it takes a lot of fuel to carry you back and forth to the capital. Ellin's given her approval this time, but next time you might not get to set your own timetable."

Gee, thanks. "So are we still OK to leave in an hour?" she asked. "Or does someone else need to set that timeframe today?"

"An hour's fine, and no need to get snippy."

Maybe there was no need, Jae thought as she finished packing her things, but it was easy to do so. Her whole purpose here was humanitarian. Volunteer doctors made little money from their patients, and essentially Earth was funding everything, perhaps out of moral obligation, or perhaps to gain favour from the locals. Even her flights back and forth from Syrene were funded by Earth. But when there were only three doctors funded for an entire planet, Earth couldn't claim it was doing everything possible to help.

The tiny population (compared to Earth) just reminded Jae further that the Tygers had originated on Earth, and had made their way across via an early version of the portal perhaps thousands of years before. Any quirks peculiar to this world must have come as a result of that travel – but she wouldn't try to convince the locals of that.

Twenty minutes later she was done. She checked her watch, debating whether she had time to visit the refugee settlement, then decided it didn't matter if she made a quick visit. Marc wouldn't leave without her, even if he whined about it. So she put on a jacket and a warm headscarf, then gathered a bundle of helpful items into a knapsack – water-treatment tablets, vitamins and protein bars. One last, small item went in her pocket…just in case. Then she began the brisk, twenty-minute walk to the little settlement.

Malchiel was waiting for her at the outskirts, and she recognised his broad, silent figure even from a distance. There was something about the way he held himself, something about the way he watched her so intently that reminded her of a hawk eyeing up prey – only not at all creepy or predatory. He lifted a hand in greeting, and she felt her cheeks heat as she waved in reply. Darn it. The blushing when she first saw him was also new, and not appreciated.

"You're leaving," he said before she even opened her mouth.

"How did you know?" Jae exclaimed.

"I watched the others put your healing devices into the metal bird," he answered simply. "What else would you be doing?"

She didn't bother explaining that the shuttle was a type of airplane, because the word never translated. He understood that it wasn't alive, and she supposed that was enough. Suddenly feeling solemn, she held out the basket. "I'm just going to visit the city, Malchiel. I need to help…someone."

He shrugged, but took the basket with a nod, then set it on the ground between them. "Your time is your own, Jae. You need not explain to me." He pronounced her name like 'Shay', but she'd got used to that by now. All the locals couldn't say the hard 'J'.

But he was still watching her with those intent gold-brown eyes, and she gave into the urge to explain anyway. "But I want to tell you. We're friends, aren't we? And…" She paused, debating how much to say about Astrid. She hadn't even told Ellin or Marc, because someone was clearly up to no good, and chances were it was a human who'd have access to their communications technology.

But then she thought of how Malchiel had told her about his wife and twin teenage daughters who'd been killed in the violent Dragonfly village clearances of three years earlier. He'd told her all sorts of things over these last few days, and she'd told him things too, and well…she trusted him.

"It's my niece," Jae said quietly. "Something's happened, and she's in Syrene. She hasn't told me why, but I know there's a problem. I haven't told my people about that, because it's a secret. I've also been asked to help heal the Syrenian emir, who's near death. If I can help him…if I can get the regent more on my side…then I can tell him about you all. It's not right that you're down here."

Malchiel's perpetually stern expression softened. "What do you think the regent can do, Jae? He fills a position, but his people listen to no one except the emir. If they will not make room for Dragonflies, then the regent cannot force them to. And even if Syrene is a safe-haven, the regent cannot do anything about what happens in Mahadra. He cannot free our people there. They have to free themselves."

And that, Jae thought, was probably the worst part. "The emir might die," she admitted. "I don't know what's wrong with him, but it might be more than we can handle." Except if he did die and the Syrenians knew she'd tried to help, chances were the humans would be blamed. "But either way, you can't stay here. It'll only get colder, and you can't grow food here, and there's nothing to hunt."

He shrugged wearily. "We'll wait here as long as we can, to see if any more of our people make it this far. Then we must move on."

Jae knew they couldn't live here, but even though she was leaving first, that idea saddened her. "Where will you go?"

He shrugged again. "South again, perhaps to the Reinlands."

The Reinlands were deep south indeed, far past the cold area they found themselves in. They were inhabited by loosely connected tribes, and the climate and the landscape wasn't half as hospitable as Syrene or Mahadra. But perhaps it was the Dragonflies' only option.

She was silent for a few moments, pondering the situation. Then she slipped her hand into her pocket and pulled out the small, stick-like black object she'd put there earlier, just on a whim. "This is a tracker," she told him, snapping apart the two pieces then holding one end out to him. "If you keep it with you, I'll be able to find you wherever you are." She paused, suddenly feeling uncertain. "Will you keep it? You don't have to. I just thought that if you move on and I come back-"

"I will keep it," he said abruptly, closing his fingers over hers. "I will keep the…track-her, and should you wish to find me, you can find me."

"OK." His hand was still warm over hers, those fingers a little rough but also very gentle, and Jae felt her cheeks heat again. "Um… don't get it wet, OK? Or too hot, or too cold…"

"I will protect it with my life."

"Uh…maybe not with your life. Just within reason." But she couldn't help smiling. "I have to go, Malchiel. I hope to see you soon, but I can't say when I'll be back."

He smiled back, and this time it creased those strange, gorgeous eyes. She was very conscious that he was still holding her hand, and that these people had different ideas of what was acceptable between a man and a woman. So she pulled her fingers away from his a little awkwardly, giving one last smile. "Be well."

Syrene

Astrid wasn't good at waiting. She jiggled from side to side where she stood, onto one foot then the other, and clenched then unclenched her hands. "They landed ages ago," she whined. "Surely we'd see them by now?"

"All will be well," Benn replied placidly, but she couldn't miss the gleam of anticipation in his eyes. From their recent conversations she now knew how fascinating he found her people – the 'Earthers' and their fantastic devices. "They will be walking to us, and it is some distance."

She tried not to grumble at that, because he was right. The two of them now stood along with just one other – the emir's nurse's son. Neoli was a solid middle-aged man with a kindly air about him and that unusual white hair. He was currently standing patiently beside an empty wagon, his eyes a little wide. But then he'd actually squeaked aloud when the human shuttle had flown overhead then had landed just out of sight, over the next rise.

The three of them waited well away from the city, and it had taken them two hours to get to this spot where there was no one to see them, not even a grazing beast or farmer. Naturally people would have seen the shuttle come to land, but that couldn't be helped.

Just then a couple of people appeared over the hill. One was a man, dressed in a loose, pale tunic and trousers, much like Benn and Merima's son wore, but even from here Astrid could see how different he looked. His hair was ashy brown, very typical for a European human, and his skin seemed too pale now she'd spent all these weeks seeing only Tyger faces. He carried something under one arm. It was long and metallic and looked suspiciously gun-like.

Next to the man was a woman clothed in the typical loose, light robes of this area, and with a white scarf wrapped neatly around her head, obscuring her hair. She could have been just any local woman, dragging a barrow full of goods for trading.

But even though she was doll-sized and her features were obscured from this distance, Astrid recognised her at once. "Aunt Jae!"

CHAPTER 13

A Little Medicine

Astrid broke away from the others and ran, her own new robes flapping from the momentum, and her own headscarf threatening to fall off. She didn't care – she just slapped one hand over it and kept running. Meanwhile Jae was setting down her 'barrow' full of medical goods and she put out her arms, and Astrid ran right into them, into what felt like the tightest and most welcoming hug ever.

"I missed you," Astrid choked out, realising she was crying and not even caring. "I'm so glad you're here."

Jae pulled away, studying her with a half-smile. "I missed you too. And look at you! You could pass for a local girl if no one looked too closely." She picked at a strand of hair sneaking its way out from under the headscarf, tied casually at the back of her neck just like Vuyani's. "Blue hair, Az? But what are you doing here?"

Astrid almost choked again. "It's been the worst thing," she began. But then the man who'd arrived with Jae had come up beside them, and she clamped her mouth shut, turning her face away. He was human and probably safe, but after everything that had happened, now few things felt truly safe.

"I guess these are the right people, then?" the man said in English. "You made a few good friends among the locals."

He hadn't recognised her as human, Astrid realised. Jae seemed to figure as much herself, because she smiled at the man. "Thank you again, Marc. I can take it from here."

He shrugged. "You don't want me to help you with that thing?"

"You'd better not. We don't want anyone to see that you were even here, or to connect us with the shuttle. Not after what happened last time."

"Understood." There was a pause. "Ah, well. Call us if there's an emergency, but remember that it'll take a few hours to reach you."

"So best not to have any emergencies," Jae said wryly. "I'll bear that in mind."

The man – Marc – left, and finally Astrid lifted her head. "I guess I really do look like one of the locals."

"I guess you've got a story to tell," her aunt countered in much the same manner.

"I sure do," Astrid agreed. She slipped her arm through Jae's, then moved to pick up the barrow. But it hardly had any weight to it, instead hovering over the ground as she pulled it along. "Let's get moving, then I can tell you all about it."

"And then Benn sneaked me into the palace dressed as a boy and gave me servants' clothes, girl ones, which feels weird because I've dressed like a boy for weeks now." Astrid glanced down at her front, which now looked distinctly female even in these loose robes with their neat sash tied around the torso. "I think it's nice. It was kind of fun to do all that stuff dressed as a boy, but the constant fear of being discovered wasn't so nice." Just then their wagon went over a rut, and the three of them sitting in the back all jolted into the air a little. "Oof! And then we called you of course, and here we are."

Aunt Jae had been listening to Astrid rattle on for the last forty-five minutes with her eyes round and her mouth a little open. They were speaking in English, and they'd given the translator to Benn instead. He'd been listening with what seemed like just as much enthusiasm, and Astrid found herself warming to him even more. But after a few moments of silence, Astrid added, "Aren't you going to say something?"

Jae shook her head. "I just…I don't…*kidnapped*, Astrid? This isn't good."

"True," Astrid agreed, "but I'm used to it by now, and I'm safe. Well, until Raka declares war and starts bombing us, I'm safe. And you're here too."

"Bombing?" Jae echoed, sounding dismayed. "Surely Earth wasn't stupid enough to sell Raka *bombs*?"

Astrid glanced across to the regent, who raised one eyebrow quizzically. "Very destructive weapons," she explained. "They can be thrown from a distance or dropped from the air or even carefully set on the ground. They explode and can destroy entire buildings… or entire cities, if they're big enough."

"Oh." Benn paled, then shook his head firmly. "Raka won't

destroy Syrene. Not when he wants to rule it. And my spy didn't mention anything so destructive. He spoke of...*gons,* and *stunnahs.* Does that sound familiar?"

"Oh, yes," Astrid muttered, thinking of that awful white-haired Tyger who'd snatched her from outside the colony itself. She was lucky he'd used a 'stunnah' instead of a 'gon'. "They can kill or incapacitate from a distance, but they're not nearly as bad as bombs."

But even as she spoke, she couldn't help looking around her at the almost flat landscape, with the city in the distance. Its walls were made of the local stone, thick enough to repel an attack with catapults and arrows and spears as the Tygers would usually use, but would it stand up to more advanced weaponry?

She thought of those videos she'd seen on Earth, from those ancient cities that had been decimated by war; their inhabitants forced to flee. Syria, Iraq, Afghanistan. They'd had stone walls too, but they'd ended up in pieces or riddled with holes. She swallowed. "It would be much better if Raka never attacks at all."

"We can all be agreed on that," Benn said dryly. "That is in part why you are here, Ms Jae, and I thank you very much for coming. If my stepfather dies..." And here he swallowed... "...if he dies, then my people will have no one to stand behind. They will lose heart."

There was a solemn silence, broken only by the clatter of the wagon wheels on the loose gravel, and their white-haired driver giving occasional orders to the sturdy horse-like creatures pulling them.

"I don't get it," Astrid said finally. "Sure, I understand that your stepfather is well-loved. But what's so bad about you ruling? You're intelligent and ethical, and compared to someone like Raka, you'd do an amazing job."

Benn smiled at her, and a dimple winked in one cheek. "Could I get you to put that in writing and send it out to all the people? But your compliment matters little when the people are so traditional. They love Jireh, and they respected his father before him. They want a ruler of true blood. The emir married my mother when I was a child, because he had no son with his first wife, and my mother had proven she could bear males by having me with her first husband. But unfortunately they never had any children together. You see, I was never meant to rule. I don't *want* to rule."

"Oh?" Astrid studied him curiously. She was liking him more by the minute, since she'd never understood why some people sought power. It never seemed to lead to anything good, in her opinion. "What do you want to do, then?"

His eyes narrowed as he considered the question. "I'd be a scholar," he answered finally. "I would learn all the secrets of our people, and all the secrets of yours." He smiled at her again. "I'd love to visit Earth. It sounds fascinating."

"Depends where you go." Some parts were dirty and busy and kind of depressing. "Tell you what," Astrid offered grandly. "If you ever make it to Earth, I'll show you around. It'll be fun."

He nodded in agreement. "I accept your offer. But as we're now entering the city, would you two please put your translators back on, but hide the mouthpieces?"

Jae, who'd been quiet for some time, said something to him in the local language. Astrid picked up a few words – it was something along the lines of, 'I speak the language fluently'. Astrid didn't, of course, so she took the earpiece gratefully, since it was more important to understand than to speak anyway. She tucked the mouthpiece away in her pocket, and hoped she wouldn't sit on it by mistake.

By then they'd made their way into the city, and the noise of everyday life surrounded them. They trundled along to the palace, the two women making sure to turn their faces away from the road. Astrid noticed that Benn did the same. It would be pointless for them to go to all this effort to arrive unnoticed, only to be outed by their 'unusual' brown eyes or features.

"We're almost at the palace," Benn said quietly a few minutes later. "Ms Jae, would you come with me straight to the emir's chamber?"

"Of course," Jae agreed immediately. "What about you, Astrid?"

"I suppose I could go back to the stables to see Kopa," she ventured. "And Jazir and Vuyani."

"Ah yes," her aunt agreed absently. "The naughty raphanta and the two who helped you. They must've been very surprised to see you're female."

Astrid's half-smile froze on her face. "Uh…they don't know yet, actually. I came straight here."

Jae just looked at her, that face so similar to the one Astrid saw in the mirror, then raised an eyebrow. "Do you think it's safe to tell them?"

Astrid sighed. Really, she didn't know, but it was getting to the point where it felt mean *not* to tell them. "They're convinced I'm this 'dragonfly' thing – I told you that, right? And they went out of their way to help me."

"Dragonfly?" Jae exclaimed. "Do you mean *branzino*?"

"Uh…yeah, that sounds about right. You've heard of them?"

Jae's lips tightened, and for a moment she looked terribly unhappy. "There's a lot to talk about," she said finally. "But I'll see the emir first. You go visit your…raphanta."

So Astrid would take the chance tell Vuyani and Jazir her weeks-old secret. That should be interesting. "I will."

Neoli stopped the wagon at the quietest part of the palace, near where merchants and traders would deliver their wares. The younger Earther had been deposited at the stables, and Benn had spared only a few moments of concern before deciding she'd be fine. She'd looked after herself these past weeks – through danger and trouser-wearing and raphanta races – she'd surely handle the palace stables without trouble.

"See that Ms Jae's goods are quietly left in the room next to your mother's," Benn told Neoli in a low voice. He didn't need to explain the importance of what they were doing. The servant already knew. Besides being a *beini* and literally able to smell emotions (and if someone was up to no good), he was also better at listening than talking. Like his mother Merima, Benn had known him since childhood and trusted him implicitly.

Neoli moved as if to leave, and Astrid's aunt made a sound of surprise.

"My apologies," Benn said, realising Neoli might be taking off with goods she would require. "I have been impatient. Do you need something?"

"Just a few basics to start with," she murmured, leaning forward and picking up a loose brown satchel. It was made of a rough, locally-made fabric, and he was again grateful at how this woman had made so much effort to fit in here…never mind that all the locals hadn't responded in kind. "Shall we go?"

He moved to help her out of the wagon in the same way he would any Syrenian woman, but she'd already climbed down. He briefly felt irritated at being left with his hands outstretched, but reminded himself that she wasn't Tyger, no matter how she looked right now. She was in a strange position, this healer. She belonged to one people and wished to share her wisdom, but for his own people to accept her, she must act like them. Just enough to be believed, not so much that she'd be prevented from doing what she must.

"Were you one of those who visited the palace two years ago?" he asked quietly as they walked. "Who attended my stepfather the first time?"

"No, those were my colleagues, both men." Jae glanced up him briefly. She was keeping her eye contact limited, Benn realised, in a way she'd no doubt learned while healing. Her niece Astrid hadn't learned anything of the sort, and made eye contact as directly as a man would. "We assumed that a female doctor wouldn't be welcome, not when it was a male who was ill. Were we correct?"

Benn nodded. "It would be unusual for a woman to treat a man," he agreed. "But now we have no choice." He felt that same depression threaten to overwhelm him, the one that he'd battled with ever since Jireh had fallen so badly ill. If the two male Earthers had not been able to help two years before, how could she help now? "The sickness is worse than before," he admitted, his voice sounding hoarse to his own ears. "Your people had no medicine for him last time, but maybe this time…"

Jae's head shot up, and this time he could see she was staring at him. Truly staring. "My people didn't actually see His Magnificence last time," she said finally. "They only spoke with an advisor, who wouldn't allow them to see the emir in person. They left without dispensing medicine because they had to, not because they chose to."

Benn stopped mid-step, then forced himself to continue as if nothing was wrong. It seemed that Merima's words had been true. She hadn't remembered the Earthers visiting previously, perhaps because they'd not had a true visit.

"What was the name of the advisor they spoke to?" he managed to ask. There were half a dozen that lived at the palace, although only two or three who'd be bold enough to send the Earthers away without them seeing Emir Jireh as expected. One of them, Koln, was Jireh's own cousin, while the other, Jenina, would be easy to identify merely because she was female.

The Earther woman paused, but then shook her head. "I'm sorry, Your Excellency. I don't recall."

"Benn," he said automatically, but his thoughts were elsewhere.

The Earthers had never seen the emir, who'd grown steadily more ill. He definitely had a spy or two in his court – because that's how things worked with rulers and he had his own too – but it seemed that they might be doing more than just sending on information. But if they'd been able to interfere in such a way, then they were closer than they should have been. That idea terrified him.

He licked his suddenly dry lips. "Let's go in, shall we?"

It's just another patient, Jae told herself as she entered the emir's room along with his stepson. They'd come as quietly as they could, Jae with her head down as they'd moved through the halls and stairways of the palace, but she knew they'd been seen anyway. *Just another patient, except that if I screw up this time I'll ruin things for my entire planet…so no pressure.* Phew.

Emir Jireh's sick room was more of a suite, decorated in what she'd come to think of as typically vibrant Tyger colours and patterns. The bedroom itself was separated from the rest of the suite by a long, rippling bead curtain, and as they approached, an elderly woman stepped through, holding a bowl. "Benn," she began, then amended it to, "Your Excellency."

Benn stepped forward. "Merima. How is he?"

"He still lives," the woman replied. Her tone was flat, the creases beside her eyes and mouth were deep, and she had silver-white hair visible under her head-wrap, contrasting with the deep brown shade of her skin. Jae wondered whether that was from age, or from something else.

The regent turned to Jae. "Merima is my stepfather's nurse, and I've known her for many years. Her son brought us here today. Merima, this is Jae Townsend of Earth. As I said earlier, it's best to keep her visit here secret."

Jae nodded politely at the nurse, remembering Neoli's white hair too. Genetic, perhaps, rather than age.

"Ms Jae," the nurse said politely. Then to Benn she said, "Nothing is truly secret, sir, although of course I will do as you ask. How can I help?"

Benn gestured to Jae, and she stepped forward. "We'll start like this…"

The Earther had so very many questions to ask, Benn mused. And that was before she had even touched the emir. Once Merima had mentioned a daily medicine, Jae's ears had pricked up. "Do you have a sample of this?"

"The medicine is one provided by Palos," Benn explained. "He's the emir's oldest friend, and would never intend him harm."

Jae looked hesitant for a moment, then continued. "Sometimes the traditional remedies are good. But sometimes they aren't what's needed, and occasionally they contain things that no one should really be using…"

After a few moments the nurse shuffled around then handed over a small parcel, which Benn knew contained a mix of medicinal herbs. "It's for a daily tea," Merima told the Earther. "He's taken it since he began to grow ill, for his lungs. He would cough, you see, and had periods of fever where he would hallucinate and mutter nonsense."

"And do you know exactly what is in it?"

There was a pause. "No, I do not. But it is not for me to question Palos."

The healer's nose wrinkled almost imperceptibly, and Benn added, "He hasn't had it for the last three days, and he doesn't seem better. Doesn't seem worse, either."

Jae nodded. "I'll check him now, if that's alright? Then I'll have the medicine tested. May as well see what's in it."

Benn watched as she moved around quickly and efficiently, her expression not giving anything away. But barely two minutes had passed when he heard conversation with the guards outside the door, then the sound and rush of air from someone new entering the room.

A moment later the beaded curtain parted, and Palos entered. His slightly stooped shoulders were stiff with displeasure, and his greying eyebrows were pulled down low over his eyes. "What is the meaning of this?" he exclaimed in a low, hoarse voice – the sort of tone one used for a sickroom. He gestured at Jae, who'd barely paused in her examination of the emir's neck and chest. "A female tending to His Magnificence? A foreigner at that!?"

Benn glanced at the Earther, feeling his heart begin to pound in the way it always did at this kind of conflict. Palos was a forceful personality who was old enough to have advised Jireh's own father, and was a fixture in this palace. But today, his position had been pushed aside, because Benn had made a decision without him.

Up till now Benn hadn't bothered challenging his edicts, because he'd thought Emir Jireh would surely wake up soon and the Syrenians didn't listen to Benn, anyway. But this? This was worth fighting for.

"I had her brought in," Benn replied calmly. "Ms Jae Townsend, I am honoured to introduce the most venerable advisor Palos, a long-term friend and counsellor for my stepfather. Palos, Ms Jae has kindly agreed to-"

"Agreed!?" he hissed, his eyebrows shooting up in a rather alarming fashion. "I did not agree to this! A stranger, a female-"

"Yes, yes, she's a strange female," Benn cut in, setting one hand against his temple. Why did everything have to be such a fight? "But she has access to medicine we don't, and quite frankly-" – and now he raised his voice to speak over the other man – "…the medicine you provided didn't work, and Jireh will be lucky to last another fortnight. So you may wait here quietly and speak with us, or you may leave, and we'll speak later."

That shocked even the old advisor into silence, but not for long. He lifted his chin then said with dignity, "I am not happy with this. And if your stepfather the emir was in his right mind, he wouldn't be happy with it either. You can be sure that we will have words later." With that final statement, he left.

There were a few awkward moments of silence, broken by Jae clearing her throat, and the harsh breathing of the sleeping patient. "I would venture that the emir would want to live," she said quietly. "But that's just my opinion."

Benn scrubbed a hand tiredly over his face, thinking that if Jireh ever returned to himself, then he'd have to talk to him about Palos. The advisor had been diligent in his duties for decades, but he didn't know when to step down. Then there was another very real problem…that Raka was actually Jireh's heir anyway, because Lady Iryz was dead. And Jireh…

…well, he wasn't dead yet, but he'd need to awaken enough to name another heir, a real one rather than just a regent. "I share the same opinion," he said in response to Jae's comment. "Do what you can to make him well."

You've no idea what rests on his recovery.

Astrid made her way to the palace stables with only a few wrong turns. Even though she was largely ignored in her servants' clothing, she still felt oddly exposed. That was ironic, because she was wearing more layers of clothing as a Syrenian girl than she had dressed as Tam, or even in her usual colony daywear.

She followed the familiar trumpeting sounds through the winding buildings with their separate stalls, walled with stone or thick wood so the raphantas couldn't see each other. They behaved rather like horses, she mused, except bigger and uglier and perhaps just a little smarter.

Just then, Astrid heard a noise kind of like a trombone crossed with a deflating balloon, and she knew she'd found Kopa. She turned the corner to find him in a wide stall, with Jazir and Vuyani sitting in the straw off to one side. They were chattering happily and hadn't noticed her arrival, so she just watched Kopa for a while.

He wore a thick, padded ring around his wrinkled neck, and as she watched, he threw his head back and waved his trunk in what looked like happiness. His target? A large, shining piece of branzine metal propped up against the wall. He was playing with his reflection. That was surprising, because Astrid would have thought he'd try to fight it instead.

Then finally Vuyani noticed Astrid. She studied her briefly, her eyes catching on the loose brown trousers, long tunic and neat tight bodice, then landing on Astrid's face. Her eyes widened, and Jazir's gaze followed hers.

He did much the same glance-over, but his face was creased in lines of confusion. "Hey Tam, why are you dressed like a girl?"

"The question would be, 'hey Tam, why have you stuffed rags down your top'," Vuyani countered, her words humorous, but her tone stunned.

As for Astrid, she just pushed away the sense of embarrassment and even a little guilt over how she'd tricked them, and moved to crouch beside them. She didn't sit though; since even these stables wouldn't do light-coloured fabric any good. "No rags," she said in what she knew to be poor but recognisable Tyger. She didn't dare risk using the translator's mouthpiece, not when everything was still so up in the air with Raka. She didn't want these two knowing too much and potentially being harmed as a result. "Not boy, either."

There was a long, stunned silence, then Jazir said in an appalled tone, "Is your name even Tam!?"

Astrid shook her head ruefully, then held one hand to her lips, gesturing with the other hand at the area around them. "Shh. No friends."

"But *we're* your friends! Or are we not?"

Just then Kopa noticed Astrid's presence and let out a happy trumpet. A moment later his trunk was caressing her neck and plucking at her hair, and she giggled. "Smelly raphanta," she muttered in English. Then to the others, "No…Jazir and Vuyani *friends*." She gestured around her, trying to indicate the danger of speaking too openly in public. "No friends."

"So you're saying we're not your friends, or that you've got no friends?" Vuyani sounded affronted. "What's all this friendliness been then, just boredom? Trying to hide that you're…not Tam? Why even invite us here?"

"And you're a girl!" Jazir said, as if it hadn't sunk in the first time she'd told him.

"No!" *Grrr!* Astrid's idea to use only half the translator had seriously backfired, and she sighed, then sat down next to the two of them, fishing it out of her pocket. She put one finger to her lips in an exaggerated fashion, then set about putting the translator back together. A minute later she checked around them to ensure there was no one close by, then spoke. "You don't make it easy, do you?" she said in English.

The translator repeated her words in polite, somewhat robotic Tyger, and her friends' eyes bulged. A moment later Kopa reached for the mouthpiece, and she gently pushed his trunk away. "This is all a secret, you understand. I'm telling you this because you *are* my friends, both of you, and because I know you can be trusted. But I don't want you to get hurt because of me."

Both of them blinked. "But you're in Syrene now," Jazir pointed out. "Even if you're…a *girl*…" and here he seemed to choke on the word, "…you should be safe from the collectors."

Now Astrid was the one to choke. "Collectors?" she echoed, hearing the word translate back into the local language. Perhaps it hadn't translated correctly in the first place. "What collectors?"

"Never mind the collectors," Vuyani cut in. "If Tam's not your name, then who are you?" Her eyes narrowed. "What's that odd thing on your face? I've never seen one before."

"Ahhh…" What was there to do but be honest? Well, Astrid could have lied, but that would have been as difficult as telling the truth.

So with Kopa still plucking at her hair under that scarf, and the two siblings constantly interrupting, she managed to blurt out the most basic of facts.

No, she wasn't a Dragonfly. Yes, she was an Earther, and she barely spoke the language without her translator. Yes, she was in serious trouble because Emir Raka of Mahadra was mad at her people…and she'd appreciate it if they didn't mention they'd seen her.

"No fear on that one," Jazir muttered. "We don't want to get on his bad side either."

"I have a question for you, though," Astrid said once they let her pause for breath. "What's a Dragonfly?"

The siblings exchanged glances, and for a moment she thought they wouldn't respond. But she should have known better – no one could keep Jazir's mouth shut when he wanted to talk. "They're the bronze people," he said confidently. "You know. The weird ones with reddish hair and brown eyes like you…well, the eyes anyway. And they can take any form, not like us. Well, not like *us*, because we aren't Blessed Ones like the silver-haired folk. But like regular people."

There was a long silence where he seemed to wait for affirmation that she'd understood, and which he definitely wasn't going to get. "Uh…when you say, take any form, do you mean like a peddler or a merchant or a fighter? Or that they dress like the other gender sometimes?"

The siblings let out guffaws of laughter, and Jazir's eyes slipped down again to her tunic top…something he'd done sporadically since she'd showed up 'female'.

"Not other jobs," Vuyani scoffed. "Other *forms*. You know, like the *beini*. The Blessed Ones turn into big cats, but the Dragonflies can take any form."

"Uh…" Astrid said again, thinking of that brief, monstrous moment in Raka's palace, right before she'd been pushed out of the window. The white-haired man's face had seemed to change. And then the other day when she'd spoken privately with Benn, he'd asked one of those cats to vacate its spot so they could sit down. He'd just asked with spoken language, no gestures.

Just then Astrid heard footsteps indicating they were no longer alone, and she quickly pulled off the mouthpiece and shoved it out of sight under her headscarf. They all froze as a man in rough clothing trundled past, pushing a straw-filled barrow, and barely glanced at them before disappeared from view. But the raphanta kept playing, stroking Astrid's face and headscarf with his tactile trunk.

"Ouch!" she muttered, reaching up to try to push him away. "Kopa, that's my hair."

The naughty raphanta backed away, but there was now something silver in his trunk. The translator's mouthpiece! Astrid reached for it but he danced away, thinking it was a game…then put it in his mouth. *Crunch.* Then having chewed on it a little, he deposited the mangled, wet object back into her hand.

"Ugh. Well, that's the end of the conversation," she said glumly in English. "Thanks a lot, Kopa."

He made a happy little whinnying sound.

"That was sarcasm, by the way."

Being back to one-syllable conversations was no fun, so Astrid finished her discussion with Jazir and Vuyani as best she could. It seemed they were planning to stay overnight in the rooms provided, then go on with their usual plans. Astrid didn't know how long she'd be here, but she figured it could be a while. The emir was really sick, people said, not that she'd had the chance to see him herself. Not that it would matter if she did, since her medical knowledge was about as good as her grasp of the Tyger language.

She said as much later, after dinner when she was in the room she shared with Jae. "It was a shame because I think they were going to tell me something interesting," she commented. "As it was, I just got left thinking of…um…shapeshifters and Blessed Ones or something. But I'm sure that's not what they meant to say."

Jae's head shot up from where she'd been focused on her tiny laptop. "What sort of shapeshifters?"

"What sort?" Astrid teased. "You're not going to ask me if I ate the wrong kind of cheese at lunch to even consider such a thing?"

Her aunt smiled, but the smile looked wary. "What exactly did they say, Az? Did they mention *branzinos* at all?"

Dragonflies, her earpiece told her helpfully. "Yes," Astrid replied in sudden remembrance. "They did. They thought I was one of those…people. Didn't I mention that earlier?"

"Maybe. There's been a lot going on."

"Of course. They *did* mention Dragonflies earlier too, because they were convinced that I was a Dragonfly in hiding, and said they were going to help me. But then today they told me that…well, that Dragonflies were shapeshifters and could take multiple forms compared to the *beini,* who could only turn into a big cat." Astrid grinned a little as if joking. "And I would think they were being ridiculous, except that a few weeks ago I saw what looked like…, um, someone changing form."

Jae was silent a moment, and Astrid waited for her to deny it all, to laugh it off. But instead she said, "Isn't it strange that we're surprised when the aliens act alien? They might look like us, Az, but they're not the same."

"Sooo…you don't think it's crazy?"

"I probably would, except I was shown a Dragonfly shapeshift myself a few weeks ago." There was a stunned silence, then Jae added, "There's a lot to talk about. I'll finish this email to Sye – that's one of the doctors who tried to see Emir Jireh two years ago – then we'll get into it."

"OK," Astrid replied meekly, thinking this was one of the strangest conversations she'd ever had…and one of the most fascinating. "Does the leadership know? 'Cos when Raka kidnapped me he said that he'd sent a lock of my hair to the colony, and they'd basically brushed him off. I reckon they're up to something."

"They're *definitely* up to something," Jae muttered, her hands freezing from where they fluttered over her little keyboard. "But maybe don't take everything Raka says as gospel. Two minutes, OK?"

"Right, right." Email first. Then Astrid could finally get those answers she was desperate for.

Two weeks later

The journey from Mahadra to the Syrenian palace had felt like an eternity. Orin knew he'd been wise to travel with the merchant caravan over the mountains, but he'd been restricted to the same achingly slow pace as the other heavy-laden wagons.

He'd also taken care to act like the others, stopping occasionally once they'd crossed over to 'sell' a few of his wares. He could have slipped away, changed into *beini* form or even just ridden his steed and left the wagon behind, but he'd kept coming up with reasons not to.

The beini is too obvious. People will remember, and everyone will definitely notice a naked man walking in the Syrenian palace. Don't leave the wagon. People will notice, and you'll get caught.

But even with accidentally-on-purpose delaying his journey, Orin had still arrived in the end. The main city of Syrene was smaller than Mahadra's capital, perhaps a little messier too. The people looked a little messier as well; their clothing style distinctly more relaxed.

There were far more females on the streets, either with their husbands or even on their own, their light headscarves tied at the back of their necks rather than modestly wrapped under their chins.

He found himself looking out for a smaller than average young woman, well-rounded and curly-haired, and with an odd brown tint to her eyes…then realised what he was doing and stopped immediately. The palace, that was his goal. That would be the most highly-guarded location as well, which could be a problem if his contact's information had been wrong.

Orin traded the wagon and mount for cash and a new barrow full of colourful silks, then trundled the barrow up to the trade entrance of the palace. Two well-armoured guards stood beside that entrance, and although their heads were covered, he could spot a fellow *beini* even from this distance. In spite of what Raka said about Alsair Benn Syrenius, the regent wasn't entirely foolish if he knew that such protection was needed. So Orin relaxed as much as he could, ignoring the guards, and waited to be greeted by the servant whose job it was to buy goods, or to reject any unnecessary purchases.

It didn't take long. "What do you have for us today, friend?"

"Fine silks from the western regions," Orin replied, modulating his voice so it sounded more like these folk.

"Western regions, is it?" the servant queried. He studied Orin's barrow curiously, but apparently he recognised the code phrase, because instead of saying the obvious, 'the western regions don't make silk', he invited Orin inside. "If you'll come with me."

Excellent.

The servant left Orin alone in a small side room along with his dubiously-sourced silks, and he didn't waste a moment. The room had a narrow balcony that opened over an alley that must be part of the inner courtyard. It also held a well-worn chair and a small table with a bowl of fresh fruit and a valise of what looked like weak wine. He considered partaking from the second, but didn't dare risk losing the time nor that the drink might be drugged.

Instead he checked that no one was watching, then stuck his head out the window to check out there too. He could see people moving about, quickly in and out of his line of sight, but no more guards.

Time to go.

Orin slipped off the loose, ornate outer robe that proclaimed him either a flamboyant rich man or a seller of fine silks, now wearing only a plain, pale tunic and trousers. Off went the turban too: he turned it inside-out so its plain underside showed, then quickly tied it back into place to cover his distinctive silver-white hair. He flexed his hands a few times, stretching his muscles, then out the window he went.

Just up above the ledge was another, higher ledge; this one running around the bulk of the whole building. If his contact's instructions had been correct, then following it to the right would lead to a rounded roof with a carved branzine weathervane.

Aha…here it was. Orin paused long enough to allow an unwary servant girl to move past below, her arms laden with cloth. Then he quietly climbed from the ledge to the roof of the building, then moved across to the next part of the palace. He followed his contact's directions to the letter, and soon enough he was in a small courtyard, one filled with fragrant plants and with a beautifully sculpted fountain in its centre. He recognised it as the twin of one in the Mahadrese palace.

Just above the courtyard was another balcony. Even from here he could see the light inside the room through the balcony doors. It was dimming low, and the scent of herbs was evident. It was clearly the emir's sickroom, but there wasn't even one single guard on this side of the room.

So there was no one to see Orin as he crept across the courtyard and then leapt up onto the balcony, pulling himself over in one easy motion even as his heart pounded madly from the adrenaline, from the risk of what he was doing.

No one called out. No one had seen him.

Then he silently pushed aside the thin curtain that veiled the room from sight, and slipped inside.

CHAPTER 14

Assassin

The room was deathly silent, with the only sounds being the faint breathing of its occupants. The two of them sat, staring at each other and at what lay between them. This wasn't the first time they'd been in such a situation. Nor the tenth, nor the fifteenth, even. But right now, it felt like life and death.

His opponent slowly reached out a hand into the space between them, closing their fingers around the slender, metallic shape. Then they moved closer, just a little closer, as if to release it again.

It was too much. He'd sworn he wouldn't do it; he'd bitten his tongue as if that would hold him back. But suddenly he burst out, "Not there, Astrid! You'll lose the game."

She stopped mid-movement, the spear piece almost touching the board. "Benn! You promised you'd stop telling me when you're about to win! How can we have a proper game with you playing both sides?" Her mouth curved in a half smile. "Besides, I think this is a really good move."

Benn huffed out a breath, unable to suppress his answering smile. Sure, Syrene was probably months away from war. Sure, Emir Jireh might have improved over the last fortnight since he'd been given Earther medicine, but he was still well away from being able to reclaim his rule. And sure, Palos was doing his best to turn everyone against Benn, as punishment for bringing in an 'outsider' – and a female at that.

But today, as Benn taught the Earther Astrid Townsend how to play Chase the Castle, none of that seemed to matter, because he was having fun. "It's not a good move," he countered. "If you do it, you'll-"

"Shhh!"

"You'll lose a piece then-"

"Shshshshhhhh!" Astrid accompanied that strange noise with a wave of both hands, as if she wanted to slap them over his mouth. "I've decided on this move. I want to make it, and I want you to play like you normally would, without trying to let me win, OK? If I lose, I lose honestly. And if I win, I win honestly. Is that clear?"

This time Benn was startled into silence, and even she looked surprised by her reaction. "I'm finally understanding how Raka felt, and why he made me play so many games," she added dryly, her pretty brown eyes wrinkling with humour. "It's so *annoying* when you let me win. But unlike when I played him, you actually give me tips."

"But I don't want you to feel bad," he argued, not for the first time. "You might be disheartened." And frankly, he thought it could be quite some time before Astrid won without his input. Chase the Castle wasn't an easy game, and while it had some similarities to the Earther game of chiss, it was different enough that all her strategies didn't seem to work.

And that was assuming that she was any good at chiss, anyway. Benn assumed that she must be, or else Raka wouldn't have tried to play with her so many times. He recalled some heated games from years before when Raka had visited their court. He hadn't been a gracious loser.

That was the complete opposite of Astrid, who seemed to *want* to lose. She triumphantly slapped her spear piece down in exactly the wrong place. "Now make your move, and don't you dare patronise me and purposely leave that piece uncaptured," she ordered.

Benn sighed, because he'd have to capture that piece to play with integrity, and it seemed she hadn't thought ahead to the long-term outcome, and he genuinely didn't want her to lose heart. Then he grinned and captured it anyway, because it was just a game…and because he liked winning. "Now look how close I am to your shield piece," he couldn't help telling her. "Two moves and you lose."

"Or two moves and *you* lose," she countered. Then she picked up a small, unimportant piece from the side of her board and moved it forward. "Ha."

"Ha to you," he retorted, preparing to explain in detail why she'd made the wrong move. But when he went to do so, he realised something. "Oh."

"Yes, *oh*," Astrid mimicked. She sat back in her place on the carpeted floor, looking extremely pleased with herself. Her clothing was much the same as when she'd arrived, and her faded blueish hair was still covered by a light scarf, as was tradition in this area. But in spite of those slightly alien features, she still looked like she belonged here. "What were you saying about a bad move?"

"But…" Benn studied the board, shaking his head in genuine amusement. "You've as good as won. I mean, you *haven't* won…but I can't win either now. And all with an *esira* piece. Those are never good for anything, and you've just put it in exactly the right place so that I can't do anything. The raphanta or spear pieces, sure. Maybe even a *beini*. But this…I did not see coming."

"That's exactly why it's so brilliant," Astrid said gleefully, her smile having widened into a beam. "And while I'd prefer to call that piece a *server* rather than the other word, do you concede the game to me?"

"Of course I do," he agreed, still in disbelief. "I guess you want your prize now."

Her smirk told the whole story. "Come on, then. Let's go visit the emir, and you can tell him exactly how fabulous and wonderful humans are, and that once he's better you're coming to visit us on Earth." She paused. "Assuming I've gone back to Earth too, and nothing else weird happens to stop me. Do you think Raka knows I'm here by now?"

Benn pushed himself to his feet, then reached out to help Astrid up. Her hand was both soft and firm in his, the sort of hand that had done hard work…but not too much. Sort of like his. And like every time they touched, even that brief contact made his cheeks warm and his breath catch in his throat. She didn't seem to notice, because she never did.

So he cleared his throat, and gestured towards the door. "Leave the board. We can come back to it again, if you like."

"You didn't answer my question."

"Because you wouldn't like the answer," Benn countered. "It's the same as I told you last time you asked. Yes, Raka probably knows you're here, because there's certainly a spy somewhere in this court telling him things. And no, my spy doesn't know who the other spy is. But you're safe here, Astrid, I promise. As safe as I am." He carefully didn't mention the several failed assassination attempts against himself that had prompted him to upgrade all of his closest guards to *beini*. It was just a shame he had too much character to try the same in return.

Astrid made a very unladylike noise of scorn, one that didn't need translation. "What we need," she announced as they walked down the hall leading from his rooms to his stepfather's, "is for Raka to drop dead."

Benn choked a little, almost missing a step. It was too close to what he'd just been thinking. Surely the Earthers didn't have some method of reading minds? "What? An assassination?"

"No, I meant some kind of divine intervention," she said, sounding surprised. "Only bad people arrange assassinations, Benn. Good people just hope their enemy chokes on a chicken bone or falls off a bridge."

He went silent for a few moments. "A chek-hen bone? Is that like a gon?"

Astrid sputtered out laughter. "No, it is *not* like a gun, you doofus. It's food! Well, sometimes. By the time you get to eating it, it's definitely food."

"And what's a doofus?" Benn teased. "This word doesn't translate, so it must mean, 'too wonderful to be described', yes?"

Benn was having so much fun, was so focused on his companion, that at first he didn't notice what was wrong. He walked right through those doors and into the entry section of Jireh's rooms, loud enough to alert him of visitors, before realising that the guards had been only outside the room, not inside. And there, just through the beaded curtain that marked off the sleeping area, he could make out a pale shape over the bed – that was *not* Merima.

With his breath suddenly caught in his throat, Benn lifted one hand to part the curtain. The unfamiliar male turned to stare at him… with his hand reached out towards the emir.

The stranger definitely didn't belong there.

Astrid stood a little behind Benn, but she could clearly see over his shoulder to where a strange man stood over Emir Jireh's bed. No, not strange – that face was familiar even with his hair covered, even in this wrong location.

The next few seconds seemed to take place in slow motion. That face connected in her memory with one in Raka's palace that had looked at her many times with disdain – that had also been at the tower window – and suddenly it felt like there was no air in the room, and her stomach twisted in fear. Next moment she was holding the stun gun she'd taken to carrying around, the one she'd quietly borrowed from Jae, and she lifted it towards Raka's brother and pulled the trigger.

Zzzt.

Suddenly he was on the floor and someone was saying something beside her, but she couldn't hear over the roaring sound in her ears. The villain was stirring on the ground, so she pointed the stun gun at him again and moved to pull the trigger – but then someone was knocking her hand away, and it was Benn.

"Astrid, please!" he was pleading. "Don't kill him! We need him!"

She blinked at him, then looked again at the man lying on the floor. He was moving a little, and all she could think of was how he'd looked when he'd pushed her out of the window. *Beini.* She knew what that meant now.

But then she looked up and saw Emir Jireh propped up in his bed, his pale face etched with horrified lines, and saw the matching expression on Benn's own face. It almost made her feel guilty… almost, but not quite.

"I won't shoot unless you try to move," Astrid told Orin the Blessed. Then to Benn she said a little defensively, "This man tried to kill me! He's a bad, bad, bad…*bad* man. What do you mean, you need him? I bet he's here to kill the emir too!" Also, she was holding a stunner rather than a 'gon', so couldn't have caused real damage unless she literally hit him with it. But she was still shaking, her heart was racing, and nothing seemed to make sense.

The probable-assassin opened his eyes, blinking vaguely, then an expression of distaste came over him as he took her in. "Typical Earther," he muttered, his words slurred. "Cheat."

Ooh, that was too much! "Me, a cheat? You're the one who kept me unconscious when you dragged me back to Mahadra, weren't you?" she demanded. "For your crazy brother to play games with, then try to punish for someone else's imaginary crime?"

Orin tried to get up, and *oops* off went the trigger again. This time when the man slumped to the floor, his eyes stayed closed.

There was a silence from the appalled-looking emir, who'd only just become well enough to sit up now he'd been on antibiotics – hence Benn relaxing enough to play games with Astrid.

As for Benn, he cleared his throat. "Are you finished, Astrid?

Or would you like to kick Orin a couple of times before you listen to me?"

"Is that an option?" she muttered. Then feeling a little ashamed – because of their reaction only, not because it wasn't the right thing to do – she lowered the stunner. "He's just sleeping," she explained defensively. "But seriously, this is a terrible man. He hates Earthers, and he tried to kill me! He kidnapped me, too."

"She already said that," the emir murmured. "She does not listen well, does she?"

"Sorry," Astrid said again, "but it's worth saying twice, because you weren't listening the first time. He could have killed you too, Your Magnificence! That's probably what he's here to do."

"Actually," Benn began. "He's my-"

"Nephew," Emir Jireh cut in. "My nephew, and I intend him to be my heir. And yes, he was here to kill me..." Astrid's head just about imploded, until he added, "...or so his brother thinks. Raka sent him here to assassinate both Benn and I, not realising that Orin has been providing us information for many, many years. He sees that his brother is not a good man, you understand."

"Oh." Astrid's shoulders slumped, and she looked across to Benn, who was watching her with a wary expression. "But...did you know what he did to me? All those things I just said – they're true! But... but I can't believe he's your spy." Because she really, really wanted to kick him, unconscious or not.

"Astrid," Benn began cautiously. "It's...complicated."

"How is it complicated?!"

Benn watched Astrid warily, feeling his heart sink. He thought that somehow he'd avoid this conversation, because he'd known ever since she'd told him about Raka's awful brother, that she wouldn't understand. Based on her reaction now, he'd been right.

He glanced down at the prone man on the floor beside him, then at his stepfather, who wore a familiar long-suffering expression. "Orin's life is in danger too," he replied finally. "He did tell me he was coming, but I thought it wouldn't be yet, and the timing...it wasn't so good." In fact, when he'd walked into the room and had seen a turbaned man sitting over the bed, he hadn't recognised him at first.

"As in, you didn't expect me to be standing there with a stun-gun when he showed up," Astrid countered. She still held the object in one hand, although it was pointed at the floor now. She scrubbed a hand wearily over her face as if it would make Orin disappear. "You know what? I'm not happy, but this is nothing to do with me. This is your palace, and your stepfather, and your possible assassination. So if you want to deal with this guy, then that's up to you, and you don't have to explain anything to me."

"Really?" Benn asked, genuinely surprised. "I didn't think you'd be so…accepting."

Her teeth made a sort of grinding noise, but he couldn't see her expression as it was half hidden under her hand. Then she turned away, her head ducked so that the trailing end of her scarf covered her face too. "I'm going to see my aunt," she muttered. "Tell your friend to stay away from me, or he'll be sorry."

Then Astrid stomped out of the room – quite angry footsteps for someone who supposedly didn't need an explanation, Benn thought. There were a few moments of silence, interrupted by a slight snore from Orin, then Benn said, "I'm guessing that she really wasn't accepting after all, was she?"

Emir Jireh made a scoffing noise, the same tone he'd use whenever some fool bet on the wrong raphanta. "I thought you were smarter than that, boy. Whenever a female says something is acceptable without a proper explanation, you should worry." He tried to sit up further in bed, but seemed to tire. "Help me up, will you?"

Benn did so, feeling a wash of some kind of emotion come over him. Relief, perhaps; that his stepfather had come so far after only two weeks of taking *antee-beeoteeks*. Or something. He wasn't quite up and about yet – and his face was still pale, and his grey-blue beard untrimmed – but this was the longest conversation they'd had in months. More importantly, he'd lost that horrible hoarse rattle from what Ms Jae had called 'a horrendous, long-running chest infection'.

"I should probably help Orin up too," Benn murmured. "He must be uncomfortable."

"Bah," Jireh said dismissively. "He's a strong young man, and a *beini* at that. He'll be fine. Besides, from what I hear he probably deserves it."

Benn privately agreed, although he also understood what (and who) had driven a lot of Orin's decisions. "I should speak to Astrid though," he said. "Make sure she understands the discretion needed. Although with this palace being what it is, no doubt the secret won't stay that way. It's as poorly sealed as a cracked vase."

"No progress on finding our chatty little bird?"

"Raka's spy?" Benn shook his head. "A few dead ends only. But that's not the worst of our problems." He paused, debating whether to mention his recent troubles when the emir had only just properly awoken, and finally said, "Palos is displeased with my recent choices, sir. No doubt he will tell you about it when he next visits." He gestured at Orin once more. "And no doubt he'll have an opinion on this one too."

"Bah," Jireh said again. "Let me handle my old friend, Benn. It's probably time he learned about this one's involvement anyway. He can blame me for failing to tell him, if he must." He paused. "Except… we shall keep quiet about this one a little longer, I think. Palos doesn't need to know everything all the time, or he'll start to think he's in charge."

Benn barely held back a matching scoff – 'start to think'? – but instead nodded. "Shall I call for Merima, then? Or Neoli?"

Jireh shook his head thoughtfully. "I think we shall keep this just between the two of us for now, my Benn. Now you go and speak to your lady before she blurts it out all through the palace."

He nodded distractedly. "Yes. Astrid."

"What, you're not going to protest that she isn't your lady?"

Realising what he'd said, Benn's eyebrows shot up even as he felt his ears heat with embarrassment. "I'm going now," he said again. Then he stepped over the still-unconscious Orin, and left the room amid Jireh's laughter.

Outside Jireh's room were two of his usual guards, one of whom was also a *beini*. The *beini* shot to attention when he saw Benn. "Is all well, Your Excellency? We heard discussion, but it didn't seem that our attention was needed."

"Is that so?" Benn asked dryly. "I understood there should also be a guard inside the room, not just outside." Not that Benn was sorry on this occasion, because it would have been awkward for anyone else to have found Orin, but it didn't bode well for Jireh's sickroom to be so poorly guarded that Orin had entered through the balcony.

The guard seemed lost for a response. "We were instructed to guard outside the room, Your Excellency. Noble advisor Palos stated that our presence would be too much for His Magnificence."

Palos. Benn barely kept himself from rolling his eyes. At least on this occasion the advisor's highhandedness had worked out well. "I see. In that case, nobody should go in for the next hour or so, not even his nurse. The emir is…resting." And Benn himself would need to be back within fifteen minutes, just to make sure.

He headed to the rooms they'd gifted the two Earthers, and found both of them in the suite's parlour. Jae had an area designated as her 'clinic', but it was currently empty as no one was being allowed into the palace for medical treatment – also thanks to Palos. Astrid was sitting in one of the wicker-and-cloth couches, and her eyes were reddened as though from crying. Even though he'd called out to warn of his approach, she still jolted at his entry then looked away.

"Hello, Ms Jae," Benn said politely in the Earther manner. "How has your morning been?"

The older woman glanced across at her silent niece, then back at him. "Adequate, thank you. But I did have the testing results come in on that medication the emir was receiving, the one he had daily."

Benn's interest piqued. "Oh?" Merima hadn't given the emir Palos' concoction since the day Benn had told her to stop, and since then Jireh had only improved in health. While Benn (mostly) respected Palos, he had to wonder…

"The ingredients appear to be quite normal for this part of the world," Jae replied, "with a good portion of nirixa leaf, probably for his breathing. It has some similar qualities to *tee-tree* from Earth, and isn't toxic unless it's taken in large quantities. I understand it can cause hallucinations." She shrugged. "It certainly has limited effectiveness, though. It never would have done what was needed."

"I see," Benn said thoughtfully. "Besides the nirixa leaf, did you notice anything unusual?"

Jae shook her head. "No, not at all. But I'm not an expert on your medicines, only our own."

Well, that cleared Palos at least. Benn had hated to think it, but somewhere at the back of his mind had been the fear that the old man had grown so comfortable with his position of power – second-in-charge over Syrene – that he'd wanted to step up to first-in-charge, and had tried to remove Jireh to get that result.

It had clearly been a silly, fear-driven thought, because Palos had known Jireh since boyhood and was generally a moral man, as far as Benn knew, although stubborn. Stubborn enough to insist on an old-wives' tea to treat a dying man.

Not dying anymore, though. Jireh was sitting up and talking, thank the Maker, even though he was currently in his room alone with a sort-of assassin from Mahadra.

On that subject... "Astrid," Benn said carefully, "might we speak in private for a few minutes?"

She'd been silent up 'til now, just sitting in that seat with the *stunnah* still in one hand, but now she looked up at him and nodded. "Come into my room."

Even though he knew they were preparing for a difficult conversation, Benn still felt his ears heat a little. A Syrenian girl would *never* invite a non-related male into her room, and an honourable Syrenian man would never accept...but then Astrid likely didn't even realise her misstep. "How about the balcony?" he suggested instead.

Ten minutes later, after Astrid had listened to Benn explain exactly why he'd joined forces with the second-worst man she knew, she politely assured him that there were no hard feelings. "I'm a guest here," she told him. "If you say that he won't hurt me, then I'll believe you. But don't expect me to like him."

"Of course," Benn replied, almost stammering in what looked like relief. "You don't even have to see him again, just-"

"Don't tell anyone he's here," Astrid finished flatly. "You did say that." About ten or fifteen times.

Benn nodded. "I'd better go. I said I wouldn't leave Orin alone for long – and we have plans to make."

She nodded. "That's fine. So do I."

"Oh?"

"Going home, of course." She shrugged a shoulder. "I've started to think of this as an adventure, and it is, a little. But mostly it's just dangerous, and my family and friends will be worried. Besides, we brought Aunt Jae here to help your uncle. You don't need me anymore."

"Oh," he said again. "Of course. Well...I'd better go, and I'll...I'll call for you once it's safe to visit again."

"Of course," Astrid echoed politely. He left – finally – and she slumped back on the balcony bench where they'd been speaking, her chest feeling strangely tight. *I'll call for you.* Was that the Tyger version of 'I'll call you'? Probably, she mused, but that wasn't even the worst of what had been bothering her.

She'd been honest with Benn. She *had* made the mistake of treating this whole thing – from meeting Jaz and Vuyani all the way to this palace – as some kind of adventure-holiday, when it wasn't. Not at all. It had been a diplomatic visit gone wrong, followed by escape from captivity then living in disguise while unable to speak the language, until luck had saved her.

It was only the last few weeks that had been enjoyable, where she'd been able to ignore her own situation and the volatility of the local politics. And…she'd come to value her friendship with Benn, and she thought he probably valued it too. But not enough to risk his 'spy' on that friendship, even when he knew exactly how she felt about that spy.

Benn had explained very, very quietly that their 'new visitor' was in a dangerous situation back home, and he might look like he had freedom to choose, but actually he was at constant risk of someone else (e.g. Raka) becoming displeased and giving him the chop, because even though he wasn't legitimate, he was still in line for both thrones. And it was safer for the visitor to hold himself back and act unpleasant, because as long as he had no charm, then Raka would see him as less of a threat.

And as for the kidnapping? Well, Benn had said the visitor had woken up to find his precious sister held in a box and about to be stolen away from home, right when she was meant to be safely back in the women's quarters in the palace. Benn didn't approve of how Astrid had been treated, he'd said hastily, but he did understand some of the motivation; whether the sister had gone willingly or not.

Benn hadn't had an answer for the 'push out the window' thing, and Astrid hadn't tried to get one. Sure, Orin the Horrible would have some logical motivation for his behaviour – in his mind, anyway – but she still hated him. He'd played a big part in some of the worst, most terrifying times of her life, and she wouldn't forget that.

And while she really, really understood why Benn needed a contact in Raka's court, she couldn't help being disappointed that it was someone so awful. She still remembered the first time she'd seen Orin, and how she hadn't known his name, but he'd looked at her like she was dog poop on a clean carpet.

Humph.

Astrid got up and stomped back into the room where Jae still sat. Her aunt looked up at her, one eyebrow raised under her reading glasses. "Did you two have a spat?"

Astrid hadn't mentioned the horrible visitor they'd just had, so Jae didn't know about Orin. "Not really. I'm just…" She sighed heavily. "…I'm really ready to go home. Have you heard back from the colony yet about when they can take me?" While initially they'd been wary of giving information, what with Raka claiming the Earth leaders hadn't cared to trade her back, in the end it had been the logical solution. They'd contacted the colony, said that they had a human who was in danger and needed to go home, and were waiting for final instructions.

"Actually, I have received a message, but I haven't checked it yet." Jae put down what looked like a syringe and a piece of sponge, then took off her gloves and turned back to her small screen. "Oh. It's not from Anton. It's from Walt, the second-in-charge. *Oh.*"

"What is it?" Astrid moved to look over Jae's shoulder then quickly scanned the written message. "Oh shoot, Anton had a heart attack? It must've been a bad one if he and Eirene have gone back to Earth for his treatment." She frowned. "They've had to put their ambrilene investigation on hold too. That's not good. And this is really selfish, but what does it mean for me? For us?"

"Look at the bottom of the message. It says I should get someone at the mining station to fly you to the colony, and they'll cover the fuel." Jae glanced back at Astrid. "Well? I'll get in touch, and you can go tomorrow, if they're ready." She paused thoughtfully. "And when you do get back home, make sure you don't let the ambrilene situation get forgotten. Lives depend on it."

Astrid's shoulders slumped. She'd forgotten that too, briefly. *Oh, and don't forget to stop Earth profiting from mass murder.* "I know." She paused. "If it's too hard for someone to fly me up, I suppose I could take a drone."

Jae gave her a disbelieving look. "You mean fly yourself up in a crate, Az? Essentially post yourself just to save someone a little fuel? Even if that couldn't go wrong in a dozen ways, you're the last person to willingly climb into a box. You hate small spaces."

"I know," Astrid said again, a little more cheerfully this time. The thought of jumping into one of those programmable boxes had occurred to her more than once, especially with how difficult it could be to arrange a proper flight home. But she was more than grateful that Jae had dismissed the idea – because she really did hate small spaces.

Orin sat up against the side of the emir's bed, sipping at a cup of lukewarm herbal tea. His head was spinning, and his whole body felt weak from being shot with that Earther device. While he'd handled one himself before, it was the first time it had been turned on him, and he didn't like it at all.

Across from him, his uncle and step-cousin sat on a long, low couch. The emir was pale from the exertion of getting out of bed, but looked rather pleased with himself for doing so. Benn had been quiet when he'd returned to the room, but still watched Orin with a bemused expression.

"Just so you know," Orin said into the silence, "she caught me by surprise. Otherwise I would never have allowed myself to be taken down by a mere female, and an alien at that." It had been nagging at him ever since he'd woken and realised what had happened. How unexpected…and how *embarrassing*.

Jireh raised an eyebrow. "Ah, you are still young, nephew. You'll realise in time that even the strongest of us can be laid low by small, weak things. I suspect arrogance will be Raka's downfall, just like it was your father's. Don't let it be yours as well."

Emir Mavet of Mahadra – Jireh's brother – had been killed several years earlier at a private dinner by an elderly nobleman with an eating knife. An *eating* knife, and the nobleman had acted so quickly that even the nearest guards hadn't reacted in time. The guards had been executed for their failure, of course, and the nobleman had promptly had a heart attack as a result of the dramatics.

The thing was, Mavet had been in dispute with this nobleman for some time over the boundaries of their land, and in the end he'd just confiscated the whole lot. He'd invited the man to dinner to tell him so, apparently not considering the outcome. Arrogant indeed – and now dead.

Orin wanted to argue that he wasn't like his father or brother, but he was used to shutting his mouth and keeping his true opinions to himself. He did so now.

Across the room, Benn burst out, "Did you really push her out of a window?"

Orin blinked at him. The regent was only a couple of years younger than he was, but he seemed so…soft. So *thoughtful.* "I presume you mean the Earther girl who shot me just now."

"Unless there's anyone else that could apply to?"

Orin almost smirked at that; the idea that there was a collection of women that he'd pushed out of windows. As for the question itself – it wasn't so simple, and he wasn't used to explaining himself. "No other girls," he replied. "And yes, I did."

There was a long silence broken by a sharp intake of breath from Benn.

Emir Jireh just looked at Orin. "I presume there's more to that story than you losing your temper with an alien, for such a thing wouldn't be in line with the man I expect you to be."

Of course there was. For the most part, Orin never did anything without a reason. In this case he could see they truly expected an answer. And he really, really wanted to be the man Jireh thought he was. For these last few years with their secretive, so-brief conversations, he'd almost felt valued. Not just a surly, blessed royal bastard, but perhaps a person of true importance.

So even though he wasn't in the habit of explaining himself, he said, "My brother had lost patience with the Earthers. They had no intention of trading to get the girl back, nor of returning our own royal sister. He was intending to give her the same punishment that our father gave his own sister when she took a lover, although I do not believe he told her as much. She would have fought more, otherwise."

Orin saw the understanding dawn on their faces. It was well known in both city-states that a generation earlier, Lady Elysha of Mahadra had been walled into a tower and left without food and water until she no longer had need for either.

"While I have no love for Earthers, I saw no need for such cruelty," he continued. "Raka might have changed his mind a few weeks later – might have decided he wished for an alien concubine or even a ridiculous games-companion once more – but it would've been too late." He shrugged a shoulder. "Out the window, her chances of survival were reasonable. It was a decent drop, but the water was deep and led straight out of the city. I also told Raka that I'd heard her skull crack, so he already believed her dead."

Benn's lips tightened. "But she could've really died."

"But if I hadn't pushed her then, she *definitely* would have died," Orin countered. "There were already men coming to seal up the window, then the door. It had to be then." He sighed heavily, finally showing some of his roiling emotions. "But enough about the alien girl. I'm glad she didn't die, but if she tells of my friendship with you, then I'll regret my kindness. My brother ordered me to kill the two of you, and not to return until I've done so. So either I find some way to pretend such a feat, or I show my true allegiance and never return home. I don't have long to decide, as you know there's someone here relaying information to Raka by one of those infernal Earther devices."

"Mm, those brilliant devices which kept us in contact," Benn mused, but he didn't sound angry anymore, instead thoughtful. "You are indeed in a difficult situation. And was it a mere month ago that Raka sent you to the Earther colony in *beini* form? Another difficult situation. Perhaps he suspects you're no longer loyal, and wishes to have others kill you instead."

Orin had considered such a thing himself, but now he shook his head. "Raka has been putting me in dangerous situations ever since I was a child," he said bluntly. "He does it to confirm my inferior position. It would pay for me to be careful with my next steps, but at this point I do not believe he suspects me anymore than he suspects everyone." Because Raka did suspect everyone, and no one. Jireh was right; Raka *was* arrogant.

"And you are his heir," Jireh said flatly. "Mavet may have passed a law stating that you could never rule Mahadra, even if there were no others, but such things can be overturned." He looked at Orin intently. "As you know, I would choose for you to rule Syrene before I'd ever allow Raka to do so. He cares for no one but himself. But if you were to die, I would name Benn as my true heir, never mind what the populace thinks."

Benn's mouth twisted in a rueful smile. "As you know, I want to rule as much as the Syrenian people want me to. That is to say, not at all."

Basically, Orin was being offered a throne. He'd known this offer might come, and now it had, he didn't know what to do with it. Heir to Syrene...after Raka, which pretty much meant never. But a pang of guilt twisted his gut as he remembered that *other* important piece of information that needed to be shared. "Speaking of heirs," he said quietly, "Raka has an unborn child running around somewhere in the mountains. Attached to an escaped *esira*."

Jireh made a displeased sound. He'd been more than clear how he felt about owning another person – it was one of the reasons he and Mavet had fallen out. That, and the fact Mavet had executed their sister Elysha all those years ago. The betrothal between Raka and Iryz had been a desperate attempt to make peace between the two angry royal brothers.

But Benn just raised an eyebrow. "And would you have anything to do with this escaped *esira*, friend?"

"If I did," Orin replied honestly, "then I'd be as dead as if I'd committed treason. Raka is obsessive about his…special females, right up until they become with child. This one's a Dragonfly, though." He grinned, just a little. "I'd considered bringing her here, but didn't think she'd trust me if I made the offer. I let her slip away on her own instead. I don't think Raka knew she could change forms. *I* didn't know."

The other two men's eyebrows shot up. He'd clearly surprised them at last.

"Speaking of Dragonflies," Jireh said thoughtfully, "there was a good man who worked in the stables. Malchiel. He was clever with brown raphantas too, but he left five years ago for Mahadra, something to do with family. If Mahadra no longer welcomes his kind as you tell me, then perhaps he's returned. Do you know of him, Benn?"

There was a long, awkward silence, and Orin looked to Benn expectantly. If Jireh had been so ill that he'd missed the mass evacuation and 'collection' of the Dragonflies, then Orin definitely wasn't going to explain it. From what he'd heard, Syrene wasn't currently much more welcoming than Mahadra.

Benn cleared his throat, grimacing. "That is one thing we do need to discuss, sir. Do you recall how years ago when the Earthers first approached us, they wished to trade a certain substance…?"

CHAPTER 15
Preparations

Two days later Jae stood at the edge of the same field she'd arrived at weeks before, waving as Astrid disappeared into the shuttle that would take her straight back to the portal. They'd decided in the end that secrecy had made the danger worse – no one had known about Astrid, so terrible things had happened.

So this time they'd told everyone at both the colony and mines about her, about what had happened, and about how she'd be returning and going straight back through the portal to her brother. They'd also sent her off with a bunch of video evidence of the Dragonfly settlements, and signed affidavits about Portal-co's weapons-dealing and grave-robbing, since the ambrilene and weapons sales had to stop *now*. As for the borrowed Lady Tamzyn…yeah, that'd take some explaining, and Jae wasn't going to be the one to do it.

Next to Jae stood the young regent, Benn. He watched Astrid go with what looked like resignation. He and her niece had seemed to hit it off, right up until something had happened a couple of days earlier. They'd clearly argued (even though Astrid had denied it) then everything else had fallen to pieces, and they'd been merely polite around each other whenever Astrid emerged from her rooms, which hadn't been often.

"It's good she's gone back," Benn said from beside Jae, as if he'd been thinking on the same subject. "I think she missed her home."

"Mmm," Jae half-agreed. She gave the young man a sidelong glance. His resigned expression had changed to what genuinely looked like disappointment, and she couldn't help saying, "Will you be coming to visit Earth when your stepfather retakes his position, Your Excellency? He seems to grow stronger by the day."

Benn perked up just a little. "I'd like to," he admitted. "But I thought it would be difficult to be enter Earth for political reasons, for fear of offending Raka. Do you think I could?"

Jae shrugged. "There's no harm in trying."

Emir Jireh sat in a chair on his balcony, behind a large, sheer curtain that hid his exact location but didn't block out all that marvellous light. He felt like a plant that had been stuck under a basket for too long – shrivelled, pale and a bit desperate for air and water. But there was so much to think about.

For so long he'd been unable to do his duties, and it irked him. His people had suffered. Not the majority of them; but those apparently weaker minorities. The Dragonflies had somehow disappeared from Syrene, and it shouldn't have happened. Even worse, his nephew told tale of the Mahadrese Dragonflies vanishing too – with many of them reported to be enslaved in Raka's mines in the northeast. Worst of all, the Earthers had been robbing graves, and might not even know it…

"Curse it all," he muttered to himself. "Laws are supposed to stop this sort of thing." He thought again of Malchiel, that stableman who'd had so many interesting ideas, right up 'til he'd moved to Mahadra to be with family. He'd had a couple of daughters, was that the case? Who knew. He might be dead now, his unidentifiable remains traded to the aliens in exchange for weapons strong enough to breach the mountains. "Curse it all," he said again, because what else was there to say?

In the room behind him he heard someone new approach – the low hum of voices, then a louder, most distinctive man's voice, aged but not weak. "Don't be ridiculous, Esan! I will speak to His Magnificence, and you shall not stop me!"

Jireh almost swore again, but instead closed his eyes briefly and took a deep, calming breath. Could he pretend to be sleeping? Tempting, but it wouldn't fix their true problem. He needed to speak with his oldest, most respected advisor too, and it wouldn't be an easy conversation. *Sigh.* "I'm out here."

There was the sound of heavy footsteps, then Palos stepped into view. He looked just the same as when Jireh had last seen him – perhaps his hair was a little ruffled, but otherwise the man looked just as he always had for the last forty years, since Jireh was a boy. According to Benn, he hadn't changed his thinking a whit either. His heavy eyebrows shot up in surprise. "Your Magnificence! Are you well enough to be up?"

"Absolutely," Jireh replied a little dryly. "Earther medicine is almost like sorcery, it's that effective. What a shame we didn't use it two years ago when I first grew ill." It had started with a nasty cough that just hadn't gone away, then he'd grown weaker and weaker, with odd, confused spells where he wouldn't know what day it was, and he'd seen things that weren't there. It had been an ugly time. Ugly, and too long, but now his mind felt clear.

His comment was intended to bring about a little guilt, but judging by Palos' expression, it had failed. "You shouldn't have needed to bring in that alien muck," Palos retorted with dignity. "Simple, healthy Syrenian recipes should have been more than enough-"

"But they weren't," Jireh cut in. "And-" *I understand you may have sent the Earthers away last time,* he wanted to say, but the older man spoke over him, his eyes bulging with fervour.

"They weren't, because you were being sabotaged! We have proof!"

Jireh just stared at his advisor for long moments. Was he trying to deflect from the fact he'd given his emir inadequate medicine for years, or was he serious? Or both? "Sabotage?"

Palos leaned forward, his expression intent. "There were the same ingredients in the medicine, Your Magnificence, but I just found out that the quantities were changed. Any fool knows that too much nirixa leaf is as good as poison." His face creased almost as if he wanted to cry, but that didn't last. "Poison!"

"I…see." Jireh glanced down at his hands where they lay in his lap; looking far too frail for a man of fifty. Then he glanced over the balcony into the palace, full of his subjects who loved him…except for those who didn't. But who were they? "Do you have any idea who might have done such a thing?"

"We've got more than that. We've got a confession!" Palos nodded once, sharply, as if agreeing with whatever he was about to say.

"Who?"

"One of the few people who'd be in a position to regularly change your doses. But it was her son that's in the pay of Mahadra. He was behind all of it, it seems."

Palos didn't even have to say the names for Jireh to know who he was talking about. His breath seemed to catch in his throat. "No. Not Neoli. Not Merima." He'd known them both for his entire life. They weren't close, but they were loyal. He'd *thought* they were loyal. "And you've got proof?"

"Of course I have proof," Palos replied solemnly. "The *beini* has disappeared, no doubt because he knew he'd be arrested. The old woman is in the cells even now."

Merima in the cells. Oh, *curse it all*. This day just got exponentially worse.

Syrene, near the Kabeer Mountains

At the outskirts of the city, a small group of merchant caravans trailed their way northwest towards the mountains, heading back to Mahadra. Orin trailed near the back of the group, his turban low over his face and his single barrow full of just enough Syrenian goods that he'd fit in with the others.

His heart was heavy with what lay ahead of him, but he'd steeled himself for what he was about to do. He'd spoken with his uncle at length, and out of the few choices available, he'd taken what seemed the bravest route. Well…almost the bravest. He still didn't have it in him to just kill Raka, which would solve a few problems and create just as many. Besides, he didn't hate his brother that much.

The landscape changed from dirt to rock, scattered with a few stubborn, spindly trees. Occasionally he'd spy an animal form quietly moving about in the distance, but the few hartdeir he'd seen had been grey rather than red-brown. The Dragonfly girl was gone, he knew. Perhaps he'd never find out if she'd made it or not.

But once they were into the mountains, Orin drew back from the others and left his temporary belongings at the side of the road. He stripped down, tied a fine cloth around his neck, then changed to *beini* form. He had to get to Mahadra as fast as possible, even faster than any of Raka's spies could find out that he'd been and gone, and these merchants just couldn't move quickly enough.

He bolted.

Not far from that very point, but unbeknownst to Orin, a small, sturdy hartdeir drank from a quiet stream. Behind it, a trio of long, slender-bodied praccats crept up, aiming for its ankles. Suddenly the hartdeir's head rippled and changed, then it turned on the attackers with a snarl. It was now the same type of creature, but much, much larger. It lunged, and the smaller predators squealed and vanished into the undergrowth.

Two seconds passed, then five, then the shapeshifter's head relaxed back into the original form. *Cowardly praccats,* Chay thought grimly. But cowardly or not, they'd have killed her if she'd not quickly changed. It was just a shame she couldn't take a winged form and just fly to Syrene's capital, since the local people would know at once that she was a Dragonfly and would surely target her. Right now those locals were just as much danger to her as any pack of praccats. Such a shame, because she'd spent much of her youth in the capital, and had many good memories.

How things had changed.

For a moment she wondered if she'd made a mistake listening to the *beini* and fleeing like she had, but then immediately dismissed that thought. Even if he'd lied about what happened to the other servant and about her own danger, she'd still been a slave. It had been that way for so long she'd almost forgotten it wasn't who she really was – an unheard, useful object rather than a person.

For those three years in Raka's control she'd been too afraid to even try to escape, knowing she was unlikely to make it out of Mahadra alive, even in a winged form. She'd been convinced that the Mahadrese would shoot her down, and maybe they would have. And where would she have gone? Her family was all dead. But either way, she knew Raka had only let her live because he'd believed she couldn't shape-shift.

Anyway, there was no going back now. There was only forward… for her and her baby. Chay resolved in that moment that she'd never get caught. She would make it to the city, and she would start again.

She had to.

Mahadra

"You'd better have good news for me."

Emir Raka stood in his otherwise empty inner chamber. All the guards were outside, stationed behind walls too thick for their words to be heard through, but in truth Raka didn't need the guards. General

Naim knew well that if something happened to the emir inside these chambers, he wouldn't be walking out either.

Naim pushed back the mix of fear and irritation that all these meetings brought. The emir had such high expectations, at times unreasonably so. But today... "The Earthers' new leader has offered us a good deal for the precious gems and branzine," he replied calmly. "Enough to arm another hundred men, or for one distance *cannon.*" The Earther word didn't translate into their own language, but they now knew well what force these weapons had. Enough to break mountains, almost. Enough to defeat cities.

Raka studied him with narrowed eyes. "And this is good news? It's half what we asked for!"

"And still a hundred times what the Syrenians have," the general pointed out. "We don't need to destroy them, Your Magnificence, merely force them to surrender. That way you can take the throne, and not have to rebuild their society as well."

Raka's expression didn't change, but Naim knew by his silence that he was considering the idea. "And your spy amongst the Earthers?"

"They say that the new leader is foolish and malleable. The last one had an unfortunate stubborn streak, but the spy says that we're still unlikely to get more than weapons for a hundred soldiers this time."

"Hmm." Raka turned away, lifting one hand to stroke his clean-shaven chin. "I need time to think on this. We've had no word yet from the *beini* in Syrene. It was expecting too much that he'd complete the task I gave him." He shrugged, then moved to pull a cord hanging on the wall. A distant bell sounded. "But what can you expect from a simple bastard?"

Naim didn't answer, because the question was clearly rhetorical. But a short while later, when the door opened and a young woman in servants' clothing entered, he knew he was dismissed. She was small, shapely and extremely timid in appearance – exactly the sort Raka seemed to like. Rather like Naim's own spy, in fact, barring the timidity which for the spy was all an act. But this wasn't the same young woman who'd been here last time...

"Are you waiting for something, General?"

He'd been staring for too long. "No, Your Magnificence."

He left.

Weapons for a hundred more men. It wasn't what he'd wanted, Raka mused as he lay back in the bath, though it was something. But was it enough?

Just then a trickle of soapy water ran from his hair down into his eye, stinging a little. "Curse it!" he shouted, swiping his hand over his face. "Clumsy girl!"

In his now blurred peripheral vision he saw the new servant girl cringe away, then a dry cloth was patted over his face. "Apologies, Your Magnificence," she whispered.

"Ugh. Just let me do it." He took the cloth and wiped his own face, feeling hot with anger. "Is everybody incompetent? Can no one do the simple things I ask of them?"

"Apologies, Your Magnificence," the girl whispered again, but he ignored her. He was thinking of his previous servant, the one who'd vanished eighteen days earlier…at the same time Orin the Bastard had left on his mission. His hands clenched into fists at the memory. Had she been stolen? Perhaps not, but the timing was too suspicious for him not to wonder. And just when he'd finally got her trained, too…

Raka sat up abruptly, feeling angry again with his brother, his faithless sister, his stupid servants, his weak general. If it wasn't for the major Earther weapon he'd already quietly negotiated for, then the failures of those around him would be too much to bear. "Life disappoints me yet again."

"Do you want me to go, Your Magnificence?"

He considered the question for only a moment. "Stay," he replied imperiously. A poor servant was better than none at all…but Chay wasn't forgotten.

No, not at all.

The Portal

After all of the drama of the last month or so, returning back to Earth was surprisingly anticlimactic. Astrid had been hurried through the colony; barely even able to say hello to Suraya or her other friends, but she didn't mind. She just zipped up the jumpsuit to cover her face, fitted her goggles into place, then closed her eyes as the hum of the portal rose up around her. For a second it seemed to be all she could hear, then the silence returned and she knew she'd arrived.

She pulled off her goggles to see the clatter and bustle of 'the other side' – a simple structure built around the portal, with bright green grass visible through the building's windows. The Earth-side portal had a park built around it, even though it was otherwise impossible to access.

Soon someone was helping Astrid to get out of the chair and asking her to sign a form confirming she'd arrived, and someone else was unloading boxes from the back of the portal-device, and there was a small crowd of people behind the glass window of the building attached to the portal. At the very front stood Nathaniel. He was watching her intently, and when she met his eyes, he smiled and raised a hand in an awkward wave. Behind him was an oval-faced girl wearing a hood, but those purple Tyger eyes were visible even from here.

Suddenly Astrid wanted to cry, but it wasn't all bad.
She was finally home.

Mahadra

It had taken two weeks to travel over the mountains to Syrene in the first place. But it only took five days to run back in *beini* form; the movements of this feline body so fast and fluid. Still, by the time Orin arrived in the city of Mahadra he was rank with sweat and his four limbs were trembling with exhaustion.

He deviated into a well-used, low aqueduct, ignoring the displeased cries of the people trying to feed their animals or draw water, then shook off only enough that he wouldn't drip water on the palace's tiled floors. Raka always hated that. And as the bearer of bad news, Orin had to avoid those things Raka hated…if possible.

But sometimes it wasn't possible. So a mere hour later, Orin knelt in his human form, barely clothed in that same thin cloth he'd had wrapped around his neck, as Raka paced before him.

"Why are you back here?" Raka snapped suddenly. "It had better be to tell me of the great mourning in Syrene for the loss of their emir and weak regent."

Orin hunched lower, drawing his bare shoulders around him as if he could make himself disappear. "I'm back because I have no other place to go, brother. But I do not have good news for you." He paused, drawing in a deep breath. "Our uncle still lives."

He felt the briefest movement of air before the slap rocked him sideways; his head ringing from its strength. "Coward!" Raka hissed. "Failure! You could not do this one thing for me? My spy says you stood in the very palace, perhaps even in the emir's room, and he still lives! Why?"

"Because I *am* a coward," Orin replied in a low voice. "I am everything you said. I stood before him, ready to strike, but I couldn't do so. He wasn't as sick as people have said. He was sitting up, and he looked at me, and guessed who I was, even though we'd never met before. He...he looks like Father."

This time he was more prepared for the second slap, and he let his head swing with the movement. But not too much, or Raka would strike again to make sure it had hurt. That was how he treated people. So Orin waited while his brother paced and raged, and when his fury abated a little, he added, "But perhaps all isn't lost. I told him a story, and I think I may have gained his trust. Perhaps we can use that."

Raka stopped mid-pace, turning his head sharply to stare at Orin. "What lies did you tell, Bastard?"

Which lies hadn't he told? They all blurred together, but it was essential to keep them straight, or all really would be lost. "I told him I was there to kill him," he replied, raising his head to look Raka in the eye. "I told him you'd sent me, but that I wanted to make a deal with him. If he named me heir of Syrene, then I would work against you so that you couldn't bring an army over the mountains. He's heard about your Earther weapons, and he's afraid. Afraid enough to try to bargain with an assassin, and for the boy-regent to do the same."

Raka scoffed. "A bastard, heir of Syrene? He must truly be desperate." But his tone had changed, and he watched Orin with narrowed eyes. "So you fancy yourself a double-agent, Orin? Whose side do you work on?"

Orin jolted in surprise and stared up at his brother, wide-eyed. "You must know I am loyal to you," he said in a low voice. "You are my brother and my emir. You've kept me alive. Sometimes I think...I think you're tired of me, but then I know there's nowhere else for me to go." He dipped his head, and his voice became almost a whisper.

"I knew you'd be angry. I didn't have to come back. I could have run, but I thought it better to risk your anger, rather than give up on my home entirely."

Had he overdone it? He'd played this scenario over and over in his head during those five days he'd run, and so many options ended in his death or imprisonment. It *was* a risk to return – but one he'd taken.

Raka didn't respond for a while. Instead he walked across the room to the bell cord that hung on the wall, then gave it a brief tug. Within five seconds the doors had opened and a servant girl walked in, holding a tray covered in food. Raka lifted something delicious-smelling off the tray and popped it in his mouth. "Notice anything different, Bastard?"

Orin studied the girl for a mere two seconds before intentionally turning his gaze away, setting a dispassionate expression over his features. "You've lost interest in the other one, then? It had to happen some time."

"Lost interest. Hmm."

But Raka didn't elaborate, and Orin certainly didn't prompt him to. Not when he knew where Chakandra had gone, and he guessed that Raka didn't really know, or else Orin would have had worse than a couple of slaps.

The girl set the tray on a nearby table, then when Raka dismissed her, she hurried to the door. It closed, then he said, "You're a coward and a failure, Orin. But you aren't entirely stupid…and you are blood. So I'll give you just one more chance, and it will be your last. Is that understood?"

Orin nodded, because he'd hardly say 'no'. "What do you need, Your Magnificence?"

"Everything," Raka replied simply. "Everything that was stolen from me. And you are going to help me get it back."

PART TWO

Dragonfly

CHAPTER 16
Fear & Anticipation

ONE YEAR LATER
Earth 2041 AD

Syrene

It was early morning on the outskirts of a tiny north Syrenian village; the time when the sun hadn't yet fully risen over the surrounding hills so the world was cast into shades of grey.

A boy in his mid-teens sleepily watched a herd of grazing karaks at the furthest heights of the Kabeer foothills. On the surface he was just another karak herder, sent out by his family for this rather solitary and dull job. But in truth he'd been chosen because this high plain overlooked one of the roads that crossed the mountains between Mahadra and Syrene. He'd been given the task of watching the road for any suspicious invasion-like activity, and alerting the nearby Syrenian army outpost if he saw anything.

It was a fool's job in the boy's opinion, because this road was far too winding and slow compared to the other options in between city-states. If he was going to invade his neighbour, he'd take the direct route. Anyway, in the three months he'd been doing this job, there'd been nothing to see except mountains, grazing animals and the occasional traveller.

Or so he'd thought. Today, his attention was caught by a plume of dust appearing from over the mountain road, barely visible in the early light yet moving faster than any rider he'd seen before. Then when the boy crept closer to find out what was causing the dust, he saw that it wasn't sent up by a mere couple of travellers.

Instead there were dozens upon dozens of wagons rumbling along the winding road. But they weren't like any wagons he'd seen before. They didn't seem to be made of wood, for starters: instead some kind of mottled green and yellow metal. Each one was wide enough to block the entire path, and the open backs of each was filled with dozens of armed men, holding weapons of a sort the boy had never seen before.

They were moving far, far too fast.

Almost paralysed with terror, the boy ducked behind the low rocky ridge, his heart pounding double-time as the vehicles rumbled below, on and on and on, seemingly forever. Then when he could finally move again, he leapt up and sprinted back towards the army outpost, leaving his herd grazing peacefully behind him.

He'd take a shortcut.

The palace, Syrene

Benn sat in a quiet internal chamber along with half a dozen of Syrene's most important figures. Even though he was no longer regent – as Jireh was now well able to do his job as emir – Jireh considered him important enough to attend this early morning meeting anyway.

Strangely enough, the other advisors had also given Benn more respect over this last year, perhaps because their emir did. Or perhaps it was because they'd spent almost twelve months trying to stave off war with Raka, who might be the official heir to Syrene, but who didn't seem to have any inclination to wait for Jireh to die of old age like most heirs did.

So far, so good. But as for Benn, he was tired of endless preparations for battles that might never come, and of the constant tension in the air. Everyone was just trying to live their lives normally, but how could they when every report from their spies just confirmed the increasing danger they were in?

Orin was incredibly fortunate that Raka hadn't yet realised he was a spy for Syrene, and that he'd been sabotaging Raka's attempts for months. And they were all incredibly, desperately, painfully fortunate that Raka hadn't yet taken those Earther weapons he'd amassed over these last few years and just driven right into Syrene, crushing all resistance along the way…

"…escaped *Branzino* slaves, so we've discovered the location of three of Raka's mines," Advisor Koln was saying. The advisor was Jireh's second cousin, and looked rather like him with his neat, greying beard and straight eyebrows, although they were very different in personality.

With his attention recaptured, Benn focused back on the conversation around him. They'd been talking about the ongoing effort to locate the missing Dragonflies, which was almost as crucial as finding out when and how Raka planned to attack. After all, what good was a ruler if he didn't take care of all his people?

"But even though we know the whereabouts of at least two thousand Dragonflies, we can't use them," Koln continued. "They're under heavy guard up north, often held by soldiers with Earth weapons, and we can't spare the men to free them."

Ever since they'd made contact with the first Dragonfly escapees, they'd been discussing the possibility to adding them to the Syrenian army. It was quite a talent when most of them could turn into a flying, fighting machine. But…

"We won't *use* them," Jireh interrupted, giving the advisor a stern glance. "We would free them because it's the right thing to do. If they want to fight – if they're *able* to fight, then they're most welcome to."

Koln looked abashed, but Benn thought that was probably from being scolded by his emir rather than any real guilt. He was one of those who didn't quite think of Dragonflies as people: the kind of thinking that had led to their persecution in the first place.

"At least Raka has stopped trying to make ambrilene," Benn pointed out. That had been good news, if it was true. It was bad enough to realise an entire people group was being rounded up and forced to work in slavery; mistreated and guarded so well that their natural defences became useless. It was far worse to think they might've been killed in the hope that money could be made from their bodies.

From what he'd heard, it was only the very oldest of the Dragonfly graves that produced ambrilene, and those were now tragically empty. Those who'd died in the village clearances of the last few years were just that – dead bodies that even the Earthers wouldn't touch. He shuddered at the thought.

Jireh nodded at the only woman in the room; a weather-beaten, wiry elder with hair pale from age rather than being *beini*. "Jenina, what's the report on our riders?"

Jenina had been married to the head of Syrene's riding army for years, then when he'd died a decade ago, she'd been kept on for her own knowledge and the respect that most held for her.

"Every capable rider in Syrene is ready to fight," she replied. "We have those closest to the Kabeer mountains training with the Earther weapons we've salvaged, but…" She looked down, deep furrows appearing between her eyebrows. "The men are still uncomfortable with the use of *gons*, and even the best-trained raphantas panic when they hear *gon*shots."

There was an uncomfortable silence in the room. It was the same thing Benn had heard last week, but it just reinforced the unsettled feeling he'd had for months: any true battle between Mahadra and Syrene would be short, loud and bloody…

…and they'd be absolutely slaughtered.

Just then the door opened and Palos entered, followed by another man in late middle age. General Alte had been elevated from Head of Guard position by the advisors during Jireh's sickness. At the time, 'General' had been a formal position rather than a meaningful one, and Benn hadn't cared who took a role that might never be needed. But now that war seemed unavoidable and imminent, Benn rather thought he disliked Alte's narrowed eyes and constant agreement with Palos.

But then Benn and Palos hadn't been getting on so well of late. The only relief was that Jireh no longer seemed enamoured of him either.

"My apologies for our lateness," Palos said, bowing elegantly before the emir. "We received a report from the north-eastern outpost that needed urgent consideration."

"I see," Jireh murmured. "And what of the report?"

"Nothing, Your Magnificence," General Alte spoke up. "Some fool saw a wagon train and thought it was an invasion. Fortunately, the truth was identified before any true harm was done."

The two men took their seats as a servant who'd come in behind them began to set drinks out on the table.

"On that matter," Palos said, "I have something to say."

Benn exchanged the barest glance with his stepfather, noticing Jireh's very slightly raised eyebrows. Palos *always* had something to say, although he'd eased off just a little after Jireh had a stern conversation with him back when he'd first returned to health.

That was around the time that Merima's son Neoli was accused of tampering with Jireh's medicine. The dose of nirixa leaf had been more than double the safe amount, which would have given even a sane man hallucinations and health problems. For Jireh, who'd already been weak from his 'chest infection', it had been far worse.

They'd said that Neoli had been paid by Raka to make his uncle sicken. Benn thought that *someone* had paid him, but the truth tests by other *beini* had been inconclusive. Not knowing if his nurse's son was guilty or not, Jireh had simply ordered Neoli to be held in the palace. Not quite in the dungeons, and in a room with reasonable facilities. Merima had left her position in protest.

They'd have to work that out too. Benn knew that if Neoli was innocent, then he'd spent many months being held for no reason and should be compensated. If he was guilty, then by law he should be executed. It wasn't an easy decision, so it was one that had been put off again and again.

But Palos had launched into today's spiel. "…as I said last week, it is most urgent that some kind of concession is made to Raka, Your Magnificence. We cannot stave off invasion forever, and he *is* your heir. Let him be declared as such before the people once more. Maybe that will be enough for him to leave us be."

"Let Raka come tramping around our Syrene?" Jenina said in disgust. "Watching everything with a possessive eye, looking for our weak spots, waiting for our emir to drop dead so he can walk into this palace? We may as well send up the yellow smoke of surrender right now, before a battle even begins!"

"His Magnificence isn't yet old," Koln added. "There's still plenty of time to sire another heir, as I've said repeatedly."

And as Benn and Jireh had also discussed repeatedly, if Jireh was to marry and try to have another child, it would likely tip Raka over the edge into invasion. As would Jireh formally naming either Benn or Orin as his heir, which he'd wanted to do for a long time.

"Raka *is* currently the heir," Palos argued, "and we're in imminent danger! There's no place for pride at a time like this!"

"Indeed he is the heir," Jireh agreed, sounding utterly unimpressed. But then they'd had this discussion many times, and Palos never seemed to accept Jireh's answer. "And as I said two days ago when you suggested the same thing, our previous attempts to placate him have failed. He wants more and more from us, from Syrene, and he won't be satisfied until he's sitting on my throne as well as Mahadra's." He took a deep breath, then let it slowly out through his nostrils. "We've spoken enough for today. All of you may return to your duties…except you, General."

The others filed out, Palos with a hint of attitude to his step. Benn picked up his goblet absently and sipped at it, then made a face. Spiced wine with too much spice – made to the older folk's taste rather than his own. He drank it anyway, since he'd been coming to these meetings for months and the drinks were always the same.

There was a silence as the door closed, then Jireh said, "General, is there anything you want to tell me now the others are gone?"

That was a question Jireh had been asking for months, too; giving Alte a chance to speak up without affecting the morale of the others.

The general's answer was similar today as every other day. "Things look the same," he replied. "But they can change quickly. As always, we must be ready."

Jireh sighed, then waved a hand dismissively. "Thank you. You may go." Then when the emir and Benn were finally alone, Jireh let out a long, weary sigh. "How much is left unsaid in those few sentences, hmm? I tell you, Benn, it's not easy being a ruler. I don't know why Raka wants it so badly."

"Because he doesn't care about doing a good job or who he hurts?"

"Mmm. I'd say so."

There was a companionable silence as the two of them sipped at their drinks and picked at the almost-full platters. Really, it was too early for a meal, and Benn felt as exhausted as if it was late at night. The constant tension had been wearing on him terribly, he mused.

"Any success with the Earthers?" Jireh asked suddenly.

Benn shook his head dolefully. His stepfather meant 'was there any success with getting weapons, transports, or armed men'. "Nothing official, of course, although I hear Ms Jae has been smuggling goods to the *Branzino* settlements down in the cold lands."

"Of course she has," Jireh agreed. He sighed again and slumped forward, resting his arms on the table. "Did Jenina really say something about the yellow smoke of surrender?"

"She certainly did."

"Huh. I didn't realise the people expected us to still use smoke signals." Jireh frowned, his eyelids looking heavy. "When was the last time we did that? Oh…black smoke for my father's death, then blue smoke when I was made emir. Many, many years ago."

Oddly enough, Benn thought, the emir had become far less traditional since his recovery. Benn vaguely remembered him being a good-natured yet solemn man, focused on tradition and pleasing the people. Now, not so much.

But Benn didn't want to see the black and blue smoke rising from the palace chimneys again. Not if it meant Jireh was dead and Raka crowned. Although somehow, he doubted he'd be left alive to see such a thing. "I'm so tired," he murmured to himself. "When this is over, I'm going to have a nice long rest."

He looked across to where the emir was now resting his head on his folded arms, and realised that he wasn't the only one.

Anyway, who needed to wait for it to be over? They could have a little rest right now…

Just east of the southern mining facility, Syrene

"How many?" Jae asked.

"Fifteen this time, including a child," Malchiel replied solemnly from where he stood at the door of the tiny, solitary medical centre. "Escapees again."Jae's mouth tightened at that news – that while fourteen of the Dragonflies who'd escaped Raka's mines far to the north were adults who'd been mistreated, one was a *child* who'd been forced to work. But she'd almost become immune to this now, after all these months of such refugees arriving.

She turned and went to the storage crates piled up along the building's interior. The first two were empty – the last half-filled with blankets. "We'll need more," she murmured. "We weren't expecting so many."

At last count, the tiny Dragonfly camp had stretched into a sprawling tent settlement of over one thousand people. Men, women and children, many of whom had been living in precarious circumstances over the last few years, since they'd been driven out of their homes in Mahadra and had failed to find new places to stay in Syrene.

But more recently they'd been getting escapees. So, so many ragged, starved, exhausted escapees from those same mines. It seemed that the guards had made a point of keeping their forced workers weak, or else they would have escaped much sooner. When a good three-quarters of the imprisoned population could in theory just change form and fly away, you'd have to take steps to stop them being able to. Jae was still fixing up those who'd had such steps taken on them, since they tended to be in bad shape.

She felt Malchiel move up beside her, and he bent to lift an armful of blankets. "Food and water," he said succinctly. "The needle. They need it."

By 'the needle' he meant any kind of injectable medication. Jae didn't bother going into detail – he'd shown he didn't care *how* the medicine worked, although his sister Rechal had become quite a handy nurse's aide. She seemed fascinated by the idea that women could be healers with more than just herbs.

"Coming up," Jae replied. "But we're going to need to more." She lowered her voice. "Are any of them…in good shape?"

Malchiel's eyes brightened at the code phrase for *possible fighter*. "At least six or seven."

Almost half. That wasn't bad at all, Jae thought, but she didn't continue the conversation. Not while they were here in her medical centre, where everything was recorded and could be viewed by Earth.

After Astrid's very public campaign last year back on Earth where she'd 'made a big fuss about ambrilene' in her words (or approached major news sites with evidence of what it actually was, in Jae's words) Portal-co had shamefacedly agreed to send aid to the displaced Dragonflies.

Jae figured it was just a tiny portion of the profits they'd made off ambrilene in the first place, but it was feeding and clothing a thousand miserable, wrecked, desperate folk. Really, it could be the difference between life and death, even if it was less than it should be.

But Earth – or Portal-co – had flatly refused to send any kind of weapons, even though they were urgently needed for defence. Jae had seen snippets of the news down in the nearby mining facility. Their CEO self-righteously claimed that they'd sent very few to Raka in the first place, that they'd been intended for hunting and to make 'the lives of the alien natives easier', and that now knowing their 'regrettable mistakes', they certainly wouldn't be funding an alien war, thank you very much.

Jae thought it was much worse that they'd armed one side and not the other. Sure, she'd seen what happened when an advanced culture sold weapons to a less advanced one – Earth's history books showed that the less advanced culture would proceed to shoot their enemies, then the advanced culture, and anyone who survived would probably be scarred by the experience.

But Malchiel had taken the news with his customary composure. 'Dragonflies aren't weak,' he'd said, 'and we will show them.'

That was why almost a year after Jae's last family had disappeared through the portal to Earth, she was still here. She'd become more and more invested in the Dragonflies' cause. Almost more than they were sometimes, she thought as they left the building for the Dragonfly settlement. "I heard from Jireh," she said once she was sure they were out of range of any recording devices. "About resettling your people in southern Syrene."

"Oh?" Malchiel's eyebrow raised.

They'd discovered some months ago that this Dragonfly man knew the emir – had been his stablemaster years ago, in fact. Since Emir Jireh was apparently mad about raphantas, they'd become quite friendly. Unsurprisingly, Jireh had seemed excited to hear that Malchiel was alive, but had deferred the idea of his old friend returning to Syrene 'until we know my mad nephew isn't going to invade and kill the lot of you'.

"As expected, he seems keen on the idea," she continued, a half-smile curving her lips. "But like with you retaking your stablemaster position, he thinks it would be better to wait and see how things play out with Raka. It might not be safe otherwise."

Malchiel shrugged. "As I expected. But most of those in the settlement here would refuse to return to the cities anyway. Not until they too feel it is safe."

Jae had figured as much too, and his lack of disappointment almost made her smile. Almost, since there wasn't a lot to celebrate at this point.

But they still had hope. Even if they couldn't openly do anything, the Dragonflies were stronger and more determined than almost anyone she'd come across. They were bruised but not crushed by their challenges. They were resolute.

And…they had a plan.

Straight after being dismissed from the emir's council chamber like a naughty child, Palos stood on the highest wall of the palace with General Alte beside him. "Give me the spyglass," he said, hearing his voice shaking. "I must see that nothing has changed."

Alte silently handed over a long, beautifully made cylinder of wood and glass. Palos lifted it to his eye, scanning the horizon just as he had a half hour earlier when Alte had first come to him. And there it was – the line of tiny dark shapes in the very distance, visible even in the early morning light. He could hardly make them out from here, but the shapes reminded him of a wagon train.

But he knew they weren't a wagon train.

Palos bit back the curses that wanted to spill out, and his anger once again turned towards his ruler. His blind, stubborn, ruler who insisted on seeking help from the Earthers, even though most of the trouble had been caused by those unnatural aliens in the first place. "Jireh didn't listen to me."

"Of course he didn't," Alte said, studying the horizon with an unconcerned expression considering their situation. "He never does. But now you have a choice. Soon the whole city will see the Mahadrese on their doorstep, and they'll try to fight unless they see that Jireh has already surrendered – which he surely will not do. You know that if there is a battle, there will not be a good outcome. So now you can be the hero of this story, Palos, or the fool."

He had already played the fool, Palos thought angrily. Fool enough to trust Alte's pleasant smiles and willingness to obey, and not realise it was a mask to cover the fact he'd been paid by Emir Raka for years. Now Palos was being asked to make such a terrible decision, to decide whether to surrender before anyone even raised a spear. And if Palos acted to protect Syrene now just as he'd been trying to do for many years, then most likely he'd be condemned anyway. There was no way to win.

"I could send up the yellow smoke as you've asked and tell everyone to open the gates; to allow Raka's army in without challenging them," Palos said through gritted teeth. "But my authority would be overridden the moment Jireh receives word of the army approaching. If they move even five miles closer they'll surely be seen with the naked eye."

"Earther wagons move faster than you can imagine," Alte said placidly. "And whoever drank the wine in the council room is surely sleeping now. It was heavily drugged."

Palos breathed in sharply through his nostrils. "As if the nirixa leaf wasn't bad enough, now you have to poison my emir again?" He hadn't even had a chance to tell Jireh the truth that Blessed Neoli had been set-up, and hadn't been altering the medicine at all. It had been a servant paid by Alte, who'd been paid by Raka.

Palos felt three times a fool.

Alte shrugged. "Actually, Emir Raka's father Mavet was the firstborn. It was Mavet's father's decision to split his kingdom into two city-states, one for each son, rather than let Mavet inherit it all as he should. So in truth, Raka should already rule Syrene. Jireh is not a true emir at all."

Palos shot him a glare. He'd known Jireh and Mavet's father Emir Avner, and he'd agreed with the decision to split the kingdom. Mavet had been…unstable. Cruel. And Avner had made the division law, which made Jireh the true ruler of Syrene. But Palos didn't bother saying this to the traitor here, since Alte had clearly shown he didn't care. "If that is what you must tell yourself to sleep at night."

"Enough chatter," Alte said briskly. "Make a decision. Will you surrender Syrene while its false emir sleeps, and save the lives of thousands? Or will you alert the city to the imminent invasion, and thus seal their doom?" His eyes narrowed slyly. "If you choose the second option, you'll also have to explain why you didn't mention any of this before, when you've known Raka's plans for weeks."

Palos's chest felt tight, and he could feel cold sweat break out on his head and neck. That was precisely why he hadn't spoken up earlier – because he knew that Jireh would make a decision without properly considering the facts, and because he'd be held responsible for keeping his silence till now.

He had to make a decision. He, Palos. Not anyone else, and it was the hardest thing he'd ever done, with so much at stake. With his eyes fixed on the wagon-train shapes in the very distance, he said coldly, "Call your master on your tainted Earther device. I shall speak with him."

It was a strange thing, Palos thought later. He and the traitorous general stood on the palace wall, huddled together overlooking the city and out towards the Kabeer mountains. There was no one else in sight, but he expected that any onlookers would see what looked like a couple of men having a quiet conversation before breakfast.

They wouldn't see the tiny flat shape that Alte held in his palm, filled with the tiny grey face of Raka of Mahadra. Like a most excellent painting, but one that moved.

Palos had barely restrained the urge to bow to the little screen. "Your Magnificence," he said. "You said you'd give us more time to-to allow you to be presented in your correct place as Syrenian heir." He'd said that he wouldn't invade yet. That they'd have another chance to satisfy him.

"That was two weeks ago," Emir Raka's tiny voice came through a grid of little holes in the device. *"And I have waited many years for what's mine. Now, I will accept nothing except your unequivocal surrender."*

Palos' chest squeezed again and he felt lightheaded. He set a hand to his chest, just above his heart. Alte had already told him what was being asked, but hearing it from Raka was somehow so much worse. "I...I am a loyal Syrenian subject," he stammered. "I will serve whoever sits on the throne, and serve them scrupulously. But...your uncle Jireh is a good man. If...if we surrender, then you must swear he will be unharmed."

Raka's tiny face didn't change expression. *"I swear it. But only if I see yellow smoke billowing from the palace within one hour, and if the city gates are opened for my army. If I hear of a single arrow being shot at my men, then I shall take that as your betrayal, and that of my usurper uncle."*

Now he was calling Jireh a usurper, Palos thought blankly. Just like Alte had said; Raka had moved to claiming that Jireh had no right to the Syrenian throne. That was an unhappy development. "One hour?" he echoed hoarsely. "It's not enough time."

"And yet it is all you shall have," Raka retorted. *"This conversation is over. One hour – or what comes next is on your head, old man."*

The little device flickered then the emir's image vanished, leaving Palos feeling as though he was about to keel over. "I need to sit down," he groaned.

"As you like," Alte said coolly. "Fifty-nine minutes."

No. There was no time to sit down. At the very least, everyone on the outskirts of the city would need to flee, because Palos didn't trust Raka's promises of safety. There hadn't been a battle for decades. The last one had been when Emir Avner had fought the eastern tribes and won, driving them away from what had become quiet Syrenian towns.

They weren't ready for this, but he had to act anyway.

Benn was trying to sleep, but it felt like a giant was shaking his bed. Someone was shouting in his ear, and he was so dreadfully uncomfortable… He forced one eye open. "Whuh?"

"You must flee!" someone with terrible breath shouted right in his face. Tight, bony hands gripped his shoulders. "Raka's army is at the palace gates! If you do not leave at once, you are dead!"

Now that would wake anyone up. Benn blinked, shaking himself awake and sitting up at what he realised was the council room's table. He must have fallen asleep, and his head was still heavy. And Palos – good old Palos – was screeching from mere inches away. "What?" he managed to get out. "How?"

Across the table, Jireh was upright but bleary-eyed. They both focused on the old advisor as he babbled out a horrendous tale of betrayal, lies, invasion and imminent danger.

"Raka gave us an hour?" Jireh repeated, his tone flat. "Even if we were drugged, and even if any troops could possibly move across Syrene so quickly, why are we only being woken now when Raka's soldiers are already inside the city?"

Palos' pale lips tightened into a straight line. The whites of his eyes were showing all the way around, and in this moment he looked every one of his eighty-something years. "You are not yourself, sire. I could not trust that you would make decisions in your own and Syrene's best interests. Not when so much was at stake."

"That was my choice to make," Jireh gritted out. "Mine as emir. Palos, you have forgotten your position!"

"Yes," Palos agreed, sounding surprised at the idea. "Yes, I believe I have."

Benn managed to stand. His head still felt too heavy, but as he looked around the windowless room, it seemed that everything was the same as it had been when he'd fallen asleep. He moved towards the closed door. "We're going to need to see this."

"Not that way!" Palos said urgently. He turned to Jireh. "Your cousin has gone to greet the invaders, wearing your robes and crown. We must take the secret exit."

Benn had almost forgotten there was another exit. That was why they'd always meet in here – because you could use the passages that led right through the palace. As far as he knew, only the three of them were aware that the passages existed.

"Advisor Koln?" Jireh looked blank for a moment, then scowled fiercely. "My family does not put themselves at risk in my place!"

Benn scrubbed a hand over his face, imagining the arrogant noble playing the part of emir. "Koln will play Jireh well, but it won't fool anyone for long," he said flatly. "Let's go see this invading army, shall we?"

CHAPTER 17

Invasion

Ten minutes later, Benn stood in a narrow passage along with Jireh and Palos, who was noticeably trembling. It was dark in here in spite of the light that shone through the tiny holes in one wall, overlooking the grand courtyard that the palace gates opened into.

The courtyard was currently filled with Syrenians guards in their royal blue uniforms, their pointy-topped helmets shining in the late morning sun. They stood in formation, dozens and dozens of them, weapons at ease as they faced the gates.

They didn't look at ease though. Not at all. Neither did the ornately-robed man standing in their midst. Advisor Koln really did look like Jireh from here, Benn thought numbly.

Worse still, two pillars of yellow smoke streamed up from the top of the palace wall, from fire pits on either side of the gate. It was unmissable even in this bright daylight.

If everything had seemed too silent from inside the council room, here it was anything but. Benn could clearly hear raphanta screams – maybe human ones too – and the uproar of a city that was almost certainly being invaded. The occasion *bang bang bang* of Earther weapons was heard over the chaos, and beyond the wall he could see grey-clad soldiers moving through the streets, their round-topped helmets noticeable even from here.

And he could see Syrenian civilians pressing back against the buildings, trying to make space for the soldiers to pass, trying to hide in corners – glancing back towards the palace which apparently was giving up a signal of surrender, and had been for some time judging by what Palos had said.

It apparently wasn't so easy to make an entire city surrender. You could tell them what to do, Benn thought despairingly, but you couldn't make every last person give up hope.

Then as they watched, the palace gates began to open.

"This is wrong!" Jireh hissed. "I should be out there!" He turned to Benn. "You stay hidden, my boy, and prepare to leave if anything happens to me. But-"

"It's too late," Benn interrupted dully. "Let's see what happens."

Maybe it would be alright, he mused. Maybe an invaded city's rulers didn't get executed when the invader was family.

Except a year ago, Raka had sent Orin to kill them both.

Yep. They were going to die.

Rulers usually rode beautifully-painted royal raphantas. Today there was no raphanta; instead in trundled a sort of covered wagon with hard metal sides and shining glass windows. The Earther wagon moved by itself, without being pulled by any kind of animal, and it emitted a roaring sound as it came in, like a beast was hidden within its dark frame.

Mahadrese soldiers rushed in on either side of it, dozens of them. They all held Earther *gons*, every last one of them. Then doors opened in the wagon's sides and more Mahadrese soldiers climbed out, also holding *gons*. Benn's breath caught at the sheer number of them – considering Earth wouldn't openly give Syrene even half a dozen to save themselves.

"Weapons down!" one of the soldiers shouted at the Syrenian palace guards. "Weapons down, or die!"

Benn noted that the Syrenian guards looked to their 'emir' for approval. When Koln nodded, the Syrenian spears were laid down on the ground.

Then Raka stepped out of the wagon. Benn hadn't seen him in person for several years, but even from here he looked very familiar. Rather like a dark-haired, more slender Orin, Benn thought. Richly-clothed, arrogant expression – but still somehow ordinary-looking for someone who'd caused so much trouble.

"Not one shot fired," Raka said. His voice was only just audible from here. "I said that not one shot should be fired, or you would lose your immunity, uncle."

And then as if in slow motion, Benn saw one of the Mahadrese soldiers beside Raka lift his *gon*. There was a *bang-bang-bang* and Koln fell backwards to the ground, red patches suddenly blossoming on the front of his pale tunic.

Someone was whimpering. Benn realised a moment later it was him.

"See?" Palos choked out. "See? He will kill you, sire! You must flee before someone tells him that was Koln instead of you!"

Jireh couldn't seem to answer for a while. "This shouldn't have happened," he whispered. "Koln…I should be out there."

"And make your cousin's sacrifice for nothing?" Benn countered. He felt numb, as though his mind was trying to make sense of everything that was happening, but his emotions hadn't come into play at all. Most of those outside seemed to be in the same situation – almost nobody had moved, seemingly in shock at the sudden violence. "Uncle, it's better to be a live vagrant than a dead emir. We should go now while we've got the chance. While we're alive… there's still hope."

Outside, one of the Mahadrese shouted, "JIREH IS DEAD! LONG LIVE EMIR RAKA OF SYRENE!"

The other soldiers took up the cry, and Benn watched as one by one, the stunned Syrenians moved to their knees.

"Long live Emir Raka of Syrene!"

Somehow the three men made it down to the underground tunnels that led to the city sewers, which then led out of the city if you knew which route to take. Benn stumbled along, shedding his rich outer robes as he went, feeling like this must be happening to someone else. Almost not noticing the smell down here…but only almost.

Then they were finally outside the city walls, meeting a white-haired man who held the reins of two sturdy, sway-backed grey raphantas. Both wore bulging saddlebags on either side and were already saddled for two riders each.

"Neoli?" Benn exclaimed. It felt like the first emotion he'd been able to express in hours.

"I took the liberty of releasing him…once I knew what had really happened," Palos panted. He was now grey-faced, his arms wrapped around himself, and looked a minute away from dropping. "The bags contain gold, jewels…and food. If you leave now…you might escape."

Might.

"You aren't coming?" Benn asked. Jireh was silent.

Palos shook his head, the movement looking painful. "I…will wait here. Someone has to…keep things in order while you're away."

Was he a traitor? Benn wondered suddenly. Was he worse than an overbearing, overstepping advisor, and instead one who was trying to remove his emir by a method more polite than murder?

But then he heard a booming voice, so unnaturally loud that he knew it must be some kind of Earther speaking device. It was a Mahadrese male saying over and over, *"Jireh is dead. Bow before your new emir and live. Long live Emir Raka. Jireh is dead. Bow before-"*

And so forth.

Benn and his stepfather got on the raphantas with Neoli, none of them making a sound even though they surely wouldn't have been heard over that ongoing, awful announcement. Then as the raphantas trotted away, then began to run (proving that Palos had chosen well for an escape route) Benn looked over his shoulder.

He saw Palos sitting at the base of the city wall, looking tiny and feeble against the massive stone structure. Then above that, above the city wall, were columns of smoke. A dozen of them from every gate of the city and from within the city itself – surely the palace walls too.

But the smoke wasn't yellow any longer. It was as black as tar, and as Benn watched, the colour began to change to a deep blue, one that hadn't been seen in decades.

A new emir had been crowned.

Earth, approximately five weeks later

At six am Astrid hauled herself out of bed to the sound of her alarm, staggered down the hall to the bathroom, then as her brain slowly switched on, she realised it was Saturday. "Damn," she muttered to herself. "Forgot to turn the alarm off." Naturally she crawled back into bed, and when she woke again, the house was full of sound.

Through the thin walls she could hear the low hum of conversation and the faint sizzle of what was probably bacon frying or possibly even pancakes, depending on who was cooking. The sun peeked around the edges of her black-out curtains, bright enough that she knew it must be mid-morning, and when she rolled over, the digital clock on her bedside table displayed 10.33 a.m.

Eh, it was probably time to get up, she decided, since her part-time job started at midday. Astrid got dressed in a short-sleeved T-shirt and jeans, ran a brush through her longish hair, then wandered out to the small living area. "Morning."

Nathaniel looked up from where he stood at the stove. "Good morning, my fellow disgruntled former colonist."

"Very funny, princess-stealer," Astrid shot back. If he was going to quote news articles at her, then she was going to quote them right back. Sure, when she'd arrived home fresh from the Syrenian palace and had proceeded to blast Portal-co's wrongs all over the internet, she'd had a few insults thrown her way. 'Disgruntled former colonist' was one of the kinder ones: a quote from Portal-co's old CEO, back when he'd still had the job. Back before she'd shown the world the evidence of Emir Raka robbing graves, and of Portal-co selling weapons to the Tygers.

Funnily enough, a lot of people wouldn't believe the 'shapeshifter story', even with video evidence from the Dragonfly settlement, and affidavits from Aunt Jae, Jireh, Benn and Tamzyn. But they did believe that Raka had been robbing graves and buying weapons, and it had been enough for ambrilene trade to be made illegal. That had been a real win, and one that was much appreciated considering how few things had gone right.

Speaking of things that had gone well – just then Tamzyn entered the room and gracefully sat down at the breakfast bar/dining table. Although it was Saturday morning, she was immaculately made-up with her dark blue hair in looping plaits at the back of her head. She wore no translator, and her long-sleeved dress was nice enough that Astrid would wear it to a party – and in fact had done so once. "Good morning, sister," she said in careful English. "Did you sleep well?"

Yes, Astrid now had an alien ex-princess for a sister-in-law. More amazingly, Tamzyn actually seemed content. "I did, thank you," Astrid replied in the same language, making sure to pronounce her words clearly. She'd learned that if she spoke too fast when Tamzyn wasn't wearing a translator, the other girl would get a panicked expression and lapse back into her native language. "I didn't mean to sleep so long. Did you sleep well too?"

"I did, thank you," Tamzyn replied in much the same formal manner – except that her eyes darted sideways to where Nathaniel was frying eggs. Her golden cheeks turned red…and Nathaniel grinned in response.

Astrid rolled her eyes. The two of them had legally married only six weeks ago, after months of Tamzyn being in limbo here on Earth as a sort of semi-legal houseguest. It turned out that while there were plenty of places willing to teach an alien royal English, or to offer her money for interviews, she…well, didn't exist, legally, because there was no place she'd been born on Earth. Or so they'd been told. No birth certificate, no passport. No tax number, for goodness sake.

Luckily somewhere along the line a helpful bureaucrat had managed to make her presence here official – an official refugee – and the flow-on effect was an official registry wedding too. Now the two of them were acting like newlyweds even though they were just in this tiny two-bedroom cottage along with Astrid, and really, it was sickening. Kind of sweet too, but definitely sickening, Astrid thought.

"You'll need plenty of energy for that party tonight," she said in Tyger, feeling proud of how the words came out almost fluently. She and Nathaniel had both made a point of learning the language after returning to Earth. It made Tamzyn's life easier, and besides, Astrid hoped one day to return to the other world. "Tamzyn, you'll be the guest of honour. The locals don't get too many royals, let alone royals from another planet."

Tamzyn looked embarrassed at that too. "As I have said, I am no longer royal. I am but the disgraced sister of an emir…and I am Nathaniel's wife."

"Yeah, well, there aren't that many disgraced sisters of emirs here either," Astrid pointed out. "But I won't argue with you. I've got to eat then get to work, because the traffic's no good at this time of day."

The small town they lived in was a couple of hours from the nearest city, and only half an hour from the portal that led back to the other world. But at this time of year, when the town was full of students on segways and holidaying cityfolk, the narrow streets had more cars than they could comfortably manage, and the journey time to work doubled.

"Here, have the first meal," Nathaniel offered, and a few moments later a plate with two eggs and a strip of bacon landed in front of her.

"Thanks."

Astrid ate then made her way to the slightly battered ute that she'd inherited upon arriving back on Earth. She'd known that her parents had left a few assets back here, which came in handy when otherwise she'd had nothing except memories and a single suitcase… and Nathaniel's gold winnings from the Tyger pit-fight. The little house that she now shared with her brother and Tamzyn belonged to a distant relative, which they were renting at a low cost. Handy, since they were currently all students.

Astrid was studying engineering, specialising in the sort of equipment they used in the colony and the mines. (Not that she was fixated on the colony, or anything.) Tamzyn had resigned herself to living in exile, and was studying the English language and modern culture, which occasionally had her horrified. She seemed to enjoy the classes on the histories of the major world cultures, including Europe, the US and China.

As for Nathaniel, he was studying international relations, the Tyger language, and political science – the perfect trio to become a cross-world diplomat…after Raka decided to bless his and Tamzyn's marriage rather than try to get revenge. Astrid figured Nathaniel would probably die of old age before that happened, because Raka definitely wasn't the forgiving type.

She lingered on that slightly grim memory as she drove across town to her work at a local orchard, then as she moved between the trees, quickly selecting both the perfectly ripe fruit for export and the not-so-perfect fruit for selling locally. Fruit-picking didn't pay well, but they'd hired her without a reference and it helped pay the bills for now. Besides, she enjoyed lingering in the shade cast by the thickly laden trees, with damp green grass underfoot. It was so very lush, so very *Earth* that for a moment she wanted Benn to see it.

They'd had no contact since Astrid had left Syrene a year earlier, but she remembered how much he'd wanted to visit Earth. She wondered again if he'd ever get the chance, and felt a little pang that it might never happen, or that she'd never find out even if he did.

Things had been…weird with the colony. Anton's heart attack had hit him so hard he'd stayed on Earth to recover, but Percy had decided to remain through the portal with his not-so-new girlfriend. Anton's wife, Eirene, moved between the two locations, still with that slightly panicked manner that she'd always had. Astrid didn't feel a pang of hurt thinking of them again – now just irritation. Perhaps time really did heal all wounds, or at least hardened them up a little.

So now Walt was the head honcho at the colony, in charge of all the information that went in and out, but she didn't know what to think of him. There wasn't much information being transferred through the portal. Not any, really, and she'd barely heard from Aunt Jae except that six weeks earlier she'd been moving between Syrene, checking on the now-healed Emir Jireh, and a little settlement of Dragonfly refugees living just outside of Earth's southern mines. She was supposed to visit Earth in three months' time, so Astrid figured they'd catch up properly then.

They still didn't know who'd pretended to be Astrid and had sent 'I'm OK' messages back to her family and friends when she really, really hadn't been OK. Nathaniel thought it had been Anton, and that he'd faked or exaggerated his heart attack when things went badly. But then he'd never really liked Anton. Astrid wasn't sure what to think – whether Anton was a sort-of enemy or not, and whether a person could even exaggerate a heart attack – so she'd just put it out of her mind, until times like now when it crept back in… She'd done all she could to shut down the ambrilene sales, had even done the brave (or trashy) thing and had gone to the media, and it seemed to have worked. But how would she really know?

"May as well think about Benn some more," she muttered under her breath as she carried her pouch of shining apples along to the processing container. "Or that shapeshifting jerk Orin. Or that *non*-shapeshifting jerk Raka…or even the people back in Raka's palace who are still stuck with him, like that poor little slave girl. Now *that's* a good use of energy."

"What was that, Az?"

Astrid squeaked and almost knocked over her barrel, but caught it at the last moment. "Sorry, Tess," she said to the other orchard worker, who was watching her with an eyebrow raised. "I thought I was alone. Just talking to myself."

"Must be grim conversation," the other girl said cheerfully. "You look like you've just smelled a fart."

That good, huh? "Do you ever wonder about people that you meet once, then will never see again?" Astrid asked.

"Sure. It's all part of travelling. Some old friend you want to look up?"

Astrid shook her head. She hadn't told Tess about her rather exotic travels in the other world, and Tess hadn't worked out that she was 'that' Astrid with the alien sister-in-law. Keeping quiet on that matter was part of making sure Tamzyn's life was pleasant, because for a royal, she really was an introvert. "No, not particularly. Just pointless thoughts."

"I think you're desperate for company," Tess retorted. "Now come over here, there are loads of apples on these two trees."

Astrid followed her, then they spent the rest of the afternoon gossiping as they worked. Tess was a tourist on a working visa, and she'd work at the orchard for a few weeks, then travel, then come back to work some more. She was friendly and very, very chatty, and it was easy for Astrid to just listen and not think about the other subjects, the ones that had no answers.

She finished her shift then got back into her ute to drive home, purposely diverting her thoughts away from those questions and to the party tonight. A wealthy businessman who also regularly donated to her university was celebrating his wedding anniversary, and he'd invited everyone who mattered. That meant Tamzyn because she was both alien and (ex) royal, Nathaniel because he was her husband, and Astrid because she was officially 'the translator'. Astrid was sure Nathaniel had insisted she come along so she wouldn't be left out. Who knew? Perhaps it would be fun dressing up for once.

Just then a light flashed above her windscreen. *"Incoming call,"* the vehicle's polite, automated voice said. *"Withheld number. Do you wish to accept?"*

Ah, even in this old vehicle she still had better technology than in the other world. There, it was like you were stuck in 2005, plus aliens. "Accept," she replied cheerfully. 'Withheld number' usually meant someone official, or more likely from the portal. "But no visual, I'm driving."

There was a slight crackling noise as the call connected, showing that the reception must be terrible…and making her certain it was someone calling through the portal.

"Astrid? Is that you?"

She frowned. The voice had been crackly, kind of high-pitched, and unfamiliar. It didn't sound like Suraya or Aunt Jae, who were the only ones who'd call her otherwise. "Yes, it's me. Who's this?"

"It's Percy."

There was a long pause as Astrid tried to make sense of that. She only knew one Percy, but why would *he* be calling her? "Uh…why?"

There was a coughing sound, then his voice came out lower, but still husky. Upset. "I know you don't want to talk to me, but I don't know who else to go to. Is Hana there?"

"No! Why would I have Hana with me?! We're not friends, you know. Isn't she supposed to be at the colony with you?"

There was a sound like Percy was blowing his nose, then he said in a low voice, "She just disappeared two days ago. Walt said she went back through the portal, and that she'd asked him for permission. But she didn't tell *me,* and when I checked the records, there was nothing. I think…" His voice choked a little. "I think the locals took her. You know, like they took you last year. For revenge, because of the Lady Tamzyn thing."

Astrid's car wheel skidded a little, and she realised she'd driven too close to the edge of the gravel road that led from the orchard into the town. She quickly pulled over, then activated visual mode. A small screen slid down over her windshield. As expected, the image from the portal was blurred and only black and white, but it was clearly Percy. And he was clearly serious – not a hint of humour was in his expression.

"Percy," she said as patiently as she could manage, "did you have a fight with her before she, um, disappeared?"

"No! We don't fight at all. We're happy together." His face crumpled, and he pulled away from the camera just briefly.

"How lovely for you," Astrid said a little dryly. "But why do you think the locals took Hana? And without wanting to be mean – why would I be able to do anything about it, even if it's true? You should speak to Walt, or whoever's in charge now." If it was true – and she really hoped it wasn't for Hana's sake – then she was helpless.

"I just told you that Walt said she went through the portal!" Percy exploded. His voice suddenly went high and rapid again, a clear sign he was upset. "I didn't even want to call you, but there's no one else. No one. Mum says she must've taken off, and no one else at the colony will listen, even when I remind them of what happened to you. Most of them don't even believe what happened to you! But I do, because you're not a liar, and I thought it was weird how you just left, but then how did Tamzyn get through the portal if you'd gone with Nathaniel in the first place? And how would you have come back and got down to the mines anyway? And-"

"Percy, please!" Astrid interrupted. Her mind was whirling, trying to make sense of what he was saying. Back when she'd been kidnapped, it had seemed like the colony had been silent, that they'd been pretending nothing had happened to avoid ever facing the problem.

Then when she and Jae had spread the information around – both north and south – and she'd been taken back to the colony, she'd been greeted by Walt, Eirene and a couple of others only. They'd had her suitcase, and they'd not even given her the chance to speak to Suraya or her other friends. They'd marched her straight to the portal – for her safety, they'd said – with the promise to sort things out once she was through. There'd been the briefest mention of Tamzyn and everyone's safety…but then nothing further.

"Are you saying," she asked carefully, "that people think I was never even kidnapped?"

"It's not proven," he replied, sounding a bit more like his usual self. "People think you left on your own to see your aunt, and that you were making a fuss. Because if you'd dress as a boy to go to the New Year festival, you've clearly got no boundaries."

"Hey! That's so unfair!"

"I didn't say I agreed with them," Percy countered. "Don't punch a hole in the viewing screen. But do you see my problem? If someone was lying about what happened to you, just so they can keep trading with Emir Raka, then they'll lie about Hana too. They don't care about her, especially not since Mahadra annexed Syrene and Raka doesn't need our weapons anymore."

Astrid was tense in her seat, but his last words made her jolt forward. "What did you just say?!"

"They don't care about Hana. She's just a girl and she doesn't have any real skills, and-"

"No, about Mahadra annexing Syrene," she cut in urgently. "What are you talking about?"

Percy blinked at her as if he was shocked she'd even question such a thing. "It happened weeks ago, Astrid. Raka's army just walked into Syrene, and the Syrenians didn't challenge them. They couldn't, and after Emir Jireh died Raka was the legal heir anyway. But back to Hana – As, I'm not even 'sposed to be talking to you. I just have access because Mum goes back and forth through the portal, and if they find me-"

"Emir Jireh died?! What?! When?!" He'd been well! Jae had told her he was well!

Percy went to reply, but then his eyes widened and he quickly glanced off-screen. "Someone's coming. I'll call you back."

Then the call shut off, and Astrid was left sitting in her ute, her hands fisted at her sides and her breath coming in ragged, panicked pants. Jireh dead? Syrene annexed? This was bad! And how did she not know about it?

Even as she thought that, she dismissed the question as stupid. Except for contraband calls like the one Percy had just made, or when she'd come through last year along with a bunch of videos, the leadership completely controlled any information that came out of the portal. For that matter, the leadership on *this side* controlled the information as well – either side could cut it off, and no doubt had done so. In this era where so many nations were still recovering from devastating wars of past decades, it wouldn't look good for Earth to have sold weapons to a much less advanced society, and for them to have promptly invaded their neighbours.

Ah, but Jae…and Benn…and Jireh…

"Call Nathaniel," Astrid ordered her car-phone.

But after several seconds passed, the automated voice replied, *"Nathaniel is unavailable. Would you like me to leave a message?"*

She shook her head, and heard the *beep* meaning the attempted call had been ended. She'd talk to him at home, anyway. Maybe they'd know something she didn't.

But when she arrived, the house was empty. The note-screen by the door read, *Hi Astrid, we've gone out for a walk. If you read this, then we'll meet you at the party at seven – Nate.*

Feeling a little hopeless, Astrid slumped into a chair and glanced up at the clock. It was after six, she realised, and she'd need to get moving if she wanted to be on time herself. For a moment she wanted to pull out, to refuse to go until she had a definitive answer on what had happened on the other world, but the smarter part of her knew she'd be better to attend. Sitting at home would only make her more upset, and there might even be people at the party who could help. At least Nathaniel and Tamzyn would be there.

So Astrid grabbed a snack from the pantry, then quickly dressed in a 'nice' dress she'd recently bought on a shopping trip with her new sister-in-law. It was fancier than she was used to, sleeveless with a square-cut neckline, a narrow skirt and shimmering fabric, and she finished the look with a light coat of makeup and a loose bun at the back of her head. As she returned to the ute, she caught a brief glimpse of herself. She looked so different from how she'd been a year earlier. Living with a fancy ex-royal had probably impacted how she presented herself, plus months of bacon and eggs for breakfast.

But then a year earlier, she'd dressed up as a boy. So really, it wasn't too hard to improve on that.

Mahadra

Orin had been captured. Caught in the act of stealing Earther weapons from the storehouse with the intention of sending them down south to that rather large escapee settlement. He'd say it was embarrassing, except that he'd been miraculously lucky not to have been caught before now. And since he was about to die – as painfully and creatively as Raka could arrange for a repeatedly treasonous brother – there really wasn't any point in pride.

Embarrassing, ha, he mused. Try terrifying, and inevitable.

He tugged once again at the manacle connecting him to the cellar wall, more out of the desire to do *something* rather than any chance it would give. It hadn't the last three hundred or so times.

The metal chain clanged against stone, and the guard standing two paces from Orin's feet scowled and prodded him with his spear – the sharp end. "Quiet, Bastard."

Orin sighed, but quietly. This particular guard had the pale eyebrows and distinctive scent of a fellow *beini*, and had already shown he didn't mind using that spear.

Just then he heard footsteps outside the doorway. They were in the cellar of a noble's house, one with a previously unused set of manacles. His whole body stiffened with tension, but the voice he heard through the door wasn't his brother's. Then the door opened, and he saw General Naim walk into sight.

Orin relaxed a little, feeling confused. He was definitely still going to die, but the fact that it was Naim rather than Raka? He didn't know if that was a good thing or a bad one.

Time to find out.

South of Syrene

Five days ago, Jae had left the refugee settlement and the mining facility behind, heading for Syrene's capital along with many others. Now the capital lay just ahead of them, and they'd have to carry out the plans they'd carefully made over these past weeks and months.

There was very little room for failure.

All in all, Jae had spent almost a year at the refugee settlement. It had become almost a regular settlement in that time, with fields being prepared for crops and half the population making plans to live there long-term. That had been completely at odds with the other half of the population, whose plans were most certainly *not* to remain long-term.

People had still been flooding in when she'd left, and she estimated that they'd gained a good two hundred new refugees in the last three weeks alone. Not from the Dragonfly work camps though – instead from Syrene, where Raka had finally given up on playing nice and had just driven right in, firing randomly as he went. (Metaphorically. She'd heard the soldiers were firing, not him personally – but in her opinion, he may as well have been doing the shooting.)

There'd been an influx of people fleeing Syrene on foot with whatever they could carry. Not just Dragonflies either, but the more standard blue-haired folk who felt they were in danger from the new government of Raka. They were weary, hungry and angry…and Jae had felt the same way seeing them.

Keep your distance, her boss had warned. *We're here to help…but we can't feed them all or be seen as politically involved. They have to look after themselves.*

Well, yeah, but what kind of cold person could stare at hundreds of desperate families, then try to find some kind of explanation for their situations being their own fault?

The sort who was feeling overwhelmed, Jae figured. She'd been getting close to that point herself…until someone entirely new had joined their numbers, changing everything.

That newcomer had fit in rather nicely with Malchiel's plans, though. And that had led them to today, where they had to act out those plans.

Jae thought they'd probably arrive at Syrene's capital in the middle of the day, and her aching feet only made her want to get there sooner. Except once they were there, they'd face everything that had forced them out in the first place – an uncaring populace made far worse by the homicidal new emir. Could their plan really work?

Jae shivered a little, as much from nerves as from the cold, and she wrapped her plain shawl more tightly around her head and shoulders. She moved closer to Malchiel, who was dressed only in a light pair of trousers and his usual head wrap. His golden-brown skin had an almost gemlike tone to it even in this semi-darkness, and she knew he had partly shifted into a mild version of his Branzino form. Probably to save him from the cold, and as preparation for 'the plan'.

"We'll be separating soon," he told her. "We'll be in groups of three or four as planned, then we'll meet again inside the stock gate."

Jae nodded. Part of the reason for her own local clothing was that she'd be one of the 'stockherders'…the others would be the stock.

Thank God for shapeshifters, hmm?

Next to Malchiel, a middle-aged man with a grey-streaked beard nodded at Jae. Jireh looked both better and worse than how she'd seen him last year, back when he was recovering from his illness. He'd be getting back into the city in quite a different way, but when you were trying to replace a deposed ruler, sometimes you had to get creative. "Are you ready, Ms Jae?"

"Ready enough," she murmured. "You, Your Magnificence?"

"I have to be ready," Jireh replied, his expression sombre. "So I will be."

That seemed to be all there was to say. Today, they had no energy for conversation, but in the weeks since Emir Jireh and his stepson had arrived at the southern settlement, they'd spoken about everything.

Well, Jireh had. Benn had been promptly dispatched to the colony to plead for assistance, along with a fortune in gold and jewels. Jae thought it was doubtful Portal-co would officially aid him, even with that kind of money, but he might get assistance from one of the rich businesspeople who'd like to get richer.

But even if Benn did manage to trade for an army's worth of weapons, it'd be too late to help with their current plan of attack. Even though Jireh hadn't explicitly said so, Jae thought that Benn had been sent away for his own safety as much as for trading. Raka seemed to dislike his step-cousin even more than his uncle – and he'd tried to shoot Jireh in cold blood.

"Has anyone heard from Benn?" Jae asked quietly. Dragonfly scouts in acrypid form had been flying back and forth between their travelling groups, careful to avoid any towns. It had got to the point where she'd hear wingbeats and immediately expect to see a shapeshifter arriving from overhead. She'd actually been shocked when they'd seen some real acrypid birds the other day – she'd almost forgotten they existed.

Malchiel answered. "Last report is that he was taken through the portal to Earth. We've heard nothing new."

Jae's shoulders slumped.

"But at this point, perhaps that is a good thing," Jireh mused. "Perhaps our chances are better if Raka thinks there is truly no resistance against his conquest." He sighed heavily, his expression for once showing his distaste. "That murderous cur. I can't believe I was going to let my sweet girl marry him."

Jae's eyebrows shot up. Like everyone, she knew well that Raka was to marry Iryz, Jireh's daughter. (She was also his first cousin, but inter-family marriage was pretty normal for the Tygers, just like in many places on Earth. No extra thumbs in sight, right?)

But she saw Jireh's eyes meet Malchiel's, and his expression turned rueful. "Ah, but this is the least of his offenses, yes? Then let us go with Heaven's blessing today, and avenge those we've lost."

Too late Jae remembered about Malchiel's own twin daughters who'd been killed along with his wife and many other *Branzinos* when Raka's soldiers raided a Mahadrese village. What an incredible loss. She'd never had children, but she was tremendously fond of her niece and nephew. Losing her brother and sister-in-law to an accident had been bad enough, and she could only imagine what he must be going through.

If she was him, she'd want to avenge their loss. She'd want to hang Raka by his toes, as well as all those who'd supported him, because it took more than one person to create a genocide.

But to have that vengeance without unacceptable bloodshed and further pain, it would take great timing and a lot of luck for everything to work out right.

No, more than that, Jae thought. It would take a miracle.

CHAPTER 18

The Party

Earth

The party was in full swing when Astrid arrived. The large house – a mansion, really – was lit up with strings of decorative lights visible even in the dim light, and the sounds of laughter and faint music drifted towards her through her vehicle's open windows. She parked her ute next to a luxury car, and barely cringed at the contrast.

She made her way through the front door, introducing herself to a grey-haired gentleman in a tuxedo. She assumed he was the host – who she'd never actually met – so treated him accordingly. "Have you seen my brother and his wife?" she asked, trying to temper her impatience. "They said they'd meet me here tonight."

The man's face lit up. "Ah, Princess Tamzyn? I haven't seen her yet, although we're all most excited to have her visit tonight. True royalty, and alien too!" He paused. "And Mr Townsend too, of course."

"Of course," Astrid echoed dryly, not pointing out that Tamzyn considered herself a *former* royal, and that her real title was 'Lady'. "I'll just go inside and wait for them, shall I?"

She was halfway through the door when he added, "Oh, but Mrs McFarland is already here, out by the gardens. You'd know her from the colony, wouldn't you?"

It took a few moments for her to work out that 'Mrs McFarland' meant Eirene – Anton's harried wife and Percy's mother. People inside the colony didn't tend to use their last names, because there were so few of them. She brightened, because chances were that Eirene would know more than either Nathaniel or Tamzyn. "Thanks!"

He let her go without any further questioning, and she went inside, her sense of urgency reduced now she knew the others weren't here yet. She checked her phone again, but there'd been no response to her messages either.

Astrid wandered around the lower floor of the mansion, admiring the tiled floors and high ceilings, dodging other guests, with her eyes open for one particular person. Then she spotted Eirene on one of the balconies that led out to the garden.

The woman was deep in conversation on her phone, her face creased in lines of worry or displeasure, and her neat salt-and-pepper hair bobbed with each emphatic movement. A pair of enormous gold earrings hung chandelier-like under her bob. They must be fake, Astrid figured, since only the extremely rich could afford so much precious metal on their person.

Eirene snapped her phone shut just as Astrid approached, glancing only briefly towards the younger girl with a tight smile that didn't reach her eyes.

Was she really going to pretend Astrid wasn't there? Astrid coughed, pushing back the mix of annoyance and embarrassment she now felt. "Eirene. Nice to see you."

Eirene glanced back at her, brow creased in confusion, then did a double-take. "Astrid Townsend! Is that you?"

"Uh…yes? Of course."

Eirene blinked at her, scanning her from her high-heeled shoes up to that carefully pinned hairstyle. "You look very…nice."

"Oh. Thanks." Astrid beamed with pleasure, but then wondered exactly how she'd looked the last time they'd met, to now have such a contrasting response. She hadn't seen Eirene since she'd come back through the portal a year earlier. "You look nice too. I like your earrings. Is Anton here?"

"No, he's not doing so well." Eirene's lips tightened in an unhappy line. "He's at home resting, but wanted me to represent us both tonight. I'm here on behalf of Portal-co, you know." She frowned, but thankfully didn't mention that Astrid wasn't exactly Portal-co's favourite person after the exposé last year. "And you're here because…?"

"I was invited because Nathaniel and *Lady* Tamzyn were," Astrid replied cheerfully, deciding that having an alien ex-royal as sister-in-law was handy for bragging rights at least. "But actually, I wanted to talk to you. I just had a call from Percy, and he was very upset. He said some things-"

"Percy called you?" Eirene exploded, her eyebrows shooting upwards again. "*My* Percy called *you*?"

"Yes, your Percy," Astrid replied, pulling back a little to avoid the spray of panic-spit. "I don't know any other Percys. He said he called me because no one would listen to him about Hana going missing, and-"

"That girl," Eirene cut in again. "That girl was always going to be trouble, but boys will be boys, won't they? What did he tell you – that she was kidnapped or mysteriously went missing and so forth, and everyone except him thinks she's left of her own free will?"

"Er…yes. More or less."

Eirene shook her head. "My poor, stubborn boy. I *showed* him the video of her going back through the portal along with Walt's nephew. A good-looking boy, and now that Anton's stepped down as mayor, Percy doesn't have those connections to keep Hana interested. I told him. I *told* him that a girl like that doesn't care about anyone but herself, but would he listen to me?"

It seemed the other woman expected some kind of response. "Uh…no?"

"Exactly. He wouldn't listen, and now he's got a broken heart." Eirene nodded, her mouth twisted like a prune. "And I've got enough to problems with Anton and the admin mess over in the colony. I don't need teenage romantic dramas on top of it."

Astrid didn't point out that at around twenty-two Percy had well and truly left his teens behind, and while she'd never liked Hana – really, really hadn't liked her – and had expected her to behave like this, she couldn't help feeling a bit sorry for her, getting on Eirene's bad side.

But she thought again of her own experience, of how someone had hidden the truth about what had happened to her, and she had to persist. "Did the video show Hana's face? Or was it just a person in a portal suit? Because you know what happened to me."

"Yes, it showed her face, Astrid," Eirene replied impatiently. She folded her arms, tapping one finger quickly against the long sleeve of her gown. "I don't know why he'd even think to ask you of all people, and why he wouldn't listen to his own mother. It's not as if you can go back through the portal without permission. You can't even send an email to the colony anymore, not after what you did last year."

That, unfortunately, was true. But now the conversation had gone in a direction Astrid hadn't planned, and Eirene looked an inch away from leaving, so Astrid turned it back to what had really bothered her. "Percy said that Mahadra annexed Syrene," she blurted out.

"Some time ago. Is that true?"

The other woman stopped her impatient tapping. "That's not public knowledge," she said tersely. "We're still coming to terms with it ourselves."

"So it *is* true!"

Eirene took a step closer, her voice lowering. "As I said, it's not yet public knowledge. Now I know you aren't always the most discreet girl, but in this matter you need to keep quiet, do you understand? No blurting it out online! No interviews, alright?!"

"I won't say anything, I swear! I only spoke up last year because lives were at stake – but now I need to know what happened!" Astrid felt tears burn the back of her eyes, thinking of all the things Percy had said and wondering about her friends and family still back in Syrene. The insult about her being indiscreet barely registered. "Is Emir Jireh really dead? What about Benn – the regent – and my aunt Jae?"

Eirene looked around her at the otherwise empty balcony, her gaze fixing on the guests moving closer as the inner rooms and gardens filled. For the first time since they'd begun speaking, her expression seemed to show true sympathy. "Last we heard, Jae was down at the southern mines again. There's no reason why she wouldn't still be there. As for the takeover…it was practically bloodless, Astrid. One moment there were two city-states, and the next, we saw vids of this army surrounding Syrene's capital. Then they opened the gates. No challenge whatsoever."

"*Practically* bloodless?"

Eirene hesitated. "They say that the Syrenians surrendered the moment they saw Mahadra's army. I don't *think* anyone died…but I don't know the details."

Mahadra's army, that had been equipped by Earth. Nice one, Portal-co.

But Astrid had already made her opinion known about the selling-aliens-weapons thing (and Eirene well knew it) and there wasn't much to gain from restating it. But she knew that the Syrenians must have surrendered because they'd known they were desperately outclassed. Because they wouldn't have wanted bloodshed, or to see their people mown down by the unbeatable Earther weapons in the hands of Raka's army. She couldn't blame them – spears and shields had no chance against guns. "I see," she said, hearing her voice thick with unshed tears. "And the Syrenian royals?"

"Emir Raka didn't waste time declaring his uncle dead and himself ruler of Syrene too, and that's the last we've heard of it." Astrid's lip trembled, and Eirene added quickly, "But I'm not the one to tell you about it, because I wasn't there. Why don't you ask that Tyger boy who'll be here tonight? The old regent, Alistair Syrene."

Alistair who? It only took a moment for Astrid to realise who Eirene was talking about. "Alsair Benn Syrenius is here?!" she exploded.

"Of course," Eirene replied a little impatiently. "He was a last-minute arrival, but our host is so proud of having two alien royals, even if they're exiled, that he's telling everyone. Maybe you didn't get the message."

"Benn isn't royal," Astrid said automatically, but her thoughts were whirling. Benn was here. *Here.* She wondered if he'd remember her, if he'd make time for a conversation for her peace of mind. Chances were he'd escaped here, if Eirene was right about what had happened in Syrene. He'd probably be trying to get support against Raka, she decided, although if few humans knew what had happened, it wouldn't be easy.

"It hardly matters," Eirene said dismissively. "Now it's been very nice talking to you, but I have things to do tonight. Remember to keep that information to yourself, yes?"

"Of course," Astrid replied, but her attention had drifted already. Benn was here.

She had to talk to him.

Syrene

The city was surrounded. Outside the walls, Raka's army camped in tents spread across the plains in every direction. They weren't attacking because the city gates were open – there just wasn't enough room for all of them inside – but their very presence made it more than clear that the Syrenians were now conquered. Their city had fallen to their enemy, and with only a handful of arrows fired.

Plenty of Earther weapons had been fired back, though. At last count there were a dozen dead. A small toll considering how bad it could have been – except to the families of those killed.

Of course, Chay thought grimly, if you asked Raka then he'd say he'd merely taken his inheritance, and politely, too. After all, his uncle Emir Jireh was dead, and Raka was next in line. Everyone knew that.

Sure, everyone knew it…just like everyone knew that the well-loved Jireh had died in 'mysterious circumstances' in the middle of that short, violent takeover, and that he'd have given the city-state to almost anyone else except his nephew Raka. 'Everyone' also knew that someone inside the Syrenian palace had ordered the gates opened and the army to stand down, and not to fight against the unbeatable alien weapons that Raka had traded his honour for.

And while most people wouldn't know Raka like Chay did, it was certain that they also knew that he was not a good man to cross. That would be why in spite of the decades-long animosity between the two city-states, no one was challenging him now.

She also figured that like her, they'd rather live. That was why she didn't use the city streets, even though the Mahadrese soldiers kept it 'safe', and even though the new, strictly-enforced curfew didn't begin 'til sundown. Instead she was down here in the sewers, where the water ran from the city aqueducts and less appealing places, creating a stinky, dark haven.

From these tunnels carefully carved by generations past, she could get from one side of the city to the other, her *Branzino* heritage allowing her to move easily in the darkness. She could even squeeze her way out into the moat on the western wall, if she didn't mind the decent drop into the puddling remains of that moat. If the fall didn't kill her, the soldiers would. As Raka said, 'loyal Syrenians don't flee their city'. Or as she and her friends said, loyal Syrenians didn't get *caught* fleeing.

Chay shivered in spite of the tunnel's warmth and wrapped her rough, ragged cloak closer around her face and shoulders. It had been carefully stained brown with mud and animal fat, and the latter meant it stunk to high heaven. Add a little dirt on her own face to go with her dyed blue-purple hair, and hopefully even Raka's finest *beini* guard would give her a wide berth.

Up ahead, a narrow beam of light from an overhead grate marked the halfway point to her home and cast the spaces around it into deep shadow. She pushed her barrow of goods carefully forward, temporarily blinded as she moved through the light, and thought of what waited for her there. In spite of the stench and the uncertainty and the physical discomfort, she had that one, little, important thing that made life seem worthwhile. Funny how things turned out, she mused-

Eep.

Chay's barrow wheel hit something in the darkness. Something soft yet heavy that emitted an odd squeaking noise. She paused, squinting into the gloom, but couldn't make out what was in front of her. She backed up a little, then pushed forward again harder. There was a groaning sound as the wheel struck again, and her heart sank.

She carefully backed the barrow away, then shuffled forward until she was close to that darker shape within the darkness. Now her eyes were recovering from walking through the light, she could see it was long and solid – big enough to be a body. "Are you alive?" she whispered.

Groan.

Chay wrestled with feelings of relief and dread. Relief that she wouldn't have to deal with another dead body – the ritual cleansing after touching such a thing would be difficult while in hiding – but dread that she'd have to risk bringing another stranger into the sanctuary. Who knew what sort of person this was? It was a man too, judging by his voice and body size.

But she wouldn't leave him to die. "Can you get up?"

There was a brief silence, then the person groaned again. What looked like an arm lifted briefly into the air, then flopped down onto the ground.

Chay sighed, then squinted at her very full barrow with its sacks of dense root vegetables carefully balanced inside. "You'd better be worth this," she told him. It was his life for a week's dinner, and that wasn't a trade she made lightly.

South of Syrene

Jae leaned back against the worn cliff face, wriggling a little in the loose gravel to make herself comfortable. It wasn't much of a place to spend the night, but at least it wasn't raining. Across from her dozens of others were in similar situations, each with their loose, oil-slicked cloaks pulled up against their faces to guard from the cold. But many of them no longer looked so human…

There were no children. They'd all been left behind with those remaining in the southern settlement where it was safer. Because what Jae and the others were going into definitely wasn't safe, and might even be crazy.

She sighed heavily, then shivered a little.

"Do you need another cloak?" Malchiel asked quietly. "I would make a fire, but you know why we cannot."

Because it would alert people to the fact that they were here, moving closer and closer to the overrun city, rather than fleeing it like they had earlier. If you pushed people hard enough, they started to push back… "I'll be fine," Jae replied. She nodded at him, glancing over his own thin, simple clothing. "But you must be cold yourself. You're wearing less than I am."

He stretched out an arm to show that his skin texture had changed. It was now smooth and hard-looking, and shone like amber in the faint evening light. "I have changed a little. It is enough."

"Oh." Jae waited as Malchiel settled down next to her, a hint closer than most Tygers would consider proper. But after all these months, the two of them were past such things. "How does it feel?" she asked. "Changing, I mean?"

His golden-brown eyes narrowed thoughtfully. "Like putting on a new set of clothes," he answered finally. "Some forms are more comfortable than others."

Jae had heard he could take as many as a dozen different forms, although she'd only seen the humanish one, the big bird, and this one. She indicated to his inhuman skin. "And this, your true form, is more comfortable? You can change fully, if you want to. You don't need to stay in…" She was going to say 'human', but realised they didn't think like that. "…in man form for my benefit."

He smiled just a little. "Once, my people's true form was the *Branzino*. But now, after all these centuries of breeding with the blue-hairs, we're like the others. More like you, Ms Jae, except that we can strengthen ourselves when we need to."

"Oh," Jae said again, considering his statement. She'd known that some Dragonflies considered themselves the 'true people', and the 'blue-hairs' as some sort of invaders who'd borrowed Dragonfly gifts. It lined up with the official Portal-co theory, that all life on this small planet had come from Earth originally.

Well…not quite all life. The Dragonflies must have been here first, because there was no one like them back home. When in their true 'Branzino' form they were humanoid in shape, but were covered in those bronze-coloured plates instead of skin. They also had large, functional, dragonfly-like double wings which could disappear in an instant when they changed back to human form. It seemed that the name 'Dragonfly' had been gifted by the blue-haired folk, perhaps in memory of Earth's insect. Jae found it all very strange, but not as scary or ugly as she might have imagined.

"Must be nice," she said in response to his earlier comment. "Making yourself stronger like that, when all humans can do is shiver, or put on more layers."

As soon as she'd spoken, she wished she could take the words back. *Must be nice.* She knew well that even though the Dragonflies were physically stronger, they were massively outnumbered. Add to that their peaceful natures, and they'd not had a chance when their neighbours and governments had turned against them. Malchiel estimated that as much as a quarter of all Dragonflies had been killed in the last ten years, most of them in Mahadra, and including his own family. It was an ugly, ugly story.

The irony was that he'd had a solid job in Syrene years before, and he'd taken his wife and children north to stay with their extended family, none of whom now existed. But that was before it all got so very, very bad. They just hadn't realised what had been happening, he'd explained once before, since letters weren't easy to send. Not like the humans who could communicate across miles without speaking a word. So they'd gone up to Mahadra, and then they'd discovered why there'd been a long silence from their own family…

But Malchiel didn't slam her for her insensitivity. Instead he just replied, "It has its uses."

Jae smiled at him, then looked across at the camp under the darkening sky. There were so many people, and most of them were just like him. It was tempting to feel feeble and a bit helpless in comparison, since without human technology, she was far, far weaker.

But human tech had its uses too, and she was in just the right place to get them what they needed right now. Not guns, not vehicles…but about two hundred cans of grey spray paint.

Earth

Benn's here.

Now that Eirene had told her, Astrid couldn't think of anything else. He was here, at the party. At some wealthy old human's wedding anniversary. On Earth.

Wow.

She'd parked herself in a corner of the enormous main living area, on a fancy yet uncomfortable couch. She was sheltered on two sides by potted ferns, although she had full view of both exits and the bathrooms. No one would come through here that she wouldn't see.

She idly admired the clothing of passers-by, the men in their tuxes in classic black and white or more modern bright colours, and the women mostly in full-length gowns of equally lovely colours. It looked like jewels were coming back into fashion, she mused, as well as more ornate styles.

Just then her gaze landed on a good-looking trio moving down the curving staircase. Two blondes, one young enough to be the other's daughter, with a young man in a colourful tuxedo in the centre. Purple, now that was an interesting choice, because it made his longish dark hair look almost blue as if reflecting the coloured cloth-

Astrid sat bolt upright. The man was smiling, and he had a dimple in one cheek. His hair was shorter than last time she'd seen him but still covered those Tyger-pointed ears, and the human-style tux had thrown her off. But it was definitely Benn. She could even see the edge of his translator where it curved against his jaw.

As if her very thoughts had called him, he glanced across the room and met her eyes. There was a moment where she waited for him to smile, to show recognition if not surprise, but he didn't. Instead he smiled politely at her, then turned away, back to the younger blonde on his arm.

Oh. *Ouch.* She hadn't expected him to run to her with open arms, but would it be too much to expect more than a vague, polite smile?

"A drink, ma'am?" A waiter had paused in front of her mostly-hidden couch, and she lifted her wineglass, showing it was half full. The waiter moved on.

Ma'am. He'd called her ma'am. Across the room Astrid caught sight of her own reflection in the large glass doors and was briefly startled by what she saw. She looked grown-up, very grown-up indeed. She suddenly realised that if Eirene hadn't recognised her at first, then why would Benn?

So Astrid forced back the sense of insecurity that crept in during high-class gatherings like this, then rose to her feet, straightening her shoulders. She was as good as anyone – well, as good as some people – and the least he could do was say hello. (And tell her all of his secrets, especially about Jae and Jireh.)

At the base of the stairs Benn-plus-blondes had been intercepted by a well-dressed couple, so Astrid hung back a little, waiting for them to finish their conversation. But the moment they did, someone new stepped forward, only allowing the trio to move a few steps.

After that happened a third time, she realised she was being too polite. Faint heart never won fair alien, was that the saying? So this time, the moment the conversation seemed to be finishing, she quickly stepped forward so that the older blonde would need to run her over to get past.

"Excuse me," the woman said. Her tone was polite enough, but there was a hint of competition in the way she scanned Astrid from head to toe.

Ah, girls. If Astrid was less secure or less focused on her goal, she might have been flustered. As it was, she gave the woman a brief smile and reached past her to tap Benn on the arm, ignoring the woman's gasp. "Forgotten me so quickly, have you?" she teased in English.

"Excuse you," the younger woman said, her displeasure far more evident than the other's. "We're taking His Excellency to meet someone very important."

"Of course you are," Astrid agreed. "Everyone here is terribly important, I'm sure. In fact, my brother is married to Tamzyn, sister to Emir Raka of Mahadra. I suppose that almost makes me important too by blood, don't you think?" Her panicked name-dropping must have worked, because both blondes seemed to brighten.

"You're the girl who was in the ambrilene interviews last year!" the older woman exclaimed. "The disgruntled former colonist."

Astrid scowled, because that really wasn't what she wanted to be known for. "I'm not that disgruntled, I swear-"

"*You're* related to Princess Tamzyn?" the younger one gushed, cutting in. "I *sooo* want to meet an alien princess! She's so beautiful! Is she nice? I think she looks nice."

"Uh…" Astrid backpedalled a little, surprised by the response and trying to rescue poor Tamzyn in advance. "She actually went by the title Lady, not princess. She's very nice, but shy. Very, very shy."

"Where is she?" the girl asked, looking around the room. She seemed to have forgotten Benn, even though their arms were still linked. "Will you take me to meet her?"

"Ahh...she's not here yet," Astrid hedged. She glanced up at Benn, who was now staring at her fixedly, his eyes a little too wide. One side of his mouth was twitching. "Actually I just wanted to say hello to, um, His Excellency. We met-"

"Through the princess?" the older blonde ventured.

"Ah, actually it was-"

"Astrid Townsend!" Benn burst out suddenly, the words given a beautiful lilt by his accent.

All three women went silent, and Astrid smiled wryly at him. "Took you a while. Was it the lipstick or the hair that confused you?"

"I'm terribly sorry," he said in Tyger, "but my translator stopped working some time ago, and I couldn't make myself understood." He paused. "My English still needs work, and these ladies didn't stop speaking long enough for me to explain."

Astrid blinked at him for a few moments, then burst out laughing.

The blondes glanced from him to her uncertainly. "Is everything alright?" the older one asked.

"Just a little problem with His Excellency's translator," Astrid told her, then said in Tyger to Benn, "Don't worry, I'll get you out of here."

The sun was low by the time Tamzyn and her husband approached their destination. To Tamzyn, the fault hadn't been in Nathaniel's motor vehicle, but in her nervousness and procrastination. She did find Earther social gatherings intimidating.

"Don't worry," Nathaniel assured her. "No one minds if we're a bit late, not to a party like this." He smiled that crooked smile she loved so much. "It's a human thing. Or this group of humans, anyway."

Tamzyn smiled warmly back at him. "If you say it's true, then I will believe you." To her, one of the many oddities of this world was its sheer size – there were more people than she could ever imagine existing – and incredible variety. Thousands of languages and customs and ways of clothing oneself…if she didn't have Nathaniel and Astrid to guide her, she'd likely be overwhelmed, close herself in her room and refuse to leave.

"Good, because it's true. And you know I'm always right."

The last was said with a teasing tone, and she responded in kind. "I'm sure Astrid would disagree with you, my love, but I shall not."

One of the most beautiful peculiarities of this place was the way men and women would interact. They would tease each other, and the families she'd observed were so very casual, so very loving. Perhaps such things existed back home amongst the common folk in Mahadra, but not for her. Not in Raka's palace. For all of its wealth and ornate beauty, it didn't have the freedom and the joy that she'd found here in her new, small, simple home.

They parked their motor-chariot, as Nathaniel would sometimes jokingly call it, then made their way towards the light-filled building up ahead. "It's very large for a human residence," Tamzyn commented. "Busy, too."

"Rich people have bigger houses," he explained. "I suppose it seems more familiar to you. Maybe one day I'll make enough money that I can give you a mansion… Tammy, are you scared? It's just a party. We can turn around if you like."

He reached across and gently drew down her sheer veil from where she'd automatically lifted it to cover her mouth, a long-lasting habit from her old home where such a movement was considered modest. She hadn't even realised she was doing it. "I don't want to go home," she said hesitantly. "It's just all these people, they'll be looking at me…"

"Of course they will. Because you're exotic and royal, and even if you were just an ordinary human, you'd still be beautiful. People will look." Nathaniel smiled at her tenderly. "We really don't have to go, Tammy. Or we can just say hello to the host, smile at a few people, then go to a movie theatre if you want. What do you think?"

It was oh-so-tempting, but Tamzyn shook her head resolutely. "We will go. I will smile at people, and if they speak too fast you may translate for me. As you said, my love, we shall need all the help we can get on this world. Rich friends are help, are they not?"

He sighed. "My wonderful, pragmatic wife. They are indeed."

"Besides," Tamzyn added a little cheekily. "If we did not attend, Astrid would scold us for leaving her alone with all the rich folk. But as for tonight…if it all gets to be too much, I shall simply hide in the bathroom."

"That sounds like a plan."

And she hadn't even been jesting.

The palace, Syrene

"Emir Raka of Mahadra and Syrene."

There was a pause, and the magnificent figure in front of Raka smirked back at him. "No," he told his reflection in the polished branzine mirror. "His Magnificence, the most splendid and revered High Emir of all Mahadra and Syrene, at the very least." It would make announcing his entry a bit lengthier, but it would be worth it.

Just then there was a faint but insistent tinkling of bells in the outer room of his suite – the suite that had recently belonged to his uncle. He had a visitor. "Who is it?" he hollered.

"General Naim, Your Magnificence. And guest, as ordered."

"Full title, Naim!"

There was a pause where Raka heard Naim clear his throat, and almost…almost heard him muttering under his breath. Then Naim said more clearly, "Your most splendid and revered Magnificence."

"Come in, Naim," Raka replied carelessly. "And your little spy too." Now that they'd successfully regained his full inheritance, they no longer needed the extra eyes and ears in the Earther colony. Such things were always useful, but Raka found himself curious about what kind of person could successfully fit into such an alien society. A clever one, perhaps, or a dangerous one.

A few moments later the curtain of beads shook, and the general stepped into the room. He quickly lowered himself into a bow. A moment later a small figure followed him in. It was a woman, a young one of no more than twenty years, perhaps a few more. Her dark veil covered her head and part of her face, but even what he could see of her seemed terribly familiar.

Raka stepped around the general and reached for the girl, lifting her chin so he could fully see her face. Her veil fell back, exposing curly, deep red hair, deeper than he'd ever seen on any Dragonfly before. But then her mottled purple and brown eyes met his…

Raka couldn't help himself. He stared, and stared.

CHAPTER 19

Lost Cause

Under the city, Syrene

The injured man wasn't light, but somehow Chay managed to hoist him into the barrow, his limbs sprawling off the sides. She gave one final, regretful glance to her sacks of vegetables. "Don't worry, I shall return for you," she assured them.

"Nggh?"

Chay lifted the end of the barrow, then almost collapsed when she realised how heavy it now was. "I wasn't talking to you," she gritted out, then tried again. If only she could shift into her *Branzino* form for the extra strength it would give her – but she couldn't risk the man seeing, if it turned out he wasn't a friend. "Oof. How much do you weigh?!"

The man didn't answer. Instead his head slumped back so that he was looking at her upside-down, his eyes mere slits in his swollen face. "S'rrry."

A sudden burst of guilt pricked her, and she sighed, forcing her energy into moving the barrow forward. The man didn't smell like methuo juice, so chances were he'd been beaten…and chances were it had been Raka's men. Wasn't that why she herself was down here? "It's not your fault. I'll get you somewhere you can be cleaned up, then you move on, understand?"

He blinked at her, then nodded very carefully. "Thhh-gnyou."

Their progress was slow, but by some miracle Chay managed to reach the far end of the tunnel. But instead of turning the corner and taking him all the way home, she stopped. "See this alcove here?" she asked him quietly, gesturing at a light-filled corner, one largely empty except for a little rubble and a small puddle. A trickle of water ran down one wall from the broken aqueduct far above.

"Sss."

"You can stay here, and I'll get you some food. You can drink the water that runs down the wall. I've done it enough times, and it hasn't killed me yet. But you have to stay quiet. Understood?"

The man nodded, his face silhouetted against the light, and he leaned forward as if he could step out of the barrow. For a moment she actually thought he might achieve it…but then the barrow tipped over sideways, and he spilled out. *Groan.*

"You're not up to walking about yet," Chay scolded him, albeit quietly. "What happened to you?"

He huffed out a sigh. "R'ka."

"Of course," she muttered. *Raka.* She set one hand under his arm, then hoisted him up onto the ledge. This close she could almost smell his skin under the strong smell of old blood, mud and waste. She sniffed a little, trying to identify his race. "Are you a *Branzino*? Or someone who just supported Jireh?"

The man shrugged a little, shuffling so he sat against the back of the alcove. Now the thin stream of light was fully above his head, illuminating his battered features and showing what the darkness had previously hidden. Chay bit back a gasp. Someone had *hated* this man. Most of his face was swollen black and blue, and what wasn't swollen was coated with dry blood. Hanks of red hair stuck to his temples, and for a moment she thought it was Dragonfly colouring before she saw the silver patches. A *beini.*

"Not a Dragonfly," she managed to say instead, suddenly overwhelmed with pity. "Another ill-fated supporter of Emir Jireh, then. You stay here. I'll be back."

He made a huffing noise that could almost be laughter, one hand flopping sideways as if to say, *where would I go?*

And Chay had to say, in that moment she wasn't even thinking of her vegetables.

Earth

"I should probably be sorry that you can't repair my translator," Benn said, "but I find that I'm not."

Astrid smiled at him across the small table. They'd shuffled their way out here, dodging the other party guests until they'd found this small, secluded alcove. Had Benn briefly wished he was more famous, that people had more respect for his position? Now, after having experienced the absolute fawning that some Earthers would show for even a temporary title like his own, he was happy to be largely ignored.

Except by this one person, of course. "You'd be sorrier if I hadn't been practising my Tyger," she said, her speech a little slow but very understandable. "I just wish I'd thought to bring my own translator. I don't need it much any longer, especially now Tamzyn's English is improving."

How had he never realised what a lovely lilt the Earther accent would give to his own simple language? Especially coming from someone like this. A year could bring about many changes, it seemed. Somehow Astrid had changed from a pretty, gangly girl to a lovely, still-slender woman…

…Who was currently saying something with her lovely, red-tinted lips. "Are you even listening to me? Or is my accent just really bad?"

"No, no," Benn quickly assured her. "I mean yes, I am listening, and your accent is fine. It's just…you do look very different, Astrid. In a good way!" He blinked at her. In the half-light her eyes had a hint of gold, like darkened branzine. "In a very…beautiful, terrifying way."

Her cheeks reddened. "Uh…really?"

"You were always pretty," he continued, although he now felt like he was digging a rapidly deepening hole. "But today, with the kohl around your eyes and the red-"

"*Ohh,* you mean my makeup looks weird," Astrid cut in, rolling the aforementioned terrifyingly beautiful eyes. She'd interspersed her words with English, but he understood. "Here, how's this?" She quickly lifted a thin piece of cloth – so fine it shredded in her hands – and scrubbed it over her mouth, removing most of the colour. Then she did something to her hair that made it fall loose around her shoulders, silky and longer than last time, in this wonderful brown shade you'd never see on one of his people…

"No, no, that's worse!" he groaned. "Now you look like yourself again!"

"I think you're teasing me," she said with a laugh. "Just like old times, huh? Except this time it's *you* who's fleeing from Raka. You look different too, you know. I almost didn't recognise you at first in human clothing."

Benn glanced down at his oddly simple, yet rather uncomfortable Earther formal wear. "I came through the portal with only the clothes on my back, so of course I had to build my wardrobe here." And he hadn't been teasing her at all, but it seemed pertinent not to linger on that point. He was starting to feel rather foolish.

They'd quickly run through the important points already – yes, Syrene had been conquered by Mahadra, and yes, he'd had to flee, and no, Jireh wasn't dead. He'd fled along with Benn, assisted by grumpy Palos who'd not quite been a traitor, but definitely an arrogant, over-reaching advisor. But in the end, he might have saved their lives.

Benn didn't know what had happened to Palos. Last he'd heard from the city, no one seemed to know where he was.

That they'd escaped at all seemed a miracle. That they'd made it south to safety, then that Benn had made it with their valuables up to the Earthers to beg for aid – and *then* that they'd sent him through the portal to their own world – well, that seemed just as miraculous. But now, in this odd place with its celebrations that seemed so very far away from his own home's challenges, they had time to linger on details.

"You've had to rely on the kindness of strangers," Astrid said, sounding horrified. "And most human strangers just aren't that kind. Lucky you're exotic and good-looking, huh?"

His eyes widened, and he felt his own cheeks heat. He coughed. "Yes…lucky. But it wasn't all just the kindness of strangers. The suitcase of gems I brought with me helped too."

"Suitcase!" Astrid almost spat out the drink she'd been sipping at. "That might explain Earth being so welcoming! And here I thought it would be an impossible task for you to drum up enough support to take back Syrene. As I told you, I think public support for ambrilene is gone now, and Portal-co says they've stopped trading weapons with Mahadra, but Raka's army still has what it has. I don't know how to fix that."

"Kill Raka?" There was a long, horrified silence so Benn finally added, "I was teasing, Astrid. I do recall you saying something similar back when you stayed at the palace in Syrene."

"Yeah…" She looked pensive. "But it really would solve a lot of problems, right?"

He'd wondered much the same thing. "I believe that abandoning one's honour in such a way – by committing murder! – never works in the long run. Justice will eventually prevail. But actually, no it wouldn't solve my problems. It would keep your brother's wife from being pursued, perhaps, but she'd never be welcome back in her home. The Mahadrese army already occupies Syrene, and apparently a lot of Mahadrese believe the two city-states should be rejoined. If Raka died without Jireh having enough support to reclaim his position, then Raka's general would step in and claim the throne. If the general died, the next man would."

He shrugged, suddenly feeling overwhelmed. He'd come here out of desperation, and because the alternative of giving up seemed unthinkable. But while many Earthers seemed sympathetic, it wasn't enough for them to promise soldiers and weapons enough to overthrow Raka. And they'd need many…so very, very many. "Jireh's making some kind of plan back in Syrene in case this fails, but I think…I think it might be a lost cause, Astrid."

"Don't say that." Her voice was a mere whisper now; her expression in lines of dismay. "It might look that way, but…"

"It definitely looks that way," Benn finished for her. It was a conversation he'd had with himself many, many times before and after the invasion. They'd lost control of the Syrenian people when Jireh had become unwell, and Palos had stepped into a role that Benn had never been able to shake him out of.

Yes, Palos had surrendered Syrene on behalf of Jireh which he clearly had no right to do…but Benn wasn't sure that if given the chance, Jireh wouldn't have done the same thing to save Syrenian lives. "Jireh might have to spend the rest of his life in hiding," Benn continued flatly. "Living with whoever will harbour him, or in ragged settlements like the one your aunt visits. And for all that you despised Orin, he was a tremendous help in delaying the takeover. But he hasn't made contact in weeks, not that I could respond if he did. Last I heard he'd been found out by General Naim. And…"

He sighed heavily, then carried on, "…Maybe Raka won't be so bad to my people. He's…controlling, and his expectations are restrictive compared to Jireh. Of course the Dragonflies are in terrible danger, assuming there are any left. And a dozen guards were killed in the takeover, so any others who seem too loyal to Jireh would be in danger too. But except for those things…maybe it'll be alright."

Astrid had been watching him intently this whole time with that same horrified expression on her face. That hadn't changed.

He sighed again, leaning back into his seat. Had he really said, *It'll be alright, except for all the dead people?* "I'm talking a load of nonsense, aren't I?"

He waited for her to say 'of course', but instead she ducked her head. "It's not over yet, Benn. You've got your suitcase of gems and your exotic almost-royal title…who knows what could come of that?"

That was nonsense too, but kindly meant. In that moment, Benn needed that kindness. "I have several meetings arranged with prominent Earthers- humans, I mean. I expect I should be at one even now. Would you like to meet me afterwards? I had no way of finding you here before, but now we've made contact, it would be good to talk some more." At least if the meetings went as poorly as he expected, he'd have someone to encourage him.

"I would," Astrid agreed. "Do you have a phone? I'll give you my number."

"I do." He retrieved the little device from a pocket of his *tuks*. It was like a much-improved version of his communication device from Syrene, the one he'd used to speak with Orin. "I was told that if you share numbers, you can find a way of following a person. In case one got lost, I mean."

"Ah, you'd be talking about the phone-tracker function." She nodded emphatically, clearly understanding what seemed to him like magic. "Nate, Tamzyn and I all use it, although since they're newly married I try not to bug them. It's a safety thing, you see, since I think she's still a bit scared someone will manage to nab her even on this side of the portal." She grimaced. "It's in the back of my mind too, I suppose, which is why I took up self-defence lessons again… but anyway, do you want to set it? If we tried to meet but got lost, it could help you find my phone, see?"

"Ah. Clever." Benn watched as she tapped her finger against the lit-up little screen and images rapidly floated about. "So if I want to find you, I touch your face? On the device, I mean."

"And so forth," she agreed. "Now you'd better go to your very important meeting full of very important people, and I'll see you afterwards, yes?"

"Not if I see you first," he promised, then frowned in confusion as she laughed and laughed.

Eh. Humans.

Not if I see you first.

Astrid was still laughing about that final comment long after Benn had gone to his meeting. Not just from how he'd inadvertently implied he'd avoid her, but also because of the baffled expression on his face when he couldn't figure out what was so funny.

"Getting a bit hysterical, Az?"

She looked up to see that Nathaniel had a) arrived at the party, b) discovered her sort-of hiding place, and c) misplaced his alien wife. "I just ran into an old friend. Not a native English speaker," she told him, then explained the joke.

He made a face. "It's not *that* funny. Also…are you crying?"

"No. Noooo." Astrid sniffed, then realised that for a non-crier, she sure sounded like one. Perhaps the joke hadn't been so hilarious after all, and she was just reacting to the events of the day. "*Oh*…I found out a few things today, Nate. Not good things, and I don't know what to do."

Nathaniel sat down beside her, his expression suddenly serious. "Tamzyn's gone to the bathroom, so she'll be a while. You know how fussy she gets with her appearance when she's anxious. Tell me what happened."

So Astrid summarised everything from Percy's phone call, to missing Hana, to Jae and Jireh, and Benn being here with a broken translator because his crazy cousin took over his home with weapons Earth provided. "So Benn's here to get some kind of military support, and for his safety, I suppose," she finished. "But…it doesn't look so good."

"Hmm." Nathaniel's expression was grim; almost as grim as it had been the day he'd found her in a Tyger pit fight. "Have you ever heard of Bonny Prince Charlie, Az?"

"No. Why?"

"He was a Scottish prince who lost his throne hundreds of years ago. He got an army together to take it back."

She brightened. "How did it go? Should I look him up to get some tips?"

There was a silence. "Not so well. So…maybe don't look him up. Just…" He paused. "Without Jireh, then Raka really is the heir to Syrene. And if Raka says that Jireh never should have inherited Syrene at all, that it should have gone to Raka's own father, then Earth might agree just because it's easier than trying to get Jireh back, right or wrong. I hate it, but I don't know how much success your

Benn will have getting Raka removed from that position, especially when Earth was basically the one to put him there."

Astrid ducked her head mutinously, because what he was saying made sense, and she didn't like it. Not at all. "He's not my Benn," she said instead.

"He's more your Benn than anyone else's on Earth," Nathaniel countered reasonably.

"That's probably true," she allowed. Remembering another odd part of their conversation, she felt her lips curve. "Ha, he said I was terrifyingly beautiful all made up like this. Would you believe it?"

"Ugh, no. Now *he's* the hysterical one."

"I don't know," Astrid teased, jumping onto that happier subject – torturing her brother. "It seems aliens find us Townsends exotic. All this…brown hair, and brown eyes. Wow."

"Yeah." Nathaniel sighed. "Our colouring would make it harder for Aunt Jae to hide on their planet, though."

Astrid's shoulders slumped again. "She'll be down at the mining station. Benn says she was OK when he left, and that was just two weeks ago."

"I'm sure she's fine." There was a pause. "Unlike Tamzyn, who really has been in the bathroom a long time. Perhaps I should go flush her out."

"Very punny," Astrid said dryly. "She might've got stuck talking to someone." Her eyes widened suddenly as she remembered that younger blonde's excitement. "Ugh. Actually, maybe she does need to be rescued. I'll go find the ladies' bathrooms. You save our seats, OK?"

Unsurprisingly her brother didn't fight her on that matter, probably happy enough to let *her* storm whatever bathroom had been allocated as the ladies' loos tonight. Astrid located them soon enough, not too far from the seat she'd taken earlier.

Time to flush out a princess – pun intended.

The Palace, Syrene

Naim's spy looked up at Raka with familiar purple and brown eyes, the two colours swirled together in her irises. She looked so remarkably familiar that he could only stare, and stare, and stare… But unlike the other one, this girl didn't drop her gaze.

"Naim," Raka clipped out when he'd finally got over his surprise, "do all Dragonflies look the same?"

"I do not believe so, Your…most splendid and revered Magnificence." The general shuffled from his bow into an almost upright position. "But sisters do." He paused. "Hanali informs me that she has a twin sister she'd believed was killed in the village of Dahiya several years ago, at the height of the clearances."

Raka's soldiers weren't supposed to kill anyone when they'd cleared those villages of their Dragonfly inhabitants, but of course accidents happened. More so in the middle of such chaos. It seemed more surprising that both twins had survived, and in such fine health.

This Hanali had an ugly Dragonfly name, Raka thought. If she'd been his, he would have changed her name just like he had Chakandra's. He studied this new girl with narrowed eyes, then reached out to tug her veil off her head. While her hair was a deeper red than Chakandra's had been – dyed, surely? – her features were almost identical. And Naim had been in Raka's chambers enough that he must have seen Raka's former *esira*. There was no way he couldn't have known there was some connection.

"What an odd coincidence," Raka said sharply. "A servant of mine was first captured in Dahiya some years ago by a soldier who thought he could hide a pretty girl away rather than have her die like the others. He was made an example of, and I also decided that to dispose of her would be…wasteful."

The spy's eyes widened at that statement, but only briefly. She said softly, "I was told last year that if I cooperated then I would see my sister Chayali, Your Magnificence, and that she…serves in your palace. I have done everything I was asked."

"Were you." Raka turned to glare at his general, now knowing without a doubt that Naim had been aware the two girls were sisters. "Why was I not informed of this family connection before now?!"

"My humblest apologies," Naim replied, his gaze dipping to the ground again. "I do not make a practice of studying your special servants, so it wasn't until it was too late that I realised the… resemblance. I did not mean to offend by my omission."

"This girl has been spying on the Earthers for over a year," Raka said flatly. Because of course Chakandra had left not long after that. Naim had had more than enough time to tell the truth. "You told your little spy a year earlier, but not me? She has the ridiculous *Branzino* colouring, but I cannot see how she would blend with their people. What haven't you told me this time?"

Naim turned to the girl. "Show him," he ordered.

The girl's eyes flickered, then their colour changed, deepening to almost solid brown. Her facial features changed subtly too, becoming more defined. She lifted her hair over one ear, revealing its tip was now rounded rather than forming a proper point.

"Hanali cannot take other forms like some *Branzinos* can," Naim continued. "But she can make small changes, enough that she fits in amongst the Earthers. As for her speech, she was taught their language by our friend at the north colony, who helped her to further fit in amongst them. She claimed to be from another city-state within Earth, an, er..."

"Ukraine," Hanali finished for him as her features relaxed back into that far more familiar, round-faced version. "Earthers from that place speak a different language than most who trade at their northern colony, so they wouldn't expect me to speak fluently-"

"Spare me the details," Raka cut in dismissively, but his mind was working furiously. The spy was a pretty girl, but she lacked the timidity that had made her sister so much more appealing. Besides, he didn't like used goods, regardless of how pleasant they looked. And the fact that Naim had hidden information from him for a full year...it made him very, very angry. "I suppose you've brought her back now to be your little pet again, General."

The general shrugged a little. "Her work among the Earthers is no longer required now that we have reclaimed Syrene, Your Magnificence. Pardon, Your most splend-"

"Yes, yes," Raka interrupted. Then to the girl he said, "I suppose you're expecting to see your sister, hmm?"

"As promised," she agreed.

"Hmm. And yet the general here didn't mention that *Chayali* – or Chakandra, which is the far better name that we chose for her – in fact went missing almost a year ago."

Hanali choked a little and she shot Naim a hate-filled, shocked glance. Now amused, Raka continued, "She left the palace. Apparently it wasn't good enough for her, and no one's seen her since. She was last seen somewhere in the Kabeer mountains, but she's probably dead now. A little thing like her wouldn't last a week on her own."

The redhead's spine stiffened, then she turned from Naim, her expression settling into a disrespectful sneer as she looked at Raka. "*Chayali* is far stronger than I. She always has been, and I will not believe her dead until I see her body. Not after I spent almost three years thinking she'd been murdered by your soldiers back in Dahiya, along with the rest of my family. I only regained hope that she lived a year ago, when your general told me so."

Raka stared at her evenly, feeling the heat of anger rush through him. But his voice was steady as he said, "Even after all this time, my Blessed soldiers know to look out for this one runaway slave. They have orders to bring her straight to me, at which point I plan to make her very sorry for crossing me." He paused, noting how the blood left her cheeks. "Unless you are tired of living, general's pet, I recommend you mind your tongue."

Hanali swallowed audibly, then bowed her head in belated submission. "My apologies, Your Magnificence."

He stared at her, his hands held loosely behind his back.

"Most…splendid and revered Magnificence."

"Good." Raka turned away from the girl, back to Naim. "Your pet will keep her Earther guise until further notice. If anyone asks, she's being held hostage pending the return of my much-missed royal sister."

"Yes, Your most splendid and rev-"

"She can go now," Raka interrupted. He moved over to the nearby wall and rang the small bell. Seconds later, two guards entered from the external room. "Take the girl to the dungeons," he ordered, "but she's not to be harmed. And bring me Sepha."

They obeyed, of course. Then it was just Raka and his general, who didn't ask why he had just called for Naim's second-in-command. Raka sat down at a nearby table, then opened one of the carved wooden drawers. "Naim, what do people say happened to Alte, Jireh's general?"

Naim's eyebrows drew together as if confused, then his expression relaxed into arrogant neutrality. "I hear he was killed by his own people, who cannot abide what they consider a traitor."

"And what do *you* say happened, General?"

There was another brief pause. "I understand he was no longer useful to Mahadra, and so was disposed of."

"Mm. No longer useful." Raka finally found what he'd been looking for; a small, slim metal shape the length of his hand. "That man was useful, and would have continued to be since his men listened to him, just as they listened to the old man Palos. He would have even led those pursuing that cowardly uncle of mine, curse his still-beating heart.

"But *I* cannot abide traitors, Naim. I cannot have them in my palaces, even if they betrayed others on my behalf. I've learned my lesson with that bastard brother of mine, and there will be no second chances."

With that final statement Raka whipped the Earther weapon out from the drawer, pointing it at General Naim. "You've been useful," he told him, "but I can't have you holding back information from me."

"Your Magnificence!" Naim pleaded, but even as he spoke, he was reaching for his pocket. Another weapon, perhaps?

So Raka pulled the trigger.

BANG.

Fifteen minutes later when Sepha arrived, he saw the red marks on the floor where the body had been, and Raka saw his face pale. Raka told him casually, "You're now general of my army. Don't disappoint me like your predecessor did."

The new General Sepha made earnest assurances, then was dismissed as Raka moved to stare out of his window. He stood back far enough that he wouldn't be caught by any stray arrows or bullets from nearby rooftops – he hadn't strived to become emir just to be assassinated. Setting his hands comfortably behind his back, he studied Syrene's skyline.

This city wasn't as grand as Mahadra, perhaps, and that view of the now-empty racecourse was quite distracting. Fortunately it was almost blocked out by the billowing columns of blue-tinted smoke that had burned for weeks now, heralding the new emir. Raka resolved to keep them burning for the first year of his rule, and definitely until Jireh was truly killed – but he'd have to find the man first.

Raka had discovered within two days that he'd had a worthless advisor executed rather than his uncle, but he'd kept that secret except amongst his most trusted guards. Still, he'd had several Syrenian guards executed anyway, in theory for treason, but actually just to make him feel better. It wouldn't do for the Syrenians to think they had other options for their emir, or that he was soft in any way.

He frowned, remembering another disappointing, worthless advisor. Ancient Palos – advisor to Raka's own grandfather Avner

– had been good enough to open the city gates, thus reducing the bloodshed, but no doubt infuriating Jireh while he was at it. Raka had hoped to execute him anyway since he was quite popular with the locals, but the old man had gone and died all by himself. Servants had found his body in his own chamber, his heart apparently having given out.

Disappointing. Perhaps it was better not to have advisors, Raka thought, since they inevitably irritated him by agreeing too much – or not enough. He'd rather not have generals either, since it seemed men in that position grew too comfortable with the power and wished for more – and they had the backing of the army already.

Hmm. Best to change his general every year, he decided. Just in case.

Just then Raka felt a sharp vibration in the pocket of his robe. He pulled out his Earther communication device to see he'd received a message.

The requested package is on its way.

His heart leapt, and a satisfied smile curved his lips. Finally, something was going right.

Under the city

Chay hurried her way along the darkened tunnel, turning left then right then left again until she reached a brown cloth hanging from the carved stone wall, just next to a cluster of light beams. She paused, then tugged on it twice.

A few moments later a section of the tunnel wall was pulled away, revealing a skinny figure lit from behind by torch light. "What are you selling?" they asked.

"Three sacks of groundroot, freshly dug," Chay replied. The sentry duly let her in, and she pushed back her filthy cloak, stepping inside the sanctuary. The door was pushed back into place on its sliding wheels, and she said a little irritably, "I've been living here for six months, Tynin. You don't need to ask me for the code *every* time."

The youth shrugged. "You look different with your hood up."

Sure she did. More likely he was just enjoying his small position of authority, even if it was just opening the door for the thirty or so fugitives who hadn't yet managed to escape the city. There'd been only a dozen of them at first: all Dragonflies who couldn't or wouldn't hide or flee, working carefully together so those who could pass as blue-hairs could keep their homes and shops on the surface, and the others would only come out at night.

Chay had been incredibly lucky to find them upon arriving in the city. Her cousin Jenniel, who had normal, naturally blue hair from her non-Dragonfly mother, had still been living in the same place she'd been in back when Chay had lived in Syrene along with her family. She'd recognised Chay immediately, even with the ragged clothes she'd managed to 'borrow', and had sneaked her in.

Chay had given a basic explanation of her capture and time at the palace, then her escape three years later, and they'd agreed that she had to be hidden, for her sake and the baby's. They'd say she was a widow, and maybe in years to come she'd be forgotten, and she could find a husband and have a normal life once more. But although everyone except Jenniel really did think Chay was a widow, she wasn't so sure about the future husband or the normal life. For now, she'd settle for living another day. "Where's Jen?" she asked Tynin.

"In the nursery. Where are those vegetables you were supposed to be bringing?"

"Back in the tunnels, just by the double-grate below the central markets. I promise I'll bring them back tonight, but I have to do something first."

She hastily made her way through the winding series of cave-storerooms that currently served as home, dodging people with hair in shades of red and brown and occasionally blue, until she reached a large alcove-like room hung with curtains. A row of wooden crates blocked off the only open side, and the sound of children's chatter filled the air. There were three women and seven children of various ages, and it was *loud*.

Chay pushed aside the crate serving as a door, then carefully closed it after her. The last thing they needed was one of these small ones escaping into the tunnels. Even though today she had an important task to do, she still found her eyes searching for one particular precious face.

"You're back. Did you get the vegetables?"

Chay jolted a little in surprise, then forced a smile for her cousin. Everybody wanted food – but fair enough, since they'd die without it.

"They're a ten minute walk away, hidden in the tunnels. I'll go back for them, but I have to tell you something. I was just looking for…"

"Your favourite person?" Jenniel said dryly. "Sleeping, believe it or not."

"Then my favourite person can stay asleep," Chay replied. She knew how hard it could be to get certain infants to sleep during the day, especially when there was noise around them. "I have to go back out again at once anyway." She quickly described the man she'd found. "I didn't tell him about the sanctuary, but there's a good chance he'll die if he's not cared for." Jenniel listened thoughtfully, then nodded. "You know the rules. If there's any chance he might have been followed…"

"I know about Raka's Blessed soldiers." Chay's lips tightened. It had been hard enough back when it was just her that needed to stay hidden, but these past weeks since Raka had taken the city, she knew they were being actively hunted. Ordinary soldiers were enough of a problem, but Raka used *beini* with special gifts and even better senses, and it made them extremely dangerous to the fugitives. "If we're found, I'll keep our secrets. I know what's at stake." Besides, she was good at keeping her mouth shut. She'd done it for three years as a slave, and relearning to speak her mind had been difficult.

Armed with cleanish rags, a small flask of precious methuo juice and some only slightly stale bread, Chay made her way back down the tunnels. Unsurprisingly the man was still slumped against the wall where she'd left him. His eyes were shut, but they opened as she approached.

"I've got food, water and medicine," she said briskly. "Tell me what hurts the most, then you can eat while I tend you."

The man made a horrible expression and a gasping noise that she realised a moment later was a laugh. "Everything hurts. Start wherever you like."

"Very well. Here, have some bread. I see you've found your voice, but I recommend you keep your mouth shut for the next little while."

Chay had said it because she knew it would hurt, not because she wasn't interested in conversation. But sure enough, over the next half hour while she tended his wounds as well as she could, their speech was limited to groans from him, and instructions from her. But the supply of bread disappeared quickly, and not all the methuo juice made it onto those wounds. But then alcohol was good for pain, too.

"That's all I can do now," she said finally. "Nothing appears to be broken, but I'm no healer. Perhaps in the morning you'll have strength to walk. Do you have somewhere you can go?"

The man's face was still swollen and bruised without its coating of blood, but his eyes had never left her face. "Nowhere," he murmured. "Would you send me off so quickly?"

"I don't even know who you are," Chay retorted. "And in case you haven't noticed, I'm hardly equipped to be taking in strangers."

"Not so strange." The man breathed in heavily, blinking as though he wanted to sleep. "But you've become…bold this last year. Where has the shy little Chakandra gone?"

Even though his words were rasping, that name took a moment to register in her mind.

Chakandra. Her slave name, so surely this man was one of Raka's guards – or even one of the courtiers who'd somehow offended the emir, if he was in such a bloodied state.

Chay's heart skipped a beat, and she felt herself grow cold with fear. But she focused on keeping her voice steady, even as she drew a narrow blade from under her cloak where it was tucked in her belt. "You've mistaken me for someone else, sir. I don't know that name."

The man's swollen mouth made that horrible shape again – a sort of smile – and he breathed in deeply again. "Don't bother lying to a Blessed One. Even if I hadn't known your voice, I know your scent, even under that horrible cloak."

"Indeed." Chay again cursed that quirk of nature that gave the Blessed only two forms, but unlike her people, most excellent senses even in their human form. She smoothly pulled the worn blade from her cloak and pressed its tip against the man's neck. "It would be a shame if I spent all that time tending your wounds, only for you to die at my hand. Tell me, who sent you? Is there someone following you?"

He just stared at her, and she pressed the knife harder, until a drop of dark liquid showed against the paler shade of his skin. Feeling chastened, she withdrew it a little, but her tone was still harsh. "Tell me, or you'll be sorry!"

"I saved your life twice," the man said very quietly. "Does that count for nothing?"

Chay sat back, pulling the knife away in confusion. There was no one who could claim such a thing, except perhaps… "Orin the Blessed?!"

He nodded, but the movement seemed to cause him pain. "The very one, although I don't feel so blessed right now. There's not an inch of skin that hasn't been pummelled."

That was the truth. She'd been sitting right here in front of him, but still hadn't recognised him until now. "What...what are you doing here?"

CHAPTER 20
Taken

The girl's expression was so fierce as she threatened him, even in the dim light of these tunnels. She seemed older somehow, even though only one year had passed, and then there was that dreadful cloak…

Orin sighed. "I was being prepared for execution, a simple beheading apparently being too gentle for a traitor such as myself. But the soldiers who brought me here to Syrene were foolish enough to merely tie me in a tent. I freed myself, set the tent on fire, then escaped."

He grimaced, finding some humour in the situation even though as he'd said, *everything* hurt. Even his fingernails ached, and they would until they grew back. "I've known of these tunnels for some time, although I don't recall actually making my way down here. And then along you came." He grimaced again, this time in an almost-smile. "Unbelievable."

"So…you *weren't* following me?"

"Just trying to survive." Orin studied her round little face, still so pretty in spite of their foul surroundings. A touch of spite, or perhaps hurt, made him add, "Perhaps it was fate giving you the chance to save my life, in exchange for how I saved yours twice. You still owe me one more."

The girl's lips thinned into a mutinous line. "I don't see how it was twice."

"Once when I told Raka you weren't with child…and once again when I told you my chest was empty." He smirked at her. "And you promised me that you couldn't take any other forms. Perhaps you *are* a good liar after all, Chakandra." His nose wasn't always good enough to identify a hastily-told lie, even though he and other Blessed liked to pretend it was. It made people more likely to be honest.

"That's not my name!" she burst out. Then she continued more evenly, "I accept that you saved me, although I'm not convinced your motives were pure. So now, I won't kill you, but the moment you're able to walk-"

"My motives?" Orin cut in. "They were simple – to stop my brother destroying yet another precious person."

The girl whose name wasn't Chakandra stared at him, her mouth open, and he realised he'd said far more than he'd meant to. But right now, when soldiers most likely *were* on his trail, what did it matter? "Do you remember how I told you about Xandrea?" he asked quietly.

"Yes." She scowled. "Was that story even true?"

"Every word of it. But what I didn't tell you was that I loved her, and she loved me."

Not-Chakandra's eyes widened. "But you're-"

"The most chaste bastard brother, just as my royal sister must also be most chaste," Orin cut in wryly. "Well do I know it. But one doesn't need to touch someone to love them. She was so…sweet, just a low servant, and she saw me as more than this odd, untouchable part-royal. And I saw her for who she was – so very, very precious." He shrugged, the memory still painful, although dulled by time.

"I tried to hide my affection for her, but I failed. Raka noticed, so naturally he had to take her for himself, just like he did everything I ever cared for. And then, just like a child with a broken toy, he disposed of her once she no longer fit his requirements. After that I swore that I'd bring my brother down, even if it took my own life to do it.

"I've lied to him over and over, I've worked with Emir Jireh and the regent for years, whatever good that did, and I've spent months sabotaging or stealing the Earther weapons he traded your ancestors' bodies for. All it gave us was a delay. Jireh's probably dead, and I likely will be soon enough. They're searching for me even now." He paused. "But…you still live, so perhaps it wasn't all for nothing."

Those last words fell heavily into the silence, broken only by the faint sound of their breathing. His more so, Orin allowed, since his ribs hurt like fire and his belly seemed to be one big bruise. "You don't have to tell me anything about yourself," he added, "but perhaps just your real name?"

At first he thought she wouldn't answer, but then she seemed to shake herself. "It's Chayali, but most people call me Chay." She frowned. "Not in the palace, they didn't. But I wasn't treated like a person there. I was a *thing,* an animal, and I didn't even get to choose my own name! I didn't dare change forms, not even to try to escape, and I couldn't even speak for fear of punishment. Is it any wonder I now speak the way I do?"

"You're very brave."

Chay's eyes narrowed as though she was debating whether to believe his words – but then he'd never been kind, had he? He hadn't dared to be. But then she lifted her chin. "Yes. And it sounds like you were too, if you've been honest with me."

"I have."

"I thought…I thought you despised me, because I was a slave."

Orin shrugged. "It didn't pay for me to be kind to anyone or anything, especially not you."

"Oh." She opened her mouth as if to say more, but just then she heard something: the sound of busy movement in the distance, echoing down towards them so very clearly. Shouts, footsteps. "Soldiers!" she cried. She leapt to her feet, slipping one arm under his elbow. "Get up!"

On instinct Orin leaned forward, but the pain that shot through him made him crumple. "I can't. I've used all my strength. Run now, Chakandra. I mean, Chayali-"

"Oh, who cares!" The girl let out a panicked sound as she jittered on the spot, seeming undecided whether to stay or go. Then finally she crouched down, leaning into him. "I won't make it far enough," she whispered harshly. "We're the only ones here, is that clear? I'm just a homeless girl living in the tunnels and stealing to survive. I know nothing, and there's no one else around." When he didn't answer immediately, she hissed, "*Understand?*"

"I understand." But despair was coursing through him. They'd been found. *She'd* been found, and her fate surely would be no better than his, unless Raka was truly feeling generous. But chances were he'd think they'd planned this; he and Chay. "Run," he told her, "or they'll suspect you're hiding something. Change forms and flee, if you can." He'd noticed she hadn't told him what had happened to her babe. Perhaps it had died…but his gut told him otherwise.

She ran, but when a blur of torchlight and footsteps and weapons surrounded Orin less than a minute later, he knew she'd been right. She wouldn't make it. Despair turned into fury, and he used the last of his strength to partially shift forms, focusing on his head and arms.

He tried to leap for the nearest figure, but he was too slow, too weak from pain, and he saw the blow coming even before it landed.

CLANG-ouch.

The darkness rushed in.

Earth

"Tamzyn?"

Astrid had waited twenty minutes and checked every ladies' toilet on this floor, but the girl who came through the polished wooden door most definitely wasn't an alien ex-royal. "Oh. You haven't seen Lady Tamzyn, have you? You know, the-"

"Of course I know who she is," the girl cut in. "Everyone knows. I saw her about half an hour ago, talking to some grey-haired lady with giant earrings. I heard her say they were going to the conservatory, which is at the back of the building." She shrugged. "Do you want a selfie with her? Because I asked for one, and she just looked at me like I was crazy."

But Astrid barely took that in, having focused on the first part of what she'd said. "Giant earrings? Were they gold?"

"Yeah, like freaking chandeliers. A bit tacky on an old lady like that, but-"

"Thank you," Astrid cut in absently, then headed towards the back of the mansion, pondering why Tamzyn would have spent half an hour with Eirene. They'd never met before as far as she knew, and the ex-royal tended to be shy when outside her comfort zone. In places like this, she never stayed away from Nathaniel for long.

Astrid wandered a little until she reached the back of the building. Two sets of French doors opened onto a tiled colonnade that ran along the back of the mansion. There was a garden just in front of her, the boundaries of the property in the distance up ahead, and to her left was a large, glass-walled room that backed onto the mansion. It looked like a conservatory to her, but it was in darkness.

There were no strings of decorative lights out here, only the occasional old-fashioned lamp post set in the darkened garden. Not a good place for a conversation. It wasn't even a particularly nice evening, with the sky clouded over and only one single drone in the air with its blinking orange lights breaking up the darkness. It looked to be heading towards the portal, she noted curiously.

Just then Eirene came into sight, around the corner from the front of the conservatory. Her head was down over her phone again, and the light from its flickering screen lit her face ghoulishly in green and white. No Tamzyn. Astrid just stood where she was, watching the woman move closer, and waiting to be noticed. But Eirene must have been very focused on what she was doing, because she was practically in front of Astrid and still hadn't looked up.

"Hi again," Astrid said.

Eirene shrieked, and her phone went flying and landed on the grass, screen up. "Astrid! You gave me such a fright! What are you doing out here all alone?"

Astrid moved quickly towards the phone, feeling a little abashed since she'd figured she might startle the other woman, but hadn't thought it would be so bad. "I'm looking for my sister-in-law. Someone said she was out here with you." She picked it up, noting the single message displayed across its surface. *The second requested package is on its way.*

"Don't touch that!" Eirene snapped, snatching the phone from Astrid's hand.

But Astrid had already seen the recipient's details. *Port-co* then a string of numbers that didn't really matter, since it was the code at the start that confirmed where the message was going. "Smuggling things to the colony under the cover of darkness?" she joked. "I suppose that drone was yours, then…"

Her smile died on her lips, because Eirene's face had taken on an awful expression, like an appalled grimace, and in that moment Astrid just knew something was wrong. What, she didn't know, but something. "Uh…are you alright?"

Then the next few moments seemed to happen in slow motion. Eirene reached into her handbag and pulled out a slim dark shape, then lifted it towards Astrid. Acting on instinct rather than anything else, Astrid batted it out of her hand. It landed on the grass near where the phone had fallen, and even in the dim light its identity was clear.

It was a stunner.

"Heeey," Astrid dragged out, dismay now warring with confusion in her mind. "Were you going to use that?"

The other woman just snarled in response, then lunged for the stunner.

As if watching all of this happen to someone else, Astrid stepped forward and kicked the stunner out of her way. It skidded forward to disappear under a low, perfectly trimmed shrub. *Thank you, self-defence classes.*

But Eirene just gave her an anguished look, then scrambled onto her hands and knees on the grass.

The second requested package is on its way, the message had read. Astrid put that together with the way Eirene was suddenly acting like a psycho, and trying to *stun* her....

"I have a really bad feeling about this," Astrid said aloud. And beyond that feeling was the feeling that she really, really wasn't panicking like she ought to… Moving quickly, she followed the stone path along to the front of the conservatory, calling Nathaniel on her phone as she did so. The door turned out to be locked, so she followed the edge of the building a little further.

Then she found something tucked around the corner, where no one in their right mind would think to look. It was a full-sized winged delivery drone, complete with a large, square plastic transport crate. The detail screen was showing it was empty, but the delivery address was already listed in glowing green letters on its small screen. *Port-co*, followed by a string of numbers she'd bet were the same ones as on Eirene's phone.

Portal colony.

"*What is it, Az?*" Nathaniel's voice came small and tinny from her phone, and she lifted it to her ear, almost crying in relief that he'd answered.

"Nate, have you found Tammy yet?"

"*No, you were the one going to get her. I think she must have fallen asleep in the loo-*"

"I need you to come now!" Astrid burst out. "Come to the conservatory around the back of the mansion, and don't delay! Oh, and watch out for…Eirene."

The woman herself was now standing at the edge of the building, looking a little worse for wear. She held the stunner that Astrid had stupidly – *stupidly* left her with, and a little red light blinked repeatedly at one end as she pressed the trigger.

"Out of battery," Astrid said flatly, but she had the most dreadful sense of despair coming over her. "I guess you've already used it today for packages one and two, huh?"

"Astrid? What's happening?"

"I think Eirene's done something terrible," she replied, still watching the woman who was futilely pressing the trigger. "Check your phone tracker. Is Tamzyn still in the building?"

"Why wouldn't she be?" Nathaniel began, then a moment later: *"Oh, #@$*! She's over by the portal!"*

Eirene let out a frustrated cry at hearing that, finally tossing the stunner aside, then moved as if to run. But she was thirty years older than Astrid, and probably hadn't been training four times a week in case of future kidnapping attempts like Astrid had. Feeling fury rush through her, Astrid stepped forward and swung her leg around low. Her semi-formal dress stopped her from making the full movement, but she still managed to trip the older woman, who sprawled with some force onto the grass.

"What have you done with Tamzyn?!" Astrid roared, crouching down in front of her and leaning into her face.

"I don't know what you're talking about!" Eirene shouted back. But then as light shone out onto the nearby wall and footsteps sounded, she shouted, "Help, help! Elder abuse!"

A few seconds later a tall figure came into view, silhouetted from behind from the light of the mansion. "Astrid?" she heard Nathaniel say. "Are you OK?"

With her heart pounding with panic, Astrid said urgently, "I came out here looking for Tamzyn 'cos someone said she'd come out with Eirene and I saw her phone and she's been sending deliveries to the portal and she tried to stun me and we've got to get Tamzyn!"

"That is a blatant lie!" Eirene argued as she sat up. "She's making things up again, just like she did last year!"

Nathaniel ignored her. "When did this happen?!"

"I don't know, but we've got to go *now*, Nate, or it'll be too late! The drones are pre-programmed, and they'll send her wherever Eirene wanted her to go!" Astrid had been shouting, but she knew that there was really only one place that Eirene would be sending Tamzyn. Maybe those huge gold earrings weren't fake after all.

She saw despair come over his features, then resolution as he set his jaw. He nodded. "Let's go."

"Just a moment." Astrid marched over to Eirene, then grabbed the woman's phone right out of her hand.

"Hey!"

"Don't give me that, you kidnapper! You're going to be in *so* much trouble," Astrid told her furiously. "As soon as we get Tamzyn back, we're going straight to the police!"

"AZ!"

"Coming!"

They sped the whole way, Nathaniel's newer vehicle going as fast as its speed-control settings would allow. By some miracle they weren't stopped, and the fifteen-minute journey took a mere eight minutes.

"It's too long," Nathaniel said in agitation. "We're too slow. Is she still here, Az?"

Astrid checked her phone again. The tracker with its little glowing dot saying 'Tamzyn' still showed on her screen, but as she watched, it blinked then vanished. "She's just gone through," she said in a hollow voice.

"Call someone! Call Brian or Suraya or Walt at the colony, but don't let her get taken!"

As he'd been speaking, his car had auto-dialled all of those people, and little holographic screens shot up along the top of the windscreen, showing the status of each call.

Unauthorised call.

Unauthorised call.

Unauthorised call.

"You know we aren't allowed to call them," Astrid cried. "We're blocked. We have to get there ourselves!" And they'd pray that someone would let them through the portal at once, because that could be just as much of a challenge.

The vehicle screeched into the delivery bay for the Earth-side portal building, and both of them leapt out as it came to a halt. Astrid almost stumbled in her gown's narrow skirt, but then she gave it a good tug – *riiip* – and kicked off her high heels, then sprinted after her brother on the smooth concrete.

She saw him reach the first set of doors, then pause briefly before turning sideways and slipping through into the lit-up building. A moment later Astrid reached them and realised what he'd done – the security doors had been locked in place, with about a two-foot gap in between. No one was in sight. She didn't question her good luck, instead turned sideways to squeeze through after Nathaniel.

She caught up with him in the control room. It was almost a perfect replica of the colony side, right down to the few buttons and the screen that recorded everything that had been sent through and received.

"Four minutes ago a drone delivery went through," he said, studying the screen for mere moments, then moved towards the door separating them from the portal itself. "Send me through, Az."

She glanced at the screen, reading *82.5 kgs crop fertiliser*, then frowned. "The weights must be off, because Tamzyn isn't that heavy."

But Nathaniel had already strapped himself into one of the portal-device's seats, and he scrunched his eyes shut. "Go, Astrid!"

She quickly shut the door, then pressed the *go* button. A moment later the inner room was filled with crystalline light. She scrunched her eyes shut too, then when she opened them again, the room was empty. He'd gone through.

Where was the controller who'd usually be here, she wondered? More importantly, could she get herself through without another person to press the button?

Just then she heard footsteps from outside. There was a gentle breeze as the door was opened, accompanied by a faint scent rather like grass clippings mixed with skunk.

"Hey!"

Uh oh.

The colony

The portal's light flashed and for a moment Nathaniel felt like his molecules were about to drift off in every direction. But that sensation didn't last, and next thing he heard the alarm confirming a safe arrival. He opened his eyes, blinking a little at the residual light, then stumbled out of the seat into the colony's delivery area.

"Nate, is that you?" He turned to see a young man standing safely over the painted safety line, staring at him. "What are you doing here, and where's your safety gear?"

"Brian!" Nathaniel exploded in relief. Out of all the people who might have been on duty, it was a friend. "There's a drone that's just come through the portal. It's pre-programmed for delivery-"

"Yeah, there's one just in the other room. What's the big deal?"

"Tamzyn's inside!"

Brian's jaw dropped, but he didn't protest as Nathaniel raced through the doorway. But there were stacks and stacks of crates lined up along the walls and around the floor, and Nathaniel could spot three different drones already in action. "Which one is it!?"

"Um…this one came through twenty minutes ago," Brian said, pointing at a big grey crate with a flashing green screen. "But there's a problem with its battery, so we just replaced it. We were about to send it off." He shrugged helplessly. "The label says it's just mining equipment!"

Nathaniel's heart plummeted. "What about the one that came through five minutes ago?"

"That one went straight through," Brian replied, his face creased with worry. "Was there really someone inside?"

There better not have been, Nathaniel swore to himself, or else he'd tear this world apart until he got his wife back. But he still approached the nearby drone crate with shaking hands, pulling his phone out and displaying the 'track' function. It didn't work so clearly on this side of the portal, but it seemed to be saying that Tammy was right…here. *Oh please, please let her still be here!*

"The crate's locked!" he cried in frustration a few moments later.

"It's a high security one," Brian explained apologetically. "I can get the key-"

"Yes, get the freaking key!"

"Getting it, getting it," his friend murmured, but he moved quickly.

Ten seconds later the crate's seal popped with a beep, and Nathaniel pushed back the hydraulic lid, cursing it for not moving faster. Inside the metre-by-metre space was a thick pile of packing material, and with his heart pounding, he dug through it with shaking hands until he hit cloth. He yanked off the cloth, and the whole pile of material came with it.

And there she was, curled up in the space with her head almost pressed into her knees, and the pattern of the fabric marked on her soft cheek.

"*Ohhhhh…*" Brian breathed. "There's a girl in the box."

"Help me!" Nathaniel cried, and as if shaking off his shock, Brian leaned forward to help lift Tamzyn out. She seemed so small and fragile as they lay her down on the hard floor, still partially curled up.

With trembling fingers Nathaniel checked her pulse, but he couldn't feel anything beyond the warmth of her skin and his own shaking. "Get the medic!"

But then miracle of all miracles, her eyes fluttered open, then fixed on his face. He just about wept. "Tammy?"

"Nathaniel?" she whispered in Tyger. "Why are you painted like a rainbow?"

It was such a nonsensical thing to ask, that even in his immense relief he leaned back a little. Had her mind been injured? But as she stretched as if trying to get up, he saw that his hands were splattered with swirls of pink, green, blue and orange. The colour extended all the way up his arms and over the rest of his body, and he realised absently that he'd gone through the portal without coveralls, and his face must look the same way.

Too freaking bad, he thought. But still, a wide smile split his face. Tamzyn was safe. And it was all due to a nosy sister and a flat battery. "I was in a hurry. How do you feel?"

"Like I could sleep for a week," she murmured, reaching up to touch his face. She had the dreamy expression she'd get when she first woke. "You've got an orange nose. You look very foolish."

"Why thank you." But he just grinned wider.

Just then there was a familiar beeping sound; that of another package arriving. Perhaps real machine parts this time. But instead, ten seconds later a colourful figure came racing through from the portal device. It was Astrid, still in a dress and with her longish straight hair streaming down her back, but she was also multicoloured from the top of her head down to her bare feet. There were two skin-coloured circles around her eyes. She, at least, had worn goggles.

"Oh, thank God," she cried emphatically, her gaze falling on Tamzyn. "She's still here!"

"Flat battery on the drone," Nathaniel told her. "How did you get through?"

"The portal controller had been having a weed break. I told him I'd get him in trouble if he didn't send me through, and that he'd be arrested for kidnapping." Then Astrid shrugged. "I guess I didn't need to hurry so much, huh? Do I look as bad as you do?"

"The colour's getting worse by the moment," he replied cheerfully. "We'll be stained for weeks, too." "Oh good." But she was grinning now, the relief surely hitting her as hard as it had him, and she slumped to the ground next to him. "How's Tammy?"

"Tired," Tamzyn murmured.

"Sleeping off the aftereffects of being stunned, no doubt," Nathaniel answered. "But someone must have been watching over us, Az. Her drone came in some time ago. The one that was just delivered was something else. I should have known eighty-two kilos was too heavy."

Or perhaps if he'd known, he might have lost hope, so it was better that he hadn't.

"Brian was here, and he's gone to get a medic," he continued. "I think we'll have some explaining to do. I just hope that Eirene was the only one who was involved."

"Maybe she was trying to trade Tamzyn back for Hana," Astrid wondered aloud. Her expression was thoughtful. "I didn't have a chance to tell you any of this, but Percy called me in a panic earlier, saying that he thought Hana had been kidnapped by the Tyger locals. I confronted Eirene tonight, but she told me that she had a video showing Hana had chosen to come back through the portal, and that Percy wouldn't believe it. I accepted that, but now I won't believe anything she said." She shook her head, her brows lowering. "Oh, and it gets worse. Percy said that Raka used Earther weapons to take over Syrene. People think Emir Jireh is dead, and Aunt Jae's back at the mining station."

"That's terrible," Nathaniel breathed. Even with his joy at Tamzyn's last minute rescue, he couldn't help but be appalled at Astrid's news. "And your friend, Benn?"

"Oh, that's the good news! Percy was wrong, because Jireh and Benn are both fine – although keep that to yourself, please. They all made it down south, and Benn went through the portal to Earth to see if he could get some help. He was there at the party tonight…" But then Astrid's face froze, and her words petered into silence. "*Ohhhhh….no.*"

"What is it?" Nathaniel asked. He sat cross-legged on the ground with Tamzyn sleepy-eyed in front of him, and he was splattered with colour like a monkey had tried to create an impressionist painting. But Astrid could see he didn't understand.

"It might be nothing," Astrid said carefully. "It's just that Eirene's phone said there were *two* parcels. Tamzyn was only one of them."

"Oh..."

With her good mood abruptly gone, she pulled out Eirene's phone and scrolled through the recently sent messages. The last one was the same as she'd seen. *The second requested parcel is on its way.* The one before that was to Anton, assuring him that he wasn't missing anything at the party, and that Eirene would bring him a treat on the way home. The message previous to *that* was sent about half an hour before the last, so about the time Tamzyn went missing. *The requested parcel is on its way.*

The second parcel wouldn't be Benn, Astrid told herself even as she picked up her own phone and opened the tracking function. It wouldn't be him, because a woman like Eirene surely couldn't capture two young people in one single evening. She was middle-aged and anxious, and not at all threatening...

Which had made her so much more effective at kidnapping, Astrid realised a moment later when she saw the truth spelled out on her phone's small screen. She turned to the others. "We had a nice chat, Benn and I," she said in a hollow voice. "Then he went off to meet someone important, but not before he added his phone to my tracker. See? Here it is."

She held up the screen. When used on Earth, it displayed tiny streets and parks and buildings, all packed tightly together. But here, she saw only the tiny outline of the colony, then a little glowing dot moving further and further away. *Benn,* the screen read. *14 KM away. 14.3 KM. 14.7 KM.* "I guess the important person he was meeting was Eirene," she added desolately.

"He must be in the drone that just went through," Nathaniel exclaimed. His eyes were wide with horror. "Where do you think he's going?"

"To Raka, of course!" Astrid exploded. "Eirene must have been working with him for ages! She must've been the one who covered up what happened to me, and she seems so bloody weak and *anxious* all the time that no one would've suspected her!" She could feel herself trembling, her hands clenched at her sides. "Nathaniel, Raka's going to kill Benn. I'm sure of it!"

Syrene

Chay knew she couldn't outrun the soldiers. Not in this form, and she didn't have the time to take another. She'd never been the fastest shifter, and fear just made her freeze up and stay in her human form. But she tried her best to escape anyway, taking the first left turn and running as far away from the sanctuary as she could.

They caught up somewhere around the bend, not too far away from one of the exits into the city. She heard someone or something running closer and closer, not sounding at all human, then suddenly she was knocked hard to the ground. A low, deep growl in her ear told her exactly what had caught her, and she couldn't push back the pang of fear that shot through her.

"I'm not fighting!" she cried. "Don't hurt me!"

"Dragonfly," she heard one man say to another in Mahadrese tones. "Bring her." Then to Chay he said grimly, "If you fight or you even show a hint of changing forms, you're dead. Understand?"

She nodded meekly, keeping her head down as the Mahadrese soldiers pulled her to her feet and tied her hands behind her back, but her mind was humming. At least two of them were Blessed, she figured, pondering her chances of fighting them off and escaping. But even if she *did* escape, it would have to be through the city, because she wouldn't lead them past the sanctuary. And even if they didn't catch her, they'd just shoot her down with arrows or even Earther weapons. She'd seen it happen to others.

The soldiers walked Chay along until they emerged from this narrow entrance to the tunnels, almost hidden under a bridge, and she blinked at the sudden brightness of daylight. She caught a glimpse of a silver-haired Blessed in Mahadrese uniform, then quickly ducked her head again so her hair covered her face. Her horrible, helpful cloak was gone, left in the tunnels, and she needed a veil. She hadn't recognised any faces, but she didn't dare take the risk they'd recognise *her*.

"Where's the cage wagon?" she heard one of the soldiers ask another.

"Back by the cattle markets," the second replied. She heard him spit on the ground. "Didn't think the Bastard would make it so far, not in his condition."

Cage wagons and spitting. Lovely. Chay thought back to how Raka would talk at length about his great plans for Syrene once he 'reclaimed his inheritance'. Perhaps those two things *had* been in the plan, but he'd never mentioned them to her.

They were still standing in the dry streambed that ran through this part of the city. Some years ago the water had been diverted, hence the existence of the tunnels she'd been hiding in. The tunnel entrance was almost invisible from here, but she still saw the other soldiers drag out another figure a few moments later. This time it was a great cat, hanging limply from the grip of two other soldiers. Its white fur was smeared with blood and dirt, and one of the soldiers was still holding an unsheathed sword, its blade marked red.

"You weren't supposed to kill him," one of the soldiers holding Chay said reproachfully. "The emir is going to do that."

The nearest of the new soldiers scoffed. He wore a light helmet without a faceplate, and his pale Blessed hair showed a little under the helm. "He's not dead; just has a knock to the head and a cut or two. He'll live for the execution, not that it matters in the end."

"It'll matter to *you*, Uzyn, because you'll be the one taking the blame," the first soldier argued. "I told you to use chains instead of rope, but you wouldn't listen."

Uzyn gave some insulting retort, but then his gaze fell on Chay. "Who's this?"

"Some piece of Dragonfly dirt. Does it matter?"

But she'd seen the expression in his eyes, so his next words came as no surprise. "Yes, because that's no ordinary piece of dirt, that's the emir's old pet." He sneered. "Maybe today's our lucky day after all."

Chay's heart sank to her feet. It looked like today wasn't *her* lucky day. No, not at all.

An hour later, when all the attempts to escape the cage-wagon they'd been shoved in had failed, and they arrived at the Syrenian palace, Chay wasn't just feeling unlucky. No, she was feeling like the most ill-fated person to ever walk the planet.

Except for having one small, beautiful person still sleeping back at the sanctuary. If only that beautiful person survived, she told herself, then none of the rest would matter. If only Raka didn't want to see them, and left them to live their life in freedom and safety, she could put up with anything.

Just then a palace guard came up to the cage and studied the occupants with apparent disinterest. Chay didn't recognise him, but he wore the uniform of the Mahadrese palace rather than the Syrenian one. "The emir will see them now."

No!

"But the Bastard's half-dead," one of the soldiers who'd brought them said. "Should we throw some water on him first or something?"

"The emir said *now*," the palace guard countered. "Do you want to be the one to tell him no?"

The answer was no. No, they did not. So out they came, even though Orin was still battered and unconscious, and Chay's legs were numb from sitting in the too-low cage.

Time to face the real monster.

CHAPTER 21

Haste

The colony

"Benn's in that delivery drone," Astrid exclaimed in horror. In her hand, her phone's tracker was updating every few seconds. *BENN IS 18.9 KM AWAY. 19.2 KM. 19.5 KM.* "We have to get him back!"

Brian had walked back into the room just as she was speaking. "The medic's stuck in room 6," he began. "Can you take your girl to him?"

"Brian!" Astrid shouted. "How do you turn the drones around?! Someone's inside one!"

Brian's eyes bugged wide, and he shook his head. "Astrid! Uh… they're secured drones, so they can't be turned around. They only go where they're programmed to go, then you can send them back. It's their whole job!"

"Well, it's a stupid job!" she shrieked. "Benn's on his way to crazy Emir Raka, and he's dead if we don't get him back! There must be some way around it!"

Brian was still shaking his head, his face pale and his expression one of utter horror. "I'll…I'll go get Walt," he stammered. Then he turned and ran from the room again, leaving Astrid alone with her brother and still-dopey Tamzyn. Lucky, lucky Tamzyn to have had a flat battery on her drone.

Nathaniel met Astrid's eyes. His own eyes were wide, but his expression was a picture of hopelessness. "Maybe Walt can help," he suggested, but even he didn't sound like he believed it. "Maybe we can go back and try to make Eirene abort the delivery."

Astrid slumped to the ground in sudden, dismayed exhaustion. She shook her head. "It'll be too late," she said dully. "Think how long it would take to get back there, find Eirene, and bring her back, even assuming that no one stops us and that she even agrees to help us! And she won't. We got lucky with Tammy, Nate. That won't happen twice. By the time we'd get back, Benn will practically be at his destination. And you heard Brian: those things aren't designed to be changeable."

"Then what?"

Her shoulders slumped. "I don't know. There must be *something* else."

Nathaniel watched her for a long moment, and Tamzyn stirred in his lap. "My head," she groaned in Tyger. "Hurts."

"Az, I need to take Tammy to the medic," he said softly. "Are you going to be alright here?"

Astrid shrugged, unable to say yes, but not wanting to hold him back. It wasn't as if he could help her now.

He left, and she climbed to her feet and moved over to the delivery control station. It was a labyrinth of buttons and screens. She recognised a few of them – operating the doors, for example – but wouldn't know where to start with something like a secured delivery drone.

"I have to try," she said under her breath. "I *have to.*" Because if she didn't, then she'd be the world's worst friend.

The sound of light footsteps behind her made her jolt. She spun around, her hands in fists as if prepared to fight. And there was Percy, dressed in what looked like the same grey tunic he'd worn when she last saw him.

He leapt back, his hands in the air. "Whoa! What happened to your…everything?"

"Portal," Astrid snapped. "I don't have time for a conversation, Percy. Someone's in serious trouble!"

He stepped forward again, his expression intent. "I know. I was listening through the door and I heard everything you were saying… even about my mum…but I can help. That's why I'm here."

Her eyebrows shot up. "Really? You can stop a secured delivery drone, right now?"

"Kind of…" he hedged. "But it's not easy. I've got a security override key from Dad since he doesn't need it anymore, but you have to touch the drone that you want to override."

She held up the phone with its moving tracker. "It's twenty-three k's away, Percy!" she cried. "How are we supposed to do that?"

He looked a little twitchy now, but he seemed to jitter with excitement. "I'll tell you how," he replied rapidly, "but you've got to keep it quiet that I helped you. And you've got to promise to help Hana."

"What? Hana?"

"They've got her, Astrid! I told you that! Swear you'll get her back for me, and I'll help you go."

Astrid paused, blinking. It seemed the stupidest thing to agree to, because how on earth – on this world – was she going to do it? But she couldn't say no, either. "I'll do it," she agreed quickly. "Now, how do we catch the drone?"

Percy huffed out a deep breath. "OK. So you're not going to like this…"

All things considered, Percy wasn't so stupid after all, Astrid thought ten minutes later. He'd been smart enough to keep a general override key from his father, and to hide it from his controlling mother. He'd been smart enough not to believe his mother about Hana – and Eirene *certainly* hadn't shown him any video footage of the girl leaving freely. He'd been smart enough to learn how to reset Tamzyn's empty drone, since that was already programmed to go to the same place.

He'd also been smart enough *not* to volunteer to chase down Benn's drone. "If it goes sour, the locals will probably treat you better than me because you're a girl," he'd said nervously. "Here, have a weapon." He'd handed her a stunner. "Sorry, I couldn't get to any guns on time."

Astrid had disagreed with his comment about being treated better if caught, because terrible men could do terrible things to females, things that were better not to think about. But she'd taken the stunner and had agreed to go, because there was no time to think, and Benn's life was on the line.

But if Percy was smarter than expected, then she, Astrid, was the one who was stupid and desperate enough to shove herself into a drone's storage crate *which was a really small, dark space!* and to let him close the lid over her head, although it wasn't locked.

She was currently curled up with her multicoloured legs tucked underneath her and her head awkwardly crooked to the side, resting against the roof of the container. The precious override key was in one hand, the stunner was in her lap, and her phone was in the other hand, its screen lighting up the entire space.

"I'm going to let it go now, OK?" she heard Percy say through the crate's wall, his words sounding muffled like he was speaking through water.

"OK!" Astrid shouted back, even though she really, really wasn't OK. In fact, she could feel her breathing becoming shallower and faster by the moment. It was too dark in here. Too small. She couldn't breathe, and she could feel the drone's engine roaring to life; feel the intense drag as it picked up speed faster than she could have imagined, and could feel her head begin to spin as she tried to stave off a full-blown panic attack.

She had just enough focus to realise that this might have been the stupidest thing she'd ever done.

Syrene

The last (and only) time Jazir and Vuyani had visited the Syrenian palace's trade gate, it had been busy and full of people. Buyers and sellers had been everywhere outside the palace walls, with merchants coming right up to the gates to look through or to sell goods to the guards. Jazir had watched as some of them had been turned away, some had been purchased from, and others had just shared a good laugh with the guards.

But those guards had been wearing Syrenian armour and Syrenian helmets with their neat point on the top. Funny, he'd never even thought about what colour their uniforms were around the branzine metal armour, but now he realised that the Syrenians usually wore shades of blue.

Today, as he and Vuyani watched from a distance, he could see the guards around the palace wore grey fabric under their armour. Unlike the usual pointed helmets, their helmets had smooth craniums, and the weapons in their hands were obvious even from this distance. They were black, silver or occasionally green: long and thin on one end, and thicker at the other end where the guards held them.

"Ooh," Jazir breathed, undecided whether he was impressed or horrified. "Those are *Earther* weapons, Vuy. Look at them."

"I'm looking," his sister replied, her tone brusque but quiet. He glanced across at her to see her eyebrows were drawn low over her eyes, her expression one of displeasure. "I knew about the takeover. We both did. It's just…so hard to see it like this."

They'd spent the last several months at their little house in the western parts of Syrene, in a somewhat isolated little village. Now it had a new well *and* a new roof, it proved to be quite comfortable, and they'd focused their efforts on the seasonal crops that could be processed and traded for more goods to take in their next trading round.

There'd been plenty of gossip to be had amongst their neighbours, and Jazir knew that Vuyani had also enjoyed spreading the story of 'helping' the regent, and winning all that gold. If the parts about Earther-Dragonfly Tam had to be brushed over, then so be it.

But their home was isolated enough that they'd only heard about the takeover a few days earlier, when they'd reached another village just outside Syrene's capital. It had been all everyone could talk about – their new emir, the new taxes that were already being instituted, and whether they were happy about it or not. Jazir had quickly figured out that those who *weren't* happy about it should keep their mouths shut.

Speaking of which, even though their covered wagon had stopped a good distance away from the trade gates, he could see they'd caught the attention of one of the guards. The man crooked his head sideways and narrowed his eyes at them. "State your business, or move on!" he called.

Jazir glanced at his sister nervously. They'd originally planned on visiting the palace again to see if they could sell spices or polished stones for jewellery, since the quality of their goods was now far better than they could have afforded in the past, but suddenly that idea didn't seem so appealing. "Uh…"

"Moving on," Vuyani called back to the guard. "Apologies." Then she ducked her head and lifted the reins, flicking them to move their karaks along. The animals snorted and obediently began to move forward, tugging the heavy wagon behind them. But she'd been too slow, because now one of the other guards had spotted their wagon and was stepping forward.

"Move it!" Jazir whispered, his stomach twisting with unease and his heart beginning to pound. "He looks the sort to rob us then call it tax." If they lost their goods, even half of them, they'd struggle all winter. They might even have to go back to a one-karak wagon, and then they'd be back where they'd started.

"I'm trying," she hissed back.

But just then, the pounding in Jazir's chest grew louder until he realised it was actually hoofbeats and had been the whole time. There was a lowing sound, and next thing the open space between them and the palace gate was being filled with karaks. And not big, strong, long-haired wagon-pulling karaks like theirs, but the smaller, short-haired sort that were left in fields for months at a time, then sold for their meat and hides.

But when those karak were brought to market, there were usually just a few at a time. Now there were *dozens,* all milling around and banging up against the gates and pooping and ignoring the shouts of the guards...

"What the..." he breathed. "Can you see the herders?"

"No, but we'll keep moving," Vuyani said quickly. She flicked the reins again, and this time their karaks picked up the pace, perhaps disturbed by their nearby cousins.

It took some time before they were out of sight of the palace, and on one of the quieter streets, just big enough for their wagon. "That was strange," Jazir commented. "I've never heard of karaks being herded past the palace, and definitely not that many. Do you think that was just an accident?"

His sister watched the distant streets with suspicious, narrowed eyes. "I don't know," she replied finally. "But in case it wasn't, I say we get as far away from here as we can."

Chay had wondered many times how she'd react if she was ever recaptured. She'd hoped never to face the situation, since even the thought of it had made her feel ill, but she'd hoped that she wouldn't shame herself by crying or trembling.

Right now, the circumstances were almost as bad as they could get, but she wasn't crying *or* trembling. No, she was just walking quietly behind the guards, her hands still tied in front of her, and her head dipped so that her dyed blue hair fell over her face.

Chay felt like she was shrivelling inside, like all her courage and personality and even her voice was being folded up and forced back into the little box called *esira,* and she hadn't even seen Raka yet. Her footsteps didn't even make a decent sound on the stone floors, not like theirs did.

Clank-clank-clank-clank was the sound of the guards' footsteps. There was a scraping shuffle from Orin, who was still a bloodied, limp rag of a *beini*. And for her? There was almost no sound, because she was walking too quietly, too carefully, with those old leather scraps she called sandals.

I hope he kills me quickly, a little thought popped in. *I can't go back to being nothing.*

The terrible thought surprised Chay a little, but she didn't have time to dwell on it because in the next moment she was being led through a door. The guards ahead of her paused outside a high, beaded curtain, but only for a few seconds before she was being led through that too.

She closed her eyes.

"His most splendid and revered Magnificence, Emir Raka of all Mahadra and Syrene!" someone announced in a Mahadrese accent.

Chay didn't need the kick to the back of her knees to remind her to kneel, but she got it anyway. Her body automatically folded as if remembering all the times she'd done something similar; her fists tightly held in front of her as if they'd be any kind of support.

He'd changed his title. That was typical of his arrogance, but she still couldn't look at him. At least the carpeted floor beneath her had an interesting pattern.

There was a long silence, then she heard him speak, his tone icy-cold. "Is the Bastard dead?"

She felt the guards around her shuffle. "No, Your most splendid and revered Magnificence," one of them ventured. "He put up a fight, but he is still alive. Some cold water would help to wake him."

"Then go wake him," Raka snapped back, "and come back once you've got something worth punishing. This filthy rug of a *beini* isn't much good to me."

There were murmured apologies, and in Chay's peripheral vision she saw some of the guards leave the room, along with poor, rug-like Orin. She hoped he didn't wake. Better to be a true rug than face whatever punishment the emir had for him.

Then the sound of footsteps drew closer. These ones were louder, although not like the guards', and had a surety about them that she'd recognise in an instant. She saw leather boots draw nearer, their beautifully-worked material embroidered with ornate designs. Was that a gem or two she spied amongst that pattern?

"So the faithless servant returns." Raka's tone was disgusted, like whenever he'd talk about the boy-regent, or his now-dead uncle. "Look at me, Chakandra."

She couldn't help herself. As if on strings, she lifted her chin towards the sound of his voice, but she couldn't open her eyes. She just couldn't. Because if she did, then he'd see everything there; everything good and bad and confused that she felt for him.

"LOOK AT ME!"

Chay's eyes shot open, and there he was in front of her. So very close, bending down over her so that she could see the tiny hairs in his nose. So handsome, so familiar, but the disgust on his face had never before been directed at her.

For a moment a wave of regret and resentment rocked her. She swayed where she knelt, and she could only hold his gaze for a few seconds before glancing away. She didn't speak. She felt small and shrivelled and like she was *nothing*.

"Was your life with me truly so dreadful that you had to abandon me for my brother?" Raka spat. "How long were you unfaithful to me, hmm? From the beginning? Did the two of you laugh at me, Chakandra?"

She tried to speak, overcome by dismay at his completely inaccurate accusations, but he carried on. "My concubine and my only brother, betraying me in the most terrible of ways. You could have had a wonderful life in my palaces, Chakandra, but instead you chose to flee as if you were suffering. Now look at you. Covered in mud and faeces. Living in a sewer." He leaned forward again, and she felt his breath on her cheek, smelled the fragrance of that same old perfumed oil he used. "Was it worth it? I hope it was, because you are going to pay for every moment of humiliation I felt as a result of your absence."

Finally he stopped speaking. Misery and confusion swirled around in Chay's head, along with a desolate hope. Did he really think she'd been capable of that kind of thing? Had he actually cared so much that she'd left? Had she misstepped by believing Orin as she did? (Did he really think she smelled like faeces? Because that was just the clothes!)

After several seconds of silence, he sneered. "Nothing to say? Of course not. Get her out of here."

Two soldiers moved forward, and Chay finally found her voice. "Wait!"

Raka raised a hand, halting the soldiers. "Speak, if you can."

She could now see another dozen or so people in the room, courtiers by the looks of them. A white-haired guard stood just behind Raka with an expression of distaste on his face. Not Orin, but where Orin used to stand. There were so many things she could have said then, starting with the fact that she'd never been with anyone else. But instead what came out was, "You called me your concubine."

Raka scowled. "A slip of the tongue. You were a slave. You *are* a slave."

Yes, but he'd *said* concubine in front of all of these people. If he'd done the same a year earlier, Chay never would have left. She would've been safe, and her child would have been safe too, as offspring of a confirmed, low-level wife. "A slave can hardly be unfaithful, then," she continued, her voice small but clear. "As a slave, I owe you nothing but hatred and fear." She grimaced, shaking her head in dismay. "But I *was* faithful to you. I didn't need to be, but I was."

He stared at her for a moment, then glanced back at the white-haired guard. "Does she speak the truth?"

The guard drew in a deep breath. "I smell no lie, Your most splend-"

"Yes, yes." Raka cut him off with a wave of his hand. "Then why did you leave?"

Because she'd been afraid. Because she'd been with child. Because she'd been forgetting who she was, and that this man was and always had been her enemy. "Because you would not name me concubine," Chay replied finally, "and because I was starting to forget that you destroyed my family, and was starting to think that my place really was serving you. I could not betray them in such a way."

His eyes narrowed, but he glanced again at the Blessed guard.

"I smell no lie," the guard said, "but there is something not quite right."

Curses. It wasn't quite a lie, but it was a definite deflection. And now that the Blessed was watching – and *smelling* – she had to tell the perfect truth.

But Raka's mouth twisted into a sneer. "So your rapid departure had nothing to do with being with child? I can only assume that if Orin lied to me about so much, he would lie to me about that too."

Truth. Truth. Truth. "There was no child," Chay tried.

"Lie," the guard cut in.

"Very well, there *was*, but it died-"

"Lie."

"Try the truth, Chakandra," Raka snapped. "Before I lose patience. Death can be slow, or it can be quick. You choose."

She was shaking and crying now, but she managed to stammer, "Jesha is just a baby, Your Magnificence! She's harmless! You don't need to hurt her, please!"

There was a brief silence. "I smell no lie," the guard said quietly.

"Hmm." Raka studied Chay with narrowed eyes, his head tilted to the side, and his hands looped gracefully behind his back. "A girl child. Blessed?"

Poor Jesha. Poor, little, sweet-natured baby Jesha. Chay thought about lying to protect her, then finally shook her head. "No," she whispered. "Just an ordinary, unthreatening baby girl."

"And where is this ordinary baby girl, Chakandra?"

Chay dropped her head. She thought of poor Jeniel, and the rest of them who she'd inadvertently betrayed. "With some peasant folk. Good people who don't know my history," she replied quietly. "They think I'm a widow."

"I smell no lie," the Blessed guard said.

Oh, thank God.

But Raka was silent. She waited for him to pronounce death and destruction over her and the child, or to say anything, anything at all to the news that he was a father. But instead there was an odd little sound, almost like a bell. Raka jolted upright, his face brightening, then stuck out one hand, palm upwards. A servant hastily handed him a small, brick-like object, and he tapped at it a couple of times.

Then his smile grew. "Ten minutes until the first delivery arrives," he announced. "Then you shall see what happens to those who betray me."

His words made no sense, but at least he wasn't talking about hunting down little Jesha. So Chay let the guards drag her to the side of the large room, then she tucked her head into her knees and waited.

Outside the Syrenian palace, overwhelmed guards tried desperately to herd the fifty or sixty karaks away from the gates, or at least not be crushed by them. The animals weren't doing anything harmful. They were just milling around, but were completely in the way.

Much too late, a baffled-looking herder came onto the scene. His cheeks and nose were ruddy from what the guards thought was probably a lunch of methuo juice, and he didn't look nearly as sorry as he should at the situation.

"A thousand apologies," he called across the mooing, disorderly mass of animals. "My *something something something…*" But the rest of his explanation was lost in the noise.

The guards didn't care about his reasons, just that he remove his animals as soon as possible. The herder proceeded to do so, but that took longer than it could have if he'd had anyone to help him. Meanwhile, a large crowd of laughing, gawking spectators watched from outside *and* inside the palace gates.

Finally the karaks were mostly heading towards the market, except for one or two strays who trotted off in the opposite direction.

One of the rumpled, harried guards saw the escapees, but decided against saying anything due to the trouble the herder had caused.

But in all the chaos, nobody noticed that quite a lot was happening under their feet. The passages down there were hardly used by anyone at all, except for those who already knew they existed. And those people knew of the hidden exits all across the city, including the cattle markets, the palace…and outside the city wall too.

And somewhere underfoot, there was an Earther woman quietly setting up a speaker system. She worked alone in the semi-darkness, and next to her was an enormous pile of empty cans of non-toxic grey spray-paint.

Enough to colour a small building, or, say…fifty or sixty animals?

Benn woke up to darkness. He had the most tremendous headache, as though he was being squeezed from different directions, and a real crick in his neck. One of his legs felt numb, and a voice was muttering from somewhere around his midriff.

"Benn. Benn. Breathe. Gotta breathe. I can do it. Eight-point-four k's. Eight-point-two k's."

He blinked and tried to sit up, but he couldn't move, and the darkness didn't lift. "Whaz hapning?"

"Benn!? Are you awake?"

He blinked again as he identified the owner of the voice. "Astrid? Issit you? Where are you?"

There was an odd, scritchy shuffling sound, then she replied, *"Um…long story. You know I'm calling you on your phone, right?"*

Phone? Phone…ah, that was right. Earther technology. So she wasn't actually sharing this space with him, but merely communicating into it. With every passing moment, Benn woke up more, but with that wakefulness came an increasing sense of fear.

"Astrid," he said carefully, "I seem to be in a box. Why am I in a box?"

Benn's voice was blurred from the poor phone reception and probably also from being stunned, but Astrid could hear his growing panic. Her own heartrate, already too high from being trapped in this death-box (*oh God why had she agreed to getting in here?!*) picked up further, and she had to force herself to breathe deeply and slowly. *Relax.* In her lap, her precious phone's screen glowed with the knowledge of Benn's closeness, and lit up the tiny space.

"I've got good news and bad news," she replied carefully. "The good news is, I'll probably be getting you out of that box in about… oh, seven minutes?"

"Seven minutes?" She heard him breathing harshly, each pant short and shallow even though his voice was muffled. *"Seven minutes is bearable. But why am I here?"*

Yeah, that was the bad, possibly hysteria-inducing news. "Um… so you know those drones that humans use to send parcels? The flying ones with crates attached?" The humans had gone to great lengths to avoid the more populated areas, but by now Benn had definitely seen this popular method of delivery.

"*Yes…*" He paused. "*Oh no. Am I in one of those?*"

"Ah…yeah. You were, um, kidnapped. But I'm in one too," Astrid hurried on, "so you're not alone. Not really. Mine's going a lot faster than yours, and I've got a key to get you out. All going well, I should catch up with you in…six minutes, then we'll get out and turn around."

There was a long silence as Benn most likely processed the fact that his tiny prison was high in the air. She waited for him to ask all manner of questions – because if she'd been him, then boy, she would've had a lot – but he just said in a small voice, "*I suppose it's too late to tell you to be careful.*"

Yes, it was too late. Really, really, really too late. "I am being careful," Astrid replied, "but it's hard to be stuck in these things, isn't it? I'm glad you answered your phone, or had it set to auto-answer, because I'm not good with small spaces."

"*I didn't think I minded them, but I've changed my mind.*" She could hear the attempt at humour in his voice. "*I suppose we're on our way to Raka. Will you tell me what happened?*"

Now the answer to that wasn't good news either, but focusing on the conversation kept Astrid's own panic at bay, and she recounted everything she knew. In the meantime, those numbers on her phone tracker kept going down until she knew they'd soon be within sight of each other. Unfortunately, what she hadn't told him was that they'd also be within sight of the city of Syrene. According to this map it was barely ten kilometres away.

"Hold on," she cut in suddenly, interrupting his tale of shock over Eirene's nefarious behaviour. "Benn, I've just about reached you. I'm going to open my crate."

"*Alright. Be careful.*"

She'd be careful, indeed. Astrid carefully tucked her phone, the stunner and the override key into the sealed base of the crate, then reached for the little latch she knew would open her crate fully. Then she pressed her bent shoulders and head against the lid. For a moment it seemed as if it wouldn't give, but then suddenly the lid lifted and flung open, and she was sitting upright for the first time in what felt like hours.

The wind was streaming in Astrid's face from the speed of the drone's movement, and the sound of its engines filled the air around her along with the rapid beeping of the alarm, telling her to shut the lid. She ignored it and peeked over the edge of the crate, trying to move her stiff, aching limbs while she took in her surroundings.

There was bluish-purple sky above her, scattered with streaky clouds. Below her the land seemed to stretch on forever: brown and green and blue, covered with odd wrinkles and little brown crumb-like shapes.

A moment later she realised those were hills and tiny buildings, so she blanched and sat back in the drone. "Ooh. I'm incredibly high up..." The tracker had shown her all sorts of things, namely that Benn's drone should be very close, but it hadn't given her the sheer height she was travelling at. She suddenly imagined the drone doing a corkscrew spin in the air and herself sailing out, so scrunched her eyes shut.

"*Astrid?*" she heard Benn say from the phone. He sounded worried. "*Are you there?*"

"I'm here." She huffed out a long breath. Gathering her courage, she peeked back out over the edge of the crate. According to her tracker, he should be right about...*there.* "I see you!" she shouted at the phone. She waved down at the other drone, about ten metres below her and the same distance ahead, then remembered he couldn't see her at all. "I'm going to steer closer, then latch onto your roof, OK?"

Benn's answer was snatched away from the roaring wind in her ears, but Astrid figured it had been agreement. But here was the part that she and Percy had only breezed over – how she was supposed to actually get hold of the other drone when she was so very high in the air, and moving so rapidly. Luckily she'd had plenty of time to examine the override key while shut inside her own crate. It was like a tiny old-fashioned phone mixed with a car key. Using it would take lots of guesswork, and probably just as much good luck.

She checked the override key again. Last time its small screen had only shown the number of her drone, but now she could see a different number blinking at the bottom of the screen. She quickly tapped at it, then when the number flashed orange, she tapped 'link'. A moment later the number was green, and suddenly the same number of options appeared for the second drone as she'd had – speed, height...destination.

Astrid cheered aloud. It looked like Percy had been wrong about needing to touch the drone; she just needed to be close to it. "Benn, I've got you!" She tapped at 'destination', but the button for 'change' was greyed out. *Press confirmation button on drone casing,* the key's screen instructed her.

On 'drone casing'? Argh, this meant she *did* have to touch the thing! Percy had been right after all, although she certainly wouldn't be telling him so. "Ah…just a minute."

Astrid tapped madly at the key's screen, hyperaware that every passing minute meant they were growing closer to the city before them. Their altitude was reducing too, and her full attention became focused on that tiny screen, while trying to steer her own drone close enough to the other that she could reach that casing.

Finally she drew alongside it, close enough that her drone's stubby wings struck Benn's, causing both drones to wobble briefly. They were now at the same speed, and the city drew up beneath them. It was now near enough that she could make out individual windows on the buildings, and see the inner citadel's high wall up ahead. She realised they'd be there in mere minutes.

A surge of fear and frustration rushed through Astrid, and she got to her knees, reaching out as far as she could to grip onto Benn's drone. But the casing was too smooth, without any handholds, and she couldn't spot this essential 'confirmation button' that her override key kept telling her about. Over and over again, her attempts failed.

"Astrid?" she just heard Benn say. *"Everything's shaking about. Are you well?"*

"No!" she shouted at the phone. "I can't get to the freaking button!" And that meant they were both going to end up on Raka's doorstep – which had previously been Jireh's doorstep. Oh, this was bad bad bad bad bad-

Feeling furious, she directed her drone as far left as she could, while still pressed up against the right side of Benn's. *Turn, turn, turn, you stupid thing!* she ordered it. If only they could crash-land outside the city, she could get Benn out and run for it. Fleeing had worked for her before.

They were close now, so very close to the ground. She almost felt like she could have jumped out of her crate to land on the roof of one of the buildings skimming by underneath – if she didn't mind breaking her legs, or leaving Benn behind. No, there was only one option, and time was almost up.

For a moment it seemed like she'd succeed in turning them both, but then her drone abruptly skidded upwards, sending her flying into the side of her crate. The whole thing lurched sideways horribly, and she shrieked as the lid slammed shut over her head, clipping her temple. *Whack.*

"Astrid? Astrid!?"

"Owww…Benn! Are you OK?" Her drone was still rocking madly, but it seemed to be settling down again, and she felt around for the latch. It seemed to be jammed, and he wasn't answering. "Benn? Benn!"

"I think I'm fall-"

The phone line went dead just as the latch clicked and Astrid's lid flipped open again. Shaking with adrenaline, she pushed herself back up, searching desperately for the other drone. She couldn't see it anywhere – was it below her? – so she fumbled to check the phone tracker again. For a moment her phone's screen showed the two drones in almost the same location, but then she could clearly see that his had stopped moving, while hers continued on.

That was when she saw the hole in the wall of a large building below. She was rapidly leaving it behind, but when she caught a glimpse of the crumpled grey drone inside, and what might have been smoke, she went cold.

She'd tried to save Benn, but it looked like she might have killed him instead.

CHAPTER 22

Accusations

Benn's drone had crashed. *She'd* made him crash.

Those terrible thoughts left Astrid numb for just a few seconds, but long enough that the high citadel wall skimmed by beneath her. She was going far too fast, and if she didn't slow down now then her landing would be as if she'd dropped a bomb on this palace…and she'd be paste.

It took all her focus to slow the drone down, and beneath her she could now see people in the streets. A few of them turned their heads to see her pass by, but the majority didn't even seem to notice. *Destination ahead,* the override key informed her. *One minute.*

Argh! Astrid was suddenly alert again. She crouched in her spot and desperately looked for somewhere to jump out. The walls of the Syrenian palace were up ahead, and she balanced on the edge of the open drone, searching for a convenient awning or pile of hay, or even a pig pen for goodness sake! But all she saw was a herd of grey, pointy-horned cow-like animals, and then she'd missed her chance and she was over the palace grounds.

Argh argh argh argh argh!!!

Lower, slower, she told the override key desperately.

The drone drew lower but barely slowed, and this time Astrid wasn't so fussy. As soon as she reached the next building that was within a body's length of her, she jumped.

Orin thought of himself as a very good actor. He'd been forced to be ever since childhood, when showing the wrong emotion would bring about a hard slap or insults, or worse, a beating. But the way he'd slumped his entire body, refusing to shift back to human form or even twitch to show he was conscious, even when he'd heard his brother's voice? Masterful.

But even he couldn't feign unconsciousness for long when his head was held underwater. He thrashed, his whole body burning with the need for air, then quickly shifted back to human when he realised the cat form couldn't fight upside-down. They pulled him out of the water barrel, of course, then clapped chains on his new form, complete with one around his neck.

"He's got more energy than I thought," one of the soldiers commented. "Back he goes."

Orin was taken back to what was presumably the same room he'd been in earlier. He wouldn't know, since his eyes had been shut. Now he could see through the slits between his swollen eyelids that the room was large, with high patterned-glass windows. Inside was a small crowd of courtiers, some of whom he recognised…along with Chayali and his brother.

His brother. *How can he be punished,* Raka had shouted, *if he's not awake to know it?*

It looked like now was Orin's opportunity to be both awake *and* punished, unfortunately.

Just then Raka glanced across the room. He met Orin's eyes for the barest moment, just enough to give him a look of utter disgust. "Leave the traitor over there, out of the way," he ordered the guards, waving dismissively at the entire west wall of the large room. "Something more important is about to happen."

Orin's eyes widened. Something was more important than torturing a betraying brother? Wonders – and luck – never ceased. But when they dragged him to the side of the room and dumped him there, he found himself watching with interest.

Raka was holding what Orin recognised as an Earther communication device, and he watched its flashing screen with narrow-eyed satisfaction. "In mere moments," he began, "we shall-"

Suddenly one of the high windows shattered, the sound as intense as an Earther cannon firing. People screamed as glass rained down over the room, and something large came flying through. It skidded across the room, almost knocking down several guards, then slammed to a halt against the distant wall. Plaster came raining down over it, destroying a previously lovely mural, and as the dust settled Orin saw what it was.

A large, smooth-sided grey box, as big as one of those wooden chests they'd use for trading silk, with crumpled fin-like shapes at its sides, and a spinning circle that even now flickered and sparked like flame in a fire. It was one of the flying devices the Earthers would use to deliver goods, although this one looked worse for wear.

It had come in far, far too fast.

Around him, everyone was standing frozen as if stunned, and Orin tried to take advantage of that by lunging upwards, towards the nearest guard. But his limbs proved far weaker than expected, and the guard moved quickly, smashing the butt of his spear into Orin's forehead. "Stay down!"

Ow. Alright, then.

No one else seemed to have noticed Orin's failed escape attempt. Across the room, Raka stood in front of the damaged box, his shoulders hunched and fists clenched in a way that said he was about to lose his temper. And then on cue… "Somebody open this for me!" he roared. "NOW!"

Two servants stepped forward at the same time, but after a few futile attempts to lift the lid, Raka rolled his eyes. "Get out the way." They moved, and he pressed a small object against the box's lid. There was a hissing sound audible even from here, and then he stepped back again. "There."

Now the servants could open the lid, although of course no one pointed out that Raka had clearly held the key the entire time. But the lid swung open, and it seemed the whole room leaned forward to see what was inside…

"It's empty," one of the servants murmured to the other.

There was a collective intake of breath, because 'empty' was *clearly* not what the emir had intended to find.

But then the other said a little nervously, "No, no, look." He leaned inside and pulled out a little black brick-like item, then presented it to Raka. "Your most splendid and revered Magnificence…was this what you wanted?"

There was a long, tense silence as the emir's face grew redder and redder…

Astrid crept along the stone pathway, pressing against the side of the building in a desperate attempt to be inconspicuous. But how could a barefoot human, coloured like she'd been attacked with a dozen paint pots, ever look inconspicuous *anywhere*? She didn't even have a working weapon, she thought desolately, since the stunner's light had blinked red then died. It was out of battery, but she'd kept it anyway. She'd also accidentally left the override key back in the crate. That…was a problem.

She was lucky she still had her phone, she reminded herself. She was lucky she hadn't twisted her ankle when she'd fallen. She was lucky she hadn't been spotted yet. Unlike Benn…

Astrid pushed aside that thought, because she didn't *really* know what had happened to him. He might be fine, if shaken. He might be conveniently found by a kindly shepherd or whatever they had out here, and escorted to the nearest safe location.

He might not be dead.

Really.

She heard footsteps from around the end of the high building, and flattened herself against the side of the wall again. But then a guard stepped around the corner, mere feet away from her. His jaw dropped, and for a long moment he just stared at her, unspeaking.

Astrid stared back, noting that his face under his round-topped helmet seemed young, and that he held a spear. He was so close that she could have reached out and touched him.

"Whaa…." the guard finally stammered. His eyes were fixed on her bare, colourful legs. "Are you…a performer?"

Astrid latched onto that explanation with relief. "Yes! Yes, I'm a performer," she agreed in careful Tyger. "I am…lost."

"Oh?" He finally looked up and met her eyes, and his dark blue eyebrows rose. "Oh. You have *brown* eyes."

She froze, because she'd learned that having brown eyes was never a good thing in this place. But she didn't get a chance to defend herself, because he leaned in a little, his voice lowering. "Are you here with the others?"

There were others? "Ah…."

"Follow your instructions, and don't meet anyone's eyes," he continued in that same low tone. "Where are you trying to go?"

Astrid blinked at him, unsure whether to feel relieved or worried by the fact that he was helping her. Could she really be so lucky? "The stables," she replied finally. She'd considered her options since she'd landed, and had thought that even finding the drone (and then successfully steering the thing) seemed far more dangerous than just getting out of the city. If Kopa was still in the stables where he'd been a year ago, then perhaps she could escape that way.

The guard didn't even ask her why she wanted the stables. Instead he made a 'follow me' gesture, then began moving down the pathway. She followed, of course. She was scared, but at this point striking off on her own seemed the more dangerous option.

They'd been walking for less than three minutes when he led her around a corner, then paused at the top of a flight of solid-looking stone stairs. From here Astrid could see across a quiet stretch of well-trodden dirt to the familiar buildings on the other side.

"There they are," the guard said in a steady, louder voice. "Go and find the rest of your group, and try not to get lost again."

She nodded in agreement, feeling baffled and yet so very grateful. It was clear that he'd known she didn't belong (because with her looking as she did, what idiot *would* think she belonged?) but he'd still helped her. "Thank you."

He nodded back, then turned away and disappeared back around the corner.

Are you with the others? he'd asked when he'd seen the colour of her eyes.

Of course she wasn't, but now Astrid was curious about what he'd meant. Here, brown eyes meant either human or Dragonfly. So depending on who the others were, maybe she *would* join them.

Strength wasn't having the most people, Jireh knew. It was having the right people in the right places.

Currently, Raka was in the throne room surrounded by his most loyal guards and hundreds of both Syrenian and Mahadrese nobles… but mostly Syrenian. He was inside the palace, whose well-guarded walls were further strengthened by the walls of the inner city – the citadel. Then beyond that were the outer city walls, and beyond *those* were the majority of Raka's well-armed soldiers, ready to rain fire down on Syrene if Raka gave the order. Then far, far beyond the soldiers were the Kabeer mountains, and Raka's own city-state full of people who were either truly loyal to him or too scared not to be.

That was quite some distance between Raka and his greatest strengths, Jireh thought with grim satisfaction.

In contrast to Raka, Jireh was surrounded by an entire city-state full of people who loved him, who trusted him, and who would be quite happy to see him back. Closer still, he was in a palace where he knew every room and its secrets…and every noble and their secrets. Half of them were related to him, anyway.

Closer still, he had fifty very loyal fighters around him. They only held basic weapons, although for many of them, their own bodies were the weapons. They'd been instructed not to fight unless essential – and then only to disarm. He wasn't here to kill. He was here to take back his home, for himself and his people.

But besides those fifty fighters, Jireh also had another thirty brave *Branzinos* who'd stripped down, taken karak form and let themselves be painted grey. The plan was that they'd mingle with some real karak in the market, make a break for it and cause a long, noisy distraction at the front of the palace while Jireh and the others slipped inside.

So far, so good. They'd put a lot of hope into the Syrenians still being loyal to Jireh's memory – or to the knowledge that poor, heroic Advisor Koln had in fact been killed in his place. That hope had been proven correct today when every last servant (and a courtier or two) had seen Jireh's face, had lit up with shock and joy, then had quietly taken off to spread the plan throughout the palace. In theory, even one set of loose lips could ruin that entire plan. That was why they had to move fast.

Jireh looked across the wide, darkened servants' hall to where his chief Earther ally was quietly fiddling with what she'd called a 'playlist'. "Are we ready?" he asked softly.

"It's looking good," Jae Townsend replied in the same tones, her eyes a little too wide. "I've connected to the same sound system Raka was using. I don't think anyone here would even know how to stop me. But we only get one shot at this. Has anyone heard back from the bullet-thieves?"

Jireh knew she referred to those brave, stealthy folk who'd been sent off to relieve Raka's soldiers of their *boolits* as well as the fuel for their vehicles. It seemed Earther weapons had the same weaknesses as bow-and-arrows and racing raphantas – both needed a kind of 'feeding' or restocking.

"Successful," a short, stocky *Branzino* said from somewhere in the crowd. He wore only a light robe, a sure sign he hadn't been in human form for long.

"And all the Mahadrese guards are accounted for?" Jireh

continued.

"All except those inside the throne room," Malchiel said from where he stood beside Ms Jae. Jireh's old stableman looked almost the same as when he'd left Syrene over a decade ago, except for the sorrow held in his brazine-golden eyes. "And before you ask, our roof scout says all ten of them are in position up there."

Jireh let out a slow, careful breath. "Then we're ready." He nodded to Ms Jae. "Count one minute, and unless one of us says to stop...play your *'punk-rock'* music as loudly and as long as you can."

Chay sat at the side of the room almost like an afterthought, watching her captor rant and rage at a little black brick. Clearly something had gone terribly wrong, which pleased her, and she thought that whoever was meant to be in that crate that had exploded through the window, they were one fortunate person. As for her, she was shrinking against the wall as if she could vanish into it.

Suddenly Raka threw down the black brick. It hit the tiled floor then smashed into several pieces, which only seemed to make him angrier. Chay had never seen him like this, not even once. "WHY DOES NOTHING GO AS IT SHOULD?!" he raged. Then he turned, and his narrowed eyes fixed on Orin's slumped form.

Her heart began racing from the sheer malevolence in that expression. He picked up a hand-sized object from a nearby table, then began striding across the room. He raised the object and lifted it towards his brother...

Chay was trembling violently. She didn't know what the thing was, but it wasn't of this world, and she saw murder in his intentional movements. So for the first time in her life, that extreme fear caused her to shift forms rather than to freeze.

She felt the tingle of impeding change all along her limbs...and then all hell broke loose.

Astrid paused at the top of the stairs across from the Syrenian palace stables, finally switching her brain into gear, and sent an important text message.

I'm at the palace in Syrene but hiding from Raka. Heading for stables. Benn has crash-landed north of city. Please find him then find me. She considered the message briefly, then realised she'd accidentally added her entire contacts list, including Eirene and that guy she once bought a virtual reality headset from. She quickly deleted them and re-added the right people…then finished the message with, *don't panic.*

There. Sent. What she'd *really* wanted to say was 'rescue me, and don't be mad' – but they'd save that conversation for later, after she'd been rescued, and after people were inevitably mad at her.

Now that was enough procrastinating. Astrid pushed back the fear that maybe, everything wouldn't go right for her, and set off walking the way she imagined a local performer or acrobat might. As she sauntered down the stairs towards the stables, she mentally prepared for the conversations she'd have with any other palace staff – and how she could keep her eyes down and still remember her vocab – but in a strange turn of events, no one challenged her. In fact, as she walked across the dry, well-trodden dirt that led to the separate stable building, she didn't see anyone.

Astrid took that last thought back as in the distance she spotted a single guard running along the outside of a distant building, then disappearing around a corner. She heard the faint sounds of some distant clamour that oddly enough, reminded her of a particular screechy rock song that Aunt Jae liked to listen to, then-

Hhhgggrrrrnooooar!

She jolted, startled, then pushed back a laugh that wanted to bubble out. That was a cranky raphanta's trumpet for sure. It sounded a lot like how she remembered Kopa, but what were the chances he'd still be here at the palace?

Two minutes later Astrid had let herself into the empty stables. Empty of people, that was, because half the stalls were still filled with grey or blue raphantas. Most were minding their own business in the generous spaces, except for a couple who probed at her with curious trunks as she crept past. She ignored them, because she was searching for one particular, rather ugly brown shape.

"Kopa?" she called softly. "Kopa, are you there?"

Hhhgggrrrrnooooar!!

The resounding trumpet came from one of the stalls around the corner, out of sight, and was accompanied by what sounded like a solid kick to a stall door. The walls rattled, and several of the other raphantas shuffled in place as if uncomfortable. Others didn't move, perhaps accustomed to this particular animal's bad temper.

Astrid picked up her steps, but she was still cautious as she crept around the corner. "Kopa," she sang softly in Tyger. "It's your old friend, Tam. Remember me?"

A moment later she saw two knobbly brown feet slam up against the top of a stall door, and between them, a waving brown trunk. Kopa trumpeted happily. (And yes, it had been a whole year, but Astrid still remembered the difference between a happy sound and an aggressive one. As his rider, she'd heard plenty of the latter.) That gave her a little burst of happiness too, even in the midst of all this uncertainty and possible-execution-level danger, and she reached out to stroke his trunk.

"Alright, Kopa," she murmured to him over the door. "Let's hope you don't mind me being multicoloured, and that you're more steerable than you were a year ago."

The heavy beats of an early 2000's alternative rock song rang at full volume through the ancient Syrenian palace. With all the speakers that Raka had rigged up weeks ago still in action, even Jae wanted to wince at the way the hoarse vocals seemed to roll off the thick stone walls and almost vibrated through her feet.

No wonder the locals had all panicked when she'd started playing the first song, especially since she'd started it at the loudest, most obnoxious point. (Malchiel's words, not hers. Jae was a big fan of that era's tunes, since her dad had listened to them when she'd been a child, but strangely the locals *hated* rock music. Rap? No problem. Country or opera? Eh. Not too bad. But punk/alternative rock or heavy metal with its aggressive vocals and powerful rhythms? *"It makes me want to claw at my own ears,"* one of the few *beini* back at the refugee settlement had said.

With a little more testing, they'd discovered that the cat shifters were more sensitive to that particular music than even the Dragonflies, who found it unpleasant but not overwhelming. And since Raka's special forces were largely *beini,* that made their decision for them. Jae's 'retro rock playlist' would do just fine as a startling, noisy distraction as they took back Syrene.

They'd made their plan assuming Benn wouldn't be able to get military help. Even though Jae knew it was terribly dangerous to do what they were doing – that the other side wouldn't hesitate to hurt them – she'd agreed with Jireh's decisions up to this point. Even if Benn *had* brought an army, it wouldn't mean that they'd win. It could just mean that Syrene was reduced to rubble between two battling forces.

But Jae had prepared for all possible outcomes, including Jireh being killed in this attempt. So she acted as planned, moving quietly around the edges of the action and looking for anyone who might need emergency medical help. She also had a bag of zipties to act as manacles as a last resort. It would be pretty hard to clean people up if they were still trying to attack.

She reached the huge, open folding doors to the throne room and stopped in amazement when she got her first look at the chaos. She should have known how bad it was from the sounds alone, but it had been difficult to tell over the deafening music.

There might have been sixty or seventy people fighting in that one large room. A good deal of those weren't in humanlike form, but were massive tigerlike creatures or even what looked like a moose's cousin, patchy red and grey, and with spikier horns. There were several fallen figures – make that a dozen – and even as she watched, well-dressed figures fled through the half-dozen exits around the room: the very same doors through which Jireh's force had launched their surprise attack.

Was her side winning? Who knew. Jae couldn't see Raka at all, but she spotted a section of the wall which looked like it had been hit by a bomb, with plaster and rubble everywhere. Not too far from that, she saw an absolutely battered, bloodied white tyger shifter crawling its way across the floor while being harassed by a Dragonfly in acrypid bird form. Its figure seemed to ripple as it moved, as if it was flickering between man and big cat. Just as it settled on cat form, the bird shifter managed to grab hold of the much larger tyger and rose into the air.

Jae went to move forward, or at least set her hand on her weapon, because she couldn't abide mistreatment on any side. Then she realised that the tyger was in chains (quite a sight, really) and the acrypid appeared to be carrying it away…so it might even be doing the tyger a favour.

Bird steals cat. That was ironic, but possibly not as murderous as the situation appeared. But in the few moments Jae had hesitated, the Dragonfly had escaped out the window along with the battered tyger.

She was too late.

Just then Jae felt a light touch on her arm, and she looked up to meet the golden-brown eyes of one of the winged, armoured Dragonfly males. He nodded at her briefly, then indicated towards one of the doors leading to the outside. She nodded, noting that no one was watching them. But before she could follow, she had one more task to do as DJ.

Jae pulled up her playlist on her phone, then switched from a particularly energetic chorus to the audio they'd recorded before they came here. And as Jireh's confident, familiar tones filled the air at that same high volume, she headed after Malchiel.

Next stop: the dungeons.

In the form of an oversized acrypid bird, Chay scraped her way through the high, wide window. The remnants of her clothing and Orin's weight meant every movement was excruciatingly difficult, and her balance was thrown off enough that her wings banged against one side of the carved stone.

She dipped briefly and felt his heavy weight strike the ledge. For a moment it seemed certain that she'd drop him – such a distance that his back would surely break – but then with a mental apology, she dug in her talons and dragged him through.

They both landed hard on the tiled roof just a body-length below them, and Chay hastened to change back to her usual form. Her clothes were now ragged around her, barely decent, but she leaned over Orin anyway, quickly checking to see if she'd caused true injury. It was hard to tell under all that fur, and he was such a mess anyway…

He shuddered, then suddenly he was once again in a man's form. Chay held back a hiss of pity, because the transformation did him no favours. If she hadn't known who he was…well, he was so battered that she wouldn't have known who he was. Also, he was naked. She made a point of looking above the waist only.

"We're on the roof," she whispered. "The palace is under attack, but if we stay quiet enough we might get away."

Orin's one good eye shifted to meet hers. "You go," he replied in a hoarse whisper. "Take advantage of the chaos, fly away. You'll never escape if you try to take me with you."

Chay glanced over the edge of the roof. Not far below was a long, narrow walkway with a waist-high wall – the top of the thick walls that marked the central structure of the palace. Over those walls was the sort of drop that would crack skulls. She'd make it if she flew; maybe even make it back to Sanctuary before the soldiers found it – but Orin wouldn't. Even though she'd been in Raka's palace for years, she didn't know Orin well, so it shouldn't matter...except that she wanted to be the sort of person where it *did* matter.

But instead of explaining all of that to him, Chay said, "I still owe you one more rescue, remember? Now keep your mouth shut, or we'll be caught."

Orin muttered something under his breath. "There's no one to catch us right now. They're all part of the uprising, or they're fighting it." His bruised lips curved into a slight smile. "Did you know that most of your people in Mahadra were captured as slaves, not killed? I heard that hundreds have escaped Raka's mines and work camps in these last months. Many headed to the south-east of Syrene..."

A pang of almost painful hope twisted Chay's belly. She'd noticed the sudden influx of red-brown and copper forms in the throne room – who could miss it!? – but all she'd been able to think about at the time was escaping. "Hush," she told Orin, but her mind was filled with the many people she'd assumed dead, but who might still be alive after all.

She'd have to go south, she decided in that moment. Who knew who she might find? But to Orin she said, "If those Dragonflies kill Raka as he deserves, they'll only confirm my people's villainy in your people's minds. Besides, Syrene is still surrounded by half his army, and Mahadra has no emir to replace him. There'll be riots while they find a replacement."

Orin's smile didn't fade. If anything, it grew wider even as his swollen eyes closed. "Run away, Chayali. While you can."

She wanted to, desperately, and she wanted him to stop asking, because she was so tempted to just do it and leave him to his fate. But instead, when she heard footsteps on the walkway below, she flattened herself to the roof.

Maybe in some universe, the hero's trusty steed would remember the way home perfectly, and would guide their badly injured rider back home, complete with gentle nose-nudges when necessary. Astrid had watched one or two movies where that had happened.

But all it did was prove that she was not the hero, because right now her 'trusty steed' was galloping *up* yet another set of stairs, getting deeper and deeper into the palace, rather than where she wanted to go…the exit.

"Gaaahh!" She ducked her head again as he raced under yet another low archway, the sort that would wipe her off his back if she hadn't been so quick. "Kopa, *stop!*"

She'd tried saying this in English and Tyger so many times and had been completely ignored. But this time the raphanta came to a sudden halt, setting his head down. Taken by surprise, Astrid went flying head-over-heels off his back – *splash.*

Ow.

She struggled to right herself, quickly realising that Kopa had dumped her into a fountain, which he was now drinking out of. He hadn't done that naughty trumpet-laugh he sometimes did, so perhaps the way he'd thrown her wasn't intentional. Either way, she was now soaking wet, and sore from the hard landing.

Wet. Hmm. She took a moment to rub at her coloured arm, checking if the swirling marks faded at all, but wasn't surprised when they didn't. There was a reason people wore coveralls in the portal, because the colour could take weeks to fade. But really, Astrid reminded herself, she had bigger problems right now.

"You really are a useless, naughty animal," she told Kopa in as sweet a voice as she could manage. "You've got me deeper into the palace rather than getting me out of it."

The raphanta just kept drinking, so she sighed and climbed out of the fountain. Her clothes were dripping, and water ran from her sopping hair down onto her face. She wrung it out a little, then took stock of her new location. The stables had been at ground level, and now she was at least two storeys up, with a low wall blocking a decent drop to her left, and a building to her right. Glancing over the wall she could see the mosaiced floor of the level below, and as she watched, several people ran past. She just caught a glimpse of armour and cloth, but it was their words that stuck with her.

"Your beloved Emir Jireh is back."

The spoken Tyger came loud and clear, and to Astrid's pleasure she understood it just fine. But it only took a moment to realise that she hadn't heard those people speaking at all – instead she was hearing Jireh himself, at maximum volume over what was surely a speaker system.

"Even now, my loyal people move through the palace, claiming back what is ours," the voice continued, echoing from somewhere down below. *"Loyal Syrenians, subdue those who do not belong here, but do not cause unnecessary harm. Our Mahadrese brothers, lay down your weapons and you will not be injured…"*

Jireh's spiel carried on for another minute before starting all over again, and Astrid's mind was spinning with excitement. If Jireh was here, then Raka might not get the chance to string her up by her toes after all, or whatever he did to people he really disliked. Not if the palace was under attack, sort of, and Raka and his soldiers would be taken up with fighting off the reverse-invasion force. That would explain why the place seemed so empty, and it might also save her life…

Leaving Kopa behind, Astrid hurried along the raised pathway, her ears pricked for any more conversation or even the sound of fighting. She could hear *something,* but it seemed to echo all around her, impossible to pinpoint.

BANG. BANG. BANG.

Astrid shuddered. Now those were definitely gunshots; the last thing she wanted to hear in this place. But where had they come from?

Raka slipped back into the shadows, pressing himself into an alcove as a trio of soldiers ran past. They wore Syrenian armour, but that meant little right now. Some of his guards wore Mahadrese garb, some Syrenian, but when everything had gone to chaos just now, he couldn't tell who was on his side.

His hated uncle's voice rang through the air, making slick promises that if true, would destroy everything Raka had worked for these many years. He clenched his fists in silent fury, the hard metal of his Earther weapon cutting into one hand. If he'd remembered rightly, he only had two more shots before he'd need to reload the *gon*. With the palace swarming with Dragonfly vermin and traitorous soldiers, he'd need far more than that. He couldn't even contact anyone on his *fone*, since he'd smashed the cursed thing before realising he'd need it again. That useless old Earther female who'd caused his humiliation would have to grovel before he forgave such an insult.

Raka still couldn't quite believe what had taken place. One moment he'd been about to kill his treacherous bastard brother – who'd looked satisfyingly beaten-up – and the next the most dreadful noise had erupted. It had been these…banging beats, and shrieking voices, and something rather like the screaming of a thousand seabirds all at once; the cacophony so immensely overwhelming that Raka had actually dropped his weapon in fright and slapped his hands over his ears.

Then suddenly the throne room had been full of far too many people…and animals…and fighting, and he hadn't even seen it start. He'd turned to see two of his best *beini* guards on the ground, writhing with their hands over their ears as hideous red and grey toned *Branzinos* launched right at them.

Feeling like everything had been happening in slow motion, Raka had picked up his *gon* and fired several times in the *Branzinos'* direction. But before he'd had a chance to see if his aim had been true (or to give his useless guards a good kick of disapproval) another guard had taken his arm. Raka didn't remember what the man had said, just that he'd led him to a nearby door and had shoved him through it without even checking what was on the other side. Then the door had slammed shut, and Raka had been left alone in this darkened hallway. Half the torches were out, and although no one was in sight, he could hear shouts and the sounds of battle echoing around the nearby corner.

He'd hidden, of course, which led him to this moment.

Raka jittered in place, his jaw clenched with fury and the need to keep silent when everything inside him wanted to roar with rage. He was the cursed *EMIR* of cursed *MAHADRA AND SYRENE, so why was he out here alone!!??*

Just then a figure in grey slipped out of the nearest door, looking back and forth in the hallway. Uzyn's gaze fell on Raka where he stood in the shadows and his face lit up with relief. "Your Magnificence!" he burst out. "You're still here! We must get you out at once."

Raka was relieved to see his guard too – enough that he decided not to shoot him for incompetence. Not yet, anyway. "Where would I have gone?" he bit out. "I don't know my way around the servants' corridors. Now get us out of here, fool!"

The guard obeyed, since he was at least an obedient fool. But as they moved quietly from alcove to alcove and room to room, and as the halls began to look more familiar, a plan began to formulate in Raka's mind. He'd always known that more than just a *gon* or *cannin* might be needed, so he'd traded accordingly. He'd even brought that greater weapon here, although had never imagined he'd truly need it.

But someone had to be punished for what was happening here. *Everyone* had to be punished.

He came to a halt outside a familiar-looking set of stairs. "This leads down to the stables, does it not?"

"Yes, Your Magnificence. They are only a few minutes away."

Uzyn moved as if to keep walking, but Raka held up a hand. "I have a duty for you to perform, my last, loyal guard."

The guard looked wary, especially when Raka recounted what he needed to do. "You…do not wish me to remove you safely from the city?" he asked, his pale brows low. "You wish me to go to this weapon in the dungeons instead?"

"I think I can remove myself from the city," Raka snapped back. "A single dark-haired man without an outer robe will get through this chaos just as effectively as two. I'll ride a raphanta or even a bloody karak if I have to. Now give me your sword, then get down to the dungeons as I just told you. The Earther weapon won't set itself off."

Or at least the Earthers had promised it wouldn't. They'd shown him lovely images of a chest-sized device that could destroy an entire city in minutes, with such force that it would change even the sunset for days. So of course Raka himself shouldn't set it off; he might not get away in time.

Uzyn swallowed. "Your most splendid and revered Magnificence. If I do not have my sword, then I may not make it to the weapon. Perhaps I could lead you out of the city, then someone could come back…"

"Keep your sword," Raka said generously after brief consideration.

"But give me your dagger." He had one of his own, but it wouldn't hurt to have back up.

Two minutes later Raka was minus his outer robe *and* his last guard, and was striding down the winding halls that led to the stables. Even through the ever-present anger that consumed him, his mind felt strangely clear.

This shouldn't have happened. Everyone had failed him.

And if he couldn't have Syrene, then no one could.

CHAPTER 23

Pay the Price

Chay crept to the edge of the tiled roof, glancing either way to ensure no one was in sight, then carefully let herself down onto the stone path below. Orin had told her to fly away, and in the end she might have to, but going back to her acrypid winged form would be her last resort. She'd been taught well that people didn't like 'different', because they often confused it with 'dangerous', and her acrypid form was certainly different. It also wasn't impervious to arrows, let alone whatever kind of Earther weapons Raka's forces had got hold of.

Because if the Dragonflies with their many forms had been captured and enslaved, then they couldn't be so dangerous, could they? Except there were still so many left, so many who'd also come to retake the palace… Maybe she'd know someone. Maybe she wouldn't be alone after all; just her and her precious, illegitimate child.

Chay felt a flutter of joy in her chest for the first time in years at the thought of others like her, but she quickly quashed it. She was still in the middle of an enemy-occupied palace, and she had to escape before she could start celebrating-

"Chakandra."

Chay froze. There was no mistaking that voice, nor the anger in his tone. She slowly turned to face Raka, her hands clasped in front of her as if they'd be any form of protection. Surprisingly he stood there alone, no outer robe and not a guard in sight, although he held one of those wicked Earther weapons – pointed towards her. Her heart sank. He must have seen her shift forms, because how could he have not seen that?! So now he must know that she'd lied and actually was one of those hated form-changers, and it must be all over for her…

"Where is your accomplice?" he asked coldly. "Waiting to ambush me?"

Chay's eyebrows shot up, and when it became apparent that he wanted a reply, she stammered, "Do you mean your brother? He isn't my accomplice. I don't *have* an accomplice."

Raka studied her with narrowed eyes, then to her amazement lowered the weapon. Just a little, but enough to show he didn't consider her a threat.

Perhaps he *hadn't* seen her change forms after all, Chay thought in amazement. He hadn't even seemed to notice that her clothing had gone from ugly to mere rags...

"I'm leaving this ungrateful, worthless city," he said abruptly. "You'll come with me now." He moved as if to walk away, then when she didn't follow, he turned back to face her. "Chakandra. Come with me now, or die."

She'd heard his command but her feet still wouldn't move. Just like before, like every time in his presence she seemed to freeze up; become small and weak and even her voice would fade. But she managed to ask, "Are you going to kill me if I do not come with you?"

Raka paused as if taking in her posture and mood. He lifted one eyebrow. "In a manner of speaking. A terrible Earther weapon will be used very soon, and this whole city will be rubble as punishment for Syrene's treachery. They had me as their emir, and they *dared* to challenge me?" His eyes narrowed again. "You say you were faithful to me. Prove it now and come, or perish with the others."

He wanted her with him, Chay realised in astonishment. Or more likely, he was taking advantage of what he thought was in his hands. "The city...rubble...?" she stammered. "You'd let everyone here die? Even those on your side?"

"They failed me," Raka snapped. "As you see by the fact that I'm reduced to such things. But I won't argue with a mere *esira*. You follow me, or stay. I don't care."

He truly didn't care, Chay realised then. He hadn't even mentioned his child, who she'd made clear was living in this city that even now he was threatening. Somehow, in spite of everything that was happening, the disappointment was immense. "You care for no one except yourself," she said in a low voice. "Even if you hadn't been responsible for the destruction of my family, I would never again give myself into your hands. I will stay."

For a moment it seemed as though Raka was disappointed, but then his expression changed into his usual smirk. "As you wish."

The emir turned as if to move away, but then stopped again, glancing over his shoulder. "You know," he said conversationally, "in the game of Chase the Castle, the *esira* piece has little value. The king is everything, and even if I lose Syrene, I've already won in life. So really, I don't need you. But I find that I don't want anyone else to have you either."

Then he raised his hand. He was still holding one of those vicious Earther weapons, the ones that could leave small, perfect holes even in rock, and he pointed it at her again. His finger moved and-

"STOP!" someone screamed.

BANG.

Chay felt a sudden sharp pain on her temple. She reached up a trembling hand to touch the spot, and came back with red-tipped fingers. It was a graze. Just a graze.

But Raka was swearing and looking at his now-empty hands, and in unison they turned towards where the voice had come from. Chay felt as if she was underwater. Her movements were so slow, and her mind was foggy with shock – had he really tried to kill her? – but even that shock couldn't explain what was standing not ten feet away from her.

What in the world...?

Astrid stood frozen, her hand still outstretched in the same posture from where she'd thrown her stunner. Yes, *thrown*, because the stupid thing was out of battery. But what was she supposed to do? She'd come around the corner to see the horrible emir himself, having what turned out to be a horrible conversation with that nice little servant girl...or ex-servant, if she'd heard correctly. It had confirmed her suspicion that Jireh was definitely trying to retake the palace, and was probably winning. (Hooray!) But then Raka had raised his gun to *shoot* the girl...

Astrid's aim had been good enough to knock the gun out of his hands, right over the low wall bordering this walkway, and his shot had gone wild. The girl now had a streak of blood skimming one temple, and her large eyes were bulging with shock as she stared at Astrid. The beastly emir was staring too, and for a moment they all just...stared.

"Is it the dress?" Astrid joked in Tyger. Her fear – or the bizarre situation – made her mouth run away from her. She glanced down at her legs. "But the, er, paint helps, right?"

The servant girl (Chakandra, that was it!) shook her head just a little, her eyes growing even wider, if that was possible. She began to shuffle back, away from Raka.

"Astrid Townsend?" he breathed, his eyes still bugging too. "You're alive! Why are you…" Then his eyes narrowed. "You survived, so you came here to attack *my* palace, dressed as some foolish jester?! Did you imagine this was a good disguise?"

"No, no, no," Astrid countered hastily, raising her hands in the air. "I didn't attack at all! Actually, I came in a box. Long story, and I won't go into it now, because…um…"

Because as she'd been speaking, Raka's expression had changed from angry to incensed. "*You* were in the *drohn!*" he accused. "You stole my sister again!"

"What – no!" Just then it occurred to Astrid that she might not be armed, but neither was he, and currently there was no one to capture and/or kill her. In her peripheral vision she could see Chakandra sneaking away, so thinking to distract Raka further, she said quickly, "OK, maybe I did. You almost got her, you know. It was really close! But Nathaniel and I found out what Eirene was doing, and freed Tamzyn at the last minute." She couldn't hold back a smirk. "She won't be coming back here."

Raka snarled. "And the boy-regent?"

Astrid's smile dropped a little. "He's not coming here either," she replied flatly. "We intercepted the second drone. Unfortunately I still managed to come here instead…but have you considered that murder isn't the answer to your problems? I mean, if you'd just been nice to Emir Jireh rather than trying to assassinate him, he'd probably have formally made you his heir…"

That last comment must have been a step too far, she realised, because now Raka looked an inch short of implosion. His head was tilted slightly back, his eyes were too wide, and there were white lines around his nose and tightly-drawn mouth. "I'm going to kill you," he stated, and his tone was surprisingly normal considering those ugly words.

Then he reached under his jacket and pulled out a long, curved dagger. It had a lovely jewelled handle, but the blade gleamed pinkish-gold and looked so very, very sharp.

"Oh," Astrid said weakly. "Are you sure?"

He lunged at her, and she shrieked and ducked away, then sprinted in the opposite direction from Chakandra. Her heart was pounding, the stone floor was painfully rough underfoot, and panicked thoughts were rushing through her mind. *He's got a knife, oh God help me he's got a knife!* and; *he really did try to kill that poor girl!* and; *did I really ask him if he was sure?!*

Astrid was guessing that yes, he really, truly *did* intend to kill her, because she could hear his footsteps pounding behind her, and images kept flashing through her mind of that knife and his furious expression. He had the advantage of shoes and just a little height, but perhaps if she could outlast him and lose him somewhere in the palace...

She didn't have a weapon anymore. She only had her phone tucked into a clever pocket in her dress, but that was no good right now except maybe to throw as a last resort, and besides, she couldn't reach it while running.

Up ahead was a blind corner, so when Astrid reached it she swerved hard right, her feet skidding on the rough stone floor. She felt a hand brush her hair and shrieked instinctively, propelling herself forward into a faster sprint along this next stretch of pathway. He was close, she realised. Too close! Just up ahead was another blind corner, and she sped up, determined to make this corner faster than the last. She could hear him breathing behind her...

She swerved to turn right again – and hit a stone wall.

The shock was immense, and she bounced off it to land hard on the pathway, her whole body aching from the impact. She couldn't breathe. The pathway had ended...she couldn't breathe.

Astrid heard Raka's triumphant laugh, and then he was on top of her; that curved blade coming down sharply towards her chest. She had just enough presence of mind to roll away, and a moment later she heard the clang of metal hitting the stone ground.

He cursed, and she reached up to grab at his arm holding the dagger. She managed to grip his wrist just as he came down in another strike, and for several moments the blade was there, so very close to her chest. Her hands were trembling and she was sobbing as she held him back, her entire world having shrunk down to this one place, this one moment.

But he was strong, and had gravity on his side. The blade dipped lower and the tip pierced her skin. She cried out.

Raka laughed. "See," he told her triumphantly, his voice ragged from exertion. "You may be an unnatural alien female, but you are still not a match for me, Astrid Townsend."

He dared to insult her as he was killing her? A sudden burst of fury broke through her panic, and pulling on her training, she brought her knees sharply up against her chest. The blade lifted away, and then she kicked out with both feet as hard as she could. Raka stumbled backwards – relief! – and she followed, pushing herself back to her feet.

For the briefest moment Astrid intentionally focused her thoughts on their position; on her own mental library of possible actions. Then trying not to overthink things, she followed through with a movement; slamming her bent left arm down hard on his knife-hand, and sharply bringing her right hand up towards his throat.

Raka's head snapped back as the heel of her hand impacted his jaw, and buzzing with adrenaline, Astrid dug her fingers into his wrist bones. He cried out and dropped the dagger, then she brought her knee sharply into his gut.

Then suddenly someone – some*thing* – flew in front of her, knocking Raka away, back against the low wall overlooking the drop. It looked like a short person wearing a suit of gold-orange armour, complete with a double set of gossamer-thin wings on their back. But the armour seemed to be *under* some plain clothing…

The person slapped Raka across the face – then again – then again – and Astrid could hear the *crack* of their hard hand striking him.

Oh, *wow*. Someone had a lot of anger to work through, she thought with a grimace. She carefully stepped back, away from the two of them, and found the dagger on the ground by her feet. She picked it up, holding it loosely in one hand as she watched the two of them.

Slap. Slap. Slap.

Astrid cringed a little as the emir's face moved with each strike. He looked dazed, as little as she could see, and he was struggling a bit but was definitely on the losing end of this attack. She debated whether she should intervene, or even run away herself, but in the end just stood there next to the wall, watching His Magnificence Emir Raka get bitch-slapped to within an inch of his life. And the thing… the *person* sitting on his chest and striking him over and over…they didn't make any sound the whole time.

But then Astrid recognised the clothing and the stature, and a number of little clues finally made sense in her mind. "You're a Dragonfly!" she burst out. And that must make her…Chakandra.

The person finally stopped slapping Raka, but one hand gripped his now-bloodstained collar as she looked over her shoulder at Astrid. The armour-like impression continued into her face, but *that* was like a cross between a bug and a mummy wrapped in amber-dipped cloth. Two big, dark brown eyes dominated a face with a tiny little mouth and button nose, like a cartoonist's idea of a cute bug-person. Except bugs didn't have pointed ears like an elf on steroids.

Astrid gulped. Considering that Chakandra was slapping Raka rather than biting, stinging or impaling him, then perhaps she wasn't going to hurt Astrid either. But it was Astrid's first meeting with a giant bug-person, and she was nervous. "Uh…please carry on."

But the Dragonfly shook her head, shuddering, and then suddenly she was Chakandra again. Her eyes were too wide and her lower lip stuck out like a toddler about to cry, and her dark blue hair was wild around her shoulders. "He was hurting you," she said in a small voice. "He was going to kill you."

"He was trying to," Astrid agreed, watching Raka warily. His nose was now bleeding (whether from Chakandra or Astrid herself), and his expression was dazed. "I think we need to get out of here before he gets up and finds someone who'll kill us on his behalf. Do you know where to find the exit? Or even any of Jireh's people would be fine, assuming that there are some here. I was trying to get out on a brown raphanta, but he just took me further into the palace."

The other girl's brow furrowed. "You rode a…what?"

As if on cue, Kopa let out a long, furious trumpet from somewhere in the background, and Astrid winced. "Long story, Chakandra, but I think you've got a tale of your own too." She indicated to the fallen man. "Shall we go?"

"My name is Chayali. Chakandra is the name this beast chose for me when he brought me to the palace." The girl said it matter-of-factly, but she stood anyway.

Astrid grimaced. *Come on, Raka. Was it really not enough to enslave the girl – you had to steal her very identity too?* "Chayali, then. It's nice to finally hear your voice. Do you think…oh look, it's Kopa."

The rapahanta had charged into sight around the corner, and was now racing towards them, along the length of the walled pathway. He wasn't slowing down.

"Kopa!" Astrid called out, then again in increasing panic. Surely she couldn't have survived Raka's attack only to be accidentally squashed by a misbehaving animal. "Stop right now!"

Chakan- *Chayali* backed away, an expression of dismay coming over her face. "You were screaming," she whispered. "It must have heard you."

Clearly. Astrid grabbed Chayali by the shoulders and shoved her into the corner behind her. Then she set her hands on her hips, trying to make herself look like a barrier. *Please don't run over my new friend.* "KOPA! STOP RIGHT NOW!"

At the last moment the raphanta screeched to a halt, his trunk waving back to expose those nasty, needle-like teeth. He trumpeted challengingly, then rushed right past Astrid anyway…to where Raka had stumbled to his feet. She just saw a smaller, curved shape of another knife in his hand, but then Kopa reared up on his hind legs and came down again in that classic aggressive move she'd seen him use so many times before.

But this time, when he hit Raka mid-chest, the man fell backwards…and there was nothing behind him.

Several seconds later they heard a *thump* on the tiled floor far below. Kopa leaned over the now-empty railing, letting out another challenging trumpet, then turned back to Astrid, stretching out his trunk to play with her multicoloured hair. *I win,* his mannerisms seemed to say.

Yes, Astrid thought numbly. *You really do win, because Raka's not coming back from that.* She didn't want to even look over the edge. She couldn't even speak. But several moments later when Chayali hadn't spoken either, she whispered, "Do you think anyone saw that?" And could they convince people that the emir was murdered by a raphanta, without said raphanta being executed in punishment? Raka *had* been holding a dagger…

Chayali shuffled over to the low wall and leaned over it to study the space below. Then when she stepped back, she wore absolutely no expression. "Look for yourself."

Astrid didn't want to, but she stepped around Kopa's playful nuzzlings and stood next to the wall, just close enough to see the area at the base of the wall, two storeys down.

Ugh, there was Raka, sprawled in an unnatural position on the marble floor. It didn't take a medical professional to see that he was dead.

But worse, spread around his body were a dozen soldiers dressed in purple and green. They were dead silent, their shocked expressions most likely matching Astrid's own, and when they looked up, she knew they'd seen her.

This wasn't good.

To Jae's surprise it had been almost easy to reach to the dungeons, as no one had even tried to stop them. It seemed that once the music – and Jireh's recording – began to play, everyone who could, moved upwards to either join the fight or get away from it.

So now she moved quietly from cell to squalid cell, working to free each occupant and give them whatever help she could. From what she'd heard, these dungeons were full of political prisoners – people who'd displeased Raka. Who knew what had happened to the real criminals.

All in all, things could be worse. Maybe that was because Raka had only held Syrene for a matter of weeks. Still, Jae would be talking to Jireh about the state of his dungeons. *Phew*, they reeked!

She was tending the blistered feet of someone who'd had a run-in with a very hot pavement or a very nasty jailer when Malchiel suddenly came in. He held a torch – the sort that was basically a burning stick – and his armoured Dragonfly form melted back from his face until he was able to speak normally. "Jae, you'll need to see this."

Jae followed him down the narrow hall to a different cell, a tiny, somewhat clean one all on its own. Inside was a silver-haired man in a grey uniform. He sat on the ground next to a large wooden barrel, his wrists and ankles tied with plastic zipties, but otherwise appeared unharmed. "I wasn't going to do it," he said mutinously, his Mahadrese accent distinct. "I'd be killing myself too. It's madness."

Malchiel caught Jae's eye then nodded towards the barrel. "Inside that is an Earther device that could destroy this entire city. So don't set it off, please."

Jae's breath caught in her throat. Her imagination went crazy with images of the worst weapons Earth had created and used in the last century. But when she reached the barrel and carefully lifted its lid, all she saw was a sea of red cylinders and wires.

She swore, and both men stared at her intently.

"Bad?" Malchiel asked.

"Yes, but…" Her initial panic waning, Jae carefully examined the barrel's contents, taking care not to touch anything. "OK, this is weird. It looks like dynamite, which is an explosive used a couple of generations ago on Earth. It's still occasionally used in mines to spark other explosives, but not that much, which might be why it was sold to Raka. Earth didn't need it anymore. It is dangerous though, and if this much was set off I think it *could* wreck the palace, although probably not the city…"

"So we should leave?" Malchiel prompted. His whole posture was on alert as if ready to grab her and sprint away at any moment. "Can you turn it off?"

"That's the thing," Jae continued, studying the barrel in confusion. "I don't think it *needs* turning off, although keep your torch at the other side of the room, alright? I don't want to risk having open flame near it, but it just doesn't…look right." She carefully lifted one of the red cylinders marked *EXPLOSIVE*, trying not to catch any of the other wires as she moved it. She sniffed at it.

"Smells like wood," the Mahadrese *beini* said from his place on the floor. "And something else."

That was exactly right, Jae realised. It *did* smell like wood. Then when she gently probed at the wire surrounding the cylinder, it came right off along with what looked like red paint, leaving a plain tube with a rough texture underneath. "Hey…" she said suspiciously. "I think this is…"

"A fire starter," Jae confirmed a few minutes later when they'd carefully sliced off the end of the cylinder to reveal a rough, wood-like substance. No wick, no explosives. Just wood. "It's a trick."

"It's not a great weapon?" the bound guard asked, sounding almost disappointed. "It wouldn't destroy the city with a great *marshroom* cloud?"

Jae half-laughed, feeling giddy with relief. It seemed that in spite of Portal-co's terrible acts in selling guns and even eighty-year-old cannons to the Tygers, they hadn't taken that final step and sold them bombs. Thank God. "Certainly not, although it could warm your house and cook your dinner just fine."

She was about to launch into a detailed explanation of what she thought that Raka thought he'd been sold, compared to what was actually in this barrel, but then a Dragonfly boy stuck his head in the door. He was still covered in patchy grey paint, showing he was one of those who'd volunteered to be the initial distraction outside the palace, but Jae couldn't remember his name. "Malchiel," the boy said, his eyes wide. "You've got to see this!"

Ugh, what next? Another bomb…an *actual* bomb this time?

But when Malchiel left the room, Jae followed him, leaving the bound Mahadrese guard with the barrel of fake dynamite, worthless for anything except a cosy fire.

The boy led them down the corridor to an area they hadn't visited since they'd thought it was empty. "We're looking for the keys," he explained.

Keys?

Malchiel stopped dead outside a cell, the open sort with a wall of metal bars rather. Jae almost ran into his back, but she still saw the cell's occupant a moment before they spoke.

It was a redheaded young woman, petite and pretty, with a rather world-weary expression on her face. But when she saw Malchiel her eyes widened and her whole visage seemed to change to something much younger and much sweeter. "Papa?"

Astrid stood in mute horror at the top of the wall, overlooking a group of guards surrounding their now-dead ruler, who'd clearly fallen to his death. And she was up here, looking like an abstract artist's idea of a clown, and standing at the place he'd fallen from…

If she thought she'd been scared before, then this was a new, knicker-wetting kind of terror.

Then one of the green-clad soldiers stepped forward, raising up his spear. "Long live Emir Jireh!" he shouted.

"Long live Emir Jireh!" the others echoed.

Astrid just about collapsed in relief. She backed away from the wall out of sight and stammered to Chayali, "Oh, thank God! I thought we were about to be executed for regicide!"

The other girl was silent, probably still in shock herself. "A brown raphanta," she murmured finally.

Astrid scratched her head, studying Kopa in bemusement. "He's not a…a *Dragonfly*, is he?"

Chay just stared, then shook her head. "A Dragonfly would be much smaller," she replied, as if that should have been terribly obvious. "So no. But brown raphantas can be terribly protective, even though they're just animals. Emir Jireh kept one in the palace stables, years ago…"

Oh. "Well, we should find Emir Jireh," Astrid said more decisively. "The sooner, the better."

Feeling like she was in a daze, she made her way down the long pathway and the multiple sets of stairs leading back down to ground level. Kopa proved to be better at going up than down, as he lost interest and wandered off down a side passage. Astrid left him and kept walking while Chayali lagged behind, looking as though she desperately wanted to be anywhere but here. But before they had reached ground level, she'd slipped away.

Astrid couldn't blame her. Even though Jireh was here and emir again by default, and Raka had been a real monster, she was feeling terrified that he was dead, that she'd been present at his death, and that she was still in a hostile, literally alien location. Oh, and she was seriously underdressed by their standards, and also covered head to toe in rainbow swirls. And then there was Benn…

But she didn't even make it back to ground level before being met by a group of people. Some were soldiers, and some were most certainly not, and one man even had that reddish-brown hair that she now knew meant he was Dragonfly. Astrid stopped, and she was debating what to say when someone pushed through the group. It was a woman dressed in simple servants' clothing, with a pale headscarf obscuring her face. She tugged it down, revealing familiar high cheekbones and worried-looking brown eyes. "Astrid?!"

"Aunt Jae!" Astrid rushed forward into her aunt's arms, feeling overwhelmed and happy and sad and a bit confused, but that perhaps everything would be alright. "I'm so glad you're here!" she babbled in English. "It's been the most terrible day, and did you see what happened to Emir Raka? He was trying to kill me, but I swear I hadn't touched him when he fell, and I think he's got a bomb planted somewhere in this palace, and-"

"A bomb," Jae echoed with an odd laugh.

"Yes, it sounded like it," Astrid hurried on. "So you should probably get someone onto looking for that. But there's something I need to do. Can you get me some transport out of the city, like, right now?"

Jae arched an eyebrow. "Because of the bomb or Raka's death?"

It took a moment for Astrid to realise what she meant. "You think

I'm trying to escape- no, not at all! It's worse." Because to her, it was.

Chay stood at the side of the room, half-hidden in the shadows with a shred of her ragged clothing drawn up to cover her head and part of her face. The palace was milling with so many people: wearing Syrenian and Mahadrese soldier's garb, or servants' garb, or even just dressed like ordinary folk. Then there were the Dragonflies…

She watched them avidly, examining each face to see if it was familiar, and was disappointed every time. What was she expecting? she scolded herself. Four and a half years earlier she'd gone with her mother and twin sister to visit cousins in the Mahadrese village of Dahiya while her father remained back in the capital. Things had been dangerous, messy, with their people being blamed for all manner of stupid things, from the poverty of their blue-haired neighbours, to the failure of karak to give milk.

Then came the law changes meaning that no Dragonfly could own land…nor run a business…nor buy anything in the markets. It had been madness, and her family had intended to quietly meet in Dahiya then return to Syrene where they'd come from.

But then the soldiers had come in the night. Chay remembered the screams and the violence; seeing her mother cut down and desperate villagers fleeing in every direction, many changing forms, but being shot down. She'd lost sight of her sister – lost sight of everyone even as she'd fled for the forest. Panic had made her unable to change forms, so she'd been a weak, trembling girl alone when the soldiers had found her.

They'd taken her back to their camp, and she'd assumed from their secretive behaviour that she wasn't supposed to be there. That was made clear when the young emir – Raka – had visited the camp the following day and had seen her as she attempted to escape. He'd ordered the soldiers killed for their presumption in keeping a prisoner and had 'rescued' her to work as an *esira* in the palace.

At the time Chay thought it had been because all Dragonflies were meant to be dead. But now she realised that the Dragonflies were meant to be slaves…which meant that some of her family might still be out there somewhere.

Chay's eyes skimmed the bustling, noisy crowds, and her heart leapt as she spotted a vaguely familiar face. The blue-haired, older man reminded her of someone from Dahiya. Her aunt's neighbour, perhaps?

Chay started to move towards him, thinking he might know what happened to others from the same village. But just then a new figure came into sight in the tiled hallway. He wasn't especially tall, but he was broader than the average blue-hair, and he walked with a particular movement that she recognised even before she saw his familiar auburn hair, and his sharp, equally familiar features. Chay's throat tightened with sudden tears, and she began moving forward even before she saw the small female figure held closely at his side, wrapped under his arm.

Then Chay cried out in amazement, and the sound was like a sob. So quiet, but the female – Chay's sister – clearly heard her even in the midst of the chaos. Hanali turned to stare across the empty space, and then she stepped forward, away from the man.

Her heart singing with overwhelming joy, Chay dropped her temporary veil and ran towards her sister and father.

Finally, the world had shown her incredible kindness and mercy. They were supposed to be dead, but they were alive.

CHAPTER 24
Heirs & Emirs

"**H**onestly, sometimes I think you try to give me a heart attack," Jae scolded.

She sat with one arm tightly hooked through Astrid's, and her clinging posture contradicted her words. The movement of the wagon they rode on made them sway steadily from side to side. Astrid had borrowed a hooded cloak to cover her head, and she hoped that onlookers would see them as just two local women travelling with family. If one didn't look at Astrid's colourful face, of course.

Jae continued, "The only worse place you could have been was in the palace dungeons, hanging upside-down from the ceiling."

Astrid finally looked away from her phone tracker, which showed Benn was still in exactly the same place he'd been for the last two hours. That didn't look good. But they'd be there soon enough, and she'd brought a doctor. For now, it was the best she could do. "Wait – did you say *upside-down*?"

"Mm. Not a pretty sight, because all the blood rushes to the head. But seriously, you show up coloured like you've mismanaged a portal transfer, and next thing Raka is dead. Oh, and there was a possible bomb in the palace." Jae shook her head, her eyes still wide. "Of course that last part ended up being just a trick – and once I find the jackass human who sold Raka that barrel of wood and pretended it was a nuclear weapon, I'm going to shake their hand. But I don't think I've been so stressed in months, Astrid, and I've been in hiding! I even just helped a deposed royal retake his throne!"

"Yeah…" With everything else that had happened, Astrid had hardly had energy or time to focus on the 'oh help there's a bomb' issue, which fortunately turned out to be a *non*-issue. It seemed that although Portal-co had been happy to trade modern guns and stunners with a culture not at all ready for them, they had drawn the line at supplying proper bombs or God forbid, nuclear weapons.

But now she knew that the bomb was a non-issue, and that she wasn't going to be executed for her part in Raka's death, those worries had been forgotten. All she could think about was Benn. Trying to change the subject she said, "So…it sounds like you've spent a lot of time with this Malchiel guy. Good friends, are you?" Astrid had only been teasing, but her eyebrows shot up in surprise when Jae blushed…a lot. Now for someone with a tan complexion, that was saying something. "*Oooh.* Going native, are we?"

But rather than denying it, Jae just lifted her chin. "I wouldn't be the first Townsend to do so, Miss 'good friends with the ex-regent'. Now speaking of going native – what did Nathaniel have to say about you coming here? I can't think he would have known."

"Nice diversion," Astrid said dryly. She quickly checked her messages, since the last one she'd sent had been to explain that she was 'with Jae now and totally fine so don't panic, please'. "Oh, he's replied to my message. He doesn't seem too happy with me."

"Let me see."

Astrid held out her phone, showing the last two replies reading, *WHAT.* And then a minute later, *CALL ME!!!!!!!!* "I've already told him not to panic," she said defensively. "He's not good at listening."

Her aunt gave her a long, expressive look, her eyebrows raised.

Astrid shuffled in her seat and checked on Benn's phone in her tracker again. It read, *BENN IS 0.04 KM AWAY.* "Oh look, we're practically here," she said hastily, pointing to a familiar-looking run-down building in the distance. From ground level it appeared to be some kind of barn, and there were other buildings in better condition nearby. A cluster of herd animals milled around a trough of water in the building's shadow.

"Nice diversion," Jae said, mimicking Astrid's earlier words as their wagon drew to a halt. "But you'll have to call him, just as soon as we're done here."

"I know." Her heart was racing and the most terrible feeling of dread sat in her belly, but it wasn't fear of calling her brother. It was of finding that drone, and what was left of Benn. She steeled herself as she got off the wagon, lifting the borrowed cloak to cover the lower part of her face. Local women didn't tend to cover up quite this much, but local women also didn't come in these particular skin tones.

There was no one in sight, so Astrid made her way across the uneven dirt towards the building. One side was split open – that was where the drone had vanished inside – and as she drew closer, she could hear what sounded like low level chatter.

With Jae and their driver behind her, she paused at the open section. Inside was dim enough that she couldn't see anything, and she could smell dried grass and animal poop. "Good day," she called in Tyger. "Is there anyone inside?"

The chatter abruptly ceased, then a low whisper began.

"I've come in peace," she added, feeling a bit like the alien off one of those classic Earth movies. But then to the locals, that's what she was. "My friend was injured, maybe you've seen him? Be-"

"Astrid!" came a familiar cry from inside the darkened space. "Dearesht friend! You came back for me!"

She froze, a little taken back. The voice sounded like Benn, but he didn't slur his words like that. She squinted into the space, making out some vague shapes inside as her eyes began to adjust. "Uh… Benn, is that you?"

"Yesh! Yesh, it's me!" She heard another low, hurried whisper from inside, and he said more irritably, "No, no, she's fine. Fine. Let her come in."

"But she's *an alien!*" the other voice said urgently, now audible. "The Earthers don't look like that! I saw one once, and they're *brown!*"

Astrid's heart had soared when he'd confirmed his identity, although he sounded worse for wear. But he was alive. *Alive!* "Benn, can I come in?" she asked, her voice sounding a little shaky to her own ears. She figured it was probably from the effort of holding back (mostly) happy tears. "I've got my Aunt Jae here to help you, if you're injured. I thought…I thought you might have been…"

"What? Dead? I've a nashty knock on my head, but no harm done."

"You certainly are hurt," another other unseen person whispered. "Your head has a lump as big as your fist."

"Oh. 'Cept for that."

Oh, for goodness' sake. Astride decided Benn sounded tipsy rather than injured, and she was tired of standing out here like a fool. She switched on her phone's torch and directed it inside the building, then stepped in herself, ignoring the unhappy cries of whoever was inside. ('Argh, the light!')

Inside the building she could make out what looked like empty stalls. One side of the building was piled up high with bales of hay, and there was a trio of figures sitting on the floor. There were a couple of local boys wearing the usual tunics and loose trousers, and next to them was Benn. He still wore his tuxedo, although he seemed to have lost the jacket, and a bulky white cloth was wrapped around his head, half-covering one eye. The boys watched her warily, one of them crouched as if to run, but Benn beamed at her and waved.

"This is my *frrend* Astrid Townshend," he told the boys, his tone still distinctly slurred. "She'sh an alien, but I rather like her anyway. Pretty too." He frowned at her. "What'sh that on your fayshe?"

The boys just stared, and Astrid flushed a little as she heard Jae and the driver come in behind her with more lights. As her eyes adjusted, she could see everything. "Long story," she gritted out. "How badly is your head hurt?"

"Mm. Don' no." He smiled loopily. "Tomy and Jetan gave me some medishin. I feel *fine*."

"We found him trapped in a box," one of the boys said defensively. "We got him out, and thought he was dead. But then he wasn't. We've been giving him something to help with the pain."

Jae, who'd moved past Astrid to crouch beside the ex-regent, screwed up her nose. "Would this medicine contain methuo juice, per chance?"

"And a few herbs," the other boy confirmed.

Astrid rolled her eyes, relieved. Methuo juice had a higher alcohol content than whiskey. It was a popular drink here, and it surely would help dull the pain. And his memory. And his liver function. But she was also annoyed, because she'd been terrified he was dead, and instead he was…drunk. "You didn't message me back," she said a little accusingly.

"Oh. My phone ishn't working, shee?"

Benn held out the device, and she studied it briefly for damage before holding down the power button. A moment later it flickered into life, apparently unharmed. "It was off," she said dryly.

"Oh. Shorry."

Astrid sighed, but really, she wanted to bounce up and down in excitement. He was alive! She hadn't killed him! She wanted to hug him, but wasn't sure where he was injured, and was getting strange enough looks from the locals already.

But just then her phone rang. The two local boys reared back, staring at it like it was a venomous snake that had appeared from nowhere. She felt the same way – because it was Nathaniel calling. She answered, of course…and quickly regretted it.

"ASTRID WHY DIDN'T YOU CALL ME?" Her brother promptly

launched into a tirade that had her holding the phone away from her ear. Something about her recklessness and suicidal tendencies and stupidity…

She winced, wondering whether she could just hang up on him, when Benn reached across and picked the phone out of her hand. "Thish ish Alsair Benn Cyrenius," he said into the receiver. "Your shister's actions shaved…*saved* my life. If you have a problem with that, you may take it up with me." Then he ended the call.

Astrid's jaw dropped, and she stared at Benn in admiration. "I can't believe you just did that."

"The shouting was hurtin' my head," he admitted, wincing as Jae unwound the cloth, revealing a good-sized goose egg. "But I'm alive, and sho…*so* are you, so he's got nothing to complain about."

Astrid considered that, debating all the possible ways she could counter that answer. He didn't yet know what had happened at the palace… "Sure," she said finally, taking a seat beside him on the hay-covered floor. "We're alive. That's all that matters."

And then, because she was so relieved that she felt like she would burst, she wrapped her arms around Benn in a hug – never mind what anyone else thought.

"Ohh, that's nice," he said, sounding a little vacant and startled. "I'm happy to see you too." Then he patted her on the arm.

Astrid just laughed.

The palace, Syrene

The palace was in chaos. The word was spreading about who'd come back, and who was dead – the Mahadrese takeover being over before even two months had passed.

But Chay was blind and deaf to all of that. Instead she sat in a quiet alcove, huddled tightly with her twin (complete with overly-red hair) and her father, who looked somewhat more worn, and yet far more joyful than when they'd last seen each other.

"They said you were dead," he kept saying, tears streaming down his face. "You and your mother, both killed in Dahiya by Raka's soldiers. I couldn't believe it when I found Hana earlier. How can you be here too?"

An incredible coincidence, yes. A divine one, really, since what were the chances of three of them surviving the destruction, and finding each other again in such a way? But this was a conversation Chay had been dreading. She hadn't had the chance to think about it before, because she'd seen her family's dear faces and had run towards them thoughtlessly. But she didn't want them to know…

"I ran," she replied instead. "I was caught, and one of the soldiers asked me why I hadn't tried to change forms and flee. I said I couldn't." She shrugged a little, feeling transported back to that terrible time. Just like then, she felt numb, and she struggled to keep the painful emotions at a distance.

"They didn't realise I meant that I was too scared to," she continued, "not that I couldn't actually change forms at all. They decided I was…harmless, and took me back to the army camp. But Emir Raka was there…and he…took me to the palace as a servant."

There was a brief silence, and Chay wondered if they were hearing everything she wasn't saying. She wanted them to know…but she didn't, too. She'd distanced herself from all of that by acting as if she truly was a widow, and by seeing her precious baby as separate from all of that too.

"So your tendency to freeze up when you're scared worked in your favour," Hana said with a little smile. "They thought you were defective like me. How long before you escaped the palace?"

Chay looked down. "I've been hiding in Syrene for over a year, with cousin Jenniel and some others." As if suddenly remembering, she sat abruptly upright. "Oh! I have to go see her at once! Will you come with me?"

Of course they would come. But as they walked, Chay turned the conversation to her family. Her father had been hiding in the mountains and various villages for years, it appeared, and Aunt Rechal and their young cousin had been along with him. He'd been south of Syrene, right near an Earther mining camp, for over a year.

"If I'd known, I could have come to seek you out," Chay murmured. "But then we might never have found Hana." She squeezed her sister's hand.

Hanali, it appeared, had a similar experience to Chay in some ways – while being completely different in others. She'd been taken to the work camps in the mountains along with many other Dragonflies, most of whom couldn't take winged forms to escape. Those who'd tried had been shot down.

But Hanali had never been able to take other forms, not like most Dragonflies. Instead she could able to make small changes to her face and body, to make herself look like other people. Hana thought of herself as defective, but Chay thought she was amazing.

Amazing enough to have been noticed by Raka's old general, Naim. Chay got the strong impression he'd saved Hana from death for dishonourable reasons, but when he'd discovered her unusual abilities, he'd turned her into a spy. She'd spent years in different places, colouring her hair and passing on information as requested. Then, they'd even sent her to the Earthers, pretending to be one of their own…

"Just think, sister," Hanali said with a tight smile. "If we'd been uglier or stronger-willed, our stories would have been very different."

Chay's hand tightened on her sister's, and her gaze dropped to focus on where she was walking. They'd almost reached the nearest tunnel entrance, but she couldn't look at her father. He'd been mostly silent as they'd spoken, but while they hadn't given details of their captivity, it didn't take a genius to work out why they'd been taken… and others had been left. It wasn't honourable, not at all, and she once again felt the full weight of her past captivity. Would he think she was tainted?

But then she felt his arm go around her shoulders. He leaned in and murmured, "My strong, beautiful daughters chose to live rather than to give up in defeat. I'm so very, very glad that you did. Raka and Naim are dead, and you are both here. It seems their evil has been used for good."

Chay's eyes pricked with unshed tears. "I have a child," she blurted out. "We're going…my baby's with Jenniel…but she thinks I'm a widow."

There was a pause as Hana squeezed Chay's hand, but then Malchiel's arm tightened around her too. "Ah," he said softly. "A child to replace those stolen."

"But…I wasn't married," Chay persisted, thinking: *aren't you disappointed? This isn't what you wanted for me!*

"Even if a ruby is stomped into the mud, it still retains its value." Her father leaned in to kiss her on the head, then paused. "But perhaps a dirty ruby just needs a good clean, little bug, before it can be fully appreciated. And I don't know what you've been rolling in, but you…need a good clean."

Chay laughed aloud, pulling away in embarrassment even as her sister grinned. It seemed the stinking cloak had left its mark on her. But the darkness had lifted, at least a little. "I will, I promise. But first – let me show you your grandchild."

Some hours later...

Jireh sat on his throne in the long, narrow hall, watching all the bowed heads before him. He held himself as stiffly as he was able, hiding any sign of discomfort from the long, busy day he'd had. That they'd all had.

But then taking back a palace was never meant to be an easy task, was it? And this here was the moment of truth – the chance for any of these combined Syrenian or Mahadrese forces to reject his leadership. With Raka so publicly deceased, Jireh was now *his* heir. He'd almost laugh at the irony, except it wasn't at all funny. The boy had had so much potential, Jireh mused, but instead he'd been a greedy, petty dictator. It sounded like an attempt at revenge had killed him, according to one of Malchiel's wee back-from-the-dead girls. (There was a lot of that going around, it seemed.)

But for Raka to have been killed by a brown raphanta – it was such an ignominious death! Although it could have happened to anyone, really. Those things were known to have a solid kick, and he'd had a couple in the stables for some time, although what it was doing high on the palace wall was anyone's guess.

In truth, Jireh had half-expected an emir would die today. Either him in his attempt to retake Syrene, or Raka at the hand of those he'd treated so brutally. Jireh hadn't wanted Raka dead – he'd hoped that he could imprison him in some splendid, isolated location and place a regent in Mahadra instead. After all, Jireh hardly could've sent his nephew back home with a firm 'please don't invade again'.

Now Raka was dead, so it was fair to say he wouldn't be causing any more problems. Jireh was sad that his own blood had died in such a way…but at the same time he felt relieved. The boy had been a right beast.

But Jireh couldn't show any of those emotions in his expression.

Not now, anyway. In front of him, all those bowed heads raised in unison. "LONG LIVE EMIR JIREH! LONG LIVE EMIR JIREH! LONG LIVE–"

And so on, and so forth. Jireh leaned slightly away from the shouts, towards the pale-haired man standing at his side. "Neoli, how long are they likely to do this?"

His new advisor Neoli was still a bit too slim from his rather unjust year in the dungeons, but he'd kept his spirit well. Today's solid meal, clean clothes and promotion probably helped too. "I've no idea, Your Magnificence, but probably longer than you'd like. They are rather pleased to have you back."

"I'm rather pleased to be back," Jireh said dryly. He meant that in more ways than one – having spent several years with his mind or body being unsuitable to sit on this throne. Still, he'd wanted *Syrene* back, and peace with Mahadra. Not to rule both city-states! What a shame Raka had to be such a fool, or that Orin had been forbidden the Mahadrese throne. He *could* fight that rule that his brother Mavet had laid down, but it wouldn't be easy.

Well, in the meantime Orin would be regent of his brother's city-state, and heir to Syrene. Jireh could do at least that much.

The cheering continued, and Jireh fixed a smile on his face even as his mind flickered over the day's events and things to be done. He'd dispatched people to close off the passages under the palace and the city, since that was a clear security risk. And he'd brought Raka's general here – Cypher? Sepha? – to ensure that the remaining Mahadrese army didn't undo today's good work. They'd given up their weapons, but he'd be a fool to think that meant the danger was over.

It didn't pay to be a fool if one wanted to keep one's throne. Jireh knew he'd made mistakes, but he'd also been given a second chance. He intended to make the most of it.

It was almost two hours later when Jireh finally managed to escape the throne room. He made his way to his personal suite where he found the new regent of Mahadra in much the same place he'd left him. Orin lay on the bed, almost unrecognisable due to all that bruising, but looking somewhat better than when he'd been scraped off the palace roof, apparently dead.

His eyes were now open, and were fixed on the small bundle held in the arms of Malchiel's daughter Chayali, who still wore the same ragged clothing she'd been in all evening. Behind her sat her almost identical sister, Hanali, along with Jireh's long-lost stable master-slash-advisor.

"This must be the newest little lady," Jireh said cheerfully. Out of everything that happened over the last few months, finding new family was a blessing. It was a shame he couldn't just pull a proper Mahadrese heir out of the woodwork too, since that would solve a lot of problems. Why his brother had to forever ban poor Orin from the throne, he had no idea… "What is my great-niece's name?"

Chayali's head shot up as if she hadn't heard him approaching, and she pulled the baby closer to her chest, her big purple-brown eyes wide. She didn't answer.

"Jesha, wasn't it?" Orin said in a hoarse voice.

"You should save your strength," Jireh told him. "I have the Earther doctor around here somewhere…" Orin rolled his eyes, apparently not understanding the value of such people, but Jireh turned to the silent girl. "Jesha is a good Syrenian name," he told her firmly. "Does she have red hair?"

But the girl just kept staring, and finally she whispered, "Why do you say lady?"

Oh, so that was the trouble, Jireh realised.

He glanced at Neoli, who cleared his throat. "The late Emir Raka acknowledged Chayali Ban Malchiel as his concubine in this very palace earlier today, in the presence of many members of both royal courts."

Chayali's eyes grew wider, and Jireh added, "Perhaps he didn't intend to do so, but it shouldn't be too hard to confirm you were his only concubine, or the closest thing to it. In that case, wee Lady Jesha will be Mahadra's newest royal."

"But she's half Dragonfly," Chayali's twin burst out, looking appalled. "She'll never be accepted by the nobility, no matter how she looks." Jireh blinked at her, and she drew back as if startled by her own outburst. "Apologies, Your Magnificence," she murmured.

He waved a hand dismissively. "They'll accept what we tell them to accept," he said firmly. "Now if Jesha had been a boy, then we might have to try a bit harder since he'd have been the new emir. But what's one more lady?"

The three Dragonflies exchanged unreadable looks, and Jireh's eyes narrowed. "What is it?"

"Your Magnificence," Chayali began, finally finding her voice.

"Jesha is the name of my cousin's child, not mine. I used her name earlier to protect my own child." She held out the quiet bundle in her arms, finally revealing her baby's face. "This is my son, Joset."

For several moments Jireh just stared at the sleeping child, stunned. The eyebrows…the set of the features… He was like a tiny, adorable little Raka.

It seemed like the problem of a Mahadrese heir had already been resolved.

It was the end of what felt like an incredibly long day, but Astrid was somehow still full of energy as she recounted the events via video-call to the portal colony. Luckily, the Syrenian palace had retained various devices for contacting the Earthers, and so she sat in a quiet room, happily taking the chance to clear things up with Nathaniel, who was still on the Tyger-side of the portal with Tamzyn.

"…And then even though Jireh had just named Orin regent of Mahadra, he had to go back and say there was an heir," she told her brother excitedly. "And Chayali is now a lady too! Or emir-mother? Is that a thing here?"

"It isn't a thing," Tamzyn said from behind Nathaniel's shoulder. She looked as stunned as the others all had. "But she will be… honoured."

Astrid blinked at her. When she, Jae and Benn had made it back to the palace, they'd found all sorts of amazing things had taken place. The surprise baby emir was her favourite so far, but perhaps her sister-in-law would find it much harder to accept. After all, 'Chakandra' had been Tamzyn's slave too. Well, kind of. Close enough.

"Seems that it's making some wrong things right," Astrid said. "Do you think she'll have a hard time?"

"Some people will not let her forget who she was," Tamzyn said slowly. Then surprisingly, suddenly, a smile curved her lips. "But I think…I think this is the most wonderful, unexpected outcome. My brother tried to crush and control this whole people group, and instead has planted one in his own place."

Yeah, Astrid had thought so too. Serve him right, the murderous maniac. Having a half-Dragonfly son was a worthy revenge, even if he'd, er, *planted* that one himself. But she didn't say as much, since

Tamzyn was still struggling with the idea that her not-so-loved brother was now dead, dead, dead. (And that death was nothing to do with Astrid! Oh no, not at all!) "And you can go home to Mahadra too," she said brightly.

Tamzyn and Nathaniel exchanged a glance on the small screen. "Yes," Tamzyn agreed, "but not straight away. We'll see how the situation develops."

Just then Astrid heard someone clear their throat behind her, and she glanced back to see the *other* big surprise of the day. (Well, one of many.) "Is Percy nearby?" she asked. "I need to tell him something."

Not two minutes later, Percy's worried face filled the screen. "Astrid! Did you find Hana?"

"In a manner of speaking." Then Astrid handed over the phone to the other girl, trying not to stare too much as her soft features sharpened until they became a not-so-Ukrainian ex-spy. But now Astrid knew everything that had happened to this girl, so she couldn't hold her own grudges too strongly. After all, Astrid herself had pretended to be a brain-damaged alien male for several weeks to save her own life. Could she blame Hanali for following the role she'd been given to save her life in turn? Even if that role had been to target Astrid's own less-than-devoted boyfriend.

But the conversation seemed too personal even for her, so she walked away to sit with Benn at the other side of the room. His enormous bandage had been replaced by a slightly smaller one, and the alcohol fumes had worn off. Now he looked tired…and happy. "That's a solemn expression for someone dressed as a rainbow," he teased.

Astrid couldn't help smiling back. "I was just thinking about how for me, all this started with Percy and Hana. And now it seems to be finishing that way too, but nothing's how I expected."

"Hmm. Well, *I* was thinking of how you once beat me in Chase the Castle, remember?"

She narrowed her eyes. Was he still tipsy? "What does that have to do with anything?"

Benn laughed. "I meant you won using an *esira* piece, the piece that everyone overlooks. And here…" He waved a hand at the room at large, which was actually empty except for them and Hana…li. "The *esira* wins. See?"

"Uh, *no*. Maybe that methuo juice is still affecting you, Mr Ex-regent."

He rolled his eyes, but didn't explain what he'd meant. "And never happier to be an ex, thank you."

Astrid gave him a sidelong glance, but he didn't seem to understand the connotations of what he'd said. She thought of Percy and how she probably would have settled for him, if fate hadn't stepped in in the form of Hana. Because if she'd settled for Percy, she wouldn't be here sitting with someone who she liked infinitely more. "So things will take a while to get back in order. But what will you do once you're free again?" Something with her involved, hopefully…

"Explore Earth, of course. Did you not say you'd show me around?"

She blinked, startled by how closely that aligned with her own thoughts. Her mouth curved in a smile. "I did, didn't I? Well, I can't go back on my word."

And so even though she was sitting in borrowed servants' clothing (again) and dyed odd colours (again) and waiting for everyone around her to make decisions (again)…Astrid found that she didn't mind one bit.

The future was bright, and she was happy right where she was.

Epilogue

Earth, six months later

The desktop screen flickered and then lit up in shades of grey, the only colours that could make it through the portal. But today it didn't matter, because the reception was passable, and the screen was big enough to show both Nathaniel and Tamzyn's faces.

"Good morning!" Astrid sang. "How's our newest ambassador?"

"I'm just Portal-co's contact, Az," Nathaniel countered, but he looked pleased at her greeting. Or so she thought. The picture was a little fuzzy, and his face looked odd. "Companies don't get ambassadors. Only countries get those."

"I was talking to Tammy," Astrid said with only a hint of sisterly smugness. "She's the new Mahadrese ambassador to Earth, remember? But sure, congratulations for replacing Walt. Even if he wasn't as bad as Anton and Eirene, he was still dodgy enough to sell a barrel of wood and claim it was a nuclear bomb. It was about time he left."

"Thank you, Astrid," Tamzyn replied earnestly. "But my position is not yet finalised, although I am very happy to see my friends again here in the Mahadrese palace."

And she did look happy, Astrid noted. It wasn't surprising, considering the time Tamzyn had spent in exile. Now due to her new role, Tamzyn was expected to regularly travel through the portal between worlds (wearing proper coveralls, of course) and couldn't be happier. And Raka? Well, Tamzyn hadn't seemed to mourn him for long at all. The fact he'd been trying to kill her might have been part of it.

"And it *was* about time," her brother added. "For both of us, but for Walt too. He might not have been involved in the kidnappings and hiding the truth about ambrilene, but he was dirty enough in the way he was secretly trading with Mahadra and keeping the money for himself. I'm just glad we've all got a new start now."

Astrid was glad too. It felt like finally, some wrongs had been made right…and the fifteen years Eirene got in prison for kidnapping didn't hurt, either. It was probably a good thing that Percy and Hana had split, because that difficult history would always be between them. Besides the secret identity and being told to date him thing, of course.

But Astrid didn't say any of that, because this wasn't about her. It was about her older brother, and his oddly different-looking face… "Hey, you're growing a beard!"

Nathaniel's shoulders hunched a little defensively, but he stroked his slightly fuzzier jawline. "Of course I am. The Mahadrese respect men who have beards. Only boys shave."

Astrid raised an eyebrow. She'd seen plenty of men without beards in her time through the portal, both young and old. Besides, what about the insult to Benn, who was also clean-shaven? "You sure about that, Mr Fuzzy?"

He flushed a little, but straightened as if to hide it. "Astrid, sometimes you're just so asinine."

Astrid stuck out her tongue. "Asinine? I don't know the meaning of the word." She really didn't, she thought privately. She resolved to look it up the moment she finished the call. "Now let's get to the real point of this conversation. We have a new romance, people. I want to know everything!"

"You mean about the regent – Orin – marrying the Honoured Mother Chayali?" Tamzyn queried, one perfectly-plucked brow quirked. "Now she's finally moved back to Mahadra, and I can see my darling little nephew every day!"

Astrid held back a grin. Tammy had gone a long way from looking down her nose at the former slave, to lavishing affection on what was honestly the cutest kid Astrid had ever seen. Brown eyes. Blue hair. Pointy little ears! "That's great, but I was actually talking about someone else."

"What other royal has a romance to discuss?"

Astrid hadn't said anything about royals. She mentally lowered her estimate of Tamzyn's open mind and teased, "Maybe Emir Jireh and that aunt of yours, Ruzaza. They'd make a nice couple, don't you think? It would strengthen ties between the city-states, too."

There was a very long silence from the other side of the screen.

"Do you mean the Most Chaste Lady Ruhazia?" Nathaniel asked, sounding appalled.

"Yeah, that's her," Astrid agreed, feeling a little defensive. "What's wrong with that idea?"

The other two burst out laughing in unison as Benn came in from the other room with a glass of water in each hand and a smile on his own face.

"What?" Astrid demanded. "Why is everyone laughing? Her name is really hard to remember!"

"Well, I know your people consider our culture backwards," Benn said, the smile making his dimples deepen. "But even we do not make siblings wed. Ruhazia is Jireh's sister as well as Tamzyn's aunt."

Oh.

Astrid pouted as she waited for the others to stop their hysterical laughter, and then cut in, "I wasn't even talking about them anyway! I meant Aunt Jae and Malchiel! Have they finally admitted they're together? The suspense is killing me!"

Tamzyn finally stopped smirking enough to respond. "I too believe they would make an acceptable couple, especially now that the stableman is an advisor to my uncle. But I have heard nothing formal."

Astrid did scowl this time. "But Nate, I asked you to ask her," she whined.

"And Aunt Jae just blushed, and said it was none of our business," Nathaniel replied calmly. "There's your answer."

"I'll call that a yes," Astrid decided happily. "Don't you think so, Benn?"

Benn shrugged, and Nathaniel cut in, "I think you've got bored of being a simple student, with no racing or anyone trying to kill you. That's why you're obsessed with other people's lives, Astrid. Either that, or you need a boyfriend."

"No way," she protested, feeling her cheeks heat while concertedly *not* looking at Benn. She'd met a couple of guys at university who'd seemed interested, but she couldn't return that interest. Not while he was still single, and in spite of how he only seemed to see her as a friend. Even though she'd taken on flatmates, and he now lived on campus for his own studies, they spent a lot of time together. Nice, *nice* time together...but just friendly. "I do not need a boyfriend. I'm perfectly happy as I am."

"Are you sure?" Nathaniel teased. "I hear Percy's back on the market again, and back on Earth, too."

Astrid opened her mouth to scold him soundly, but Benn spoke up. "Astrid and I are dorting," he said firmly. "Percy will have to find himself another girl."

Everyone went silent.

"We're *what??*" Astrid stammered.

"Ah, sorry, *dating*. That is the word." Benn looked pleased with himself. "I am still learning, but I am determined that I will be fluent in English soon enough."

She studied him in shock, trying to work out if he was serious. But for someone with such an excellent sense of humour, he didn't seem to be joking right now. "You do know what dating is, right?" she asked finally.

"Oh yes. My roommate has explained it to me," Benn continued. "The family does not choose the spouse. Instead, young men and women spend time together to see if they wish to marry. They share meals together, and go to theatres, and even have long, pleasant walks on the beach." He frowned. "We went to that beach last week, Astrid, but I must say it wasn't appealing. It was very cold, and the wind blew sand into our eyes. Perhaps we need to try walking again on another, more pleasant day."

She just blinked at him, and he frowned. "Or perhaps you liked the wind, Astrid?"

Astrid opened her mouth to answer, then found she couldn't. Not with two avid sets of eyes watching from via the portal. "Excuse me." She shut down the video call, then turned to Benn in amazement. "Are you saying that this whole time you've been here on Earth, and we've been spending time together, you thought we were dating?"

"Of course." In the silence that followed, Benn's face fell. "You did not…?"

How to answer that? Feeling like she wanted to giggle and scream at the same time, Astrid replied carefully, "Benn, I'd be happy to date you. I didn't realise you wanted to date *me*. You know…you know there's more than just friendship to dating, right?"

His eyes widened a little. "There is?"

"Sure. If you want to find out if you'd like to, um, *marry* someone, it takes more than just long walks on a windy beach."

Benn didn't answer, and feeling a bit like a predator and like a dozen butterflies were rushing around her belly, Astrid leaned forward and cupped his face. "Like this."

On the other side of the screen, Tamzyn and Nathaniel sat in silence as the other two…well, discovered that they'd wanted the same thing after all. But strangely, neither of them discovered that the video call was still running.

"I am so appalled right now," Nathaniel whispered. "I really don't think we should be seeing this." Because it was all very well to tease his little sister about boyfriends, but…ugh. Just…ugh. Brothers shouldn't have to see such horrors! He quickly shut off the video - properly this time.

"At least he made his intentions clear," his wife countered quietly. "And it was only a kiss, yes?"

She didn't seem half as upset as he'd expected, and he shot her a betrayed glance. "Tammy! What happened to, 'if you promise, then you're married'?"

"I heard no promises," she said calmly, although her cheeks flushed a little. "But as you've said before, Earth is different from my home. I'm more concerned that we couldn't give them the invitation to the Coronation festival. I thought Astrid would be so excited to be invited back, and we never got to tell them!"

Nathaniel thought back to what he'd seen before the video ended, grimacing. "I think they're excited enough, thank you. No, if they want to find out, they can just call back. Besides, the last time she was over here for a festival…"

To say it had gone badly would be an understatement. But the whole, brief war *probably* wasn't Astrid's fault…

"Next time," he said again decisively.

The End

Dear Reader,

I hope you enjoyed reading *Tyger* as much as I enjoyed writing it. I had such fun playing with the somewhat 'historical' setting of an alien culture 1000 years in the past, without needing to be at all historically accurate.

Some themes inspired by real history were the treatment and restricted lives of women, the décor (thank you, Topkapi palace), culture clash, the crazed behaviour of rulers (just about any absolute monarch in any culture), and the enslavement of minorities (or majorities, like with Sparta's *helot* slave population).

Now that last topic isn't at all light and happy, but it's also not restricted to any one culture. Throughout history, we humans have had a tendency to enslave anyone weaker than ourselves, whether other people groups or the neighbour down the road who can't pay their bills. Believe it or not, some estimates place somewhere between 21 to 46 million people in slavery-type conditions at the time of writing this book.

So while I wanted to address real issues in a fantasy setting, this novel's themes are way, way milder than what people have actually gone through. :O

On that happy note...besides being inspired by history, I literally dreamed many of the ideas in *Tyger*. The raphanta races, the characters of Benn, Raka, Jireh and Palos, and the part where Astrid dresses as a boy all came from weird but awesome dreams, the sort that stuck in my head long enough to be written down...and then written into a book. I also dreamed about the portal itself, including the way colour would stain people after travelling, and the Stockholm syndrome-ish situation between Chay and Raka.

I had fun with the names in this story. One of the things I like about fantasy or sci-fi is making up names, or borrowing real, unusual ones because of their sound or meaning. Some names in *Tyger* don't really mean anything, like Tamzyn, but others were carefully chosen to reflect the character. For example, 'Raka' is similar to the Hebrew word 'raca' meaning fool. 'Jireh' means 'powerful'. 'Benn' (Ben) means son, representing this character's relationship with Jireh.

The briefly mentioned Emir Mavet got his name from the Hebrew word for 'dead' or 'died' ('cos he's dead, get it?). The name Vuyani is of African origin, and means 'be happy'. Vuyani, like 'Syrene' (based on 'Cyrene') and 'Mahadra' weren't chosen for their meaning, but just for how they sounded. I found out afterwards though that Cyrene could possibly mean 'supremacy of the bridle'…which has an interesting connection to the Syrenian love for racing raphantas. Convenient, hmm?

Some other random facts - Mahadra and Syrene are in the southern hemisphere of planet Tyger. You might have guessed this by the way it gets colder as the characters head south. This comes from me being a native New Zealander, and accustomed to this particular climate set-up.

I also intentionally avoided locating the Earth-side of the portal, because then I'd have to take that local culture into account, and I didn't want to. It's English-speaking, so take your pick for where it might be.

Tyger was 100% intended to be a standalone novel. At this point it is…but I have ideas floating around for what would happen next. Maybe one day I'll get to writing them down, but don't hold your breath. I have plenty of other novels you can read in the meantime :D

Anyway, thanks for reading. If you liked *Tyger*, please leave a review or a rating at your favourite online retailer.

Until next time,

When life falls apart, you've got to hold it together.

Unshakeable
M. MARINAN

Unshakeable

Seventeen-year-old Iscendra's world is shaken
when she's illegally conscripted into a spoiled
Martian ruler's private army. With her entire future
under threat, it takes all her strength not to fall apart.
But when the opportunity arises for real change,
will she have the courage to risk not just her
own life, but her family's too?

A standalone sci-fi novel.
Available at major online retailers.